Praise for

THE CHEROKEE ROSE

"Few novelists can do what Tiya Miles can: conduct deep historical research to build a novel's spine *and* write a compelling lyrical story *and* lovingly tend to the altars of Afro-Indigenous ancestors. *The Cherokee Rose* is a mic drop—an instant classic. . . . An invitation to listen to the urgent, sweet choruses of past and present."

—Honorée Fanonne Jeffers,
author of *The Love Songs of W.E.B. Du Bois*

"Tiya Miles tackles such a sensitive and complex topic with incredible wisdom, grace, honesty, and research. *The Cherokee Rose* is a fascinating exploration and enchanting examination of often hidden or misunderstood histories. It's so real and yet so magical, an extraordinary journey."

—Robert Jones, Jr.,
author of the *New York Times* bestselling novel *The Prophets*,
a finalist for the National Book Award for Fiction

"Untold history blossoms vibrantly to life in Tiya Miles's *The Cherokee Rose*. A triumphant arrangement—part ghost story, part historical mystery told with modern flair. A fascinating group of contemporary women are compelled by the forces of folklore to discover their interwoven ancestry. Miles seamlessly layers robust fact with immersive fiction in a revelatory investigation of Cherokee and Black American identity—a tale of division, unity, and awe-inspiring cultural resilience."

—Afia Atakora,
author of *Conjure Women*

"A timely, necessary tale that will transport readers to a time that should never be forgotten, but is rarely explored with such a close eye. Beautifully written and impeccably researched, this is a novel for history devotees as well as those with an appreciation for the enduring nature of the human spirit. Lovely." —Asha Lemmie,
New York Times bestselling author of Fifty Words for Rain

"Dr. Tiya Miles's fiction contains, perhaps, just as much truth about our forgotten histories as her nonfiction. Her imagination—rendered with intricate and beautiful sentences and clear yet expected indications of her meticulous research—enables our moral imagination to grow. We need this." —Caleb Gayle,
author of We Refuse to Forget

"Poignant and essential storytelling. That only begins to describe Tiya Miles's work. The Cherokee Rose is a book that, with a deft hand, illuminates a little-known, yet vitally important, facet of a past we all share. A wonderful read." —Jason Mott,
National Book Award–winning author of Hell of a Book

"The history of the American slave-owning South is a history of erasures. With this novel, Tiya Miles overwrites the whitewashing, vibrantly imagining a complex and nuanced community within the Cherokee Nation where the lives of African Americans and Native Americans are interwoven in surprising and forgotten ways. But this is far more than historical fiction; it is a provocative and charming exploration of how one twenty-first century original, Cheyenne, reframes the past by the creation of a home meant to be shared." —Alice Randall,
author of The Wind Done Gone

"The Cherokee Rose is a great story, a skillfully woven mystery about the way history unfolds in individual lives. It neglects neither the

Indian nor African American side of the story. The novel's characters, beautifully intertwined, teach us that disenfranchising community members always means a loss of our own selves, an erosion of the very things that make us tribal."

—Craig Womack,
author of *Drowning in Fire*

"In *The Cherokee Rose,* the award-winning and distinguished historian Tiya Miles demonstrates her equally impressive talents as a novelist. Peopled with richly conceived characters, driven by compelling human dramas that cross cultures and ages, and enlivened by graceful and evocative prose, this debut novel is an intimate study of the tangled histories and contemporary legacies of slave-holding in Indian country. *The Cherokee Rose* asks hard questions about race, power, and belonging and reminds us of the fierce love that centers the quest for justice. We need more novels like this."

—Daniel Heath Justice,
Canada Research Chair in Indigenous Literature
and Expressive Culture, University of British Columbia

"An enchanting examination of bloodlines, legacy, and the myriad branches of a diverse family tree."   —*Kirkus Reviews*

"With both modern-day and historical characters equally believable in their desires and life journeys, this novel tells a little-known story that is complex and captivating."   —*Foreword Reviews*

"[A] wrenching yet enlightening saga. Readers will be taken with the way this novel blends past and present."   —*Publishers Weekly*

"With the character arcs and the exploration of an often-overlooked area of history—the Native American ownership of African slaves—this is a solid choice for book clubs that savor meaty discussions."

—*Library Journal*

The Cherokee Rose

THE
CHEROKEE
ROSE

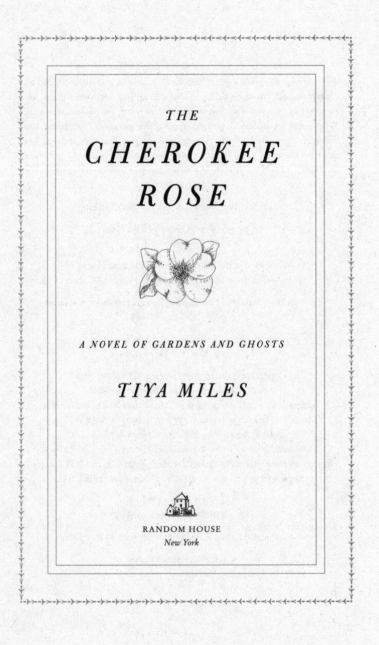

A NOVEL OF GARDENS AND GHOSTS

TIYA MILES

RANDOM HOUSE
New York

2023 Random House Trade Paperback Edition

Copyright © 2015, 2023 by Tiya Miles
All rights reserved.

Published in the United States by Random House,
an imprint and division of Penguin Random House LLC, New York.

RANDOM HOUSE and the HOUSE colophon are registered trademarks
of Penguin Random House LLC.

Originally published in slightly different form
by John F. Blair, Publisher, in 2015.

Grateful acknowledgment is made to the following
to reprint previously published material:
HarperCollins Publishers: "Women" from *Revolutionary Petunias*
by Alice Walker, copyright © 1973, 1972, 1970 by Alice Walker.
Used by permission of HarperCollins Publishers.
Oxford University Press: "Gardens of Memory" by Tiya Miles
from *Historical Fiction Now* edited by Mark Eaton and Bruce Holsinger.
Reprinted by permission of Oxford University Press/USA.

ISBN 978-0-593-59642-5
Ebook ISBN 978-0-593-59643-2

Printed in the United States of America on acid-free paper

randomhousebooks.com

2 4 6 8 9 7 5 3 1

Book design by Fritz Metsch

IN MEMORY OF

Peggy Pascoe, Josie Fowler, and Helen Hill:
"dewdrops from the sky"

FOR MY SISTERS AND OUR DAUGHTERS:

Erin Miles, Stephanie Iron Shooter, Maryanna Gone
Dubois, Nancy Azure Escobedo, Berta Iron Shooter,
Connie Rae Azure, Lauryl Azure, Nali Azure Gone, Noa
Alice Gone, Baylee Rain Iron Shooter, Dominique
Longknife, Alayah Azure, Mayliana PlainFeather,
Janice Azure, Nylenena Dubois,
and those yet to come

They were women then
My mama's generation
Husky of voice—stout of
Step
With fists as well as
Hands
How they battered down
Doors
And ironed
Starched white
Shirts
How they led
Armies
Headragged Generals
Across mined
Fields
Booby-trapped
Ditches
To discover books
Desks
A place for us
How they knew what we
Must *know*
Without knowing a page
Of it
Themselves

—ALICE WALKER,
"Women," *Revolutionary Petunias*

The Cherokee were driven from their home-lands in North Carolina and Georgia over 100 years ago when gold was discovered in their lands. The journey [was] known as the "Trail of Tears." It was a terrible time for the people— many died from the hardships and the women wept. The old men knew the women must be strong to help the children survive so they called upon the Great One to help their people and to give the mothers strength. The Great One caused a plant to spring up everywhere a Mother's tears had fallen upon the ground.

—"The Legend of the Cherokee Rose,"
Cherokee Nation Cultural Resource Center,
Tahlequah, Oklahoma

Contents

Introduction

WELCOME TO THE Cherokee Rose, a restored plantation in North Georgia with enchanting gardens and a haunted past. The white-columned manor house fashioned of ruddy, aged bricks opens into stately rooms furnished with fine antiques. The rear quarter of the home spills onto vast green grounds that encompass plots of colorful wildflowers, climbing roses, fruit trees, and river cane. As beautiful as this estate can be in the light of dawn or shadow of dusk, it was also the site of historical atrocity. Nevertheless, this is a place where three young women of African, Native American (Muscogee and Cherokee), and European descent join forces to honor their ancestors, reclaim the past, and save sacred ground, and as a result, find new meaning in their lives. As the characters in the novel discover, this compromised historic site where traumatic historical events occurred can nevertheless become a place where they belong.

For some, this will be your first visit to the Cherokee Rose. For previous readers, this will be a return trip to a place and story that will be familiar and, at the same time, much changed. This is a new version of a novel I wrote approximately a decade ago after completing an award-winning history about a plantation of majority Black residents owned by a Cherokee family in Georgia before they (enslaved people and Cherokee slaveholders) were forced west by the U.S. government's Indian removal policy in the 1830s.[1] This version of *The Cherokee Rose* includes the same characters whom many readers have told me they came to love, as well as revised, rewritten, and new scenes. It also includes an updated Author's Note, which details the research behind the writing (with a segment on the Southern plants in the book), as well as a recent essay in which I reflect on the novel as a work of historical fiction.

This last topic—how the genre of historical fiction relates to historical study—is the one I have been asked about most consistently. Readers of *The Cherokee Rose* have asked how I approach fiction writing as opposed to historical writing, what tensions I experience as an author working in both forms, and the benefits and costs I associate with each approach. I find deep satisfaction in plying the crafts of both history and fiction, and I feel that each allows for the open exploration of historical themes and stakes. In scholarly historical writing, argument, sources, context, and clarity are paramount, while in fiction writing, characters and the events of their lives in relation to the story take precedence. If history is intended to enlighten readers about change over time based on argument and evidence, fiction is intended to take readers on an emotional journey through identification with characters. The emotional truth that fiction writers can sometimes capture is often just out of the scholar's reach due to the unforthcoming nature of historical sources. This distinction between history as explanatory and fiction as emotional is a lesson I have had to learn through trial, error, and practice, as my desire to convey information, transmit cultural ideas, and wrestle with social issues at times overtook my development of characters and their interpersonal relations in the previous version of *The Cherokee Rose*. Still, I believe that both history and fiction do theoretical work, and that both historical and fictional roads lead to enlightenment about the human condition and how we have and have not, should and should not, shape our communal lives—a fundamental subject of our time and all time. In my approach to both types of writing, I aim for the same kind of revelation—a realization that history matters to the present in both positive and negative ways, and that engaging the past can lend unexpected richness to life. I see the past—including personal and collective memories, and individual and group histories—as a powerful tool in our human kit for living meaningfully in the present and preparing intentionally for the future.

My works of history (which focus on race, slavery, women, and the environment in the United States) are always about the present and future as well as the past, and the same can be said for my fiction. Indeed, my brand of "historical fiction" might be more accurately described as time tandem fiction or historical bridge fiction, because of my attention to contemporary characters living modern lives that are always influenced by dynamics of the past, whether or not they know it. And while I am honored that professors of U.S. history and Native American studies have assigned *The Cherokee Rose* in courses, I want this novel to be a pleasure to read for anyone with an interest in women's lives, family formation, racial identity, historic places, Black and Native American ties, genealogical research, spiritual conviction, or gardens. And this story may also appeal to mystery readers, romance readers, LGBTQ theme readers, and people with an interest in ghost lore, which, as I have written about extensively elsewhere, is a means by which Americans access ideas and express concerns about unresolved issues in the national past. Many of the ghosts profiled in regional tales and local tours represent larger experiences of crisis and trauma such as colonialism, war, and social disruption, hence the plethora of Native American ghosts and haunted "Indian" burial grounds, Civil War soldier ghosts, young bride and widow ghosts, incarcerated ghosts, and ghostly figures on the margins of society who were victimized by powerful people in life. Through the ghost—the aggrieved person who returns to expose a wrong or settle a score—contemporary readers and tourists can confront troubling aspects of social history in a way that feels intellectually and emotionally safe.

This book is about a haunting. There is, at the same time, a joyful element to *The Cherokee Rose* that springs from the bonds people form even in the most unlikely and difficult of circumstances. This sense of joy surfaces in the book through platonic and romantic moments of intimacy—between family members, friends, mentors, students, ancestral spirits, and would-be lovers, and between people and the natural world (particularly plants). Each of these intimacies must unfold on tarnished ground (in this case, plantation land) because this is the place where the characters find themselves due to historical forces, and indeed, where we find ourselves, as inheritors of American racial legacies. I believe that even the most stained places on our national landscape—like plantations where African and Indigenous people were exploited—are features of our shared cultural heritage that can be renewed and reclaimed to tell new stories of resistance, love, and hope. And indeed, these places must be confronted and reinterpreted, rather than erased and abandoned, if we are to acknowledge the wrongs of the past and move forward together. The experience of the women in the contemporary story line of this book suggests that such a transformation can only be built on a foundation of truth-telling about what occurred in the past lives of America's places.[2]

The Cherokee Rose was born on the research trail when I was a graduate student in the late 1990s. I was among a small number of PhD students and early career academics who were working to revive and update the study of African American and Native American historical intersections, with a particular focus on the nineteenth century and the enslavement of people of African descent by citizens of Indigenous nations in what is now known as the American Southeast and Oklahoma.[3] Although we were inspired by the early scholarship of famous Black historians like Carter G. Woodson (the founder of Negro History Week, which became Black History Month) and influenced by ethnohistorical (conjoined historical and anthropological) scholarship by Native American history specialists of the 1970s through the early 1990s, we were raising new questions about the experiences of African-descended people in Indigenous spaces, about gender and mixed-race families, about race and law, and about how colonialism shaped these and other dynamics. While I was traveling through Oklahoma, Georgia, North Carolina, South Carolina, and Tennessee to conduct research for my dissertation and the two books on Cherokee slavery that followed, I found myself just as fascinated by the other people pursuing this research for personal reasons, especially genealogists and tribal members, as by the archival materials I was uncovering. It was clear that contemporary people in all walks of life—and not just eager young scholars like me and my colleagues at the time—cared deeply about this history. The stories of those who found it immensely important to trace their family lines and heritage places to Indian Country became the loose inspiration for the contemporary characters, composites of sorts, in the novel. And many of the tensions and incidents of wishful thinking and disappointment described in the book are drawn from my observations of people I encountered in state archives, at conferences, and at community events.

Drawing from these observations as well as knowledge of my own family lore about Native American ancestry (which I have critically examined elsewhere), a significant tension in the novel twines around an African American longing to connect with Native American heritage, which is romanticized and co-opted in American culture more broadly.[4] Many African Americans have family stories and strong convictions about possessing Native American ancestry. These convictions are not always based on historical reality. Certainly, a minority of people who identify as Black and would be visually identified by others as African American do come from families that included an Indigenous member in the past or had strong historical ties with Native individuals or groups in the past; but this does not necessarily mean these individuals are Native American, which is a general (and hence misleading) term for kinship and political citizenship in specific Indigenous nations within the present-day boundaries of the United States. Claiming to be Native American when one is not, a practice termed "playing Indian," has a long and troubling history in American culture that coincides with the deterioration of Native nations' political autonomy and the dispossession of Native people's land. While African American claims to Native Americanness may have different origins and aims than Euro-American claims and

Latino/a/x claims, such as the desire to associate oneself or one's family story with freedom from slavery, the negative effects of such presumptions—an undermining of genuine Native American status—still follows. The borders of racial and tribal identity are sensitive and at times contentious, which *The Cherokee Rose* explores.

And for the tens of thousands of African-descended individuals who are indeed Native American (Black and Indigenous, with present and active kinship ties and/or citizenship/belonging in a tribal nation or tribal community), acceptance has not always been forthcoming from other Native Americans who "look" Native, mixed-race Native and white, or white. A damaging strain of anti-Black racism among some Native Americans, perhaps especially within nations that formerly owned Africans as slaves, has only been openly acknowledged in writing by some Native intellectuals, such as the Osage literature scholar Robert Warrior and the Louisiana Choctaw ethnic studies scholar Brian Klopotek, since the early 2000s. In the wake of the national "racial reckoning" that began after the killing of George Floyd by a police officer in Minneapolis in 2020, more Native activists and scholars (without Black ancestry) have begun to articulate and contend with this reality of anti-Black prejudice in Indigenous communities. Afro-Native people have, of course, been experiencing and discussing these dynamics for decades.

A second major tension among the characters in *The Cherokee Rose* stems from Black women's complicated relationships with one another. Two of the main characters in the contemporary timeline of the novel are mixed-race Black women, and three of the minor characters are Black women. These characters struggle with one another over very real personal issues in African American women's lives: interracial relationships, colorism (the privileging of light skin), featurism (the privileging of European-adjacent features in beauty standards), body size issues, and social class differences and biases. I have heard from Black women readers that vicariously experiencing the conflict among the Black women in the novel, and the way they express (or suppress) that conflict, was cathartic. The resentment that Black women sometimes direct toward one another stemming from the pain they feel in a society that does indeed reward lighter skin, straighter hair, slimmer bodies, and European features, simmers beneath the surface of interactions and can hinder healthy friendships. My model for thinking about these issues, which are prominently on display on social media platforms today, has long been Audre Lorde's classic essay "Eye to Eye: Black Women, Hatred, and Anger," where she exposes the problem with directness and sensitivity.[5] The characters of *The Cherokee Rose* do not solve these dilemmas but they move through them toward greater understanding of themselves and others.

Much has changed in our social and political landscape since I first hit the research trail in Georgia and Oklahoma over two decades ago and later began drafting the original version of *The Cherokee Rose* when my now thirteen-year-old child was a baby. These changes have inspired me to revise and expand the novel for this new edition. For decades, the Cherokee Nation of Oklahoma excluded from citizenship descendants of the group known as Freedmen—men and women that Cherokees had formerly enslaved under Cherokee law. The Cherokee Nation and its representatives often avoided discussing this history and deflected responsibility for immoral actions. This rigid stance was disheartening for Freedmen and -women descendants, for their advocates in the Cherokee Nation, and for scholars studying slavery and race in Cherokee history. At a conference on Indigenous slaveries held at Yale University in 2016, I shared my view that the Cherokee Nation was squandering the opportunity to embrace Freedmen and -women descendants and thereby set a positive example for other Indigenous nations that had owned Blacks as slaves. Today, after a tortuous legal and political path that included organizing and lawsuits by Freedmen descendants and their supporters, as well as pressure from the federal courts in 2017, the Cherokee Nation is setting that standard. There are now more than 8,000 people of Freedmen/women descent with full citizenship rights in the Cherokee Nation. In June of 2020, the Cherokee Nation removed

Confederate memorials from Capitol Square in Tahlequah, Oklahoma, with the support of Principal Chief Chuck Hoskin, Jr., who described the decision as an act of "healing" in a period of "racial strife" for the country.[6] In 2020, Principal Chief Hoskin acknowledged that slavery was wrong, issued an Executive Order on Equality to ensure all citizens' rights, founded the Cherokee Freedmen Art and History Project, and appointed Marilyn Vann—an activist and Freedmen descendant of the extended Cherokee family that owned the plantation where this novel is set—to a high-level governmental commission. In a 2022 program about the Freedmen issue, Deputy Chief Bryan Warner began his remarks with the sentence: "Simply put, Freedmen history *is* Cherokee history."[7] A visit to the Cherokee Rose offers an illustration of this statement, even as it conveys the conviction that Black history, Indigenous history, and women's history *are* American history. Here on this fertile ground, as hallowed as it is tainted, new definitions of self, family, community, and nation can grow.

*

This edition of *The Cherokee Rose* would not have been possible without the keen eye and bottomless support of my editor at Random House, Molly Turpin. For this novel and two other books, I am also grateful to my agent, Deirdre Mullane, who always had faith in this story, placed the book years ago and again in 2022, and is herself a passionate gardener. My agent Tanya McKinnon has been assigning me fiction craft readings behind the scenes for three years, for which I am also grateful. I have been blessed by a bouquet of messages from readers over the years, some of which influenced these revisions. One of those readers is Alyssa Napier, a gifted graduate student in education at Harvard University and aspiring editor and social issues discussion convener who read the book three times, gave me invaluable, detailed feedback, and reignited my love for these characters. More than any other person, Sharony Green, a historian and reader, kept the fires of this story burning over the years by teaching the book, inviting me to speak with her students, and wearing Jinx's preferred footwear—cherry red Converse—to class. I am grateful to the Cherokee scholar Adrienne Keene for updating me on developments in the Cherokee Nation around issues of race, and for inviting me, together with her cohost, Matika Wilbur, to speak about these issues in the summer of 2020 for their podcast, *All My Relations.* I have been inspired creatively by the innovative work of former and current students, all African American women, working in the fields of public history and historic house museum management: Kyera Singleton, Michelle May-Curry, Hannah Scruggs, and Kyra March. Finally, my acknowledgments for the first edition of the novel appear at the end of the Author's Note and are still heartfelt.

—Bozeman, MT, July 2022

The Cherokee Rose

PROLOGUE

Dust to Dust

-+->->-·-<-<-<-

SHE WAS A vision of ribbon and light standing before the attic window. Her spirit was unsettled. Her work was not yet done. Because she had failed to heed the warning when the digging first began, now she had to find a way to open the book of the past.

The place where the shovels tore the ground was known as the Strangers' Graveyard. Negroes were buried there, and Indians, too, and Indians who were mistaken for Negroes. The man with hard, iron eyes and hair the color of river sand was the first to break ground in the burial place on the outskirts of town. Wielding his blunt-edged shovel, he tore into the tender earth, displacing soil and sediment heap by heap. He was the leader, the master, the maker. The others simply followed, plunging into the people's bones with lock-jawed excavation machines. The Strangers' Graveyard had rested in peace for more than a century, floating out of place and beyond time. An island of brambles and spindly trees, it had been forgotten, except by those who cared for it and those who cared nothing for it. Once, many years ago, the graveyard trees had been sentries with bottles of colorful spun glass suspended from their branches. But now their protective powers had worn away, and the graves lay exposed. The burial ground was open land, good land, valuable land in the view of the man with the shovel.

Trucks dumped mounds of dirt into adjacent refuse piles, the faded bones of human remains churning beneath the wheels. A collarbone bleached and brittle. A skull with sunken sockets for eyes. Even the chalky skeleton of a small slave child. The shovel man, unperturbed, instructed his crew to lay a foundation. While workmen mixed thick cement and cut the flesh of trees to size, the man began to prowl and prod the vast perimeter of his property. His daily walks spread farther and wider until he reached the line. He eyed the river and the cane beyond his acreage, coveting the supple hill and sunkissed fields. On the day his crewmen poured cement on the site of the gutted burial ground, the shovel man crossed the border and entered the land of the Cherokee Rose. As he strode around the plantation, grasping a shovel and brittle map, he stomped upon the white roses to force a pathway.

She had crossed a border too. She had crossed the bridge of time. Watching him from the attic dormer, she peered down the slope of the overgrown hillside. Beyond the graceful brick facade and covered rear veranda, beyond the yard where slaves had toiled and medicinal plants had grown, lay buried the freedom dreams of her foremothers. The shovel man consulted his map, shifted his tool, and broke tender ground. Even she, who was without form, shivered.

She feared the overturning of secrets. She feared the abuse of the land. She feared the worst. *Matricide.*

She had but one hope. There were descendants—bone of her mothers' bone, flesh of her mothers' spirit. A way must be found to call them home to a tainted house. She would gather the scattered defenders. They would gather the buried memories. The memories would bind them together or tear them apart.

Africans once enchained on these lands believed the dust of the dead had the power to heal and the power to harm. She trusted this dust also had the power to wrest unsuspecting souls from their illusory, earthbound moorings. She held fast to the view beyond the window: garden, cane, river, roads. Dust motes floated like cottonwood spores in the dappled sunlight around her. She breathed softly against the house and felt the attic walls expand. Reaching for the brass latch that sealed the half-moon window shut, she turned its rigid, rounded thumb and pushed. Warm, sky-born air sprang into the garret. The dust of two hundred years flew into a shifting wind.

Part I

The Three Sisters

❖❖·❖❖

In late spring, we plant the corn and beans
and squash. They're not just plants—we call
them the three sisters. We plant them together,
three kinds of seeds in one hole.

—Chief Lewis Farmer (Onondaga), in Michael J.
Caduto and Joseph Bruchac, *Native American
Gardening: Stories, Projects, and Recipes for Families*

❖❖·❖❖

ONE

->->->· ·<-<-<-

JINX MICCO WALKED the path to her Craftsman cottage, breathing a sigh of false relief. It used to be that after work, when she could be alone with her thoughts, was her favorite part of the day. But that had changed around the time her latest column was printed. She fumbled in her messenger bag for her keys, ignoring the ugly garden beds beside the doorway. If her great-aunt Angie had still been tending them, the beds would have overflowed with long-lashed black-eyed Susans and heavy-headed sunflowers. But nothing grew in those old plots now except for the odd clump of scrub grass, which Jinx knew her great-aunt would have immediately plucked.

She stepped into the husk of a house, inhaling the musty smell of plaster. The place was hers now, its walls covered with a faded floral wallpaper, its furniture curve-backed and overstuffed, its rayon Kmart curtains edged in scratchy lace. Photographs of family members, framed and mounted, crowded the walls. Jinx was not a lace-and-flowers kind of person, but she had kept it all anyway. She hadn't changed a thing in this house since the inheritance—not the curtains, not the dishes, not the harvest-gold appliances. The 1920s cottage looked exactly as Aunt Angie had left it.

Jinx changed out of her cargo pants and slipped into comfy cutoff sweats. She unwound her hair from its braid to let it fall loosely around her face, a shade browner after countless walks in another Oklahoma summer. She sat in her great-aunt's easy chair and dove into one of Deb's charbroiled burgers, watching a rerun of *Charlie's Angels* on the old rabbit-ear TV. She wished she had strawberry rhubarb pie for dessert. She was sure she had ordered a slice, but instead she had to settle for a handful of Now & Laters, her annoyance rising each time she unwrapped a single candy square.

Jinx washed her dinner plate, switched off the television, and raised the stiff windows. A moist breeze ruffled the curtains as she settled into her great-aunt's study to start her evening's work.

Angie Micco had been a pack rat, collecting any and every book on Muscogee history, saving each Sunday issue of the *Muskogee Phoenix,* and scouting out past editions of old Creek-area newspapers. She had century-old back issues of the *Phoenix,* the *Eufaula Indian Journal,* the *Muskogee Comet,* and the *Muskogee Cimeter* stacked to the roofline of the terra-cotta bungalow. Leaning over an open book at her great-aunt's desk, Jinx tried to focus on her research. But she couldn't shake the nagging sense that something was wrong. Ever since her last column, she had felt out of sorts. The source of her discomfort was not internal, like a stomachache or guilt pang; it was external, like a free-floating irritant. And now she was up against a deadline for her next installment of the "Indian Country Yesterday" column she had created. Her editor, a third cousin through a second marriage, was getting antsy. *Read,* she told herself. *Focus.*

She was supposed to be researching the Green Peach War of 1882, a major event in late-nineteenth-century Creek history. "Traditional" Creeks led by Chief Isparhecher, the ousted judge who wanted to maintain a tribal government, had waged a flash battle with "progressive" Creeks led by Principal Chief Checote, who wanted to run the Creek government like that of the United States. The traditionalists were the heroes of the story, the progressives glorified sellouts. Gray was just not a color she believed in. Back when she was taking graduate school seminars, she had never been one of those hesitant students who had trouble making up or speaking her mind. One professor who she knew didn't think she belonged there had even called her work "potentially polemical." She had shot back that he was "potentially racist" and asked why no Native American historians were on his syllabus. When it came to the black-and-white of Creek history, Jinx took a hard line. He gave her a C in the class, tantamount to an F in graduate school, and wrote in the margin of her final paper that her analysis "lacked sufficient nuance."

Jinx leaned sideways and plucked the folder on Chief Isparhecher from the *People* drawer of her great-aunt's filing cabinet. She loved that Aunt Angie had kept paper files on historical figures in the Creek Nation. She skimmed an old clipping on Isparhecher and his motley crew of anti-assimilationist activists, squinting at the tiny print and pushing back a loose skein of hair. She jotted down interesting points on her legal pad. Later, she would turn those ideas into an argument and send in her next column for the *Muscogee Nation News*.

Jinx's hand itched. Her legs were cramped. The pen felt awkward in her hand. Something was wrong in her great-aunt's house that night. Something was out of balance, like a dish off a shelf, a door off its hinges, a weed in the garden.

*

"Morning, Deb," Jinx said from her perch on a stool at the L-shaped diner counter.

Deb Tom was a big-boned woman with bay-brown skin and silver hair that rolled down her back in waves. Some tribal members considered it unfortunate that she had such prominent Black ancestry, but they didn't dare show their feelings out in the open. Deb's words could be sharper than her homemade hot sauce, and the helpings just as generous. And Deb didn't hesitate to throw offending customers out of her café and on to the street corner. Everybody loved Deb's home-style cooking too much to cross her. That's why Jinx was there.

"Well, well, if it ain't Jinx Micco. Didn't think I'd see you around 'til dinnertime." Deb held a coffeepot in one hand, made the rounds refilling mugs, and took her own sweet time circling back to Jinx. "Coffee?" Deb said. She knew Jinx didn't drink it.

"I'm saving myself for Coke, and I'm here because I can't shake what you said about my last column."

Deb was a regular reader of "Indian Country Yesterday" and one of Jinx's biggest fans. But she had given Jinx flack for the piece on Afro-Creek Christians that mentioned a mission-school student back East. Deb had taken offense—unwarranted offense in Jinx's mind—at the nature of the subject matter, probably because she was a descendant of Cow Tom, a famous Black Creek interpreter from the nineteenth century. The subject of race among the Creeks made Deb touchy.

Deb placed the coffeepot on the burner.

"Are you going to tell me what pissed you off?" Jinx said to Deb Tom's back. "If you were mad enough at me to forget my dessert, don't you think I have a right to know why?"

Deb held her stance for a moment, then turned to face Jinx. "You didn't have to be so hard on her. Telling the story like Mary Ann betrayed her own mama. The way I read it, you made that lone girl responsible for the entire downfall of traditional Creek religion."

Sam Sells, a retired breakfast regular who always took Deb's side, turned his eyes away from his eggs to glare at Jinx.

Jinx lowered her voice. "The story wasn't even really about her. It was about the Methodist missionaries' failed attempts at converting Southern Creeks in the early 1800s. I had to explain that Creek traditionalists rejected Christianity, and that the Black people Creeks owned as slaves were the first to accept the faith, because that's the way it happened. Those first enslaved converts paved the way for Creek conversion to Christianity. Mary Ann Battis was just an interesting example of the larger phenomenon. A part-Creek child of a Native mother and Black father who wanted to stay behind with white missionaries while her mom was removed to Indian Territory? It made for a punchy conclusion. That's all. I think you should forgive me and let me order pancakes and a Coke."

Deb was staring, unimpressed with Jinx's argument and command of the facts. "That's exactly what I mean. *You* see her life as no big deal, but she was big to somebody. What you wrote might be all anybody remembers about that girl. They'll say she was a sellout who rejected her own mama in a nation that reckoned kin along the mama's bloodlines. And they'll say she was Black, because that's the secret sauce of your tribal traitor story." Deb threw her hand on her hip. "Benny," she called back to the kitchen, "go ahead and get Jinx's order up!"

Jinx blinked, diving for cover into the glass of icy Coke that Deb set before her. After a long moment, she looked up again. "I don't care that Battis was Black. I mean, I do care, but I don't care. She was just as much Indian as you or me."

"Don't you dare try that color-blind crap on me. I know you too well, Jennifer Inez Micco, ever since you was a baby. And I can't say I've noticed you calling any of your other Indian figures, no matter how mixed with white they were, 'part-Creek' in your column." Deb paused, then dropped the grenade she had been hiding in her apron pocket all along. "Like auntie, like niece."

"What?" Jinx exploded, causing Sam Sells to slosh his coffee over the top of his chipped ceramic mug. Deb's other morning diners were craning their necks to get a look at who was making the commotion. Her mother would hear about this before ten o'clock, Jinx was sure. "Are you calling my aunt a racist?" Jinx wasn't afraid to use the race card either. If Deb could deal it, she could play it.

But Deb was Deb; she stood her ground. "Angie Micco was a lot of things, some good and some bad. But one thing she wasn't was open-minded about people who were different." She looked intently at Jinx. "Any kind of different."

Jinx chipped her words off the ice of her thoughts, gripping the sweating glass, empty now of soda. "I don't know what you're talking about."

"I think you do, honey. I think you do. Here's your breakfast. Now, eat up and get over to work before it's too late."

*

Jinx trekked to the small public library building and stowed her messenger bag. Only schoolchildren and members of the Freaky Friday paranormal romance book club ever found their way into this outdated branch. She longed to chat with visitors about local history. But spending her half-days helping low-maintenance patrons kept her mind clear for evenings, the time when she did her writing and cataloged her great-aunt's historical files. Her library income paid the taxes on Angie's house, which didn't sit on tribal land in their checkerboard Oklahoma town where former Creek Nation lots had gone to white residents over the years. It also paid for her fruit-pie habit at Deb's, her Twizzlers habit at the 7-Eleven, and her daily Coca-Colas. For a part-time job, it wasn't bad.

When Angie Micco left her house and everything in it to Jinx, no one in the family had minded. From the time she was a tiny girl, Jinx had gravitated to Aunt Angie, circling her ample form like a small moon to its planet. There were photos of Jinx as a sixth-month-old sitting on Aunt Angie's lap, sucking on the end of her great-aunt's thick eyeglasses. At family feeds and cookouts, she toddled behind Aunt Angie, clasping soggy fry-bread chunks in her fists. Everyone said it was Angie, not the kindergarten teacher, who taught Jinx to read. At picnics in the arbor, the two of them would settle on a blanket all their own, reading old Indian Territory newspapers and reacting to the goings-on of historical figures Aunt Angie had taught Jinx to know. Except for Jinx's mother, who would pause beside them now and then to smooth back Jinx's hair and refill Angie's coffee mug, the relatives had left them to their studies.

For Jinx's twelfth birthday, Aunt Angie gave her a series of early-edition Creek history books that had been sold by the tribal college after it updated its library collection. When Jinx turned sixteen and finally asked Aunt Angie an American Indian history question she couldn't answer with certainty, Aunt Angie had smiled and said it was time for Jinx to leave the nest. At seventeen, Jinx went off to college on scholarship at the University of Tulsa. "That one's a smart cookie, trained by Angie," everyone back home had said. Four years later, Jinx set off for graduate school to pursue her doctorate in history. Aunt Angie, then seventy-six with dyed purplish hair and the same oversized eyeglasses, had ridden shotgun next to Jinx on the cross-country trip to North Carolina, telling Jinx what turns to make and which lane to drive in, even though Aunt Angie herself hadn't driven a day in her life. Eight years later, Jinx had yet to earn her degree. When her mother called to say Aunt Angie was gone, Jinx packed up the notes and files for the dissertation she would never finish and returned straight home to Ocmulgee.

"There you are, Jennifer!" Emma Langlier called when she spotted Jinx enter the empty reading room. Jinx's cheery co-worker was dressed in a floral sundress and flat-soled sandals with her hair neatly clipped, while Jinx's oversized cargo-style khakis, loose T-shirts left untucked, and cherry-red Converse high-tops with a hand-beaded design on the tongue sometimes caused older patrons to do double-takes.

"Why don't I read to the daycare group this morning while you catch your breath?" Emma offered. "Can you believe the school year is about to start? All those kiddies with their new lunch boxes and stuffed pencil cases!"

Jinx smiled her thanks, thinking about the implications of a busier workday. "Great. I'll be right around the corner. I'll process returns and neaten up the nature section. It's still a mess after that summer camp squad rifled through. I'll be in the back if you need me."

Jinx made her way to the cramped office where Emma's kitten calendar hung from a bulletin board and her pointelle knit sweater draped the back of a chair. Emma would be busy setting out puzzles and selecting stories, and their branch director rarely came in on Friday mornings. Silently promising that she would pay the time back by doing post-story-hour cleanup, Jinx sat at the computer and surfed the Internet.

"Mary Ann Battis" got no hits when she typed it into the Google search bar, but the name of the mission where she had first gone to school returned a series of articles. Jinx opened a link concerning Alabama state historic sites that described the Asbury Mission School in Fort Mitchell, next to a photo of a historical marker. The Methodist mission school in the Creek Nation, located on the

Georgia-Alabama border, had been destroyed by fire in the early 1800s. Most of the children were relocated to nearby white Christian homes, but advanced students had been transferred to a Moravian mission school in the Cherokee Nation, housed on the estate of a wealthy Cherokee chief named James Hold. When Jinx googled "James Hold," a score of tourist websites popped up profiling the "devil-may-care" Cherokee "entrepreneur" and describing his "showplace" plantation on the Georgia "frontier." Jinx clicked on a link to a recent newspaper article about the Hold Plantation museum, titled "State Cuts Pull Rug from Under Cherokees, Friends of the Hold House," and skimmed.

Apparently, the historic Hold Plantation was going to be pawned off by the state like a broken turntable that month. It wasn't as bad as when the United States government had put the Creek Council House up for sale in 1902, but it was bad enough. This plantation was the last place Mary Ann Battis was known to have lived. Traces of her might still exist among the household items or museum records.

Jinx sighed, lifting the loose tendrils of hair along her temples that always worked free from her haphazard braid. The Cherokee home would probably fall into the hands of some rich white man like most Indigenous land of any value.

"It's time for magic!" Jinx heard Emma chirp to the children now gathered in the multipurpose room. "*Mary Poppins,* picking up from where we left off, a snack, and then we'll make tissue-paper umbrellas!"

Jinx sat up straighter in her chair, entertaining an idea. Maybe the door had not yet closed. If the article was accurate, the house was still on the market. She could try calling and asking if materials could be identified, photographed, scanned, and emailed. Jinx printed out the pages from her search, circling the number of the state office that still owned the now defunct house museum. Then she scooped up and re-shelved the pile of book returns in the bin so Emma would not have to.

*

Jinx didn't stop by Deb's that night. She warmed a can of pork and beans and ate it with toast and a hunk of commodity cheese her cousin had brought over. Then she sat in her great-aunt's desk chair and reread the text of last week's "Indian Country Yesterday." She sighed in momentary relief. Her argument that Black and Black Indian Christian converts like Mary Ann Battis had furthered the cultural assimilation of the Muskogee nation was sound. Her readers could intuit that she questioned Battis's choice in shunning Creek family life in exchange for the Christian faith. But her facts were correct—of that Jinx was certain. If Deb Tom wanted to claim that her writing wasn't PC enough, that was fine with Jinx. She didn't deal in sanitized history.

Jinx opened a dog-eared book on the history of the Green Peach War. She compiled more facts in her notebook, glancing up at the windows and walls at frequent intervals, distracted by the strange undercurrent in the air. She sighed, craving fruit pie and feeling uneasy. Maybe Aunt Angie had information on Mary Ann Battis in her collection of papers. She flushed with embarrassment, glad that Deb Tom was not there to witness it, as she realized she had not seen Battis's example as important enough in her column to hunt for multiple sources.

Jinx turned to her great-aunt's filing cabinet. *Battis* was there. The wafer-thin folder held four microfilmed letters from the Creek Agency records of the Bureau of Indian Affairs. Jinx shifted toward a shelf and pulled down the general Creek history books, searching for *Battis* in the indexes. She found her listed in two studies. The authors disagreed about whether the girl's mother or father had been Black and whether her Black parent had been enslaved or free. But the authors, like Jinx, agreed that Battis chose to remain with the missionaries while her Native family suffered the trial of compulsory removal. It was the only conclusion that could be reached from the documentary record. There was nothing new here—or at least, nothing Jinx could see.

She closed the file on Chief Isparhecher, opened the top drawer of her great-aunt's metal filing cabinet, and slid the folder back inside. Then she opened the second drawer to put the Battis folder in place.

Jinx looked from drawer to drawer, realizing for the first time that these files were not in alphabetical, chronological, or even thematic order. She slung open every drawer then, running her fingers along the razor-edged folders like a blind person speed-reading Braille. Could it be that her great-aunt's biographical files were organized by race, with full-bloods positioned at the front, mixed-bloods placed in the back, and Black Creeks stuffed into a segregated second-tier drawer? Could it be that Jinx with her almost-PhD had come along and maintained the same color-coded filing system two generations later? Deb Tom's accusations against her great-aunt—against her— rang in Jinx's head.

She abandoned the study, snapping off the lamp. She brushed her teeth and pulled on a pair of boxer shorts. Her bedroom—her great-aunt's bedroom—was shadowy and still. And then a cool breeze floated through a window, mixing with the flat interior air. Jinx turned in surprise. It was early September in Oklahoma, where even night-time breezes were sticky and warm. The curtains fluttered as she watched. She reached out to touch a lace-edged hemline that left a faint trail of dust on her fingertip.

*

When Jinx walked into Deb's Diner early the next morning with her messenger bag slung over her shoulder, Deb looked at her for ten yawning seconds. "Sit," Deb finally said.

Sam Sells was having sausage and biscuits smothered in gravy. He nodded a silent greeting at Jinx from beneath the rim of his John Deere baseball cap. Jinx breathed, feeling the tightness in her gut loosen.

Deb placed a glass of Coke before Jinx on the counter, along with a napkin and fork. "I did some asking around through the dinner shift last night. Nobody talks about Mary Ann Battis much these days among the Freedmen descendants," she said. "There's still some pain there from a story long forgotten. Mary Ann's daddy—they called him Battis—was a Black man who took his own freedom. I always heard he came through Alabama Creek country on a forged government passport back in the 1790s. And her mama, well, she lost touch with the girl once the family came out here to Indian Territory. Her mama got one letter and never heard tell of poor Mary Ann again."

Jinx had not touched her glass. She shook her head. "I didn't know."

"That's only part of the story. The rest of it, we don't know either. But you could find out for all of us. You could find her grave and pay your respects. Look for people whose elders might have remembered her. Get your information from more than one source."

Jinx didn't glance at the fluffy pancakes that Sadie, one of the waitresses, had delivered to the counter. Deb was watching her too intensely, waiting to see if Jinx would accept her wild assignment. Traveling to commune with the dead and pounce on strangers to help corroborate a loose story were not among Jinx's usual research methods. But the Cherokee plantation for sale and those hypothetical house-museum records were already occupying her thoughts. Jinx realized she was curious, and more than that, she was chagrined.

"Wait right here," Deb said after watching the range of emotions cross Jinx's face. "I might have something for you."

Jinx nodded, cutting into her pancakes.

By the time Deb returned, huffing and puffing from her exertions, Jinx had finished her meal. She was sure Deb had walked all the way back to her shotgun house down the long alley from the restaurant.

Deb was holding a wrinkled manila envelope twined shut with a thin red cord. She leaned forward on the counter, exposing cleavage in the deep V of her neckline. "This was part of my great-grandfather Cow Tom's papers. The family kept them stashed away in a cardboard box all these years. I take them out from time to time, share tidbits with the Freedmen descendant groups, but I never could make heads or tails of this letter. I bet you can if you set your mind to it." Deb paused. "It might just be the push you need to finish that degree."

Jinx snapped her head up. "I didn't finish because my great-aunt died. I had to come home."

"No, baby. You didn't finish because once things got tough out there, once those university folks challenged what you thought you knew, you tucked tail and ran. Your auntie's death was hard on you, I know, but it was also an excuse for you to give up." Deb softened. "Angie Micco was right about one thing. You were born to study our people's history." She handed over the envelope. "Open it."

Stung by Deb's blunt words, Jinx hesitated, but she couldn't resist the call of that envelope. She untwined the thin cord and drew out a saffron page. The paper was cracked and brittle, flaking at her touch like the salted surface of a pretzel stick. She worried about the oil of her fingertips damaging the document. If this had been an archive, she would have been asked to wear white gloves before handling something so fragile. Down the counter, Sam Sells waved to Sadie for a refill of coffee, and behind it, Benny fried eggs and wiped his brow with a forearm. Jinx scanned the paper, taking in its prominent features: shape, texture, date, script. Antiquated cursive loops, beautiful in form, trailed across the page.

April 18, 1826

Dear Mother,
I pray this letter reaches you before much more time has passed,
whether you be in the West or still here in the East. I hope it can
be read to you, for when we last saw one another, neither of us
could speak or read the English language. My mind turns to you
on this tenth anniversary of the death of my godmother in Christ.
I could not accept the loss of her then, as I could not, a lifetime
ago, accept the loss of you.

I do not blame you, Mother. Do not blame yourself. You had no means to feed me. The mission school at the fort took me in and placed me among their pupils. At the tender age of eleven years, I was one of the eldest. I learned the ways of civilization and tried my best to be good, but ghosts haunted me at the school; fiends grasped at me. They pulled my gown in the dark, split my braids in two, unfolded my insides, and stole me from myself. I had a child. She did not survive. What was I to do?

I set the place on fire and watched it burn.

They would not let me return to you, would not let me see your face, even when you came to beg for my return, even when my uncle came dressed in white men's clothing to strengthen your entreaties.

And so I was exiled to the Cherokee Rose and given the gift of a second family.

I have lately heard the news from my godfather that our lands in Alabama will soon be claimed by that same ravenous horde who settled our lands within the borders of Georgia, and that more of our people will go west. I cannot come to you, Mother, despite my affection, which forever abides. I must remain here always, to do the Lord's work and tend the graves of my other mothers. Even as I write you, I sit in my godmother's chair, reading the pages of her Bible, worn from the tread of her finger: "Whither thou goest I will go, and whither thou lodgest I will lodge. Thou people shall be my people and thy God my God. Whither thou diest, I will die, and there will I be buried."

I seek only to do the bidding of the Lord. I pray that you and my uncle are safe, that my brothers and sisters care for you even as I would have done. I pray that the new land in the West is fertile and rich and that a future may be possible for our people.

Yours forever in the wounds of Christ Jesus, MAB

Jinx dragged her eyes from the page. *MAB.* Mary Ann Battis. Deb Tom was watching her with that same intense stare. "We've been waiting close to two hundred years to learn what became of young Mary Ann. That's damn sure long enough, even on Indian time. I believe you're the one who can find the answers. The question is, will you?"

Deb was not the first person to ask Jinx for information in the five years since she had been back in Oklahoma. People had started coming to her with their research questions the day she stepped foot in town. "Your great-aunt Angie used to say you'd know this," they'd begin as they put a question to her about a fifth cousin, once removed. "Your aunt Angie said to ask you, if she wasn't here," they'd explain when they inquired about a rift on the nineteenth-century Tribal Council. That was how Jinx came to know that she had inherited not only a house but a role as well: family historian. Because the Creek Nation was one big family of families, all interwoven through the cartilage of kinship and history, and because Jinx was not just Creek, but Cherokee, too, on her father's side, the role of family historian could be the work of a lifetime. Aunt Angie had devoted herself to the study of history and this cause.

Jinx had failed at both.

She replaced the letter in its envelope and handed it back to Deb Tom. She reached inside her pocket for a ten-dollar bill, placed it on the counter, and took one last long swig of Coke. Beneath the tinkling of the diner's bell, Jinx made her escape.

*

"When are we heading over to Deb's for dinner?" Jinx's cousin Victor, who was like a brother to her, said on the phone.

Jinx had spent the afternoon on the back porch of the bungalow typing up her column. Now she was in the living room fiddling with Aunt Angie's ceramic figurine collection.

"I thought I might go to Applebee's or cook at home. Do you want to come over? I can make Indian tacos."

"You don't cook, which makes that last statement mighty suspicious. Spill it."

"Long story or short?"

"Shorter than short, because I'm hungry."

"Deb Tom is pissed about my last column, and she wants me to rewrite it."

"I read that one. A little dry, maybe, but that's no crime."

Jinx paused. "I might have gotten something wrong."

"And you can't stand to make mistakes. I know. Ask your editors to print a correction. I see it done all the time."

"Deb wants me to go down South and trace a student I mentioned—just as an example, I keep pointing out—at the end of the column."

"A road trip? Now you're talking. Does Deb Tom pay mileage?"

"So you think I should go?" Jinx said, freezing in front of the figurine shelf.

"I think you want to go, or you wouldn't be so upset about it. And I think you could use a vacation. It's like a mausoleum in that house, and you've lived in there alone for five years. If you don't watch out, twenty years will pass by and you'll turn up on *Hoarding: Buried Alive* with a wall of old newspapers and files blocking your door. If Deb Tom is giving you a reason to get out of there for a while, I say go."

"I'd have to get time off." Jinx walked into the bedroom to pace in front of her great-aunt's dresser mirror.

"You know Eva—"

"Emma."

"—lives to cover for you. If you give me a week to arrange things, I'll come too," Victor said, then added, "Where are we going?"

Jinx smiled at that. "Georgia."

"The Coca-Cola capital of the world, and Jinx Micco's still sitting in her auntie's living room?"

"Wrong. I'm in the bedroom. Standing."

"When do we leave?"

"You're a Hotshot, and it's still fire season. You can't just take off on a wild goose chase."

"Copy that. But *you* can."

*

Jinx spent the late afternoon making plans in Victor's trailer and pledging to call him daily from the road. Since Emma agreed to cover her hours during what was already a slow time of the year, and the library would be closed on Monday for the holiday, their boss had given Jinx a full week off. If she took advantage of the long weekend and got as far as the Arkansas border tonight, she would have ten days before the library needed her back.

At home, she stuffed a duffel bag with T-shirts, cargo pants and shorts, underwear, and athletic socks. She packed her messenger bag with the Mary Ann Battis file, a Craig Womack novel, and a Nancy Clue mystery. She stuck her toothbrush and deodorant into a plastic baggie and left a voicemail message telling her mother not to panic.

She didn't contact Deb Tom. It would only make things harder if she failed.

Grabbing a fresh can of Coke and an unopened bag of Twizzlers, Jinx headed out. She climbed into her Chevy, the same truck she had driven cross-country thirteen years ago, setting off for graduate school with Aunt Angie beside her. Jinx could still picture her indominable aunt riding shotgun, with burgundy curls, soft-veined hands, and thick eyeglasses.

Headlights blazing, gas tank full, Jinx flew out of town.

TWO

CHEYENNE ROSINA COTTERELL read the auction details aloud, bracing herself for the onslaught. She had come across the notice in a North Georgia antique market while scouting for the interior design firm where she worked. The country-road market had been cluttered and dusty, and the flyer, which must have been hanging on that bulletin board for weeks, still left gritty particles of dust on her fingertips. She folded the flyer and lodged it on the table beneath the pepper grinder, delicately patting her fingers on her white cloth napkin.

"Forty acres?" her friend Toni said in her pushy attorney tone. "You can't be serious, Cheyenne. All you'd need next is the mule."

"Fourteen acres," Cheyenne corrected as her girlfriends listened with facial expressions ranging from shock to concern. "Below the Cohutta range of the Blue Ridge Mountains. It used to be a massive estate back in the 1800s, but most of it was parceled out and sold off over the years. The original plantation house is still standing, along with some cabins, a peach orchard, and a whole lot of mosquito-ridden river cane. And yes, I am serious. I'm bidding on the place next week."

"Now I *know* you've lost your mind. You can't live in the mountains, girl. You're one hundred percent city." Toni leaned back in her chair and raised the smooth arch of an eyebrow. She savored the crispy end of a sweet potato fry that would go straight to her hips, Cheyenne thought.

De'Sha nodded, sipping her chardonnay.

Layla adjusted her black-frame glasses and skimmed the state auction notice that Cheyenne had placed on the tabletop.

Cheyenne eyed her three closest friends, a tableau of Black urban chic. Toni wore a sleeveless tangerine sundress that showed off the deep tone of her shoulders and complemented her sultry bleached-blond hair. Layla was dressed in hand-dyed jeans and impossibly high heels, a look that punctuated her short natural haircut and stylish glasses. De'Sha was still wearing her crisp navy suit from work, her hair coiled in shiny black ringlets that touched the collar of her jacket. Cheyenne knew she had thrown a Molotov cocktail into their weekly dinner conversation. The four of them had met in a reading group for single Black women and instantly hit it off. Now they got together every Friday night at Aria, a hip new eatery in Buckhead with too many rich desserts on the menu for Cheyenne's taste.

"I thought that place was a public museum of Cherokee history," De'Sha said. "I remember going up there for a field trip in grade school. Is it even habitable?"

"I have to say I agree with them, Cheyenne. Isn't this a little unrealistic?" Layla said. She was a graduate student in public policy at Georgia Tech and took it upon herself to play the role of the thoughtful one in their group. "Why would you buy an old house up in the boonies? An old *plantation* house. You just got promoted to lead interior designer. Is this the right time for a job change?" Layla nibbled on a warm ginger cookie with a dollop of fresh organic cream. She had inhaled her meal and moved straight to dessert, Cheyenne noticed, indifferent to the effect on her waistline.

Cheyenne sipped her lime-freshened sparkling water. "I thought I was dreaming when I first saw that flyer. My grandmother's people came from that part of the state, maybe from that exact plantation. It *was* a museum when we were in school, De'Sha, but the building's been sitting empty for years while the director of some inefficient state office weighed what to do with it. The Parks Department can't manage the property anymore. But I can. I've always wanted to design and run a bed-and-breakfast. This, ladies, is my chance."

"But have you thought this all the way through, Chey?" Toni asked, her gold hoop earrings rocking with the emphatic motion of her jaw. "Where would you get your nails done? Where would you get a Frappuccino? How would you even find the staff to run the damn place? I hear they have a Dunkin' Donuts up in North Georgia. And a bunch of Billy Bobs. Maybe you could get used to that, but I doubt it. You like expensive coffee and fine men too much."

"Fine men?" Layla pounced. "Did I miss a breakup story while I was away at that conference? And does this mean I can have Devon now?" She paused at a look from Toni. "Yes, Toni. I take Cheyenne's leftovers. Her men are always beautiful, and you know I don't have time to meet people while I'm working on my dissertation."

"Girl, that dissertation is working you," Toni said. "What is this, year six?" She took a sip of Fresca and returned her attention to Cheyenne.

Cheyenne forked a leaf of baby arugula. "I *am* serious, ladies. Atlanta is less than an hour away in good traffic. I can drive back on Fridays for our dinners. You'll hardly know I'm gone. And you can come up to the B&B after it's open, relax for once." She shot a cool look at Toni.

"If you open a B&B, you can say bye-bye to meals at Aria and hello to a new identity as Butterfly McQueen, who got famous, I'll remind you, for playing a maid on screen," Toni said. "You'll be slaving away twenty-four seven, washing other folks' linens and handing out maps for hiking trails. Bet."

Layla tipped a finger to her chin, signaling that she was about to speak as she gave Cheyenne an evaluative look. "I think you've got the wrong take, Toni. Cheyenne's not Prissy-the-maid in her version of the story. She's Scarlett O'Hara."

De'Sha sucked in a breath of realization. "You *want* to live on a plantation. That's the point of this?"

"I want to *save* a plantation," Cheyenne said. "Because it means saving my family history."

"Which version of *Gone With the Wind* did *you* watch?" Toni pressed. "Tara was a romanticized slave labor camp, and the last time I checked, we were all Black—even those of us who think they're Native American because they have good hair and ordered a DNA test."

"We all have good hair, girls," Layla inserted in a warning tone.

Cheyenne ignored Toni's dig. She directed her words toward Layla and De'Sha. "Honestly, it *is* time for a change. I'm tired of working at a rarefied boutique, helping the society set pick out three-hundred-dollar throw pillows. And yes, Layla, I'm tired of Devon. You can have him. Buying this plantation house and bringing it back to life would finally give me real direction. Saving my family history and sharing that history with guests could be the most important thing I ever do."

"*If* your Native American ancestor legend is true," Toni said, her voice dripping with skepticism.

Layla was watching her with patronizing disbelief, De'Sha with barely disguised sympathy. Cheyenne was hurt, but she refused to show it. She knew Toni had always been jealous of her. Toni craved attention, and she was used to receiving it. But as striking as Toni was, she couldn't hold a candle to Cheyenne. Cheyenne drew open, naked stares from men—and a few women too. People were transfixed by her willowy figure, toffee-toned skin, and swirling dark tresses. The hair was her inheritance from the mysterious Cherokee ancestor whom jealous women, including Toni, loved to dismiss as mere fantasy. Most female friends she'd ever had were just like Toni—secretly wishing to see her fail, but hoping her charms would rub off on them.

Cheyenne smoothed the skirt of her Lilly Pulitzer floral dress and flicked back the ponytail she had pinned with a rhinestone-studded clip. She reclaimed the auction notice and tucked it into her handbag. She was ready to go.

"It sounds like you've made up your mind," Layla said, reading

Cheyenne's body language. "I'll come visit you, but only after you've fixed up the place. You know I don't do rustic."

"Call me if you need a small business loan," De'Sha, a banker, added with a wry grin.

"I just hope you don't regret it," Toni said, wanting to have the last word.

But Cheyenne wouldn't let her. She slid a hundred-dollar bill onto the table, enough for the sweet and salty treats her friends had been scarfing down and an ample tip for the waitress. She tossed her ponytail over her shoulder. "I'll see you in the country, ladies. Desserts are on me."

*

Cheyenne arrived home late that night, after first stopping to fill the gas tank of her silver sports coupe. She planned to hit I-75 at dawn and beat the other drivers heading to quaint inns and cabins in the Blue Ridge Mountains for Labor Day weekend. She wanted to get a feel for the Hold estate before it was auctioned on Tuesday.

Opening the door of her condo and slipping off her pumps, Cheyenne sank her feet into the shag carpeting. Her glass-walled townhouse in Candler Park was sleek and modern, with views of the city skyline. She looked around at the Eames side chairs and angular cranberry couches. Maybe she was 100-percent city, as Toni claimed, but who said she couldn't bring city to the country? The Hold House could be completely redone in a modernist style—straight lines, nickel fixtures, shagreen finishes, textured accessories. The contrast between nineteenth-century architecture and the clean look of her interior design would be to die for.

Cheyenne dropped her dress in a tent on the floor, showered, and blow-dried her hair until it fell arrow-straight. She changed into satiny pajamas, stepping over the crumpled dress. Gretchen, the domestic help whose visits were a gift from her parents, would be in tomorrow afternoon to tidy up. Cheyenne settled onto the leather couch, tucked her feet beneath her, and turned on Lifetime. The made-for-TV drama about a divorced couple's new lease on marriage after taking in an orphaned child was a repeat. It was Friday night, after all. Nothing was on. Cheyenne flipped through last month's *Cosmo,* then picked up the racy urban romance she was in the middle of. She plunged back into the story of Diamond, the gorgeous girl who grew up too fast in the Chicago projects, and Jay, the would-be poet turned drug dealer who sold crack to satisfy Diamond's gold-digging appetites. Cheyenne tried to ignore the hungry ache she felt in the pit of her stomach. A salad at Aria and a Nutri-Grain bar were all she had eaten that day. As she often found in the dim hush of nighttime after the rush of the workday had passed, she was starved for more.

*

Cheyenne had been lying to herself when she pledged to hit the road at dawn. She never woke a minute before nine o'clock. She packed her suitcases and makeup bag, dressed in a skirt and fluttery blouse, then waited in line for ten minutes at the nearest Starbucks drive-through. *Damn holiday travelers.* She sipped her light latte as she peeled onto the highway behind a line of cars. It took her thirty minutes just to clear the city sprawl on the way to her dream home in the foothills. Listening to the wistful strains of Sade's "Sweetest Taboo," Cheyenne sped up I-75 with the top down on her Mercedes-Benz and a Jackie O–style scarf tied around her head. The view of dense buildings gave way to green space; flat land rose into hills and dipped into shallow valleys.

Cheyenne's thoughts flowed with the music as she drove. She felt on the verge of a great discovery, one that could change her life. She had always been interested in her grandmother's stories about their Native American heritage, but she hadn't started tracing her roots until after her grandmother's death. There were so many things she wanted to ask, now that it was too late. To compensate, Cheyenne had become an avid participant on the *AfriGeneas* and *RootsWeb* genealogy sites, posting queries and checking compulsively for the latest additions to the Cotterell crowd-sourced family tree. She could trace her family history back to the 1860s, but then the trail went cold.

That's where her grandmother's stories came in. They explained the gap.

Her grandmother used to say the Cotterell family line had started on a Cherokee plantation two hundred years ago with a female ancestor who married a local man. The couple's children hadn't been enrolled in the tribe because of their mixed-race ancestry, but the children's names, along with those of all Black Indians on the plantation, were recorded on a secret list that no one had seen since. The Hold Plantation in the North Georgia foothills, the heart of former Cherokee territory, was the only site Cheyenne had found during her genealogical research that matched the details of her grandmother's story: a Cherokee-owned plantation near the mountains that once had Black residents and still had secrets.

Cheyenne's parents thought she was obsessed with genealogy because she hadn't found the right man to distract herself with. Her father humored her with fabricated interest in the charts that filled the pages of her *Black Indian Genealogy Workbook*. Her mother didn't even pretend to care, waving away Cheyenne's grainy prints of family census records. To them, genealogy was a hobby, but to her, it was a quest. In her family history she could find the missing pieces of the puzzle, answers to the elusive questions: *Who am I?* and *What is my purpose?* Cheyenne was a throwback, her grandmother used to say, to a lost branch of the Cotterell family tree.

She fully intended to find that branch and brandish it.

THREE

→>→>>·◄─◄◄

RUTH MAYES STARED at the ocean liner floating across her computer screen unbidden. Apparently, Holland America had slashed its Jamaican cruise fares to drum up ticket sales for the fall season. Pop-up ads nettled her, especially when they were animated to stealthily catch her eye. She edited the images she allowed into her head at every opportunity.

She x-ed out the picture of the long white boat, blocking the thoughts it elicited. Reaching for her travel mug, she took a sip of bad office coffee, then pulled off her tortoiseshell glasses and tugged a corkscrew of thick, dark hair. She leaned back into her seat, aligning her butt with the padding, shifting her swivel chair with the movement of her body. Wheeling the chair in close to her desk, Ruth dug her clogs into the floor and glanced at the architectural photographs taped to the backbone of her cubicle. She needed a house muse to help her generate a story idea.

Ruth rested her head on her forearms. It was four o'clock in the afternoon, one hour until the start of her forced vacation. She had nothing to do and nowhere to go for the next six weeks. What she absolutely could not do was hole up in her basement apartment. When she had too much time on her hands, the pictures swarmed into her mind, forming a cloud of memories that overtook her.

"Ruth, are you okay?" It was Lauren, Ruth's eternally empathetic, India-print-skirted creative director.

"Why wouldn't I be?" Ruth straightened her back and popped her glasses onto her nose, taking care not to catch them in her thicket of curly hair.

"Just checking." Lauren scanned Ruth's blank computer screen as if to make a silent point. "The sisal-mat photo spread didn't come through. You clearly need an assignment. And we need a filler story on floor coverings by end of day—something trendy, natural fiber-y. I'm thinking—hand-woven carpets!"

"Carpets?" Ruth repeated. How much lower in the story assignment pecking order could she fall?

"Five hundred words. And don't miss the deadline just so you have a reason to come in Tuesday. As much as we love you around here, we don't want to see you until the leaves have turned. Take your vacation and save the company some money."

Abode was suffering, and everyone on staff knew it. Advertising had plunged in the last year, and subscriptions had slowed as readers started cutting back on their leisure-activity budgets in the recession. For the first time in its eight-year run as a sleek Minneapolis-based shelter magazine, *Abode* was in the red. Instead of cutting staff or shutting down, senior management was asking writers to take accrued vacation time without pay by the end of the calendar year.

Ruth was an office junkie who barely alighted at home, so she had saved up six weeks of vacation in her four years with the magazine. The lost pay would devastate some of her co-workers, but Ruth's mother had left her an ostrich-sized nest egg in the form of a trust fund and shares in a company that, so far, was persisting through the downturn. Her passive income was robust enough that she could contribute monthly to a domestic violence shelter in the city.

For Ruth, it wasn't the money that kicked her heartbeat into high gear when she contemplated a forced march to vacation time, it was the yawn of open days with nothing, and no one, to fill them. She thought she should consider this internal battle with time in her journal, but she knew she wouldn't. The regular writing she did in notebooks with droll covers that she drew herself recorded what she saw and heard, not what she felt. She was making the KDP people who had started selling blank books on Amazon last year an undeserved fortune.

"Carpets are cozy. Carpets are colorful. Carpets are cocooning," Lauren was saying. "All those comfy C-adjectives that set the mood for fall. Six hundred words with an ethnic twist. That's all I'm asking."

"You said five hundred," Ruth protested, raising an eyebrow.

"I'm thinking six hundred now that we've had a brainshower session," Lauren said, smiling in encouragement. Lauren thought *brainstorm* was too forceful a descriptor for the collaborative creative process.

When Lauren moved away to make her office rounds like a peppy bohemian candy striper, Ruth stood to stretch, hoping the physical movement would help spark ideas about rugs. She walked to the wall of windows at the far side of the industrial loft, touching her hand to the brick and gazing out at the skyscrapers. She cracked one of the windows that had been sealed all summer to trap in the air-conditioning that irritated her sinuses. The breeze outside was cooler than she expected. She pulled together the three buttons of her soft, cropped denim jacket over her tangerine T-shirt that read "Probably Late for Something" in cursive script.

"Ruth! Got a minute?" The voice came from behind her.

She turned her back to the window, brushing pale dust from her fingertips.

It was Justin, the magazine's eco-stylist who had been eyeing her for months. He was one of those thirtysomething white guys with feeling eyes and attractively rumpled, longish hair. She had observed a whole tribe of his nouveau beatnik poet kind at Carleton College when she was in school.

"So . . ." He took a breath. "Since you'll be on vacation for a few weeks, and I'll be out for a few days, I thought maybe we could get together for dinner." He paused, running a hand through his messily styled hair. "And it's okay if you're late," he added with an entreating grin.

Ruth gave him a half smile, fully aware that her jacket was buttoned, which meant he had read the saying on her chest earlier and memorized it. Justin was cute, she supposed. Any woman with her head on straight might at least bargain him down to a coffee date, but she didn't meet that criterion. Where romance was concerned, she had always considered herself an outlier, not because she was bi, but because she subscribed to the *X-Files* motto: "Trust no one."

"Sounds fun, at some point, perhaps." She tried to sound optimistic. Justin really was a nice guy who sometimes brought boxes of bagels to work. "But I'm probably going out of town during my leave . . . to research a story."

"The carpet thing? Did you find an angle? I've been thinking of doing a piece on floor coverings made of recycled rubber. There's a growing industry down in Dalton, Georgia, the U.S. carpet capital." He smiled and leaned in, but not close enough to crowd her. "Maybe we could report it together. Pitch a feature story idea to Lauren."

"My carpet piece is just a filler for the November issue. Nothing special. The carpet capital, though, there's a ring to that. And Lauren's into the letter C today. Thanks for the lead." Ruth flashed him half a smile before walking away from the open window.

She could feel Justin's eyes on her ginger-colored culottes as the soft cotton shaped to her ample hips. It was one of her best features, she knew—her hip line to rump line to firm, strong thighs. The thighs came courtesy of many a long-distance weekend run, the hips and butt from her mother. Try as she had to lose weight back when she was in summer camp sharing a cabin with a Black Barbie lookalike, or when she was at Carleton rooming with stick-figure girls who fake-complained that the size twos were the first to go from the sales rack, she found that running never quite canceled out strong maternal genes. She was a comfortable size fourteen, which meant she was edging toward sixteen and just a tad slimmer than her full-figured mother had been. She still recalled the rounded lines of her mother's generous shape, the comfort she found in that constancy of softness. But the positive memory was immediately hijacked. "My Gold Coast," her father would say with a proprietary, knowing smile, tracing the curve of her mother's hips with cool blue eyes. Watching her mother's expression cloud, Ruth would frown, too, and, for reasons unclear to her small child's mind, cling to her mother's leg or hand.

Ruth shut the memory down with a willful precision born of practice, slid into her desk chair, and typed "Georgia, rugs, carpets" into the search bar. The first few links were carpet-company websites. She scrolled through their menus, jotting notes. Then she opened a link to a newspaper story about the carpet industry in northwest Georgia, the influx of Latino workers and arrival of Mexican groceries and taquerias. *Thank you, Justin.* This was the kind of material she needed to type up six hundred words of cotton-candy copy for Lauren.

If Justin was *Abode*'s eco-stylist with a regular column to his name, Ruth was its ethno-stylist, but without the title or highlighted byline. She was assigned virtually all the "ethnic" stories—on drapery inspired by Somali fabrics, the Hmong kitchen garden, new directions in outsider-art furniture design. Ruth ignored the obvious pigeonholing of her de facto job description, which she knew fell to her only because she was Black. So far, Lauren had been willing enough to keep her busy on assignment, which Ruth accepted as unspoken recompense for the narrow topical scope.

Ruth had by now developed a rote method for her filler stories. She started with online research, made a few phone calls, conducted lightning interviews, and dashed off a feel-good piece. It took her just under an hour to pound out her text on how workers in the Georgia carpet industry incorporated hints of their Latin heritage into textile designs. It was claptrap, and she knew it. The real story was labor exploitation in the heart of the industrial Sun Belt. But that wasn't the kind of story that would suit the readership of a glossy magazine like

Abode, with its sleek photos of flawless homes, emerald lawns, and wraparound porches as lacy as push-up bras.

Ruth skimmed her draft of "Aztec Influence Colors Georgia Carpet Kingdom" before pushing the SEND key to whisk it off to Lauren. It was five o'clock, but a few of her fellow writers still hunched over their desks. She dreaded going home to her too-quiet "garden level" (translation: basement) apartment, where not even potted succulents could grow. She would never explore in her journals that maybe she had selected the low-light dwelling for that very reason. Houseplants did not respond well to her. Neither did anything that grew, perhaps because she would not make the effort necessary to tend to them. But Ruth told herself she chose the place for the savings on rent, which left more of her monthly stipend for donating to women in need.

Ruth tapped her unpolished fingernails on the mousepad, trying to think of a reason to stay at the office late. As she scanned the results of her previous search one last time, her eyes fell on an odd blue link. It was an article in the *Dalton Daily Citizen* dated August 2008, just last month.

STATE CUTS PULL RUG FROM UNDER CHEROKEES, FRIENDS OF THE HOLD HOUSE

Local residents were saddened to learn that a beloved institution is being dissolved.

Georgia Department of Natural Resources (DNR) officials said Wednesday that the state-owned Hold Plantation, along with the Moravian Church mission building on the grounds, will be sold due to the budget crisis.

The Chief Hold House was built in 1804 by James Hold, the son of a Cherokee mother and Scottish-Irish father, who rose to become one of the Cherokee Nation's most prominent leaders. The house served as a political and economic center for the Cherokee people until they were forcibly removed from the area by the federal government in the 1830s. It was restored and opened as a state historic site in 1952 but was closed by the DNR in recent years.

The DNR has announced an auction of the Hold House, its contents, and its surrounding land for September of this year.

Local volunteers who hoped to raise funds to reopen the Native American house museum are calling the impending sale an "outrage." John Cook, a Tribal Council member of the Cherokee Nation of Oklahoma, agreed, saying, "The Trail of Tears was an effort to eliminate the Cherokee people, and now they're trying to eliminate our culture."

Other tribal members echoed this sentiment. "If there is no interpretation at our Georgia historic sites, who will tell that story?" said Stuart Pickup, a member of the United Keetoowah Band of Cherokees. "The Trail of Tears was an ethnic cleansing. The state of Georgia is adding insult to injury by refusing to tell the public about it. If you don't understand history, you're doomed to repeat it," Pickup said.

Ruth pushed her glasses up to the broad bridge of her nose. She opened a new window to confirm what she thought she recalled from her ethnic studies courses. The Cherokees' grueling forced march along the Trail of Tears from the hills of Georgia and North Carolina to Indian Territory in Oklahoma had taken place in the winter of 1838–39. Now, 170 years after that crime, an economic crisis was going to finish the job of wiping Cherokee history off the Georgia state map.

"Lauren!" Ruth called, jumping up from her seat and grabbing pages from the shared office printer. She plunged into Lauren's office, culottes swirling against her calves. "Am I set with the carpet piece?"

Lauren looked up with a smile from her mug of chai tea and the slick proofs fanned across her desk. She nodded. "Nice work. I'll handle the edits and proofs. Have any plans for the holiday week-end?"

"I do now." Ruth dropped the printed pages next to Lauren's proofs. "A story about a historic house built by Cherokees and run as a museum. The state of Georgia closed the place down and is about to auction it off."

"You want to cover this?" Lauren said, her face brightening at Ruth's enthusiasm. "The topic packs an emotional punch. Our readers would appreciate the historic home focus, and the ethnic minority group angle is something they would expect from your byline." Lauren sighed, handing back the pages. "But you know *Abode* can't afford—"

"I'll pay my own expenses."

"In that case, sold. Take photos. Good ones. I don't have the budget to send a photographer down there."

"You'll be showered with images of formal gardens and white-pillared porches," Ruth promised. She gave her boss a genuine smile and a pass for the outmoded reference to minorities. Native Americans were citizens of Indigenous nations. And Lauren, who was of Swedish descent and brought *kanelbullar* cinnamon buns to the office monthly, was as much a member of an ethnic minority group as anyone Ruth would encounter in Georgia.

Back at her desk, she shut down her MacBook, slipped it into its quilted sleeve, and grabbed her bunchy leather bag. She snatched the pink floral travel mug that read FUCK THIS SHIT from her desk and stopped to refill it with coffee dregs left in the staff kitchen.

As Ruth pushed through the metal door into the clear autumn day, she felt again that hint of coolness in the air. The weather was on the cusp of change in Minnesota. She was going south just in time. She strode to her Volkswagen Beetle and plopped her mug into the holder. She would stop by her apartment to pack a bag and ask her upstairs neighbor to collect her mail. She had no family members to call to tell she was leaving. She and her father rarely spoke. Even if she were to move away from Minneapolis, he might not notice until

Christmastime when she failed to turn up for their awkward annual dinner. Her grandparents on both sides had passed away. She had no siblings.

Ruth programmed her GPS with the address of the Chief Hold House and waited for her route to upload. The digital map glowed green in the dashboard. She blinked at it and breathed. She was headed down the interstate to a small, rural Georgia town near the city where her mother had been born.

FOUR

++>-+>·+<-+<

AS SHE STRETCHED to wipe the window ledge, Sally Perdue hiked up the baby. Her dust mop, dulled by the grime of countless cleanings that never seemed to make this old house shine, flopped on the end of its stick. From his seat on her hip, the baby lunged for the mop, reaching sideways with a chubby fist. "No, no, baby." Sally's voice was gentle. "This is Mama's, and this is Junior's." She handed him a rattle. He reached again for the mop, his blue eyes tracking dust set in motion by his mother's hand. Dust motes rose like dandelion seeds where they stood on the staircase landing, a space one-third the size of the trailer Sally shared with Eddie Senior.

Sally blew a puff of air through her lips. *Not much more now. Just the stairwell and the hallways, the butler's pantry and foyer. Thank the Lord Eddie Junior takes good naps.* Sally had finished the second floor while he slept in his seat. She had mopped and polished the main floor while he rode on her hip in a fancy made-in-Canada sling she had gotten as a hand-me-down from one of the former docent's daughters.

Sally cooed at her son once, twice, looking into his eyes while he gurgled. She lifted him out of the sling and bent to strap him into the bouncy seat. "Almost finished, Junior. Gotta make it pretty. Somebody's fixin' to buy this place." Sally plopped a kiss on her baby's cheek and popped a pacifier into his mouth. She pressed the button that made the seat rock back and forth, then wiped a palm across her damp hairline.

Raising the sling over her head and stuffing it into her diaper bag, Sally grasped a fold of her T-shirt and flapped it in and out. She cranked the iron handle of a leaded-glass window, hoping for a breeze. The noise of a construction truck rumbled in. *Maybe a digger, maybe a bulldozer. Mason Allen.* Beyond the dip of the elegant hill on which the old plantation house stood, the land was being cleared for a condo development.

Sally touched a hand to the paneled oak wall beside her. Its planes and ridges felt like vertebrae beneath her thumb, fragile and hollow, thinning with age. She had begged for this job back in high school— talked her way into it when she heard the previous cleaning lady had quit in a huff, complaining of an odd smell in the attic that just couldn't be gotten rid of. *A dead bat,* Sally had thought at the time. She had seen worse around her trailer, even before Eddie Senior moved in. The director of the house museum called an exterminator and hired Sally on the spot, desperate to see the place spruced up in time for the garden show that year. The pay was low, but better than what Sally made cleaning at the nursing home. And she had always wondered about this brooding house on the hill, visible for miles. She had been curious about its history even before her fifth-grade class took the tour for county kids. If she had made it to college, or even out of high school, before getting together with Eddie Senior, she would have taken a class on Southern history. But working here had given her the next best thing, a chance to soak in all that drama of the past.

The story went that James Vann Hold, the man who built the plantation when this all counted as Indian land, was the handsome son of a full-blood Cherokee mother and European father. Hold got to be filthy rich investing family money in slaves, trading deerskins and crops, and making shady business deals. He was murdered in the prime of manhood, and nobody knew who did it. Sally recalled the script by heart from overhearing the docents. They never really changed it up unless a Black person took the tour, in which case they said "servants" instead of "slaves." She had cleaned the place only a year before the state closed it down. She had been hired back today to get the house ready for auction. Sally was glad for the work, such as it was. Lord knew, Eddie Senior took a paying job only when he had a mind to.

Junior dropped his paci. Sally tucked it into her bag and stuck a clean blue one in his mouth. She dusted ornate mirror frames, wiped down silvered glass, swept the formal stairway and long oak halls. When she finished the foyer, she was parched and thought that Junior must be too. After climbing the stairs to where he sat rocking contentedly on the landing, she pulled out his bottle of formula. *What a good baby.*

The rude honk of a horn blared through the open window. *Shit,* Sally thought. *Eddie.* She flew into motion, lifting Junior and hooking him to her hip with one arm beneath his padded bottom, grabbing the diaper bag in one hand and the bouncy seat in the other. She jogged down the staircase, jostling the baby and his things while the horn bellowed.

"What the hell took you so long, Sally?" Eddie was mad, his face puffing out and in from his worked-up breathing.

"Sorry." Sally reached inside the open rear window to unlock the door and throw the bouncy chair inside. She eased into the passenger seat and held Junior out to his daddy. "Could you take him for a spell? I need to lock up."

"Jesus Christ. I told you to be ready when I got here."

"I won't be but a minute."

Sally ran back to the house and opened the double entry doors. She reached for the oval sign that hung on a hook beside the door chime's soundbox. Exiting, she pulled the doors shut behind her, turned the oblong metal lock, and listened for the click. Hearing it, she twined the ribbon of the sign tightly around the neck of a brass doorknob. CLOSED, it read. With her back to Eddie Senior, Eddie Junior, and the winding driveway that led into town, she pressed her hand to the heavy wooden door panel. "Bye, now," she whispered to the house.

"Get a move on, Sally!" Eddie shouted. "This kid of yours is gone and shit his pants."

Sally turned her back to the redbrick mansion, its eaves and porches, porticoes and columns. As she hustled down the broad front steps, a stiff breeze followed her, carrying with it the meadowy scent of late-summer wildflowers. The wind caught and parted Sally's short red hair, cooling the nape of her neck.

While Eddie careened the beat-up car around the circular drive-way, the breeze kept on blowing, flipping the sign on the door to read OPEN.

Part II

Talking Leaves

✦➤⋅⋖✦

We don't just live in a house, but with it. The houses and rooms in which we live and lived stay with us. Hopes and dreams are buried in them, as are cries of love and the bruises of violence.

—Joy Harjo, "The Song of the House in the House,"
A Map to the Next World: Poems and Tales

✦➤⋅⋖✦

FIVE

✦>-✦>-·✦-✦-✦-

THE DRIVE FROM Atlanta stretched into a frustrating trek, heightened by Cheyenne's nervous anticipation.

After what felt like hours, she found herself pulling in front of the Chief Hold House. She eased out of her car and planted her heels in the uneven gravel, taking in the view. Bold, brick, and becoming, the building seemed to greet her like a bridegroom. Cheyenne seized a breath. *Magnificent.* Even the high heat couldn't distract her from this architectural gem.

The Department of Natural Resources had arranged for a local broker to show her the house that afternoon. The middle-aged woman in a pastel pantsuit with light brown hair hanging neatly to her shoulders leaned in the window of a black SUV and smiled flirtatiously at the driver, whose face was hidden from Cheyenne. Cheyenne willed the broker to speed it up. She was desperate to get inside the house. There was no chance those thirty-eight photos on the realtor's website did the historic beauty justice.

Cheyenne undid the silk scarf on her head, shaking loose her dark sheeting of hair. She retied the slip of fabric in a soft knot around her neck and shifted her weight and one hand to her hip. She stood at a polite distance, impatiently biding her time.

"Of course, Mr. Allen," Cheyenne overheard the broker say. She caught snatches of conversation interspersed with the woman's nervous laughter.

"Well, yes, I *have* received other calls. I'm required to show it to anyone who makes a request by law . . . pro forma . . . nothing serious."

"I don't like to be let down," Cheyenne heard a male voice answer. ". . . promised . . . river view . . . a fine partnership. Let's not jeopardize . . ."

"Leave it to me, Mr. Allen. It's a gorgeous property with good bones, but it will take an army to restore it. Smart buyers will recognize that and move on to the next listing. You have a good holiday, now."

Cheyenne watched as the SUV's window rolled up to seal out the sunlight and the woman straightened her back and cleared her expression.

"Miss Cotterell?" The woman held out a hand as Cheyenne closed the distance between them. "I'm Lanie Brevard. We spoke by phone."

"Yes. If I may, who was that just leaving?" Cheyenne's lips tightened. Someone else had scheduled a viewing, and that person had an in with the realtor.

Lanie Brevard cleared her throat. "Mr. Mason Allen. A pillar of our town."

Cheyenne frowned. "He's interested in the Hold House?"

"Everyone around here is interested in the Hold House, Miss Cotterell. Surely you've read about the controversy in the papers. This estate has been an economic boon to our town for centuries. With any luck, we'll see its fortunes rise again after the auction. Let me show you the house."

She escorted Cheyenne up the wide front steps, dangling a key labeled *Hold.* The lock released, and the broker turned a knob on one of the twin oak doors that held a sign on a ribbon. Cheyenne stepped into the foyer after her. The house had a stale, closed-in smell despite the scent of cleaning products that indicated a recent mopping. The air inside felt cool and still, like a root cellar. Cheyenne crossed her arms over her chest, stroking her bare skin in the sudden chill.

The broker watched the motion. "Handmade bond brick," she said. "Keeps the house cooler than a cave. You're from Atlanta, as I recall."

"Candler Park."

"Mr. Allen does business in the city from time to time, but most of us prefer to stay here in the mountains. Our town is just right for us, fits like a hammock. Have you been up this way before?"

"Often. We toured the Hold House in grade school. It was the fifth-grade pilgrimage. And I used to spend summers on Fort Mountain at Camp Idlewood."

"I'm familiar with that property," the broker said. "Idlewood was an Afro-American camp that started as a rudimentary school for ex-slaves."

"Actually, the teachers there, *free* Black women from the North, taught reading, writing, and math. Industrial courses came later. The school operated for fifty years. In the 1920s, the child of one of those original teachers raised funds to repurpose the buildings for a camp. Professional African American families from all over the South sent their children there every summer."

"Hmm," the broker said noncommittally. "In any case, the camp is closed now. The state purchased the land to expand Fort Mountain State Park—which is just one of the gifts of the Allen family to our county."

Lanie Brevard broke off her homage to the Allens and turned to the drawing room. Cheyenne followed, pushing back the wave of worry as her Giambattista Valli skirt swirled around her knees. This was it. She was here. Inside the arms of the Hold House. She took in the elaborate carvings on the fireplace mantel, the plaster moldings that framed the walls and ceilings, and the hand-blown windows languidly filtering light.

They exited the drawing room, entered the dining room. She scanned the nine-over-nine leaded-glass panes topped with gold-leaf fixtures in the form of phoenixes rising. Dried pine needles and okra pods rested on the windowsills. An old-fashioned brick of tea sat on a saucer made of blue transferware china. The antique textiles and furnishings collected over the years remained in place. Some of the pieces had belonged to the Hold family; others had been donated by wealthy patrons. Cheyenne had read in *Southern Living* that the table settings in the Hold House were replicas of the fragmented dishware uncovered beneath the outdoor kitchen by a state archaeologist in the 1950s. The property would be auctioned with its contents intact, sold "as is." Spacious by nineteenth-century standards, boasting three stories, eight rooms, broad hallways, back and front porches, and a cellar, the house brimmed with the contents of generations. And it could all be hers. It had to be.

Lanie Brevard led Cheyenne through the first floor with chatty narration about the upstanding families who had lived in the home before the museum opened. Cheyenne tried to tune her out. She preferred to focus on the house.

In the front hallway, where a half-opened cardboard box held forgotten copies of Chief Hold House brochures, Cheyenne turned with the broker toward the wooden staircase. They mounted the grand oak steps with carved balustrades, reached a large, superfluous landing, and continued to the second story. At the front of the center hallway, a seating area flowed into a covered veranda that faced the road leading off the estate. Cheyenne turned on the crisp heels of her slender Bottega Veneta sling-backs to make her way to the master bedroom behind Lanie Brevard.

It was divided from the rest of the home by a lateral bridge that echoed the structure and form of the staircase. The oddly placed bridge connected the front and rear of the second story. It rose in an arch from the center hallway and crossed the open space of the downstairs hall. Cheyenne had read in a local guidebook that architectural historians debated the reason the bridge had been built. Some said it represented the split sides of James Hold's racial identity; others argued it was Hold's calculated attempt to keep his private life separate from the scrutiny of United States Indian agents and white missionaries.

Cheyenne crossed the elegant arch of the unusual bridge, the sharp edges of her heels digging into the floorboards. She faced the entry to a spacious bedroom and saw a closed doorway farther down the hall—leading up, she supposed, to an attic. She watched as Lanie Brevard unlatched the velvet rope that cordoned off the master bedroom, protecting its heirloom contents from long-gone tourists. Inside, Cheyenne's gaze caught first on the full eastern view of the Blue Ridge, then on the hand-worked lace canopy atop the mahogany bedstead, and next on the folding antique game table splayed with period playing cards. The room had no proper master bath, but one could be added without even knocking down a wall. She moved to a chestnut wardrobe with an inlaid rose motif on the crest. Pulling it gently open, she marveled at the little drawers inside and stroked the silk of the chest's inner lining. Cheyenne breathed in and out, gazing at blue-peaked mountaintops and feeling deep in her bones that this would be her bedroom. She turned to see Lanie Brevard watching, a sharp look in her eye.

"Miss Cotterell, I would be remiss if I didn't tell you just how much work goes into maintaining a historic house like this. It would be quite an undertaking. If you're looking for a vacation property, we have charming cabins and peeled-log homes on the market. I could show you a few right now."

Cheyenne's eyes narrowed. The woman was steering her. "I like a challenge, Ms. Brevard. I like the Hold House."

The broker paused. "Then you have the right to know that members of the original Hold family and their slaves . . . How shall I put this . . . They tended to die under mysterious, even violent, circumstances. There's no evidence that this is a stigmatized property per se . . ."

"Is this the part when you tell me the mansion is haunted? Did you feed Mason Allen that line too?"

"Of course not." The broker pulled her shoulders back and waved her hand in the air between them. "Mason is local. He knows all there is to know about this house."

A high-pitched peal erupted from the hallway. The sound was not human.

"What was that?" Cheyenne jumped, hand flying to her chest.

"It's bound to be a stray cat. The property is full of them." Lanie Brevard smiled politely.

Cheyenne fingered the natural pearl in her left ear, dropped her fidgeting hand, and set her chin. "I like cats," she lied to the broker. "In fact, I've been thinking about adopting a kitten."

SIX

‑❧‑❧‑‧❧‑❧‑

JINX BLAZED DOWN the interstate in her ruby-red pickup with a public library audiobook blaring from the speakers. The braid of sweetgrass made for her by Aunt Angie, the one she always traveled with and vowed never to burn, nestled in the crevice where the windshield met the dash.

She crossed the border into Tennessee at twilight and decided to stay over in Chattanooga on Sunday night. When she saw the billboard for the Chattanooga Choo Choo, the historic train depot converted into a pricey hotel, she imagined a long soak in a cool porcelain tub, plush white towels, and a cache of fancy toiletries. Turning off the highway, she pulled into a Super 8. After stashing her duffel and her messenger bag in a corner of the motel room, she twisted her braid into a knot, showered under the tepid spray, and dressed in jeans, a clean T-shirt, and high-top sneakers.

Jinx had to get back into the truck to find the main drag downtown, where she planned to forage for food and see what there was to see. She scooped up Coke cans, Twizzler wrappers, and used napkins, stuffing them into the crumpled McDonald's bag from that morning. She dumped the trash into a can on the sidewalk and took in the street scene around her. People were out enjoying the warm night air, savoring the last summer holiday weekend. Jinx walked among the chattering pairs and small groups, passing clothing boutiques, gift shops, and antique stores flanked by potted urns of vibrant late-blooming flowers.

On a quieter corner, she found a used bookshop with the name ONCE UPON A TIME stenciled above the entrance. Jinx ducked inside. Helping herself to a sugar cookie from the yellow plate on the counter because she never passed up free sweets, she scanned the bulging shelves. The clerk, a rosy-cheeked older woman dressed up like Mother Goose, complete with downy wings, waved at her. Jinx let her eyes linger on the employee and her costume for an indiscernible half-second before biting into the sugary wafer.

The store didn't have a section on Native American history, but the American history alcove overflowed into stacks on the floor. On the Civil War shelves, she found an out-of-print biography of Stand Watie, the heralded Cherokee brigadier general for the Confederacy. With one foot on a stepstool, she skimmed the first chapter. Watie's story began in southeastern Cherokee territory, where she was headed that weekend. He and his brother Buck had both attended the mission school run by Moravians on the Hold Plantation, the place where Mary Ann Battis had ended up after she set the fire. Jinx flipped to the index. No *Battis* there. But the book was well worth the six-dollar price. It would make for good contextual reading once she pulled into Georgia and found a place to stay for the week.

She tucked the book under her arm and moved down the aisle, not wanting to leave any stone unturned. She was examining the women's history and Southern history shelves, pulling out books to read their title pages, when she noticed a hardbound volume with needle-thin black lettering shelved behind other texts as if it had been forgotten. It was a nondescript reprint of an old Moravian Church history, seven hundred pages long, no contents page, no index, no price. Jinx swung her messenger bag onto her shoulder, holding a book in each hand as she speed-walked to the counter.

"Find what you needed?" Mother Goose said.

Jinx nodded. "But this one"—she pushed the heavy missionary

history across the counter—"isn't marked. How much does it cost?" She crossed the index and middle finger of her free hand, praying she could afford it.

Mother Goose studied her face, then the inside front and back covers of the dusty book. "That depends entirely on how much you're willing to give," she said.

*

The sky was slate dark, the air still warm, when Jinx left the bookshop. Smelling the tang of barbecue and hearing a din in the distance reminded her that she was starved. She followed the smell to a doorway framed by Christmas lights and a mounted speaker that pumped out the voice of Tammy Wynette. Inside, she sat at a picnic table covered with a sticky, checked plastic cloth and plotted out the next day's route on her highway map. When her meal arrived, Jinx folded the map and dove into a basket of brown-tipped fries and sauce-slathered ribs.

When she had finished her food, licked the tips of her fingers, and cleaned up with a wipe, Jinx headed for the wharf. She knew she had to see it before she left Tennessee: the riverside park. Cherokees had camped along the river here, at a place now called Ross's Landing, in preparation for their forced march west to Indian Territory.

Jinx took the boardwalk to the end, where it hung above the water. Blocking out the boisterous sounds of tourists and city dwellers in the background, she imagined the scene as it might have been 170 years ago. In the summer of 1838, her father's people had been herded here and corralled into rancid camps, where they sickened and died in the sweltering heat before their principal chief, John Ross, secured permission from Washington to postpone their departure until the weather cooled. Jinx pictured her ancestors inside the tent village. Old ladies with sagging eyes, grown men with flagging spirits, babies dying of heat exposure against their mothers' mourning breasts. It was as though they were all there with her at the wharf, behind a sheer curtain sewn of nothing but time. She could almost reach out to touch them, to whisper in their ears, to tell them that although it would cost dearly and always, their people would manage to survive.

The voice she heard in her head next might have been Deb Tom's, or perhaps her own conscience speaking up, awakened by the water. "And so would the people enslaved by our ancestors, who, though ignored by history, also walked the Trail of Tears," it said.

SEVEN

✦→✦→✦→ ·←✦←✦←✦

HE'S NOT HOME, Sally thought with a spike of relief when she saw Delta's faded sedan parked all by itself in the gravel drive. Delta must be working the holiday too. Mason Allen hadn't expanded his family's real-estate profits by giving folks time off for Labor Day. She bet he had his Mexican crew working right now in the empty lot that some folks whispered used to be a slave burial ground. Sally pushed Eddie Junior's umbrella stroller, grateful he was still asleep even though the wheels kept catching. Mason Allen's family home sprawled before her, three white clapboard triangles topped by red-tile eaves. It was an old Cherokee plantation house like the Hold place, built by the Indians before the Trail of Tears. Mason's family won it when the state of Georgia seized Cherokee homes in 1830 and redistributed them to white settlers in a rigged land lottery. Mason had kept the estate pristine, along with all the other property he would one day inherit from his daddy. The Allen family used to own as much land as James Hold had in his heyday. They'd even possessed the mountain that dominated the area, back before they donated it to create Fort Mountain State Park. The story went that it took a dinner in the Governor's Mansion with none other than Lady Bird Johnson to convince Old Man Allen to hand the mountain over for conservation and the benefit of the public. But Mason Allen could still have the state park closed when he had a mind to, for hunting parties, social-set picnics, and whatnot. He and everybody else acted like his family still owned half the county, one of the Blue Ridge Mountains, and practically all of the sky.

Sally leaned forward to heave Junior's stroller onto the porch. She rang the bell of Mason Allen's long white villa.

"Hi, sugar," Delta Jones said to Junior, whose bright blue eyes had just popped open when she answered the door. Delta nudged the door back with her hip, reaching down to unbuckle Junior. She and Sally both knew Mason Allen wouldn't tolerate stroller wheels on his checkerboard parquet flooring. "Come on in, Sally. You want some coffee?"

Delta was wearing her light blue maid's uniform, a cotton dress with buttons lined straight as a ruler down the front. A white apron dusted with flour curved around her ample middle. Her short gray hair was pressed and curled, shining from a recent visit to May Bell's Beauty Shop. Miss Delta always took care with her appearance, even now that she was knocking on the door of her seventy-eighth birthday.

"Yeah, Miss Delta. Thank you, and good morning. You been doing all right? Your hair sure looks nice."

"Thank you, sugar. We had a family picnic on Sunday, and you know I had to go and get my hair done for that," Delta said. "How about some grits?" she added, looking at the shadows under Sally's eyes.

"Yes, ma'am. I didn't make time for breakfast this morning. And Eddie Senior's been real busy lately. Gone a lot."

"Mmm-hmm," Delta said. "I'm through baking. Let me take Junior."

"Thank you, Miss Delta. But remember, now, he can't eat solids yet. Just formula, in the diaper bag."

"Is that what them doctors at the health clinic told you? I raised eight children of my own and three of the Allens. A baby can always use some good pot liquor. Chock-full of vitamins. I got some left from yesterday's collards. Now you go on and start that deep clean. Mason wants us half-time today. Seems like he's cutting back. That stock market hullabaloo all over the news has the rich white folks running crazy. You know where to find your supplies."

Shit, Sally thought, doing the math in her head. She did a deep clean for Mason once a month. She had been counting on a full day's job for her grocery money.

"Mr. Allen's out this morning?" Sally said, listening for the sound of his footfalls. He lived alone except for Delta on weekdays, and Gus, his three-legged hound dog.

"Afraid not. He's in the study, wrangling with somebody in New York on the telephone. He's been over at the courthouse wheedling old maps of the Hold Plantation out of poor Jasper, who surely would rather be home in bed on the holiday. He parked his truck in the garage when he got back. That's why you didn't see it. Might be he doesn't want people eyeballing his papers. He's more nervous than his daddy. Always thinking somebody's trying to outdo him."

"Too true," Sally said, handing Delta the diaper bag and kissing Junior on the nose. "Miss Delta, you're a lifesaver. I'll clean up quick." She smoothed Junior's downy tuft of strawberry hair. "You be good for Miss Delta, now."

Sally made her way up the sweeping double staircase, lifting the vacuum step by step. Mason had carpeted the stairs an eggshell white to contrast with the dark banister. That staircase was a bear to clean. She would start with the bedrooms.

"The hell I don't have it," Mason was barking as Sally passed his wood-paneled study. "You're my banker, Mort, not my nanny. Don't tell me what I can't spend. I don't care what's going on in that stock market of yours. Liquidate something if you have to. The condo project by the river is coming along just fine. I got the land for a song, and the units will sell big. We're close enough to Atlanta to draw out the yuppies. It'll generate income by springtime."

Sally peeled back the door of Mason's bedroom. She slipped inside, dragging the vacuum behind her. She freshened the linens on his bed and dusted the furniture. She used the special cloth he favored for his flat-screen TV, marveling again at the mammoth size of it. Besides the television and a leather lounge chair studded with brass prods, Mason hadn't changed his parents' room when they retired to their Florida vacation home and left him here to run the real-estate business. Sally wiped down the doors of Mason's closet, filled with dark, custom-made jackets ordered from Charleston and one or two seersucker suits for when he wanted to play the part of a Southern gentleman.

"Check with my father?" Mason's voice rose in undulating waves. "I run this company now. Land is what I deal in, Mort. Real estate. And I want that Hold Plantation. Nothing like it's changed hands around here since my granddaddy got charmed by a woman and gave away Fort Mountain. I know a good investment when I see one."

Sally opened the door to the master bathroom and lifted the lid of the john. She sprayed Clorox and started to scrub.

"My father didn't build up this family's fortune for me to come along and lose it. I will not lose it, Mort. It takes risk to play the game. Borrow the money if you have to. It'll sell below value. I'm up against a bunch of Indian lovers and a Black lookie-loo."

Sally flushed the toilet and watched a chemical-blue cyclone swirl toward the pipes. She knelt beside the spa bathtub, sprinkled cleanser in, and turned the water on. She scrubbed the rings from Mason's baths in rhythmic circles. Delta couldn't get this house as clean as she used to in her daily ministrations.

Sally felt him before she heard him—Mason's stiff blue jeans sharp against her folded back. Delta ironed them after the wash. Mason liked his creases.

"Sally." His voice was quiet. "Can't you keep it down in here? Can't you hear I'm trying to talk business?"

Sally turned off the faucet. Water sluiced from her hands and dripped from her forearms. She hated the way Mason always tried to catch her alone, tried to subtly press up against her and breathe in the scent of her hair. She never cleaned for him unless Delta was also in the house. She didn't trust him one lick. Especially now that the Hold

House was on the line and the town was wound up tighter than an old grandfather clock. Anything was liable to happen.

"Be more aware of your surroundings," Mason Allen said. "Or you might stumble into something you're not ready for." He slowly squeezed Sally's shoulder, turned his back to her, and glanced at his reflection. "You missed a spot on this mirror." He stepped back into the hall through the bathroom's second door, snapped his fingers, and commanded, "Come, Gus."

Sally heard the crippled coonhound teetering out from his corner in Mason's paneled study. Folks said it was good of Mason to keep his daddy's hound after it got shot in a hunting accident. But Sally knew Mason preferred weaker creatures so he could feel like top dog.

EIGHT

+->->->-·-<-<-<-

CHEYENNE ARRIVED EARLY for the property auction at the Murray County Courthouse on Tuesday. She had spent the weekend in the Room with a View Bed-and-Breakfast on Fort Mountain Road, studying her competition, skimming tour books about the Georgia Blue Ridge towns, and fending off repeated offers of rich morning pastries and high-carb fruit salads.

As she sat on a bench toward the front of the main chamber in the dome-roofed courthouse, adjusting her pearl necklace and checking her messages, Cheyenne eyed the anxious crowd slowly gathering around her. The room crackled with expectation. Representatives from the Department of Natural Resources arrived in inexpensive suits and ties and wearing masks of resignation. The green-uniformed rank-and-file employees of the Parks and Recreation division exuded frustration; they had turned out in force to defend their jobs and historic sites. Although the park employees and their supporters would try to have their say after waging a public fight in the newspapers, Cheyenne was sure the private sale would proceed. Decisions had been made at the executive level by the director of the Department of Natural Resources, who was appointed, not elected, and therefore had little to fear from public agitation. Golf courses and fishing lakes—big draws for tourists—would receive most of the state funding in this tight economy. Prizing revenue over what some viewed as sentimental attachment to the past, DNR officials had determined it made good financial sense to sell state history to the highest bidder. The Dahlonega Gold Museum, the Georgia State Archives building, and several other properties were also on the chopping block. The Hold House would be only the first historic site to go.

A small group of self-identified Native Americans conversed in the back of the courtroom. Reading their pained expressions, Cheyenne thought they didn't look any more "Indian" than she did. And even as she formed this split-second impression, Cheyenne felt the "Cherokee" contingent eyeing her with a curiosity akin to judgment. They would never entertain the thought that she might be Cherokee too. Because they were more white than Black, they got a pass. Their Cherokee identity was scarcely questioned by other people, while Cheyenne's was openly ridiculed even by her closest friends.

Across the aisle, the real-estate broker, Lanie Brevard, sat with a notepad in her lap. She glanced at Cheyenne and shook her head in a gesture that radiated pity. Cheyenne felt as if the whole room was watching her, as if a sign hung over her head spelling out: INTRUDER. She volleyed the stares of the Cherokee contingent, ignored the smug assessment of the broker. She held her head high, coiffed ponytail softly skimming the neckline of her raw-silk tank.

Cheyenne's gaze skated to the far corners of the room. She noticed that a spatial division had taken shape. Government officials and white professionals in shirts and ties populated the front of the courthouse. Employees of the Georgia state parks were clustered in the middle. The Cherokee contingent and some onlookers filled in the back. Opposite them on the other side of the courthouse, a few African Americans sat together. An older Black woman with pressed gray curls kept a steady, interested gaze on Cheyenne. An older man in overalls sat beside her. A woman in a paisley dress who might have been a schoolteacher had glasses dangling from a chain around her neck. The man next to her was dressed in a park-service uniform but sat apart from his fellow employees. He chatted easily with both women, making them laugh. His cropped hair lay in black waves, framing a sculpted chestnut face with angled cheekbones and a classically firm chin. His dark eyes were serious despite the levity he seemed determined to buoy in the others, as if he wanted those around him to feel safe but harbored private apprehensions.

Cheyenne felt a twinge for him, an uncharacteristic stab of empathy. He probably wanted the auction to go poof at the last minute, for a representative of the Department of Natural Resources to stand and say it was all a mistake. She pulled her gaze away from the park ranger's face, but not before his eyes found hers in the flicker of an instant.

She tapped the heel of one wine Ferragamo pump against the waxed courthouse floor. It was fifteen minutes past the appointed start time. The clock on her dream was ticking, and she didn't want one minute wasted.

Years ago, her parents had promised a down payment toward the purchase of her first home. It was an extravagance they could afford. Her father was a high-ranking Coca-Cola executive and major stockholder in the company. He and Cheyenne's mother, who came from old Atlanta money, owned a faux Italian villa in Decatur and a summer cottage on Martha's Vineyard. Cheyenne had lived in the carriage house behind the villa during her years at Emory and then while pursuing her MA in interior design at Georgia State. Moving to Candler Park had been her declaration of independence, and her parents had applauded the step. They were even more pleased to learn of her intention to use their promise of a house to start a small business. She needed her own achievements in life, her mother had opined over drinks at the tennis club, especially if she was going to attract the right sort of man: a doctor, lawyer, investor, or techno whiz with an Ivy League or Morehouse degree.

What was the holdup? Why was this taking so long? Cheyenne shot looks of annoyance at the auctioneer, who stood facing the packed house in a seersucker suit that stretched across his rotund middle. He seemed to be waiting for something to happen. And then it did. A cadre of well-dressed men barreled into the courtroom, moving like they owned the town and everybody in it. One of them, with storm-gray eyes and sandy hair, strode at the head of the pack. He had accentuated his tailored suit with a smart tie striped in Georgia Bulldog colors. *A UGA grad. With money. Wait until I tell the ladies about this,* Cheyenne thought. *Billy Bob just got an upgrade.* She took a steadying breath as the men settled into a row that had been left empty, as though reserved for them.

"What are we waiting for, Jasper?" the Bulldog said to the auctioneer.

But it was apparent to everyone in the room that he was the answer to his own question. They had been waiting for him—because this so-called public auction was predetermined. Cheyenne looked at Lanie Brevard, recalling their conversation the day before and the fragments she had overheard. *Mason Allen. Pillar of the town.* The Bulldog turned just then to find her with his slate-gray eyes. He gave her an appraising look and didn't smile. Cheyenne gripped the Blackberry in her hands. She knew determination when she saw it. He was there to steal the Hold House out from under her.

The auction began, the buzz of nervous conversation drowned out by the rhythmic calling of the auctioneer. Cheyenne sat on the edge of her bench, stiff and alert. She had accompanied her mother to Christie's auctions and watched expensive jewelry and curios changing hands, but she had never done this alone before, never made a bid for herself on something as large as a house.

"And who will start the bidding at one hundred thousand dollars? One hundred thousand for the house on the hillside and fifteen lush acres of prime Georgia farmland," the auctioneer intoned.

A man in a cowboy hat representing the Cherokee contingent bid first, lifting his hand with a pointed index finger. A low murmur of approval sounded from the back of the courthouse. This group was determined to keep the home out of private hands with the funds it had raised in its community campaign, which probably included many of the onlookers in the room that day.

Mason Allen casually threw his hand up, raising the bid to two hundred thousand.

Cheyenne bided her time, waiting to see what would happen next.

The man in the cowboy hat looked encouraged, and answered the auctioneer's prompt for an increase of fifty thousand dollars.

"Three hundred and one thousand, Jasper," Mason Allen said with quiet finality. His expression was one of satisfaction, as if he relished the moment.

The Cherokee contingent fell back against their benches, defeated. Everyone who followed the local news knew they had raised three hundred thousand dollars—an impressive figure, but not enough.

The courthouse went silent.

Cheyenne saw Mason Allen wink at Lanie Brevard.

"I have three hundred and one thousand dollars, three hundred and one thousand dollars. Who will make it four for this one-of-a-kind plantation property?"

"Four hundred thousand." Cheyenne's voice was high-pitched and shaky, like the ring of a wineglass touched to a tabletop by jittery fingertips.

Turning in his seat to look behind him, Mason Allen fixed his steely eyes on her face. He raised a hand at the auctioneer and coolly pledged half a million dollars.

Cheyenne knew the outcome was now uncertain. Her parents had set her limit at five hundred thousand, and even that was too much in their view. Just like Cheyenne, they had seen the Hold property photos online—visual evidence of the lapse in care, overgrown shrubbery, and provincial town services. But to Cheyenne, those photos didn't do the house justice. You had to be there to sense its true value. You had to feel the spirit of the house.

Cheyenne tapped the buttons of her Blackberry as she worded a hasty text message to her father and waited for his answer. "Going bid is 500k. Great investment. Go to 600, Daddy?"

Her cell phone beeped, and she lifted her hand with a cautious smile. Her father had replied within seconds. She was still in the game.

Mason Allen's face reddened. He raised his hand like an ax splitting wood. He never took his eyes from hers as he bid seven hundred, eight hundred, nine hundred thousand, more. Cheyenne saw her opponent's emotions rising with each sharp cut of his palm in the air. He could be running out of rope. They could be close to the end.

Cheyenne's fingers flew across her phone. She didn't want to give her father time to call or text her sensible mother, who would have nipped this venture in the bud hundreds of thousands of dollars ago. But she had always been her father's little princess.

She seized on the thought. "Daddy," she typed out, "it can be all mine for 1 mil. I've never wanted anything more."

Seconds that felt like minutes passed. Her cell phone beeped. Cheyenne was stunned as she uttered aloud the figure that could have bought a spectacular townhouse in Savannah's famed historic district, now that the real-estate market was showing signs of an impending crash.

Mason Allen sat back, breathing like a steam engine, his face bright red. Cheyenne heard a collective gasp. She had won her dream house, to have and to hold. And the big man on campus had been bested, maybe for the first time in his life. Her stomach tightened with the promise and the anxiety of it.

Mason Allen turned to his astonished associates with a look that could not contain his rage. He stood and strode down the courtroom aisle with a confidence born of privilege. The other men followed. The state employees craned their necks. Lanie Brevard wilted with patent disappointment.

When Mason passed the bench where Cheyenne sat, flushed by her public triumph, he paused to hold out a hand to her. "Congratulations, Miss Cotterell. The Hold House is quite a prize—and quite a challenge to secure in these elements. You've got your vermin, your floods, your wildfires, your vagrants, and the occasional violent criminal hiding out from the law in the woods. How many doors and windows are there on that big place? Have you counted yet? If I was the one wearing your pretty high heels right now, I'd run to Atlanta and not look back."

Cheyenne pressed into her seat, instinctively ducking her head like prey. Then she recognized the message she was sending. She regained her composure and raised her dark eyes to meet his. This man needed to understand that she would not be so easily cowed, that she was the kind of woman who got what she wanted. Hadn't he just seen proof of that?

"Mr. Allen, is it? Don't you worry about me. I can take care of myself."

"In that case, sleep tight, and don't let the bedbugs bite." He laughed at his own words, making show of his good sportsmanship without letting the vocal levity alter the steel of his eyes.

"Please, this way." The auctioneer was speaking to Cheyenne. She stood and saw over the auctioneer's shoulder that a cluster of people, the African American contingent in the back, had stayed to watch her interaction with Allen. One of them, the far-too-attractive park ranger, held his hat in a tight-knuckled grip and scowled.

Cheyenne followed the auctioneer, who motioned her toward a private meeting room where she handled the paperwork with Lanie Brevard and a horde of shocked attorneys and state representatives. She signed the last page and stood, smoothing the red-wine silk of her knee-length skirt. She held her shoulders upright and headed toward the courtroom doors with a sashaying walk. She didn't glance at Mason Allen, who still stood beside her empty bench, hands clenched in his pockets.

"Well, now." Cheyenne heard a voice like rustling autumn leaves as she passed through the courthouse doors and onto the broad stone steps. It was the elderly woman with silver hair and maple-syrup-colored skin. Her light blue dress was like a costume out of time, a 1950s-style maid's uniform. And if she was still standing here, she had made it a point to wait for Cheyenne.

"Just look at you, sugar."

"Excuse me?" Cheyenne said.

"Just look at you. I'm Delta Jones. Lived here all my life. And I ain't never seen nothing like that before. The Allens bumped down a notch. Where are you from? Who are your people?"

Cheyenne saw pride shining in the woman's eyes, pride directed toward her. She offered her hand and introduced herself.

"Owning the Hold House is more than a notion," Delta Jones said. "Funny thing about that place. No one can seem to hold on to it, no matter how bad they want to. The children of James Hold lost the land to the Georgia state lottery before that Trail of Tears. The Georgia militia men who drew the lots set fire to the house to smoke the family out, and then fought to the death with each other because they thought there was gold on the grounds."

"I'm not intending to go anywhere, Mrs. Jones," Cheyenne said, clutching her handbag and glancing back toward the courthouse door. "Nor am I planning to die."

She took note of the park ranger with the serious eyes standing behind Mrs. Jones, listening to their exchange. But she didn't want to make eye contact, for fear of what she would see in his face. Surely not the kind of pride that the elderly Mrs. Jones exuded, a racial pride she remembered from her grandmother's generation of Black Southern women. No. The ranger's job had been on the line, and his side, the state employees, had not even had one chip to play.

The park ranger had lost to her, just like Mason Allen. Would she see anger in his expression? Resentment? Outrage? Cheyenne chanced a glance. Up this close, the ranger's eyes were magnetic, so dark and intense that they rivaled a stormy nighttime sky. He shook his head—in disbelief, or maybe frustration—when their eyes finally met.

"Come on, Miss Delta," he said in a Southern accent thicker and deeper than what Cheyenne was used to in Atlanta. "Let me drive you back to work."

Fine. That was fine with her. She didn't need to know his name. She would probably never see him again. Maids and park employees were not exactly in her social set. The Hold House auction had brought out all sorts of people, and now they would scatter again to the places where they belonged.

"Watch yourself, sugar," Mrs. Jones called as the ranger gently led her away, touching an elbow to guide her toward the courtroom doors. "Things ain't always what they seem. Shallow waters run out. Still waters run deep."

NINE

⤖⤖·⤛⤛

JINX SLEPT IN at the Super 8, called her cousin and her mother to tell them she was still alive, and found an IHOP for lunch because she would eat pancakes anytime.

By late afternoon, she crossed the state line and found the town of Chatsworth, Georgia, sister city to the historic township of Hold Hill, where the Hold Plantation and Moravian mission were located. She followed Highway 411 through the center of town, passing an old inn, boarded up and abandoned, with a massive sign of a caricatured Indian advertising the Chief Hold Hotel. She drove past a brick law office, a flat-roofed diner, and a dive called Chief Hold Video and Tanning that shared a lot with a Marathon gas station. Indian kitsch was always weirdest in places where Native Americans used to live in large numbers. Jinx rolled her eyes, pulling into the gas station. She had read online that there were a few motels in town, mostly along the main road into the mountains. She would grab a fresh Coke and ask for directions.

"You're not looking for the Hold House, are you?" the young woman behind the register said. She held out her hand to take Jinx's money for Twizzlers, Coke, and beef jerky. "It's closed. No more tours. We used to get a lot of Indians coming through to visit the place back when I worked there. Cherokees and Poarch Creeks, mainly. Are you from North Carolina? Alabama?" The woman was in her early twenties. She had a bright Southern drawl and rambunctiously curly strawberry hair pinned back at her temples with flat barrettes. Her sunny smile contrasted with the circles beneath her eyes.

"Oklahoma," Jinx said. "What happened to the tours?"

"The museum closed a few years ago. Folks around here hoped it might reopen, but the state auctioned off the place just this morning. It's a sad case, to tell you the truth."

Sold. Jinx's hopes fell even as her attention pricked at this unexpected opinion. "Why do you think so?"

"It wasn't just General Scott who ran the Cherokees out of this valley. The local militia was in on it up to their ears. The way I see it, the state of Georgia is guilty for the part we played. The least we could do is keep the Hold House open as a show of respect for the fact that the Indians were here before any of us white folks. But I'm going on too much. I always do that, Eddie says." The young woman handed Jinx her change and clamped her lips shut.

"Eddie sounds like an idiot," Jinx said, smiling at her.

The woman blinked in surprise, then grinned. "Don't tell his mama that. She'll quit babysitting for me Tuesdays and Thursdays. Want to drink that now?" She handed Jinx an old-fashioned bottle opener and leaned forward on the counter.

Jinx popped the top on her frosted Coca-Cola, cradling the thick green glass. "Heaven," she said, taking a swig. "I'm Jennifer Micco. And I could listen to people talk about history all day."

"Sally Perdue, no kin to the governor. And I guess you could say I'm a history buff too."

Jinx leaned forward. "So, who bought the house? At the auction?"

Sally Perdue glanced around the store. Except for a couple in biking shorts quibbling over the various brands of bottled water and a lone teenager lurking around the explicit magazines, it was empty. "Mason Allen tried to buy it. He's a real-estate man and builder whose family goes back a long way here. He spent a month placing ads in the paper about his big plan to build a housing development on the old Hold property. The Cherokee Chieftains Club, he was calling it, 'where the streets are lined with gold.'"

"Sounds a little over the top." Jinx sipped her Coke.

"Not around here. We had our very own gold rush in 1829. Allen liked the idea of it, I guess—the symbol of the gold. The development was supposed to be real fancy, with a clubhouse in the original building, half-a-million-dollar homes scattered around it, and a golf course in the old cornfields and wheat fields. I bet he's steamed he couldn't get his hands on that land. Somebody else bought it right out from under him. A woman from Atlanta." Sally whispered, "A Black woman."

Jinx's eyebrows shot up. Her chances of getting into the place might have just improved. "Is she there now?"

"She came to town for the holiday weekend. Drives a Mercedes." Sally winked. "Looks like she's got what it takes to give Mason Allen a run for his money."

Jinx was quiet, recalibrating.

"You know," Sally continued, "maybe she'd let you see the place. Wouldn't hurt to ask. It's just up the road, past the four-way stoplight. You'll go up a hill and turn right at the iron gates."

"Thanks," Jinx said. "Could you recommend a place to stay around here? For cheap?"

"How long are you fixin' to be in town?"

"Just a few days."

"There's a bed-and-breakfast way up the mountain road, before you reach the entrance to Fort Mountain Park. That'll run you at least a hundred a night. But if you want cheap, I have a neighbor who rents a room in his cabin. He clears out and stays in his tent. Charges thirty bucks a day, and that includes a fair share of whatever he's got in the fridge."

"Is he a good guy?" Jinx said, her tone pointed.

"The best. Used to work at the Hold House before they shut it down. Now he gets by how he can, like most of us."

"How would I find this place?"

"It's halfway up the mountain road. A log cabin with a green door and a vegetable garden out front, just past the Ball Fruit Stand that looks like it's falling apart."

"A fruit stand?"

"The Ball Fruit Stand. Even though the sign fell off its hooks, you can still make out the words. My grandparents used to own it, but they lost the land due to taxes. Here, try this."

Sally reached below the register and then handed Jinx a canning jar wrapped in a red-checked square of cloth. "Strawberry preserves. I learned how to make homemade jams from my grandma. They used to sell the freshest fruit at that stand, sweet and juicy like you wouldn't believe, a lot of it grown right over in the Hold House orchards. There's still plenty of good fruit there, even though the state let the grounds go to pot. My jams are the hottest items in this store. My boss pretends like he doesn't know I'm selling them in exchange for jars for his wife."

"How much do you charge?" Jinx said, eyeing the jar that was already making her mind wander to pancakes smothered in jam.

"It's a gift. Stop back in before you leave town and say hello." Sally reached for Jinx's empty Coke bottle. "I'll take that for you."

"Thanks. And I'll be sure to." Jinx grabbed her plastic bag of snacks, along with the container of jam. She saw the teen loafing his way to the counter with a computer gaming magazine and stepped out of his path as she headed for the exit.

"If you stay at Adam Battis's cabin, tell him I sent you," Sally called. "I live just up the road from him, in a white trailer."

Jinx stopped in her tracks. Adam *Battis*? Then, through the convenience-store window cluttered with decals and obscured by two-liter Sprite bottles, she saw the lot suddenly fill. Three men pulled up in a roar of sound: engines, brakes, and revved-up voices. Rifles hung at the rear of their vehicles. A dead doe, her neck nearly severed, flopped in one of the truck beds. The men jumped from their cabs, cloaked in Day-Glo hunting vests. They yanked the gasoline hoses free and filled their tanks.

The teenager squeezed past Jinx, who had frozen in place, holding the door ajar.

"Speak of the devil," Sally Perdue said. "Mason Allen hunting with firearms before the season's open. He must be madder than hell today." Taking her cue from Sally, who had gone rigid as a scarecrow, Jinx fixed her eyes on the man striding toward the building. He pushed past her as if she were invisible. The smell of sweat mixed with cologne wafted from his skin in the tight space of the doorway. Jinx backed into a rack of free advertising circulars, watching the other two men follow in his footsteps.

"Why didn't you get him, Mase?" one of the men called out while he grabbed a six-pack from the cooler. The couple in biking shorts made their way to the checkout with bottles of Evian and pouches of granola.

"I told you I didn't have the angle," the first man responded in a low voice.

"Lay off," the third man said. "Mason's had a tough day. Probably doesn't feel right hunting in the Hold House woods now that some-body else holds the deed."

Mason Allen's face went red as he turned to his fellow. "If I didn't feel right hunting in those woods, I wouldn't have suggested it. I still own all the property around that estate, which is more than any other man in this town can say. I'll hunt anyplace I damn well please. Noth-ing's changed."

"Sure," the third man said. "We know that. Why don't you come over to the house tonight? I'll have Jules clean up the deer. We'll have venison, some good draft pints, and Betty's fresh chess pie. We can shoot some pool and relax."

Jinx watched Mason Allen's temper drain. He had accepted the peace offering.

"She won't last in that big old place," the second man said. "Wild animals in the woods. Pests and barn cats in the house."

"Damn straight," said Mason Allen. "She won't last a week."

With a last glance toward Sally, who was ringing up the couple's things, Jinx hustled to her truck. Turning out of the parking lot, she headed in the direction of a tree-covered mountain jutting into the sky.

*

Jinx followed the two-lane road through town, past chicken coops and an old sawmill. As the road climbed, the buildings and yards spread farther apart beside it. A forest sprang up to her left, throwing shade. Jinx spotted a dilapidated ruin of white wood and lattice, where a faded, peeling sign on the ground pictured a blush-orange peach on the stem: BALL FRUIT STAND. She peered into breaks in the trees beyond the stand and spotted a small log cabin with dark green shutters and a porch set with two red rocking chairs. She turned down the dirt road, passing raised garden beds crowded with corn-stalks, sunflowers, and tomatoes. She passed a small woodshed and parked by an old pump well.

"Hello?" Jinx called into the yard. No one answered. She climbed the porch steps and knocked on the closed screen door. Nothing. A handwritten *Guests Check Here* sign was taped to a tin mailbox on the porch floor. Jinx opened the lid. An envelope was inside. "Instruc-tions for Guests," it read. The note invited visitors to use the enclosed key to let themselves in, to put a sign on the front door, and to leave thirty dollars in the box; it also provided a number to call if they needed anything. *Trusting guy,* Jinx thought. *Or crazy guy.* She riffled through the supply of mini flashlights and one-size-fits-all rain pon-chos in the mailbox and saw a stack of creased motel-style DO NOT DISTURB signs. She was too curious to turn around and leave, too strapped to pay B&B prices. Besides, Adam Battis had to come home sometime, and Jinx wanted to find out exactly who he was. She pulled the key out of the envelope and unlocked the cabin door.

The building was designed with an open layout of around six hundred square feet. A loft bed with a futon underneath was built into the wall to the left of the entry door. A sign taped to the futon frame read FOR GUESTS. A stone fireplace was the focal point, encir-cled by a plaid sofa and a ladder-back wooden chair. Outdated gas appliances and a scratched round table and chairs made up a kitchen area in the rear corner. The space was neat and clean and smelled like pine trees. There was little clutter to offer clues about the man who lived here—no photographs on the dresser, no pictures on the wall, no dirty dishes in the sink. A bag of dry cat food hunched on the kitchen counter, but she saw no sign of a cat.

Instead of trinkets or photos or pets, this man collected books. Built-in bookshelves sandwiched the fireplace and wrapped around the living room walls. The titles were labeled by category, then by genre—*Fiction: Literary, Mystery, Speculative; Nonfiction: Religion, Science, Mythology*. The shelf by the futon was labeled *Local Interest* and held books on Cherokee history, Georgia history, plantation architecture, Southern gardening, and the Appalachian Trail. Brochures and maps had a home on the shelf, along with a laminated field guide to birds and a bin of vintage postcards marked at a dollar each. Between Mother Goose at the bookstore, Sally at the gas station, and the mysterious Adam Battis, Southern hospitality had reached heights of knowledge and eccentricity Jinx had never imagined.

She went out to get her duffel and messenger bags, then hung the DO NOT DISTURB sign on the front door. She rummaged in the fridge and cupboards and made herself buttered toast with gobs of Sally's homemade jam, uttering an involuntary "Hmm" as she bit into a piece. Jinx washed her dishes and made up the futon with the striped bedsheets folded at the foot. She heaved the heavy church history out of her duffel bag and situated two bed pillows along the back of the futon. Sitting up against them, she pushed her legs in front of her and listened for the sound of a car approaching. She would read while she waited for Adam Battis to appear.

Jinx opened the book to the title page: *A History of the United Brethren in America, Inclusive of Abstracts of the Hold Hill Mission of the Cherokee Nation, 1815–1825, kept by our brethren and sisters who journeyed into the darkness of the heathen Indian lands*. She skimmed the chronicle of church events in eastern and central Europe, Pennsylvania, and North Carolina, making her way toward the section on the Cherokee mission on the Hold Plantation:

What follows is an accounting of the Hold Hill Mission to the Cherokees. The chronicle is based on the diary of Missionary Anna Rosina Kliest Gamble, as summarized by her favorite pupil and Indian sister in Christ, Mary Ann Battis, who gave the story in a letter to the clerk of the Church before her death in 1886. The diary of Mrs. Gamble, known only to her pupil, is lost now to history. It was, the Indian sister related, full of anecdotes, sometimes even of thrilling interest, particularly those in reference to the celebrated James Hold & his contemporaries. After her mother's early death, Mrs. Gamble was raised to great success in the Bethlehem orphanage and boarding school. She taught sixteen years in the Female Academy at Bethlehem. Later in life, she was a very efficient help in the Missionary labors of Br. John Gamble and became the Hold Hill Mission's chief diarist. It is to be regretted that Mrs. Gamble had no biographer, & even astonishing that she was not her own, as she was passionately fond of her pen & wrote about almost everything, excepting herself. Her command of English, both written and spoken, was exceptional. Her gifted mind possessed a poetic fancy. She left many pages of manuscript, which we fear have been lost. Gathered here is all that remains, as recalled by her devoted pupil.

An immediate picture of Mrs. Gamble affixed itself to Jinx's mind—based, she guessed, on her brief encounter with Moravian history in graduate school, as well as a hazy image of Laura Ingalls Wilder's mother from the *Little House on the Prairie* television show. She envisioned a kindly middle-aged woman with graying light brown hair swept up into a modest bun. On top of Mrs. Gamble's head rested a thin covering trimmed with handworked lace. Satisfied with her conjured image, Jinx continued to read:

After the restoration of peace following the Cherokee War with the English in 1760, it was decided by the Church to establish a Mission among the Cherokees, but the Indians were not then receptive. In the wake of the American War of Independence, which changed the balance of power in the region, our ambassadors received a friendly reception from James Hold, a chief of the upper Cherokee towns, who said if the Brethren should open a grammar school for their children, we might come and make a trial of teaching the Gospel also. The upper chiefs came to our ambassadors, bid them welcome, & shook them by the right hand as a sign of friendship. James Hold appropriated land for the use of the Mission & directed his Negroes to assist our Brethren in enlarging an existing cabin. According to the instructions agreed upon in the meeting, we were not to concentrate on the Indians alone but to give some attention to the half Indians and the Negroes also, many of whom were slaves.

At last the Revd. John Gamble, an experienced and faithful Minister of the Brethren's Church, who had already been on a visit to Hold Hill and was well known to Mr. James Hold, felt himself called upon to accept an appointment as principal Missionary from our Church to the Cherokees. His respected wife, who had entered into the married state but a few months before, after having served for many years as principal Tutoress in the School for young ladies at Bethlehem in Pennsylvania, accompanied him. Mrs. Gamble had, two years prior, accompanied the Revd. Loskiel in a visit to our Indian Congregation in Ohio. Her mind opened to the plight of the Aborigines of America, she found herself called into Mission service. Out of interest and care for the Indians, she joined herself to Mr. Gamble, who sought a spouse to assist him in our Missionary labours amongst the Cherokees. There, by the Lord's blessings, Mrs. Gamble's gifts proved a particular benefit for the Scholars at Hold Hill.

Besides providing food and raiment for the scholars, keeping school daily, acting as physician, entertaining visitors, writ-

ing letters, & on Sunday teaching the Gospel, Mrs. Gamble
kept, in the midst of this wilderness, a botanic garden, contain-
ing many exotic and medicinal plants listed by their Linnaean
names. To her friends at Salem and Pennsylvania, besides,
Mrs. Gamble sent between twelve and fourteen hundred specimens of dried plants, & near a hundred packets of seeds, several minerals, specimens of all the Indian manufactures of cane
and a number of other curiosities.

In early March, 1815, the Gambles arrived at Hold Hill, the
plantation of Mr. Hold, which is about eighty miles from
Tellico Blockhouse, Tennessee. Mr. Hold was a half Indian but
in his dress & color & conduct was quite like a white man. Mr.
Hold had there two wives, who kept busy spinning and weaving cotton. He had ninety Negroes and a German overseer
who took care of the plantation. Mr. Hold had about one hundred heads of horses. He traveled mostly to Charleston and
Augusta, & many people came from afar to trade with him.

Mr. Hold resided in a fine brick house, the first of its kind
in the Cherokee country, with a dignified doorway and bridge-
like stairway that was much wondered upon by visitors. Hold's
house had a large and spacious yard with many beautiful roses
and shade trees, & somewhere in this yard, it was rumored, lay
a hidden treasure. The Georgia settlers say it is a trench of
pure gold buried by the mound building Indians who dwelled
in this valley in ancient times. These stories have never been
confirmed. Beyond Hold's home and fields, his mill at the
creek, & his ferry at the Conasauga, all was perfectly wild.

Jinx forgot she was reading as she tunneled deeper into the world
of the 1800s. Afternoon sunlight speckled the windows, filtered
through a bank of pines. Unseen birds called from perches high in the
treetops. Jinx drifted off to sleep with the weighty book pressed to
her chest, reducing her breathing to shallow draws of dreamlike air.

TEN

✦➤➤➤·◄◄◄

CHEYENNE FINGERED THE fine lace curtains flowing against the glass in the Hold House master bedroom. She opened the chestnut wardrobe, unzipped her Louis Vuitton suitcase, and lifted out her dresses, blouses, and skirts. As she put her things away, Cheyenne imagined what life was like here two hundred years ago, when the home was illuminated by candlelight and the man of the house would have come home riding a steed. She pictured Chief James Hold, dark and chiseled like the male models on the covers of her historical romance novels.

The house was still. The room was quiet around her except for the scratching that seemed to come from behind one of the many shut doors.

She smoothed back the dampening hair at her forehead. She left the room, crossed the odd interior bridge, and descended the staircase, thrilling again to the echo of her heels on the floors of her dream home. She made her way into the drawing room, approached a window, and drew back the golden curtains. Her eyes fell on the ornate furnishings, on the fine film of dust. She thought fleetingly of something she had heard once on *The View:* 80 percent of dust is made up of dead skin cells that people shed in the course of daily life, which meant that in any person's home—on the dusty bookshelves and windowsills—were bits and pieces of the resident's former self. Did dust from a thousand lives settle into the crevices of an old house like this one, forming sediment as deep as an archaeological pit?

Cheyenne didn't want to think so.

She untied another of her Jackie O scarves and let the hair of her ponytail fall gently to her shoulders. And before she knew what she intended, she found herself dusting the room. The silk scarf, thin and delicate, fluttered in Cheyenne's hand, caressing the indentations of the carved fireplace mantel. Dust rose and fell again onto the oak floorboards, soft as a fresh snowfall. Through the windows, she could see that dusk had stolen in and settled itself upon the grounds. High in the cottonwood trees, catydids hummed. Cheyenne draped her sullied scarf across the Tiffany fireplace screen. The lateness of the hour surprised her. She had skipped every meal that day and was starting to feel it. She wondered if she would still be able to find a takeout salad in town.

Cheyenne stepped out into an evening humid after the day's long heat. She locked the front doors behind her with the heavy notched key that Lanie Brevard had given her at the courthouse. Sweat pooled in the hollow between her breasts beneath the wine-colored silk. September was turning out to be one of the hottest on record in Georgia, with temperatures hovering in the nineties.

As she stood on the wide front porch fanning herself with an open hand, Cheyenne heard a rustling in the azalea bushes. She narrowed her eyes, scanning the shrubbery for rabbits, opossums, or rabid raccoons and vowing to buy a can of pepper spray at the next opportunity. But this was no small animal. The man who emerged from behind a utility shed raised his hand in a gesture of greeting—or maybe guilt, given that he was trespassing.

Cheyenne squinted in the dark, her heart racing to catch her panic. She backed into the porch's shadows and fumbled for the door key to go back inside. Forged of heavy brass like the others on the ring, the key was a rock in her fist. She aimed it, hand shaking, at the lock. But what had been easy a moment ago seemed impossible now. The lock resisted as the stranger approached.

He walked the curving stone path beside the overgrown formal garden, then stopped twenty feet away from the front porch. Cheyenne fished the Blackberry from her purse, stabbed 911, then swore aloud in a whisper. Her cell phone got no signal here. The ridged mountains nearby and steep dip to the river made her new plantation house a pre-tech lockbox. She realized just how vulnerable these isolated fourteen acres of hillside made her. Toni's sarcastic voice popped into her head as she imagined her friend commenting. *Gone With the Wind* meets *Halloween*.

"Excuse me, ma'am," the man said. "I didn't mean to startle you."

His deep voice and green uniform were little data feeds that let Cheyenne take a breath. She paused with a finger hanging over her useless cell phone. She recognized this man. The park ranger.

"The name's Adam Battis," he said, standing at a distance, slowly rolling the vowels on his tongue. "I'm with the Georgia Parks and Recreation unit of the Department of Natural Resources. I work here—used to. The Hold House was my responsibility, so I still keep an eye on the place. Seen anybody around here tonight?"

Cheyenne took in all she could of him through the evening shadows. He was tall and stood with a wide-legged stance that projected subtle confidence, an ease in his own skin that few men she knew possessed. His eyes flashed through the dusk with a dark intensity as he scanned the grounds.

"Besides you?" she said, raising her hands to her hips. That's when she noticed he was holding a bag of pet food and a Maglite. She zoomed in on this odd detail, putting aside for a second the thought that he lived close enough to keep watch over the place—and to watch her—a possible comfort or possible worry. "We almost met this morning. Cheyenne Cotterell. Even if I were to accept your excuse for being at my house uninvited after dark, I can't fathom why you have that bag."

"For the feral cats. This plantation's full of them, mostly in the outbuildings, though one or two have been known to slip inside the main house. They can hunt for themselves, but I don't like to think of them being out here on their own for too long. Need some help with that?"

Cheyenne knew he meant the lock. What she didn't know was whether he was a Good Samaritan or a disgruntled ex-employee who might go postal. Everyone who worked at the Hold House had been fired or reassigned when the place closed. There was bound to be some bad blood out there, some resentment at the recent turn of events.

"Not necessary. I've got everything under control. My husband is on his way from the city. I'm going to meet him for dinner now."

The man looked skeptical, then amused, or so Cheyenne thought as she tried to read his eyes without seeming to.

"I understand." He paused. "And if that husband of yours deserves you, he ought to give you a ring."

Cheyenne turned her back on him to perform raising the key to the lock. She heard the tease of a smile in his voice and knew he had seen right through her. She felt a tug of interest against her will. He was smart. And attractive . . . And unemployed. But she would probably never see him again. If he was lucky, he would be reassigned to another state park.

Being a beauty had always made her bold. She considered turning to face the ranger, offering him an inviting smile and making a return joke about the nonexistent husband—or not. Some men liked the idea of sneaking around. Fine with her. She was comfortable with one-night stands, and in fact preferred them. Until she found the catch she would marry and make her mother happy with, men to Cheyenne were like those three-hundred-dollar throw pillows: necessary clutter. She could have this country ranger dumbstruck and panting in less than five seconds and be back at work on her dream home by morning. So, why not?

Cheyenne rolled her shoulders back and turned to hit Adam with her irresistible full-lipped smile. Her loose mane of straight hair flew as she turned, spilling loosely across her breasts.

It took her only a second, instead of the five she had planned on, to realize something had changed. The path was empty. The ranger was already gone.

Cheyenne felt disarmed. When had a man failed to linger as she walked away, failed to steal just one more look at her on the sly? *Maybe he's gay.*

She bit the corner of her lip, fit her key into the lock, and reentered the house. The strangeness of the evening hadn't diluted her hunger. Instead, it had made the gnawing in her stomach grow worse. She sat on the teal divan in the drawing room, replaying the scene in her mind until precisely thirty minutes had passed. She was giving the park ranger plenty of time to clear out. There was no way she wanted to lay eyes on him now. There was also no chance she would find a decent restaurant open this late in what Layla had called the boonies. She would have to find a grocery store if she wanted to eat anything at all.

Cheyenne sighed, grabbed her purse, and headed for the Piggly Wiggly.

*

The city of Dalton was twenty minutes west of the Chief Hold House. Twenty minutes just to reach a facsimile of civilization. The Room with a View Bed-and-Breakfast, where Cheyenne had stayed on Fort Mountain Road, stocked a cooler of grocery items in its gift shop. Now Cheyenne could see why. She would have to do something similar when she transformed the Hold House—serve breakfast and afternoon tea to her guests and run a gourmet commissary.

She pulled her sports coupe into the lot at the Piggly Wiggly, a name that somehow brought two unappealing images to Cheyenne's mind: one of three dancing little pigs and another of roasted pork loin. Popular culture had lately decided pork was "the other white meat," but Cheyenne didn't trust it. She had given up pork chops and steak years ago, along with baked goods, potatoes, rice, and cheese. She had caught on early that her looks were something special, that she was, as her mother said, a true beauty. And true beauty had to be protected, just like fine art and architectural landmarks.

Cheyenne had learned that lesson well. In sixth grade, when she had started filling out, her mother noticed a ripple of flesh across Cheyenne's stomach. "Oh, no, honey," she had said. "We're not having that. Hold that belly in. A true beauty like you can't afford fat." So Cheyenne had held it in, every day, until she forgot what it felt like not to clasp her muscles like a knot of coiled rope. As she entered high school, and her breasts took shape and her hips flared out, her stomach remained as flat as a girl's. She made sure of that. When her body struck back at her, it was with hunger, a clutch at the gut that couldn't be satiated with all the celery sticks in the world. Like the clawing feeling of emptiness she felt right now that had brought her to the Piggly Wiggly.

The parking lot was nearly vacant. Cheyenne parked two spaces from a green Ford truck that looked like it belonged in an old car show. She eased out of the car, feeling again the sticky residue of the day's heat. From the seat of an idling motorcycle, a young man eyed her. He was white with bad-boy tattoos, rumpled hair, and thick eyelashes. Back in Atlanta with the safety of her friends nearby, she might have done him if they had met in a trendy club. Her mother wouldn't have approved, of course. Her mother wanted her married yesterday to a Black man from a Black family that was wealthy and fair-skinned like theirs. The guy with the tattoos smiled at her, letting his eyes roll over her figure. Cheyenne avoided his gaze, stepping quickly away.

The sliding doors swooshed. She entered the cool space, thinking this shop had been new once. Now it just looked tired, worn, and grungy, a grocery store past its prime. She picked up a basket and headed for the produce aisle, holding her purse on the elbow of her other arm. Cheyenne skimmed the signs. Where were the organics? She would give anything for a Whole Foods right now. After five minutes, she gave up, settling for pre-bagged iceberg lettuce, floppy celery sticks, and wan tomatoes that should have had a few more days in the sun.

"Good evening, Piggly Wiggly customers," came a canned voice over the loudspeaker. "Our store will be closing in fifteen minutes. Please bring your final selections to a register, and have a good night."

Cheyenne looked at her paltry basket. She would have made a poor wife back in the Cherokees' day in Georgia, when the men hunted and the women gathered fruits and nuts. She lifted a bag of wilted sprouts and found unsalted California almonds. She hurried to the dairy aisle, where she fingered a package of low-fat dip.

"You only live once. Go for the good stuff," a deep voice said.

Cheyenne whirled. Adam the park ranger. For the third time today.

He had already changed since she saw him prowling her grounds over an hour ago. His wavy hair glistened from a shower. He smelled like Irish Spring and pinesap. He had discarded the park-service uniform and was dressed in worn blue jeans, a dark green T-shirt, and brown leather sandals. She felt disheveled next to him, rumpled and sweaty, even though he was in Levi's and she was in raw silk. She also felt as if she had been caught doing something shameful.

"The dip," he explained. "You can do better than low-fat."

"I don't really eat dip." Cheyenne put the container back. "I was looking for the soy milk."

"The milk is that way." He pointed down the wall.

"Of course." Cheyenne worked to regain her bearings. This was not how things went with her. She was calm. She was poised. She wrapped men around her little finger. Cheyenne rolled her shoulders back, accentuating the swell of her breasts. "I'm afraid I may have been rude when you came to the house tonight, Adam. I wasn't expecting anyone, and . . ."

"You were right to be cautious. You can't trust everybody around here." He leaned down, resting his elbows on his cart, bringing his eyes to her level. He had five inches on her despite her tall, model height.

Cheyenne took in the contents of his cart: pork chops, drumsticks, brown rice, cereal, eggs, tortilla chips, olive oil, cat food. Impulsively she asked, "Can I trust *you*?"

Adam's eyes flickered at that. She had caught his attention. "Most of the time," he chuckled. "Listen, when you go back to Atlanta to get your things, you might want to consider installing one of those electronic security cameras."

"How do you know I'm from Atlanta?"

"It's a small town. People talk . . . And you look it."

"I look what?" Cheyenne flipped her gleaming hair and let it fall back into place. Adam watched the motion with something behind his eyes, something she wasn't used to. Amusement.

"Rich," he said.

"There's plenty of money around here, I've noticed."

"We've got our kingpins and our second-home seasonals. But most folks who live here full-time struggle to get by."

Cheyenne dropped her eyes, her thoughts going to that elderly woman, Delta Jones, in her maid's uniform and the man in front of her who was now out of a job. "About the Hold House. I hope you understand that the state would have sold it whether it was to me or someone else."

"What are your plans for the house? Weekend getaway? Rental property? Quick flip?"

"Nothing like that," Cheyenne said, noticing he had not accepted her olive branch. She felt as if she should explain, as though she needed to defend herself. And she didn't like the feeling. A word came to mind that she had never associated with herself: *shallow*. It's what Delta Jones had said to her in the courthouse, spouting riddles like some kind of oracle. *Shallow waters run out. Still waters run deep.* Cheyenne took a breath.

"My interest in the estate isn't superficial. My family has history there."

"You don't say."

"My grandmother's people are from this area, going way back, and I believe one of my ancestors lived on the Hold Plantation. I think she, or he, was on a list of mixed-race children freed by the man who owned the estate, their father, Chief Hold. I'm going to renovate the mansion and run a bed-and-breakfast there. I want to care for the place. It's not just lovely to look at. It has depth, a proud history. I want other people to see that."

Cheyenne chanced a glance at him, expecting to see further signs of amusement, or maybe the condescension and pity her own friends had displayed. Instead, she saw interest in Adam Battis's eyes, and maybe a hint of regret.

"You've heard of the list?" he said.

Cheyenne's heart kicked. "My grandmother told me about it."

"Mine, too, but I never saw evidence of any census of Hold slaves the decade that I worked at the site. Did your grandmother also tell you about the lost gold?"

"No, but I read about it in the Room with a View's guidebooks. It's rumored that when a white farmer spotted gold around here in 1828, it wasn't the first discovery, that James Hold himself had found deposits, buried a cache, and used his wealth to blackmail and bribe tribal officials, federal agents, and Christian missionaries."

Adam nodded. "It's possible. Over twenty-six tons of the stuff were eventually unearthed. And by all existing accounts, Hold was an unscrupulous entrepreneur. By 1829 the first American gold rush was on. By 1830 the Georgia governor had illegally extended the state's jurisdiction over Cherokee land to give white prospectors access. There's no sign of buried gold on the grounds either," Adam grinned, "but it makes a good story for the tourists. Look, if you're planning to stay here full-time—"

"I'm sure I'll need help around the place," Cheyenne interrupted. "Maybe I could hire you back once I get things off the ground."

Adam's dark eyes flashed, and Cheyenne wondered if she had gone too far, if he was the kind of man who would see a job offer from a woman as emasculating.

"I'm doing all right on my own. But I do have a favor to ask."

Cheyenne exhaled in relief. Her heart kicked harder beneath the wine-silk tank top. He did want something from her. *What?*

"I have a friend, Sally Perdue. She's accustomed to picking fruit in the Hold orchards. I've been taking care of the trees since the museum closed, and they're in good shape, producing well. It would crush Sally if she couldn't do it anymore."

Cheyenne blinked. "What does your friend look like?"

Adam's eyebrow rose.

"So I'll know her when I see her."

"Redhead, blue eyes, petite," he answered.

Cheyenne swallowed. She could already anticipate Toni, Layla, and De'Sha's smug looks when she recounted this story: Cheyenne Cotterell passed over for a white country bumpkin.

"I'd like to meet her," Cheyenne lied. "In the meantime, tell your friend she can pick all the fruit she'd like—this season."

"I will," he said in what sounded like a cooler tone. "Sally feels attached to those trees, after living here all her life and coming from a family that's been here for more than three generations."

"Then she'll understand how I feel about the Hold House," Cheyenne said. "Possessive." She squeezed her fingers around the metal handle of her shopping basket and turned to walk away.

"Did your grandmother ever tell you that pretty is what pretty does?" Adam said. His words, directed toward her back, landed like arrows.

*

Cheyenne closed and locked the oversized doors of the Hold House and scooted a box of museum brochures against them for good measure. Running into Adam had made her feel uneasy for the second time that night. Locked inside her new old house, alone and a little shaken, she considered what to do next. The house felt huge and empty, as if it were yawning into the hillside. She flipped on a light switch in every room as she walked through the first floor, eating a handful of almonds as she went. She drank a glass of water, then splashed water on her face at the small sink in the three-quarter bath. She retrieved the scarf she had used to dust the drawing room, rinsed and gently wrung out the fabric, and hung it on a hook.

Through the diminutive bathroom window, Cheyenne heard the rumble of a four-wheel-drive fade into the night. Her ears pricked. A truck or SUV had been nearby, maybe as close as the parking lot that the museum used to operate. Had Adam the park ranger followed her home in the vintage green Ford? Now, that would be interesting. But if he had thought to pursue her, he had changed his mind. The yard outside was quiet now.

Cheyenne breathed a sigh of disappointment that morphed into a buzz of anxiety, as her thoughts turned to someone else who drove a four-wheel-drive in town. *Mason Allen.*

Cheyenne quickly climbed the stairs and crossed the nonsensical interior bridge to the most secluded corner of the house. In the bedroom of Chief James Hold, she kicked off her pumps and unclasped the waistband of her skirt. Briskly rubbing her chilled upper arms, she changed into satin pajamas the color of ripe apricots. At the thought of apricots, Sally Perdue came to mind, then Delta Jones, and Adam Battis watching over the place. Because he knew the pull this house had on people—people like Mason Allen, people like her.

Cheyenne shivered. *Why was she so cold?* That damn bond brick.

She stood again, scanning the room, looking for a solution. In the corner she discovered a linen press with a frayed patchwork quilt inside. She unfolded the faded covering and wrapped it around her shoulders, then curled up on top of the canopy bed. Except for the distant creaks and sighs of the settling foundation, the house grew quiet around her. Cheyenne allowed her eyes to close and leaned into the pillows, trying to ignore the sensation that she wasn't alone.

ELEVEN

→>→>·→<·→<

ADAM BATTIS HADN'T come back to his cabin last night, at least not as far as Jinx could tell. She showered, dressed, and ate a bowl of his Honey Nut Cheerios while she called her cousin.

"What time is it?" Victor mumbled. Jinx could imagine him running his hand through his long, tangled hair.

"Eight o'clock my time. Seven, yours."

"Oh, you're cruel."

"You should be up anyway. You have fires to fight."

"Not today I don't. So now that I'm up, what's going on? Do they still sell Cokes with the original cocaine formula down there as a way to get folks of color hooked?"

"As in a CIA soda conspiracy? Are you serious, Victor?"

"Just Google it."

"And on to the verifiable news, I lucked into a couple of local connections, and I'm staying at some guy's cabin."

"Some *guy's* place? Now I know the Coke is drugged."

"Oh, please. He rents it out. I need to track him down after I visit the plantation today and see if he'll give me an interview. Get this. His last name is Battis."

Victor whistled. "And Deb Tom's plot thickens. Everything is fine out here, since you didn't ask. I'm holding down the fort at Aunt Angie's House of Curious Antiquities."

Jinx sighed. "Why do I put up with you?"

"Because I'm so lovable. Be careful down there. Don't let that cabin dude take you for a ride. They don't call it Dick-land for nothing."

"Dix-ie Land," Jinx said.

"Same difference."

After the call, Jinx drove down the mountain road, passed the Marathon station, and came across the wrought-iron gates Sally had described. She turned in through the elaborate ironwork opening, followed the long, paved road, and inched beneath oak trees draped in the kudzu so pervasive that people thought it was native to the South. She drove toward a gravel lot half a mile ahead, where a Volkswagen Bug was already parked. Farther in the distance but within walking range of the lot, a svelte Mercedes sports coupe nestled in front of a big brick house. The new owner, it appeared, was at home. And she had company.

*

With her Blackberry in one hand and Burberry handbag in the other, Cheyenne pushed the doors open. She stepped onto the wide front porch, leaned against a column, and was surprised to nearly trip on something beneath it. An old-fashioned picnic basket had been tucked beside the base of the column. She stooped, opened the wooden lid, and peeled back the cotton dish towel. Inside were golden corn muffins, fresh tomatoes, Vidalia onions, loose-leaf lettuce, citrus vinaigrette, a bottle of milk imprinted with the name of a local dairy, and homemade strawberry jam. The note attached read, *Peace offering. Adam. P.S. Sorry no soy.* Cheyenne brought her lips together, then smiled to herself. His gift was surprising, discriminating, and . . . gallant. It almost made her want to rise to the occasion and eat a homemade muffin slathered in butter.

Almost, but not quite. She lifted the basket with both hands and glanced toward the distant gates. Two cars had appeared from out of nowhere. A Volkswagen Beetle sat idling in the lot. A rusty red pickup was crawling up the road.

And to the left of the house, where she had seen Adam walking last night, her azaleas had been beheaded. Cheyenne sucked in a breath. The beautiful shrubs that framed her front yard were barren at the tops, their lush leaves and pink flowers lopped off like a bad haircut. Had someone taken a weed whacker or hedge trimmer to them in an act of petty vandalism? Her heart jumped when she thought of Adam. *Impossible.* When she had last seen him in the yard, the azaleas were intact. This had happened while she was away, while they were both at the Piggly Wiggly, and she just hadn't noticed in the dark.

Or it had happened in the night while she slept, after she heard a vehicle rumbling near the grounds. But who was immature enough to play this kind of trick, with an outcome so subtle that it could be missed or misinterpreted? It had to have been a wandering deer or two. She had heard they ran rampant in the country. Cheyenne was trying to decide if she had convinced herself, as a woman stepped out of the car in the parking lot, and the truck inched closer along the drive.

*

Ruth switched off the engine and emerged from her car as if from a cocoon. A wall of wet heat smacked her in the face, steaming her tortoiseshell glasses. It had to be eighty degrees out there, and it was only late morning. She stared blindly, then thought to pull her glasses off, wiping them on her T-shirt and placing them back on her nose. She was standing in a gravel lot beside a small abandoned shed meant for a parking attendant. Before her, a gravel road stretched like a ribbon toward a stately brick building. Ruth squinted at the house through the leaves of oak trees that followed the line of the road. It appeared reserved, withholding in its elegance, facing north from atop a hill. Classical in structure, the house had elements of the Federal and Georgian architectural styles. Every facet of the building, from windows to porches to tripod eaves, was perfectly proportioned to signify authority. This was the house of a patriarch. The apparent softness of its rose-colored bricks and grassy yard was simply an illusion caused by the passage of time.

The road made a graceful loop before the house, rejoined itself, and wound out toward the iron gates. A woman stood on the porch holding a picnic basket, staring in her direction. Ruth thought better of driving beyond the public lot because that might seem presumptuous. She would leave her car and approach the house on foot. She started up the path. When she passed the fifth oak, Ruth caught a glimpse of the woman's features, which were coming together in a sickeningly familiar way. *Could it be? Of course not. Please, no. Oh shit!* By the tenth oak, she knew for sure. Dressed in a supremely flattering lemon tank dress was Ruth's best friend from summer camp—the best friend she couldn't stand.

The woman's hair was brushed back into a shiny ponytail. A cluster of gems glimmered from the center of her headband. A classic Black American Princess, BAP, from birth, Cheyenne Cotterell had finally gone and gotten herself a tiara.

"Ruthie Mayes! Is that you?" Cheyenne gracefully pounced, crossing the distance between them and throwing her arms around Ruth. "I can't believe it. After all these years. You look exactly the same, girl! Rocking that natural hair, and flaunting that full figure. What on earth are you doing down in Georgia? You'll tell me the whole story later. Whatever the reason, it's a relief to see an old friend here, someone I know and trust."

Ruth cringed at the nickname she had shed years ago pronounced in that lightly lacquered Southern accent. Cheyenne had never known her, not really. And Cheyenne Cotterell was exactly the same too: exquisitely polished, perfectly shaped, and swinging the impossibly straight hair that Ruth had always suspected was a weave. It was just like Cheyenne to bury a dig in the rut of a compliment. To Cheyenne, *natural* meant uncouth, and *full-figured* meant fat.

"Tell me everything. What brings you back? You're not here to visit Camp Idlewood? Nostalgia was never a thing with you."

Ruth regretted her next words the second she spoke them. "I'm here to write an article about the Hold House."

Cheyenne laughed, throwing a hand to her chest as Ruth remembered her doing when she wanted to appear surprised. "So you did become a writer. Good for you, girl! You always did have your face buried in those notebooks. This big place is mine now. And let me tell you, I could use some company." Cheyenne glanced at a bank of azaleas with no flowers.

"Yours?" Ruth choked out the word.

"*All* mine. As of yesterday. I had a successful interior design career at Swag and, honestly, any man I wanted in the city, but life is short now that we're over thirty. I needed something more. So here I am, the proud new owner of a famous plantation. What's up with you, girl? What have you been doing these last ten years? Don't even try to book a hotel room while you're in this teacup town. I insist you stay with me. We can have a mini Idlewood reunion."

The rush of words was overwhelmingly familiar—the coyness, the bossiness, the sickeningly sweet narcissism that stunk like rotting flowers left in the vase too long.

"Has it really been a decade?" Ruth looked over her shoulder at her car. She needed to extricate herself before this got worse.

Cheyenne followed Ruth's gaze. "Is she with you?" She pointed her chin toward a woman jumping down from the pickup beside Ruth's Beetle. Dressed in rumpled shorts, with a long, dark braid looped around the back of her neck and hanging below her modest chest, the woman held her hand up to her forehead like a visor.

"I've never seen her before."

"Another tourist. I've been warned they keep on coming. Let's go inside and catch up." Cheyenne started up the stairs to the veranda.

Ruth glanced back at the woman, who had slung a messenger bag over her shoulder and was loping on long, lean legs toward the house with a purposeful look on her face. "What about her? She's already seen us standing here. Wouldn't it be rude to walk off? Let's wait so you can explain."

"Ruthie, I never explain. There's a sign. It says 'closed.' I'm sure that woman can read."

Ruth frowned. Cheyenne had always talked down to her—a high school queen bee lecturing the friendless fat girl. Ruth bristled at the memory of feeling dependent, the new kid at camp desperately want-ing to fit in. After her mother's death, her father had sent her to Idle-wood, a summer tradition in her mother's family. He said she would learn about her African American culture there. But Ruth had known he just wanted to be rid of her, especially as she grew older and began to mirror her mother's looks. She had resented being sent away by her father and then being claimed as a project by Cheyenne, the only one at camp who would toss her a bone, because their grandparents had known each other. Cheyenne ruled Idlewood. Whatever she wore set the trend. Whatever she said went. Whichever boy she wanted to date was hers for the taking. Even the counselors loved her. And now Cheyenne owned a historic riverfront home, while Ruth still lived in a basement apartment and went to a coin-op laundry.

She'd left behind the painful memories of childhood, and she hadn't come all this way to relive them now. Sighing, Ruth did the math. Seventeen hours back to Minneapolis. Six weeks in her empty apartment. The loss of the most interesting story she had proposed at *Abode.* And there was the woman walking toward them. Ruth had wit-nessed plenty of historic home tourists in her time with the magazine. She'd even jotted some descriptions of a few of them down in her notebooks. That woman was not on vacation or out on an afternoon jaunt. She was not here for fun. Her purposeful stance, the way she looked like she meant business, made Ruth wonder about her agenda.

Ruth kept her eyes on the visitor for a moment before slowly, am-bivalently, following Cheyenne up the stairs. The windows on either side of the doors cut sunlight into diamond-shaped patterns. The front lock was oblong and intricate, shielded by a slender cover. Etched into the rounded knob below the lock was the barely discernible out-line of a rose. Cheyenne went inside, holding the door she'd unlocked for Ruth. Ruth held a palm to the heavy door, propping it open for an extra moment as she gave one last glance over her shoulder at the woman walking the alley of oaks. *Knock,* she thought, as she trailed Cheyenne into the house that seemed as though it was lying in wait.

*

Jinx fanned herself in the heat, following the gravel path, shifting the weight of her messenger bag from one shoulder to the other. She reached the doorway through which the people talking a few moments ago had vanished and pressed her thumb to the antique bell. The chime echoed through the walls. Moments later, both doors swung open.

Two African American women faced her across the threshold. The woman to the right with her hand on the knob was poised and svelte with classical features, a coffee-and-cream complexion, and a crisp ponytail that caressed the nape of her neck. Jinx could picture her on the cover of a bridal magazine, holding a single white lily and dripping pearls. This one grasped the doorknob of the left door possessively and had been the one to unlock it while Jinx watched from the road. She must be the new homeowner.

Jinx had seen the second woman hold the door open, as if silently communicating with her. At around five-two, this woman was much shorter than the first and generously figured. Her tight, animated curls spilled over a cloth headband to loop around the tops of her ears. Her large eyes, a semisweet-chocolate-brown, overwhelmed the tortoiseshell glasses that sat off-kilter on the bridge of her nose. Jinx looked a second too long at those eyes, deeply dark and withholding. To break the spell, she glanced down and read the words on the woman's T-shirt: I'M A FREAKING DELIGHT. Jinx's spontaneous laugh came out as a snort.

"Can I help you?" said Ponytail, with a pointed look that indicated Jinx was entirely out of place and taking up valuable time.

Beside her, F.D.'s lips barely curved up at the left corner.

"Yeah. Sorry about that. I'm Jennifer Micco. I'm a writer from Oklahoma doing research on Creek and Cherokee history. I understand you're the new owner. I was hoping to talk with you about the history of this house and the Christian mission that used to be on the property."

"And you're with what publication?" Ponytail sounded curt, but interested.

"The *Muscogee Nation News,* my tribal newspaper. I write the history column. The Moravian mission school that used to operate here educated a tribal member. I'd like to write a profile story on her. I know the house is closed to the public, but I thought there might be some records related to the mission here."

"I had no idea the house sale would attract attention so soon. Ruthie here—she's a writer, too— wants to do a story for a home-and-garden magazine. We were just about to discuss my plans to renovate the property and reopen it as a boutique bed-and-breakfast next year. Three is the magic number, they say. Come in."

As she crossed the threshold behind the pair, Jinx felt a strange undercurrent, like a winter wind riding the back of a warm, autumn breeze. The sudden chill raised the fine hairs at the base of her neck and caused her to look toward the road just before Ponytail sent the front doors swinging shut.

"Coming?" F. D. said, watching Jinx as she hesitated. Jinx breathed and steadied herself with a look at those chocolate eyes.

"Yeah. Did you feel that? The temperature just dropped like twenty degrees."

"Cheyenne says it's the brick. I have a sweater in the car, if you need one."

"That's sweet, but I won't take the clothes off your back yet." Jinx bit her lip. She hadn't meant to sound suggestive. She noticed F.D. give her a sideways glance, checking for her expression. "Have you two known each other long?" Jinx added, steering back to predictable ground.

"Long enough," F.D. said.

"This way, ladies," Ponytail called.

Jinx followed the other women through the foyer and entered a spacious, formal room made extravagant with intricate woodwork. Artisanal carvings of snakes and panthers wrapped around the mantel; small alabaster roses embellished the wall moldings. A gilded mirror flashed the reflection of Jinx in her carpenter shorts and pow-wow T-shirt, F.D. in a long denim skirt and humorous T-shirt, and

Ponytail in a feminine slip of a dress. Wide windows flanked the mirror and the elaborate fireplace, allowing views to the lush hillside and stately lane of oaks.

Ponytail gestured toward the seats, lifted a crystal pitcher, and set about pouring water into drinking glasses. She arranged the tumblers on a Victorian folding tray whose copper joints creaked under the weight of the heirloom service. She eased into a straight-backed chair with forearms carved like cat claws, and smoothed the lap of her unwrinkled dress.

F.D. perched on the edge of a damask divan, looking noncommittal. Her legs were crossed at the knee, and she tapped one foot restlessly in the air, dangling a leather clog until it threatened to drop. Jinx found herself focusing on the woman's chocolate eyes—no, her curved lips—no, that tongue-in-cheek T-shirt.

"Are you going to sit?" Ponytail said.

Jinx looked away from F.D. and took the seat across from her host, a mahogany chair with elaborately carved cutouts and a scroll design on its chartreuse cushion.

"We've put the cart before the horse. I'm Cheyenne Cotterell. This is my old friend Ruthie Mayes. Welcome to the Hold House, Jennifer." She extended a slender hand into the cool air between them.

"Thanks for speaking with me without an appointment." Jinx's eyes darted around the room, landing on the stiff, dark furnishings with richly colored upholstery, the oil paintings depicting a bevy of women holding vases, and the two women in the flesh sitting awkwardly before her.

"I'm *Ruth* Mayes," F.D. said, correcting her friend's introduction. "No one calls me Ruthie anymore." She sat with a straight spine, leaning slightly forward to reach out a hand to Jinx. Her hand, in contrast to those distant, arresting eyes, was small, soft, and warm in the chilled room. She quickly withdrew it as her eyes met Jinx's and then skated away.

"So where in Oklahoma do you come from, Jennifer?" Cheyenne

asked, ignoring her friend's interjection. "I couldn't help but notice your shirt. Are you a Cherokee Indian?"

"I'm Creek on my mom's side, Cherokee on my dad's," Jinx said, not adding that "Indian" was the only kind of genuine Cherokee there was. "I live in Ocmulgee; it's not too far from Muskogee, if you're familiar with the state. Are you from this area? Is that why you purchased the Hold place?"

"I'm from Atlanta, but my Cherokee ancestors are from this plantation. People say you can see the Indian influence in my hair." She stroked the tip of her ponytail. "So you can see how meaningful it is to me to have acquired this property. You can put that in your article, by the way."

Jinx noticed Ruth's eyes narrow in reaction to Cheyenne's words. She looked back to Cheyenne. "May I record this?"

Cheyenne nodded. Jinx withdrew her phone from her bag and opened her voice recorder while Ruth opened a bound notebook.

"And how do you know your family was Cherokee? . . . Aside from the long hair evidence?" Jinx didn't really intend for the edge of sarcasm to creep in, and she caught Ruth's eye as she spoke. Ruth's eyes sparked, as if the subtle dig was satisfying. Jinx knew then that she had walked into an emotional minefield. But still, she took some small pleasure in bringing light to Ruth's cool eyes.

Cheyenne had felt the shade too. She tilted her chin up and inserted an over-the-shoulder ponytail toss. "My grandmother always said we came from a Cherokee plantation at the base of these mountains. It took me years to pinpoint it. I assume my family were among the group who hid out in the Georgia hills during the Trail of Tears. They didn't go to Oklahoma or North Carolina. That's probably why my grandmother encouraged my parents to name me Cheyenne. She didn't want us to lose our heritage."

"Because Cherokee and Cheyenne both start with 'Ch'?" Jinx felt her annoyance rising, blunting her will to maintain a gloss of professionalism. Cherokee Princess Syndrome pissed her off. This woman was probably about as Indian as that Chief Hold Hotel sign on the road leading into town. But Jinx knew she should check herself. She shouldn't disrespect anybody's grandma, even the grandma of a Black Indian wannabe. And she didn't need to make enemies on day one if she wanted access to this place.

"In other words, you don't believe me. And if you're guessing we're not on the Cherokee Nation Rolls, you're right. But as a historian, surely you know those government lists are completely unreliable."

"Actually, I'd say the Dawes Rolls are fairly reliable. No record is ever perfect, but they can help us verify what's true. Making a claim of Indian-ness is not the same as *being* Indigenous." Jinx glanced at the silent Ruth, who sat with her elbow pressed against a tufted pillow, observing the undercurrents of the conversation and jotting in her notebook.

"Well, now we have science to settle these questions. And I've kept you two waiting entirely too long for the grand tour," Cheyenne announced, as if this were a natural follow-on. She was so smooth at wiping away any hint of discord that Jinx wondered if she had trained for high teas and debutante balls at finishing school.

"I have an architect on retainer in Atlanta. He'll draw up the remodeling plans over the next month. I expect to keep the house and furnishings intact for the most part, though I'll want to do some modernizing and add full-sized baths. I'll preserve the reception hall where you entered, keep this drawing room as is." Cheyenne stood. "Feel free to take as many photographs as you like, but do seek my permission before printing them. I have a vision for promoting this house to draw the right kind of guests."

Ruth raised an eyebrow. Jinx shook her head.

As Cheyenne swept toward the doorway, Jinx fell in next to Ruth, noticing that up close she smelled like cherries, and her skin was the powdery shade of a cinnamon donut.

"How did you find out about this place?" Jinx said near Ruth's ear.

"I was doing online research for a story about carpets—don't ask—when I stumbled across a newspaper article. It said the house museum was being sold and advocacy groups were protesting. I thought more people should know, that greater publicity might help the fundraising campaign. I had some vacation time coming, so I drove down from Minneapolis to check it out. I didn't know I would be too late. What about you?"

Jinx felt a chill prick her neck that had nothing to do with the cold house this time—or so she thought. "What do you think, Ruth Mayes? Is this serendipity, fortuity, or both? *I* read that article. John Cook was quoted? Stuart Pickup? I'm researching a Creek student who lived here in the 1800s. She had a troubled life, and a woman I know back home wants me to find out what happened to her."

"I'm going to go for broke and choose 'both,'" Ruth said. "Is this woman back home a friend?" she added, her gaze glancing over Jinx's face.

"She's an elder, a devoted reader of my column, and a heck of a cook. For a while I thought about getting my doctorate in history, and since I write a column, folks sort of give me homework assignments."

"Sounds much more interesting than how my stories are assigned."

"People back home really care about what happened in the past, and why. Shared history is a big part of what makes us a tribe."

"Are you one of those people?"

"My great-aunt taught me to see things that way. Tribal history was her life before she died five years ago."

"I'm so sorry. You must miss her."

Ruth's eyes took on a darker cast, so sincere and shadowed that Jinx found it hard to look away. "Thank you," Jinx said.

They had turned, stopped, and now faced each other in an ornately furnished room that neither of them noticed.

"You're welcome . . . It's just . . . I know . . ." Ruth backed out of her sentence and readjusted her shoulder angle, breaking the connection.

"Did I lose you two? This way, ladies." Cheyenne raised her

voice and gave them a long-suffering look over her shoulder, gesturing like Vanna White as she exited the drawing room. A velvet rope, unhooked from its mooring, hung loose in the hallway. "This is the formal dining room. Beyond it is a butler's pantry with a modern kitchen nook—microwave, mini-fridge, hot plate—and a three-quarter bath."

Folds of gold silk drapery flowed around the windows. A portrait of a brooding, dark-haired man dressed in a deep blue vest and red velvet jacket hung above the fireplace. The dining table was lavishly set below a brass chandelier topped with dusty wax candles.

"James Hold?" Jinx asked, facing the oversized portrait that made her feel as though the eyes were sizing her up.

Cheyenne nodded. "The handsome devil. He built this estate from the ground up and ran it until his death in 1816. He got to be the richest man in the Cherokee Nation, and most of upper Georgia too. This plantation sat right at the crossroads, the frontier line where Georgia and Cherokee country met. James was murdered in a nearby tavern—drinking brandy, the story goes."

"Who killed him?" Jinx said.

"Who indeed?" Cheyenne answered.

Jinx saw Ruth jot a note in her book and then tuck it under her arm.

"That galley kitchen must have been added later," Ruth said, surveying the layout. "In a house like this, the kitchen would have been outside originally."

"That's right," Cheyenne said. "The kitchen was located out back when the home was built, to protect the house from fire. Then the kitchen structure became the Moravian missionaries' cabin, where they lived and held worship services. The plantation kitchen was rebuilt in the basement of this building, a practice James Hold would have seen in the Savannah homes he visited on business. The park service added the kitchenette for convenience. They used the original kitchen outside as storage space. I'm planning to have it connected to the main house through a glass breezeway that will frame out the garden and river below the property."

"I passed that river on the highway," Ruth said. "More than once. It's not easy to find this place."

"You never did have the best sense of direction. But you two popping in is already proving helpful. It's a trove of market research now and promises to be advanced marketing when your stories come out. I'll update the signage and include video directions in online listings." Cheyenne turned toward Jinx. "The Conasauga River—I believe that's a name from the Cherokee language—was a main thoroughfare in James Hold's day. He operated a ferry and trading post along its banks. His plantation stretched much farther then. It encompassed most of this township."

Cheyenne led them through the rear parlor, then exited French doors to wind back into the center hallway.

"This is the home's only phone." She gestured to a walnut secretary holding a coal-black telephone that looked as ancient as the house. "You won't get a cell phone signal or an Internet connection unless you drive down to the gas station at the bottom of the hill. Feel free to use the house phone for local calls."

Cheyenne glided toward the central staircase, which made a graceful turn at a landing before rising to the second story of the house. There the stairs dovetailed into a wooden archway—a footbridge indoors. The sight was so odd that Jinx half expected the floorboards to shift under her feet, morphing into a mountain stream or the River Styx. She saw that Ruth was not only scribbling notes down, but also taking photos of the walkway with her phone.

"Good eye, Ruth. This bridge is the famous architectural feature of the house," Cheyenne said. "There's only one element similar to it in Georgia, according to the tour brochures—the hanging staircase in the Owens-Thomas House in Savannah. But Hold built his much earlier and concentrated his workmen's attention on the top of the stairs rather than the middle. Obviously, these are the second-floor bedrooms. This one would have been used as a children's or guest room." The indicated chamber contained a pencil-post bed swathed in a coverlet of handmade lace, a satin-covered slip chair, and a dark mahogany sleigh bed.

Cheyenne led them across the bridge.

"The master bedroom," she said, showing them a room aglow with sunlight. "James Hold and his wife would have slept here."

Jinx stepped inside the room. Behind a floral folding screen, she saw a suitcase lying open. Fluted skirts danced from sateen-lined hangers in an unlatched wooden armoire. A chest of drawers held personal emollients and high-gloss cosmetics. A cashmere wrap was neatly folded across a needlepoint footstool. Cheyenne had wasted no time moving in.

"Does that lead to the attic?" Ruth asked. Hanging back at the threshold, she pointed to a narrow door at the end of the hall, catty-corner to the master bedroom.

"I haven't ventured up," Cheyenne said. "It's bound to be icky, and I don't have a house cleaner lined up yet."

"May I?" Ruth cracked the door before Cheyenne could answer. Jinx followed Ruth, leaving Cheyenne with little choice but to bring up the rear of her own grand tour.

The door led into a small closet full of mops with dingy heads, straw brooms, empty spray bottles, and dust cloths. Peering into the darkness over Ruth's shoulder, Jinx saw steps behind the clutter—steep, narrow, spindly steps with cobwebs at the corners. A dank smell—caused perhaps by a moldy rag or dead mouse—wafted from the top of the stairwell. A row of dusty woven baskets dangled from hooks along one wall of the dark, steep space. The baskets emitted a faint scent of tumbled earth that cut the stifling air of the closet. Jinx watched as Ruth drew closer to the baskets as if pulled by some magnetic force, sinking into the darkness of the narrow recess.

Ruth bent toward one of the baskets, stroking the two-toned weave with her forefinger. Particles of pale dust dotted her fingertip like the powder of a cabbage butterfly wing. "What are these made of?" she asked. She had stopped writing. Her pen was now lodged beneath the stretchy fabric headband near her ear.

"River cane. The place is overrun with it," Cheyenne answered.

"The weave is so intricate, the cane so thick. It's hard to imagine someone could work with this material, let alone make something so exquisite out of it," Ruth said. "My mother had a basket like this when I was growing up. She kept her heirloom flower seeds in it."

Jinx watched Ruth, filing away the detail that Ruth's mother was a gardener—or used to be. Ruth spoke of her mother in the past tense. *I know,* Ruth had begun to say when they were speaking of Jinx's deceased aunt. *Grief.* It was at least one of the unstated emotions behind this three-way conversation. Jinx added it to her mental list behind *resentment, suspicion,* and *envy.*

"That's a sifter," Jinx said gently. "Your mother was sorting with it. Separating the seeds she wanted to grow from debris." Jinx watched Ruth suck in a breath, swallowing some squall of feeling before it could escape. "Ruth, are you—"

Cheyenne cleared her throat with a studied delicacy. "We're getting rather off track. The third story is unfinished," she said. "I was told the museum never made use of it. I'll have to start from scratch up there, gut the space. It should work well as a family suite. I expect innkeepers can stick kids and their hassled parents anywhere. You didn't come all this way to write about dingy storage closets. Why don't I show you the gardens?"

Cheyenne trooped down the maze of halls and stairs, past the rear parlor and toward the back exit. "The servants' entrance," she announced.

"Or, in plain language, the entrance enslaved people used as they carried out their forced labor tasks," Ruth said, her dark eyes distant again. "Blacks were owned as property here. Or do you plan to hide this part of the Hold House history from your future guests?"

"Isn't hiding from history your department, Ruthie?" Cheyenne said with a frosty look as she opened the door and stepped outside.

TWELVE

❯❯❯·❮❮❮

HURT BY CHEYENNE'S below-the-belt comeback, Ruth tucked her shoulder, elbowed past the other two women, and stepped onto the wide-plank porch. The unkempt land before her spilled into a sea of green where tousled flowers stretched across the crest of the hill. Cheyenne was rambling on to Jennifer Micco about her Native American ancestry and the DNA test results she was expecting. Ruth shut out Cheyenne's voice and even the response of the Oklahoma columnist who was smart, funny, and had seemed so sensitive to her feelings.

She stood in awe of the garden.

She focused on the swamp sunflowers, snowy asters, salvias, and sedums intertwining with abandon in the untamed yard. Butterfly weed and Indian blanket blazed in vibrant hues. White roses sprang up among the colorful wildflowers, tingeing the stiff hillside breeze with a sweet, old-fashioned perfume. Each bloom—beside a gate, beneath a tree, along a path—was full and brilliant, knowing it would soon burn out with the full onslaught of autumn. Ruth's trust in this garden was immediate. She felt something as she stood before these plants, sewn from seed generations ago and still growing, still thriving, even though their gardener had long since turned to dust. Ruth breathed in, thinking for the first time in years of the fragrant musk that used to cling to her mother's ebony skin: lily of the valley mixed with perspiration from long hours spent gardening in their double-lot yard. Ruth sank into the memory of her mother's scent and stepped off the porch, her tin-can heart creaking open.

She crossed a patch of dirt and waded into the garden. Her feet found a path of gray river stones, winding between a weathered cabin and a row of dilapidated dependency buildings. She stopped when she could go no farther, where the slope took a steep dive to the river. The wildflowers faded into a grove of river cane that crowded out the sunlight, with thin stalks shooting up into a mass of feathery tufts all the way down to the water's edge. The reeds were as tall as trees and had the likeness of bamboo, lovely and primitive as they swayed, whispering in the wind. It was a wonder this canebrake had not been chopped down like most of the others across the region. It was a wonder the cane here had been allowed to live. *Shh, shh,* the cane stalks seemed to whisper to her. *Shh, shh.*

Ruth breathed in the loamy smell of river water flowing at the bottom of the incline. Mud. Fish. Sunlight. A picture of the St. Paul house where she had spent her early childhood flooded her quiet mind. She remembered those long hours in the garden, many hours like one unbroken thread. She remembered her mother looking out from beneath the brim of her rattan hat, smiling at her, smiling at Ruthie, the little girl. Ruthie had always been underfoot, tracing ant trails, mixing mud pies, scouting for rain-soaked worms along the garden's edge, never knowing how much her mother was teaching her there, or that it would all disappear like a faded sepia photograph. That garden was the laboratory where her mother had developed the natural products of Canebrake Botanicals, her wildly successful body-care company. That garden was also their private haven, their secret place away from the prison-like house.

Gazing at the canebrake that girdled the Hold Plantation, Ruth recognized the likeness. Around the perimeter of their yard, in soil made rich by the Mississippi River, her mother had nursed river cane from her home state of Georgia. She had never taken Ruth to meet their Georgia relatives, had never taken her to see their family's home-place, but surely her mother had missed it, loved it, wished she could return to it. Why else had she struggled to grow a little piece of Georgia in her frigid Minnesota yard? Ruth tore her glasses off. The garden blurred before her eyes, the raw pattern of color and light revealing hidden shapes. She returned the glasses to her nose, smudged and wet, and glanced back at the others.

"How much land did the Holds control?" Jennifer was asking Cheyenne where the two stood talking in the shade of the porch.

"A few thousand acres, according to the brochures. This was the working yard, where servants did their outdoor tasks—laundering, soap making, log sawing, corn shucking. I'll have it landscaped and put in outdoor patio seating. Past the work yard was the flower garden, and then the vegetable and herb gardens. There's no water view now, but when I have the cane cut back, the vista will be spectacular."

"And where were the slave quarters?" Jennifer asked, casting her gaze across the grounds.

Ruth wondered if the columnist had posed the question on her behalf. She glanced at her, caught her eye, and knew. The sense of being seen, of having her interest recognized without needing to put herself forward, made Ruth feel even more emotionally off-kilter.

Cheyenne sighed. "The servants' quarters haven't survived. In the 1950s, the state had an archaeological survey done. They speculated that there must have been at least twenty workers' cabins on the grounds to support a force of a hundred people. They were probably located a mile out, near the cornfields and gristmill."

"Have you thought about reconstructing them?" Jennifer said.

"Ladies. Honestly. People don't want to pay to think about racism on the weekends. They want to relax. And I want to pamper my guests, not preach to them." Cheyenne tossed a hand to a hip, switching her slight weight from one wedged heel to the other.

Did Ruth see Jennifer's expression change at the mention of racism? She wasn't sure about that, and while she was considering the question, she was startled to see the columnist jump off the porch, maneuvering toward her through the overgrown blooms.

"Can I join you?" Jennifer said. "You seem to know what you're looking at out here. My aunt had the green thumb, not me."

But Ruth wouldn't let herself say "yes" to that question or let on that she had even considered it. She didn't open up to people, socially or romantically. She never let them close enough to discover the emptiness inside her.

Strands of dark hair had escaped the columnist's braid and were fluttering around her inquisitive face, which Ruth noticed was the appealing brown color of perfectly toasted marshmallows. Her cargo shorts were wrinkled, her T-shirt curled at the hem. And she was smiling with a warmth that crinkled the corners of her eyes. Jennifer Micco was more than a little interesting. And she was one of the few humans, male or female, apparently unaffected by Cheyenne Cotterell's charms.

"Suit yourself," Ruth said, and then, because that sounded abrupt even to her own ear, she kept on talking. "I was just thinking this garden has a theme. Roses are growing everywhere, though they're hard to spot at first. Rambler roses, tea roses, English roses, even the powder-pink Cinderella roses my mother used to call 'the babies of the rose family.' And see those wild Cherokee roses? The ones still in bloom? They grow in places people have occupied but left behind."

"Like memories," the columnist said.

Ruth paged open her notebook to write that down. "This is definitely a rose garden. Hidden among the weeds and wildflowers, and it's been here for years."

"I didn't realize you knew so much about gardens." Cheyenne had finally reached them, carefully navigating on her wedged heels. "Maybe you take after your mother after all. It's surprising how much a child can pick up so young. Fun fact. I read a *Georgia Backroads* magazine article over the weekend that had interview snippets with people who worked here years ago. One was a Black woman who said she picked cotton on the place as a girl in the 1940s, back when it was used for sharecropping. She said the Blacks who lived in town then—

before the white residents made it an official historic township, increased property values, and drove most of them out—used to call this estate 'the Cherokee Rose Plantation.' The name never made it onto any map or brochure."

"The Cherokee Rose," the columnist repeated as Ruth opened her notebook and wrote the name down.

"I believe this is the building you're looking for, Jennifer," Cheyenne said, stepping along a fieldstone path and indicating the rough cabin behind the main house. "The original kitchen for the home that was refashioned as a missionary station, the one you asked about." She gestured toward a row of stout batten-board sheds that sat across from the kitchen and formed an enclosure of the rear acreage. "Those were the corncrib, smokehouse, and weaving house."

"And what about that?" Jennifer pointed past the southeastern edge of the garden, where an oddly shaped shelter crouched among the cane stalks. It was made of mud or clay and crowned by a conical roof. The sun shone hard on its walls and dry thatch top, as if the roof made of reeds could still absorb sunlight, converting the rays into chlorophyll, into energy, into life. Wild sevenbark hydrangea with ivory blooms trailed the perimeter of the spherical house, interspersed with milkweed plants. Golden and orange-winged monarch butterflies fluttered over the plants, giving the scene a fairy-tale glow.

"Another of the Hold House mysteries," Cheyenne said, one hand slanted upward to protect her face from the sun. "According to the state archaeologist quoted in the brochure, it's not a structure James Hold would have built. His style was classically European."

"It's old," Jennifer said. "Maybe even eighteenth-century."

"It could be African-influenced," Ruth said, thinking that her years of being assigned the ethnic stories at *Abode* might be paying off, and jotting in her notebook as she spoke. "West African houses were round. Enslaved people here might have remembered how to construct them."

"Or it could be an early Cherokee winter lodge," Jennifer said. "They were round houses too."

"It could be a hybrid form," Ruth said, wondering if anything else like it existed in the region. She stared at the habitation in the cane. Who had lived there? Had they found a sanctuary in that little earthen house? Or had it been a prison cell? She wanted to go to the structure, to touch its walls, to see what secrets lay inside. Her thoughts flashed to her colleagues in the retro brick loft of the magazine's offices. They would eat their hearts out to see this place—a classic plantation wreathed by gardens with a wattle-and-daub Indigenous lodge tucked out back. And her heart could be devoured, too, if she let it, by the melancholy beauty of a place that pulled her back in time.

"Why don't you ladies take a stroll, get inspired by the scenery," Cheyenne said. "I'll find refreshments. It's long past lunchtime, and I know Ruthie can't bear to miss a meal. It will be paradise. We'll picnic in the garden, and I'll pitch my ideas for the B&B's grand opening." Cheyenne pivoted and headed toward the house, her ponytail swinging and her slip dress swaying in the breeze.

Ruth felt a touch on her arm that was as gentle as it was brief. She looked up to find Jennifer watching her, as if she had heard Cheyenne's understated dig, as if she understood how it felt to be constantly reminded you weren't as good as somebody else. Ruth felt her skin warm with embarrassment—and maybe gratitude.

"Want to check out the old kitchen with me? It sounds like we have a common interest. I like my meals, too, the sweeter and richer the better." Jennifer smiled, then walked ahead of Ruth toward the decaying building, making a path of parted stems for them both to tread.

Ruth followed, stooping to examine the outlines of a former vegetable and herb garden. A brown-backed box turtle showed its face and blinked at her. She watched it disappear behind a watercress leaf, then thrust her hand into the leaves, parting hedge mustard from shepherd's purse. Four pairs of beaded eyes peered back at her—two turtles instead of one, tucked together like the twin hearts of the lopseed plant that grew around the exterior of the weathered cabin.

Jennifer pushed through lopseed stalks to enter the low-slung doorway. Ruth tripped over a threshold warped by the elements, righted her clog, and stumbled inside behind her. The cabin smelled like a pine forest after a rain: damp wood, wet moss, sodden earth, balsam. The walls were made of unpeeled log that had once been whitewashed. The floors were nothing more than raw packed earth. The windows were encrusted with dirt streaked by long-dried raindrops. The only pure shaft of light, dancing with dust and pollen, shone through the open doorway.

The first room was the largest of three, occupying the full front width of the cabin. This was the original cooking space, judging by its size and features. A massive chimney built of rocks rose against one wall. A hunk of tree trunk served as a mantel. Carved into the wood in the center of the trunk was a faded cross formed in the leaves of the tree of life. At the base of the chimney, a deep fireplace took up a third of the room. This had been the Hold family's hearth, the place where their meals were prepared. An unfree person had probably worked here, or perhaps even lived here. A ruddy brick oven, a later addition, had been built into the opposite wall, surrounded by shelving fashioned from elm. But any cooking elements once stowed on those shelves—cast-iron pots or trivets or cooling stands—had been lost or sold away.

Jennifer lowered herself to the floor, sitting cross-legged. Ruth sat beside her, facing the open door to catch a breeze.

"Out of the frying pan, into the kitchen," Jennifer said, fanning her face with a hand and grinning. "It's sweltering, but incredible. To think people lived here centuries ago, cooked here, prayed here, shared their lives. Mary Ann Battis, the girl I'm looking for, could have sat where we're sitting now, one day in the 1800s."

Ruth looked at Jennifer for a long moment, at her dark, thoughtful eyes. She was suddenly aware of the sweet smell of Jennifer's skin. *Was that candy?* In the silence, she could hear the sound of Jennifer's breathing—steady, rhythmic, alive.

"The girl you're looking for . . ." Ruth repeated.

Jennifer paused, tilted her head, and gave Ruth a look that began with curiosity and ended with a smile. "*One* of the girls I'm looking for. And I think it's time you know that my friends back home call me Jinx."

"Jinx?"

"Buy me a Coke." Jinx grinned.

Ruth laughed out loud, remembering the childhood saying for when two people blurted out the same word at the same time, almost as if by magic.

The noise descended in a rush, sounding in Ruth's ears. *Shh, shh.* It was coming from outside. *Shh, shh.* The river cane was whispering. *Shh, shh. Come. Go back. Come. Go back.* The rustling echoed in her eardrums, sounding like a voice that had traveled across a great distance.

And that's when Ruth saw the girl.

She was fourteen, maybe fifteen, with long, awkward string-bean limbs, honeycomb-colored skin, and brilliant brown eyes. The girl's hair hung to her back in a thick trunk of braid, tied off at the base with ribbon. She stood just beyond the cabin doorway in moccasin-covered feet, staring directly at Ruth. Ruth drew in a breath of shock as her heart sped to twice its resting rate. She felt waves of emotion wash over her as if by osmosis. Sadness, loss, longing, rage, and resentment, backlit by a sheen of love. As she stared at the vision, Ruth felt that she could *be* that young girl, that she was a helpless young teenager tossed again on the seas of her father's reckless passions. And then she knew the girl before her had no mother because of someone's criminal act. Ruth's face felt flushed, and a line of sweat slowly spread to discolor the fabric of her headband. She closed her eyes, trying to swallow. She pushed her glasses up on her nose.

She blinked, opened her eyes, and looked again at the doorway to find the girl was gone . . . if she had ever been there.

Shh, shh.

She had never acknowledged the truth out loud.

Shh, shh.

"What's wrong?" Jennifer said.

Ruth focused on breathing, *in, out,* and then put her mind to work at what it did best: obfuscating the threatening things she saw in her mind and rationalizing her feelings. She was exhausted and under stress. She hadn't slept well on the road. And she had arrived at her destination to find an unpleasant surprise: her queen-bee summer-camp bunkmate, a person she had never been fond of, now owned the place she was supposed to be writing a feature story about. And witness to it all was a striking someone whom she might . . . Ruth didn't finish that thought. It was as though she had careened into an adolescent anxiety dream. Of course she was seeing strange things.

The girl in the door was a trick of the eye, a trick of the light, a trick of her mind. Ruth had only to blink her eyes to make the girl disappear—just as she had for all those years with the memories of her mother, just as she had with the great loss that had hulled the seed of her life.

She looked up to find Jennifer watching with a look of concern and confusion.

"Jennifer . . ." Ruth started.

"Please, call me Jinx. What just—"

"Bon appétit, ladies!" Cheyenne's voice chimed from the garden path. "Chop-chop!"

THIRTEEN

✦➤➤➤·◀◀◀✦

ADAM HAD BEEN working in his garden all morning, staking corn-stalks, thumping pumpkins, and pulling weeds. The quarter of an acre in front of his cabin that he had devoted to his hobby kept him and more than a few neighbors in fresh produce all fall. The tomatoes Adam grew ranged from tiny grapes and romas to a purple, bulging heirloom variety planted from seeds saved by his mother and passed down from his grandmother. He and Sally usually chose a slow week-end to can the tomatoes in his shed with a college football game blar-ing in the background. Those jars, with their satisfying pops as they sealed, made for tasty pizza and spaghetti sauces come wintertime.

The heat had gotten to him hours ago despite the shade provided by his sunflowers, which stood like yellow umbrellas on stilts along the perimeter of the fence. Adam had stripped off his T-shirt to fling it across a stump by the woodshed. He took another swig from a water bottle that was sweating as hard as he was. The outdoor work soothed him, especially in a week like this, when everything seemed awry. The Hold House buyer was far from what he had expected. He thought he would be dealing with Mason Allen, who was tough but practical to the core—avaricious, certainly, but the devil Adam knew. Instead, he found himself tangling with a stranger—a sexy, snobby, gutsy stranger who seemed entranced by the place but for some rea-son had it in for azaleas. Adam shrugged into a smile. She was a puz-zle, that one.

The telephone sounded inside his cabin. He wanted to ignore it but knew it must be Sally. She was at home on Wednesdays if she didn't have a cleaning job, and she must have spotted him in the yard through the window of her trailer. Adam stood, the ache in his knees telling him it was past time to call it quits for the day anyway. He grabbed his damp shirt and water bottle, kicked off his Nikes, and walked inside his snug log home. Shaded by pine needles, the cabin was cool around him. It smelled like the coffee he had brewed that morning and left in the pot just in case—and like the pleasantly foreign scents of a stranger, the shampoo and lotion of his overnight renter, who had eaten cold cereal and left while he was out in the tent.

"Yep?" he said, holding the telephone to his ear.

"What are you doing out there in the heat of the day?"

"Sally. Are you spying on me again?"

"It's not spying when we're neighbors."

"How's Junior?"

"Napping. I know a thing or two about sunstroke, Adam Battis, and don't think because you're Black you can't get it."

"So you're babysitting me now too?"

"Somebody has to, since your mama's moved to Dalton and the whole town's gone nuts over the sale of the Hold House. Now tell me. What's going on over there? I know you've been to see her."

Adam paused. "I did run into the new owner—her name is Cheyenne Cotterell—at the supermarket. She says she wants to operate a bed-and-breakfast and live here year-round. She also says you can keep picking fruit in the orchards."

"That was your doing. Thanks for looking out for me. Did you tell her?"

"Tell her what?"

"Don't play dumb. Did you tell her you hope to rent some land on the place and restore the cabin your grandmother grew up in?"

Adam sighed and took a gulp of water. "It didn't come up."

"You have to *bring* it up. Lord knows, you've got as much claim to that plantation as anybody else. More than anybody else. Mason just wanted to develop the property. And the new owner sounds like she just wants to run a business. You have roots here, Adam. You belong to the land."

"This woman says she has roots, too, that she had ancestors on the plantation. Mason might have rented to me if I could have convinced him that having me run the orchards would have turned him a profit. But this one? No. She's a romantic with a backbone. She doesn't want anybody crowding in her dream."

Sally was quiet for a moment. Adam imagined her biting the fleshy tip of her thumb, like she did when she was deliberating.

"And does she?" Sally finally came out with it.

"Does she what?"

"Does she have a history on the plantation? Because your grandparents—my grandparents, all of those old folks—said your own family was there going back generations."

"I don't know her history. I'm not even sure if she does."

"When's the last time you worked on your family history research?"

"I set that aside long ago. I told you that. I looked into it, called the Cherokee Nation enrollment office in Oklahoma and tried to see if any Battises were listed on the Cherokee Freedmen Rolls. They weren't."

"One phone call and you're giving up? You haven't rented out that cabin, slept in your tent, and saved twenty-five thousand dollars for nothing."

"It wouldn't make any difference now. The property is gone, and the buyer is in it for the long haul. Nobody cares if my ancestors lived there."

"Somebody cares," Sally said. "I guarantee it. You just don't know who he—or she—is yet."

*

Cheyenne had found a shady spot beneath a white peach tree. She spread out a patchwork quilt and busied herself preparing the picnic like a copper-toned Martha Stewart. She laid out china from the Hold

House collection, corn muffins, a cake of butter, a fresh tossed salad, and vinaigrette dressing. She placed a pitcher of cool water on top of a tin tray and set out drinking glasses.

Ruth sat on the edge of the textile island, tucking her denim skirt around her calves. Jinx found a place nearby and sat quietly, watching her. Cheyenne knelt on a linen throw pillow.

"Thanks, Cheyenne," Jinx said. "Looks good."

"I can't take all the credit. The basket was a welcome gift from someone in town." Cheyenne nibbled at the crust of a muffin top, then placed it back on her plate and reached for her water glass.

Jinx spread butter and jam on a muffin, repeatedly glancing at Ruth, who was staring into the cane field and ignoring the attractive spread. "Are you okay, Ruth?" she finally asked.

"She's right," Cheyenne said. "You aren't eating, Ruthie, and that isn't like you."

"You don't know what I'm like," Ruth said, abruptly switching her laser stare from the river cane to Cheyenne.

"I know you always used to dig right in at camp, like you were starved for a home-cooked meal. So much so that I assumed that father of yours couldn't cook and wouldn't hire someone who could."

"You don't want to get into commentary on eating habits with me, Cheyenne." Ruth's voice was laced with warning. "Not today."

"What has gotten into you, Ruthie? We're just trying to have a pleasant picnic."

"I'm not thirteen anymore. Why the fuck do you keep calling me Ruthie?"

"Now that was uncalled for," Cheyenne snapped. "What has gotten into you?"

"Ruth," Jinx said, leaning across the quilt to touch the other woman's bare elbow. "Are you sure you're all right?"

"Fine."

"We just met, I know, but this doesn't seem . . . It was stifling in that cabin. You could be experiencing heatstroke. Do you need some water?" Jinx reached for the pitcher and poured the clear liquid into a glass. She held the glass out to Ruth, who took it without a word and placed it on the quilt beside her empty plate.

Cheyenne scoffed and spoke under her breath. "Try offering her an ice cream shake instead."

"I'm happy with my size, Cheyenne," Ruth said in a voice raised to emphasize Cheyenne's pretended discretion. "And with my appearance, even though you never thought I should be."

"So this is about looks? Still? Are we really reverting back to tenth grade, comparing our figures and fighting over who's cutest? You never appreciated what I tried to do for you, *Ruth*. You've always resented my trying to help, as if it was a secret, your messed-up home life in Minnesota, and how much you needed to be accepted when you came down here in the summers. Do you think I would have spent so much time with you if our grandparents hadn't been friends before your mother died? Honestly, it was charity."

Ruth inhaled sharply, a shifting look of shock, hurt, and embarrassment crossing her features. She set her face and kept her cold stare on Cheyenne. "Was it charity, too, when I was holding your precious 'Indian' hair while you threw up your meals in the toilet every other day?"

"I do *not* have an eating disorder."

"And I don't have a weight problem."

"You could have fooled me. Because you act like you carry the weight of the world on your poor Little Orphan Ruthie shoulders. We've all had hardships in life. When will you learn that losing your mother doesn't give you license to be a class-A bitch?"

Ruth shot up, knocking over a jar of jam as she stood with one bare foot on the quilt and another on the wildflowers and prickly grass.

Jinx reached out a hand to help her regain her balance. Ruth sidestepped the touch, blindly aiming her feet at her clogs as she stumbled beyond the peach tree's canopy.

"I don't need this, and I don't have to take it. Not anymore." Ruth glanced quickly at Jinx, avoiding eye contact with Cheyenne. "I'm sorry," she added for Jinx alone, and left.

*

The picnic was over. Jinx didn't finish her food. She realized, too, given what she just heard, that Cheyenne had probably never intended to eat a full meal anyway. She looked at the empty spot where Ruth had been sitting and saw she had left her notebook behind. On the blue cover Ruth had drawn a stick-figure beaver with an impish smile and large thumping tail, posed playfully over the words: *"Dam it!"*

Jinx pressed her lips together, worried for Ruth. She picked up the notebook and pen clipped to its back cover and slipped both into her messenger bag. She helped Cheyenne pack up the picnic basket and carry the things into the house, said a polite goodbye, and started up her truck.

It felt like a week instead of a day since she had arrived in Georgia, Jinx thought as the truck idled in the Hold House lot. It felt like months since she had gotten a dressing-down by Deb Tom. The longer she spent in this place, the odder things seemed, and the more her research, Ruth's arrival, and Cheyenne's property purchase seemed like occurrences far beyond coincidence.

But what was she thinking? That they had been gathered here for a reason? And if so, by whom, and for what purpose?

Jinx had never considered herself superstitious. She trusted what she could read and analyze; she was a by-the-book chick. But sometimes she felt essences, or presences, that weren't physically there—like the Cherokee travelers at Ross's Landing, and the something askew in Aunt Angie's house. And something like that—something strange that tapped into a sixth sense—had happened to Ruth in the missionary cabin that afternoon. Jinx was sure of it. Whatever Ruth had sensed or seen had been extraordinary enough to make Ruth freeze, to cloud her face with distress, to trigger feelings from the past that had erupted in an ugly fight with Cheyenne.

Jinx felt for Ruth, worried for Ruth, in a way that made her own heart go still. Ruth was now emotionally fragile and alone somewhere in these remote mountains. Where had Ruth gone? And would she come back? Jinx worried, too, that the three of them had started something that day—or something had started them. Maybe that something needed to be identified and finished, or the emotional storm that had been unleashed would take Ruth under. *Three is the magic number,* Cheyenne had said in the drawing room. That was true in the fairy tales of Western culture. But in the old world of Southern Indigenous medicine and power, four was the number of ritual magic. If Jinx, Ruth, and Cheyenne had already been called to the plantation, did that mean a fourth person was due to arrive?

Or maybe the fourth person was already there, in spirit form rather than flesh—and Ruth Mayes knew it.

The moment Jinx had crossed the threshold of the Hold House, she had sensed something was wrong with that place. It had felt too cold and empty inside despite the bright light and Cheyenne's chatter, while the missionary cabin that had been the former kitchen had burned hot with raw emotion. The place provoked Ruth's anger and Cheyenne's insensitive response. It made Jinx feel out of sorts about the chances she hadn't taken—to have a love life, to push her intellect, to live outside of Aunt Angie's shadow. This plantation, or a spirit that animated it, was obsessed with emotions of the past. Hold Hill had a ghost.

Jinx felt a chill that was fully internal this time. What kind of supernatural mess had Deb Tom gotten her into? This was a realm that Aunt Angie had never prepared her for, that she would have to navigate on her own.

She could turn toward the highway. She could get out of town. She could flee to the safety of her Oklahoma bungalow and maintain the lines of order that her great-aunt had established for her. She could leave this hot mess behind, drop the search for Mary Ann, forget about adorable Ruth, outrageous Cheyenne, and that dark and moody plantation. A part of her wanted to do just that. But instead, when she shifted the gear and turned out of the Hold House gate, Jinx found herself driving back up the mountain road.

She knocked on the pine green frame of the screen, peering in through the open door of Adam Battis's cabin. The smell of meat sizzling in a frying pan wafted out to her, and she realized she was famished.

A tall African American man with close-cut hair, serious eyes, and handsome features came to the doorway.

"You must be my mystery guest," he said in a deep Southern drawl. "I wondered if you were planning to pay up. Come on in."

"Finally, we meet. Hi, Adam. I'm Jennifer Micco." She reached out a hand to shake his and placed her messenger bag on the floor. "I was just out for the afternoon. I was hoping to stay three nights, and I was going to leave the money for you."

"Just a joke. Sally Perdue wanted me to ask if you liked the jam."

"It was scrumptious," Jinx said, following Adam into the kitchen, where he pulled a second plate out of the cupboard.

"I always keep her strawberry jam on tap—that or wild strawberries from my garden. We have a belief in my family that having strawberries in your house helps to maintain good relations. And you need that kind of guarantee when you've got strangers coming and going the way I do."

Jinx raised an eyebrow in surprise. "That comes from a Cherokee legend, about a man and woman who argue. The woman runs away, and the man finds her by following a trail of strawberry flowers. They make up and agree never to let their differences separate them again. The strawberry plant is a reminder to keep the peace, to care for others."

Adam Battis gave her a contemplative look. "Have a seat and join me for dinner, Jennifer. Want a beer?"

"I'll take Coke, if you have it. And that would be nice. Thanks."

Jinx slid into a ladder-back chair while Adam brought over two plates heaped with oven-baked fries and pork chop sandwiches. He set a can of Coke beside her and a Michelob Light in front of an empty chair that he promptly folded his lean frame into.

"This looks great," Jinx said, thinking he was a man whose cooking Deb Tom would respect. She squirted ketchup onto her fries.

"You know your mythology," Adam said, sipping his beer.

"So do you. That's some collection of books you have over there. The mythology section is impressive—Native American, Greek, Roman."

"I majored in folklore in college, went on to study forestry, then took a job with the park service so I could stay in the area. I've learned over time that it's all story-work, even the woods bit. What would a Grimms fairy tale be without the forest?"

"You're from here originally?"

"I grew up right on this mountain. My father worked at the mill; my mother sold cakes and cookies to tourists. My grandfolks, they came from the Hold place. It was called the Cherokee Rose Plantation back then. Growing up, I heard so many stories about its history. I always wanted to work there. I used to manage the grounds and physical operations at the house museum."

And then they shut the museum and threw you out of a job, forcing you to run a hostel out of your cabin. "Historic-site caretaker by day, mythology scholar by night," Jinx said. "That sounds like my work schedule back home in Oklahoma. I work at a public library part-time and do tribal research and writing in my free time. What made you stay around here when you lost your job?"

"I belong here. I have a responsibility to this place, no matter who owns the land on paper." He took a messy bite of his pork chop, smothered in onions and mashed between two slices of soft white bread. "So what brings you to the Hold House?"

"How did you—"

"Sally is a talker." Adam smiled.

"That's something I was hoping to tell you about—well, to ask you about, in fact. Have you heard of someone named Mary Ann Battis, a young Creek girl who studied at the mission station on the grounds of the Hold Plantation?'"

Adam's eyes widened. He leaned forward in his seat. "She was my great-great-great-grandmother. I'm named after her son, Adam Battis. But I never heard anybody say she was Creek. I always assumed she was Black and Cherokee. Why the interest in my family tree?"

"Mary Ann Battis was Muscogee Creek. I'm Muscogee too. People back home want to know about her history. Since I do historical research, I was commissioned, so to speak."

"So you're telling me your 'people' want to hear all about some Black Indian girl from Georgia? I'm surprised to learn that Mary Ann is a topic of interest out there, unless you're trying to make an example out of her for one of those legal cases where freedpeople's descendants get disenrolled from the tribe and have their voting rights stripped like it was 1940s Mississippi."

"I'm not the tribal citizenship police, and I don't want to be. Indians are Indians, regardless of skin color."

"That's what your family thinks?"

"That's what *I* think. And my cousin who's like a brother to me, and a lot of other people I know."

Adam looked at Jinx for a long moment. "So what is it you've found out about my ancestor?"

"Not much yet. I know she was a student at the Asbury Mission School in Alabama, and then at the Moravian mission here on the Hold estate. Her mother was Muscogee, and her father was a Black man. When her mother, uncle, and siblings were sent west during the first stage of the Creek Removal in the 1820s, she stayed on here with the missionaries. No one knows why she stayed behind instead of going to Indian Territory with her family. Did you hear any stories about her when you were growing up?" Jinx took a swig of Coke from her can.

"Only that she came to Georgia by herself in the 1800s, took up with a traveling preacher, and never made it out to Indian Territory. She died on the Hold estate just after Reconstruction," Adam said, starting on his fries. "It wasn't so unusual for Black Indian people to use their skin color as a shield back then. Soldiers were rounding up Indians for removal, but even though they thought they knew what an 'Indian' looked like, they regularly missed the mark. I guess it was the one time in American history when passing for Black was a tactical advantage."

"Is she buried on the plantation?" Jinx asked.

"Nah. There's an old Black cemetery called the Strangers' Grave-yard a mile past the Conasauga. Folks buried loved ones there during Jim Crow, when the official town cemetery was closed to them. None of the graves were marked—just a big rock here, an unusual tree there. Back in James Hold's day, enslaved folks who were sickly and died young, or who caused trouble by breaking the tools or running away, were buried beyond the main estate. It could be that's how the Strang-ers' Graveyard started, as a burial ground for Black castoffs. Mary Ann was laid to rest in there, I've always heard."

"Do you know where the cemetery is?" Jinx said. "I'd like to see it and find Mary Ann's grave."

"A local man named Mason Allen bought and fenced off the prop-erty several months ago."

"Shame." She shook her head. "There should be ways to protect that land. I remember hearing about a slave burial ground in New York City that was saved from demolition. It takes research, a lot of people working together, but it can be done. There might be evidence of the burial ground's existence in the WPA slave narratives."

"That Roosevelt project from the Depression? I thought that was just make-work for unemployed writers." Adam leaned another inch forward, propping his elbows on the table.

"They're actually oral histories taken with formerly enslaved peo-ple by government employees hired by the Federal Writers' Project. It's true it was just one of the ways to try to get people working again, and the narratives are filtered through the questions—often white in-terviewers talking to Black interviewees—but historians have found gems in there."

Jinx watched Adam's eyes brighten with interest, then fade with resignation.

"Mason's already got the foundation in place for his time-share condos," he said. "It's too late to save the graves. If things had worked out the way Mason wanted, he'd own land on both sides of the river—the Strangers' Graveyard and the Hold Plantation too. There's a local legend about gold hidden on that property. Gold lust never died down around here after the rush of 1829, and it's picking up again now, with all this talk of a Great Recession. Folks want wealth they can touch. Same old story. Greed. If Mason Allen had won the Hold estate at auction, he might have made a fortune down the line finding gold—or, more likely, selling the dream of hidden treasure."

"So you're saying her bones have already been disturbed."

Adam looked straight at Jinx. "All of their bones." The legs of his chair made an ugly sound on the floor as he stood and reached for the dirty plates.

FOURTEEN

-›-›-›- ·-‹-‹-‹-

THE HOUSE FELT empty to Cheyenne now. It had been exhilarating showing the place to people who could understand her passion for it. Jennifer Micco was steeped in the missionary history of the plantation and had hung on Cheyenne's every word. Ruth, although she was annoying about it, recognized architectural elements and could identify plants. Both of them had been eager to learn more about the house, and Cheyenne could have gone on for hours before the big, immature blow-up about who was skinnier in the 1990s. She bit her tongue, causing an uncomfortable sting to radiate through her mouth. Ruth had lost her mind and verbally attacked her for no reason. But Cheyenne had brought up the woman's mother twice, almost as if she were rubbing it in. Now, in the cool of the house with the heat of the moment behind her, Cheyenne knew she had taken things too far.

The Minnesota newspapers had covered the story of Ruth's mother's suspicious drowning death during a cruise with her husband. Cheyenne was only ten at the time, but she still remembered the gossiping ladies at her grandmother's church, the flowers on their hats shaking with the pitch of their voices as they accused Ruth's white father. And the next summer, Ruth had turned up at Idlewood, the same camp both their mothers had attended when they were girls. Cheyenne had befriended her not for the sole reason she had spouted at the picnic—charity—but because she had also been attracted by the defiant cast of Ruth's eyes. Ruth needed Cheyenne—a social butterfly—to help her fit in. And now that Ruth had come back, dispelling the stillness and stagnancy in that house with her prickly attitude and probing questions, Cheyenne wondered if *she* might need *her*. But because of Cheyenne's refusal to ever back down, she was alone again on the grounds with a dozen tiny worries about Adam Battis, Sally Perdue, Mason Allen, and yes, Ruth, pricking her like mosquitoes.

Cheyenne washed the plates from the picnic, taking care not to chip her nails and wondering how quickly she could find a house cleaner. Maybe she shouldn't have selected formal dishes for an outdoor meal, but this was her home now, and she was going to use all the things in it. Cheyenne dried her hands on a paper towel, thinking she needed to purchase nice linens. She sighed and made her way up to the master bedroom, where she changed into a watermelon running suit, white tank top, and matching tennis shoes.

There were benefits to being alone, Cheyenne told herself. She would use the time to carefully survey the house and grounds, inspect her azalea bushes up close, and find those orchards that Adam the park ranger had mentioned. She started her exploration in the foyer, looking through the literature. She rooted through the stacked boxes by the door and drew out an array of Chief Hold House booklets.

Cheyenne flopped onto the teal divan, where a sour-faced Ruthie Mayes had sat that morning. She opened one of the booklets—a history of the restoration of the Hold House. When the first house museum tour took place in 1952, the cost was fifty cents for adults and twenty-five for children. She should have placards made showcasing those darling prices, painted signs in vintage lettering that she could hang inside the guest rooms. Cheyenne wondered what those first paying guests would have thought about the million-dollar price tag in 2008.

She felt another pinch of anxiety. Her parents wanted this to work for her, but they were also cautious. They hadn't expected to spend so much on a property, and neither had Cheyenne. Her parents had borrowed half the money by taking out a second mortgage on their cottage at the Vineyard, and they intended to pass that debt along to her after she got her hospitality business up and running. She needed to make this bed-and-breakfast shine, or she might have to sell the place. Nothing could go wrong. The stories Jennifer and Ruth were writing—if they returned to complete the research—could be key for sparking interest when she opened her doors next year. Cheyenne tossed the booklet onto a cushion and stood. She thought of Layla, De'Sha, and Toni back in Atlanta. It was Wednesday. She could drive down on Friday, meet them for dinner at Aria, and stay overnight at her condo. Then she could drive by Swag and pick up some lovely kitchen accessories for the new house.

As she paced in front of the towering windows and carved fireplace, hips swinging and thoughts turning, Cheyenne caught a glimpse of herself in the mirror above the mantel. She paused, smiling at her reflection, at the smooth hair and alluring face, the svelte body that was hers and yet not hers. She moistened her lips to make them glisten, reflecting the lush pink of her tracksuit.

And that's when she saw the roaches in the fireplace. Cheyenne swallowed a yelp as she hopped back on the balls of her feet. Two dozen fat cockroaches with shiny, black segmented backs were squirming and crawling inside the grate. One or two had scuttled out beyond the ceramic enclosure to traverse the ornate Turkish rug. Cheyenne choked at the sight of their thick antennae testing the air. She hated bugs. And cockroaches went beyond bugs. They belonged to a wholly separate category of disgustingness. Her eyes darted around the room, and then she saw more. A roach was clinging to the hem of the curtain next to the fireplace. Three were climbing the Tiffany glass fireplace screen. One was crawling on the window next to the mantel.

Calm down. Think. Maybe she should have scheduled a pest inspection before signing the papers. She would have if she had been less impatient. But she had let house-lust subsume her while leading her parents to believe that she was taking every precaution with their investment. But if the home was infested, wouldn't she have seen at least one roach when she toured it with the broker? Wouldn't she have seen the sickening little beasts in the galley kitchen when she stored her groceries last night?

This was no ongoing infestation. These creeping, crawling germ carriers had been imported. She thought of the azaleas with their blooms lobbed off. Twice when she had been out of the house, strange things had happened that would have lowered the property's appeal to any buyer. Earlier that day, when the three of them were touring the grounds, she had left the back door unlocked for anyone to waltz right in. She had thought Mason Allen had just been taunting her at the courthouse when he asked if she knew how many points of entry there were in this building. But maybe he had been issuing a subtle threat of coming attractions. If he was behind this, she would not let him win.

Cheyenne wrapped her arms around herself and squeezed, cupping her elbows in her palms. She would not be run out of her house or off her plantation. There had to be insecticide somewhere in the park service supplies. She could stand at a distance and spray the monsters. And first thing the next morning, she would call an exterminator. She wouldn't relish it, but if she had to, she would have a chat in a public place with Mason Allen as soon as the house had been sprayed.

As Cheyenne backed away from the mantel, praying the bugs wouldn't get far, she heard a scratching sound in the hallway. She backed against the wall of the drawing room and peered around the doorframe. A tabby cat the color of orange sorbet sat on its haunches, tail flicking side to side with agitation. The cat's fur was long and spiky, its bright eyes keen. It meowed once, then stretched its paws forward to roll into a four-legged stance. The cat slowly ambled toward her, lean and sleek. "What the hell?" Cheyenne said quietly, so as not to shock it. *Calm down.* She had feral cats on the property. Adam fed them. She knew this. An exterminator could handle them too.

The cat appealed to her with its round jade eyes. Cheyenne backed up a step. Taking this as a sign, the cat bounded past her into the drawing room and leapt at the window, grasping a fat roach in its paw. The cat snapped the roach into its mouth, then went for one on the curtain hem. The scene was mortifying. The only saving grace was that no one else was there to see a feral feline dine on vermin in her parlor.

"Good kitty. Good, Sorbet," she whispered to the animal as she grabbed her shoulder bag and ran for the door.

*

Ruth stepped over brittle twigs, looking at the faded buildings that once composed Camp Idlewood. Released from the Hold Plantation's wrought-iron gates, she had headed blindly for the steep mountain road. After passing the abandoned fruit stand that had seemed dimly familiar, she had felt the mountainside rise beneath her tires. To the right, the road had offered breathtaking vistas where tourists gathered at pull-outs to gape at the misty valley below. And now she was here, at the place where she had spent ten successive summers between the ages of nine and eighteen.

The campus looked smaller now, its handful of Adirondack-style log structures scattered over five acres of cleared forestland. Fort Mountain State Park had purchased the land some time ago, and the buildings seemed to be in use as a crafts and nature center. Ruth made her way to the old dining hall, with its metal crank windows that slowly wound open. She breathed in the familiar smell of live pines and felt her clogs sink into the forest floor. She sat on the steps of the dining hall, tucking her denim skirt around her, peering beyond the campus clearing into the dense woods.

Since the early 1900s, Idlewood had been a tradition among Southern Black families with means, a place where girls imagined themselves as future debutantes and boys were expected to make connections that would last into the future. She had been viewed as a charity case and put in a bunk with Cheyenne Cotterell.

Ruth had not admitted to herself or anyone else that she knew the truth about her parents. So she couldn't hate her father for stealing the joy in her life. Instead, she had settled on hating Cheyenne Cotterell. Cheyenne and her well-heeled Atlanta family with all the right marriages to other Black people in their "set." Cheyenne with the colorful stories of a Cherokee ancestor that lent her genealogy an exotic twist. Cheyenne in her skinny pink tanks and J.Crew short shorts, her straight, penny-shiny ponytail doing its jaunty swing. Cheyenne with a gaggle of girls flocking around and a gang of boys gawking behind. Cheyenne and her fairy-tale existence.

Ruth remembered the first time she heard Cheyenne throwing up her grilled cheese and tomato soup in a stall of the bunk room—how satisfying it had felt to know Miss Princess found perfection only through self-abuse. She felt a twinge of remorse at the harsh thought now, but only a twinge. Cheyenne was obsessed with herself. She deserved to live with a ghost who could melt a person's personal boundaries and send their feelings into a chaotic spin. Because Ruth was sure now, after she had walked and thought, breathing in mountain air touched by the scent of pine, that a ghost is what she had seen.

But what about Jinx? The thought rushed over Ruth in a wave that took her breath for a moment. Maybe it had been fair, and if not fair, defensible, to leave Cheyenne to the fate she had chosen by buying and romanticizing a haunted plantation. But she had left a perfectly innocent, well-intentioned, surprisingly kind person back at that haunted house with no explanation—and no warning.

Ruth stood and brushed off the seat of her skirt. She looked again at the empty camp buildings, allowing the thoughts that had tortured her many years ago to push through the surface of her long resistance: her mother had walked these dirt pathways; her mother had slept inside these cabins; her mother had been a girl here, safe and carefree.

It didn't take Ruth long to narrow the list of places where Jinx might be staying. Here in town there was one option: Room with a View Bed-and-Breakfast, where Ruth herself had booked a room. She stopped in at the desk, inquired after Jinx, and learned from the clerk about a cabin rental near the Ball Fruit Stand.

*

"Battis. Adam Battis," the man said to Ruth, holding out a lightly callused hand. He was a hunk with smoky dark eyes and muscled arms that, from the looks of his place, came honestly from hard work out of doors. She was surprised to feel a twinge of jealousy. What did Jinx think about Adam Battis and his biceps? *Wait.* She knew that name, and not just because of Jinx's research subject. She vaguely remembered this place.

"Your mother used to sell amazing cookies in front of this house," she said. "I went to summer camp here. I'm Ruth Mayes."

"Camp Idlewood. Sure. My mother lives in Dalton now, with her sister. I'll pass along your compliment. Are you looking for a room? I'm full tonight, I'm afraid, but there's a B&B a few miles up the road."

"I'm looking for a person. Jennifer Micco? She sometimes goes by Jinx."

"Jennifer? She's here. Are you two together?"

"Not exactly."

"Yes," Jinx interrupted such that their words overlapped as she pulled the door back to stand beside Adam.

Ruth looked from Adam to Jinx, at the comfortable way Jinx held the doorknob.

"Come on in," Adam said, watching her. "Jennifer's renting the place for a few nights. I do the cooking sometimes and then head out to my tent. There's dinner left, if you're hungry."

Ruth followed them inside the rustic cabin lined with shelves of books. She settled in at the scuffed kitchen table while Adam warmed up something that smelled delicious. He poured himself and Ruth cups of decaf coffee and set a fresh can of Coke in front of Jinx.

"What brings you back to Fort Mountain, Ruth?" Adam said.

"I'm a magazine writer, here to do research on the closure of the Hold House and the future of the historic site."

Adam chuckled, shaking his head. "So you're researching my lost job, and Jennifer's researching my dead ancestors. It sure is reassuring to know that the press and professors are on the case."

"I'm no professor," Jinx said. "I write for myself and for my tribe, not a bunch of narrow-minded academics."

Adam paused and took a sip of coffee. "And you two were down at the Hold House today. You met the new owner."

"Cheyenne Cotterell," Ruth said, her voice going flat.

"Cheyenne Cotterell," Adam repeated. "She is something."

He was smitten, Ruth saw immediately. Just like all the rest of them.

"A strong woman," Adam said. "She's got grit. She faced down Mason Allen at the courthouse auction to walk away with those keys."

Ruth listened with annoyance as she nibbled an oven fry and cut into her pork chop. But even if he was blinded by Cheyenne's charms, Ruth had to admit that Adam could cook. She hadn't realized how hungry she was after that awful picnic. The tender pork chop met her tongue in a burst of savory flavor.

"Allen? Again? That guy sounds like a 3D asshole," Jinx said.

"He comes from a powerful family and had crazy luck in the real-estate market before the bubble burst. He saw this little northwest town as the next big development opportunity. He built luxury cabins up here in the mountains for Atlanta executives, owns an RV park for motor tourists down by the highway, and has condos underway by the river. He was planning to build a housing development for rich suburbanites on the Hold estate and acted like he already owned it. I've heard rumors that Allen was the one who put the parks commissioner up to auctioning off the Hold land in the first place. He thought he'd be the one to buy it. He didn't count on Ms. Cotterell."

"What do you think Allen will do, now that he's lost his bid?" Jinx said.

"He won't give up, I can tell you that. Maybe he'll wait her out and see if she'll sell. It's not easy to run a big, old place like that."

"Adam used to manage operations when the house was public," Jinx said to Ruth. "But doesn't it piss you off," she said, looking back at Adam, "that your family comes from that plantation, and other people can fight over it because they have the money?"

"Cheyenne claims her ancestor came from the Hold place too." Ruth realized too late that this sounded like a defense of her.

"That's what she told me," Adam said.

"How likely is it, really, that a prissy African American interior designer is descended from famous Cherokees?"

"Unlikely, maybe, but not impossible," Adam said. "More than a few Black families up here can trace connections to the Hold estate. And I wouldn't call Cheyenne prissy. She's just a little too proud."

"Mm-hmm," Ruth said, pointing the tines of her fork at him. "You just met her, and you're already under her spell." She saw a grin tug at the corner of Jinx's mouth. "What?" Ruth questioned her.

"I bet you could cast a pretty mean spell yourself. But it's possible, and I raise it as a possibility only, that you're too busy fixating on Cheyenne to realize it." Jinx softened her words with a teasing smile.

Ruth felt her earlobes warm beneath the spiral curls that covered them.

Adam shook his head, smiling. "I wish my friend Sally were with us. She would love this. Historical drama. Romantic mystery. Right here in our little town."

"Sally is a mystery buff *and* a history buff," Jinx said with a playful smile to match his. "She was holding out on me."

"Fine," Ruth interjected. "Maybe what Cheyenne says is possible. But James Hold was an enslaver. They don't have a good reputation as a category of human being. It's much more likely that he owned Cheyenne's supposed ancestor than that he married her and gave her the keys to the big house."

"And there's a third possibility," Jinx said. "If Cheyenne's ancestor was enslaved on the hill, Hold could have owned her and slept with her. It happened, though some people in my tribe like to pretend it didn't." She looked at Adam. "Was James Hold ever known to take up with Black women, consensually—or not?"

Adam hesitated. "I've heard anything was possible with him. He was known to be a violent man."

Ruth's expression had grown stiff, her voice thinning as she spoke again. "Cheyenne told us Hold was murdered. Does anybody know who killed him, or why?"

"Historians say it was his old friend turned enemy, Alexander Sands," Adam said. "The story goes that James went out riding one day with the Lighthorsemen, the Cherokee Nation militia, to chase down horse thieves. He came across Alexander, who insulted him. Old James Hold was not the type to tolerate disrespect. He whipped Alexander right in front of the Lighthorsemen. The next thing anybody knew, Hold was shot dead at Buffington's Tavern."

"Is that what you think?" Jinx asked. "That Sands did it?"

"Maybe Sands pulled the trigger. Maybe not. Plenty of people had a reason to want Hold dead." Adam spoke with a sober expression, eyes fixed on his coffee cup.

"Like Mary Ann Battis?" Jinx said, seizing on the silence behind Adam's words. "Would she have wanted him dead? I know she set fire to the mission station in Alabama. None of the literature says why, but it's well documented that Native students at government boarding schools committed arson as a form of resistance. Maybe Mary Ann set the fire to defend herself or the other children. She seems like a tough, troubled girl who might do anything when pushed too far."

"She was barely fourteen when she came to the Hold Plantation," Adam said. "According to our family stories, she became a young mother and had a baby to care for right away. I wouldn't be surprised if she felt she was trapped there, and being trapped makes people do desperate things."

Ruth's mind filled with an image then, and she let it come. She saw again the flowing skirt and dangling ribbons in the dim pearly light of the mission cabin. A troubled teenage girl stood on the line between this world and the next. River cane stalks whispered in the background. *Shh.*

Come. Come back. Ruth could not resist this call. She was being wrenched back in time, whether into her own lifeline, or the lifeline of the girl, she did not yet know.

FIFTEEN

✦➤➤➤•◄◄◄

ADAM SAT IN his blue canvas tent with the flap tied open. The air outside had shifted since dinner, carrying the faint scent of a coming rain. It was a small tent designed for one or two people. He shared the space with his sleeping bag, an empty crate that doubled as a bedside table, a stack of books, and his laptop computer, which sometimes did and sometimes didn't catch a wireless Internet signal from the Room with a View Bed-and-Breakfast up the road.

As soon as his company had abruptly left, with Ruth Mayes looking dazed and anxious, he'd tidied up the cabin and prepared it for Jennifer Micco's return. He didn't know what time she'd be back, given the odd circumstances of her departure, but she had rented the space. It was hers. Besides breaks for showers and meals, he stayed in his tent when he had a renter. That was the deal. What did they call it on the radio? The sharing economy? Folks in economic straits were turning to sharing more often these days to make ends meet. Adam did well with this arrangement, especially in the summer months. Since there was no mortgage on the cabin thanks to his parents, Adam's expenses went to food, utility bills, student loans, his mint-condition 1980 Ford Bronco, and quality gardening tools. The rest he used to take his mother out to dinner once a month and to stock his savings account.

When the state closed the museum, Adam had been twenty-seven, four years out of his forestry master's program and working at the

Hold House. Once he was out of the job he loved, he'd started renting out the cabin, saving his earnings in the hope that he might be able to buy the Hold place someday—or if not buy it, at least rent land around the old mission cabin. This was where his grandmother had grown up. The family member he was named for, Adam Battis, was born in that cabin, where his great-great-great-grandmother Mary Ann had lived. His grandmother said they descended from two lines: one African American, one Cherokee. Exactly how those lines got crossed, she hadn't known—or hadn't seen fit to tell him. But she always said two proud bloodlines linked together were stronger than one alone.

Adam sighed and stretched his legs on the thin canvas that did nothing to cushion his muscles from the hard ground beneath. He would help Cheyenne if she'd let him, and tend the fruit trees for Sally, but the hope of living there one day, of restoring his family's cabin, was a notion he would have to let go. Even knowing what he knew now, after a dive into the records Jennifer had pointed him to, he didn't have the heart to try to force Cheyenne's hand. Adam took a gulp from his water bottle and lifted his laptop back onto his thighs.

The WPA slave narratives were searchable online, digitized by the Library of Congress. Adam had found the website an hour ago and was still pondering the import of what he had discovered there. He flipped open the black lid of his laptop, reread the electronic pages he had been struggling to absorb. Five people formerly held as slaves from the Hold Plantation in Murray County, Georgia, had been interviewed in 1932. The interviewer had asked questions about their owner, food rations, physical treatment, and what they thought of Abraham Lincoln. A man named Michael Gamble was among the five interviewees. He had been born in 1850 and listed Michael and Hettie Gamble as his parents. Michael Gamble told the interviewer his family had lived in the refurbished barn of the mission station, right alongside Miss Mary Ann Battis. Miss Battis, Gamble explained to the confused interviewer, had helped raise two children on the Cherokee Rose Plantation, neither of whom was hers. One of them, Isaac Cotterell, was the child of a local Black preacher. The other, Adam

Battis, was the illegitimate son of a young enslaved woman and Chief James Hold himself.

*

Come back. The picture in Ruth's head had resurfaced the multisensory memory of the ghost sighting. And because she suspected the vision was the spirit of a girl in crisis, she had listened to the words that accompanied the image. Jinx had insisted on coming back to the Hold place with her, packing up her things at Adam's and following Ruth in her truck.

Ruth gazed out on the shadowed oaks and the burnished brick structure. The Hold House was nearly dark. Only a small arc of light shone from the master bedroom window, casting an eerie glow. Ruth parked her Beetle, imagining Cheyenne cocooned in a cluster of pillows in the high canopy bed and wearing two-hundred-dollar pajamas and a sateen headscarf and eye mask to match.

Ruth waited for Jinx to jump down from her truck. They rounded the house beneath a full white moon. A breeze rustled the branches, sending warm ripples through the humid air. They picked their way through weeds and wildflowers to the missionary cabin situated behind the big house. Ruth used her iPhone for illumination. It shone like a firefly as she held it out before her. Jinx carried a heavy black flashlight that she had retrieved from her pickup. She swung it as she walked with that steady, loping stride, dark braid swaying like the grasses beneath their feet.

Ruth ducked into the cabin ahead of Jinx.

"What are we looking for?" Jinx said.

"Not sure. I just knew I had to come back." Ruth moved to the spot where they had sat earlier that day. She lowered herself to the ground facing the doorway just as she had done the first time, nudging her glasses higher when they slipped down her nose.

Jinx squatted beside her. "What is it?" she said gently. "What happened here, Ruth? What did you see?"

Ruth turned to face her. "I saw a girl, like a shimmer in the sunlight, and I heard a sound, a sort of voice, telling me to come back."

Jinx sank into a sitting position. "Do you believe in ghosts?"

"I wasn't entirely closed to the idea, but I always thought if ghosts were real, my mother would find a way to visit me."

Jinx was quiet for a moment before reaching out to touch the tips of her fingers lightly to Ruth's back.

Jinx's fingers were warm and comforting through the thin cotton of Ruth's T-shirt. Ruth leaned into Jinx, letting their shoulders touch.

"Maybe your mother has been with you all this time. She's a part of you, right? You can acknowledge her presence as much or as little as you choose to."

"You're still close with your great-aunt," Ruth said.

"She's always been my guiding light. But as much as I loved her, will always love her, I'm starting to realize she didn't see everything clearly. She wouldn't have liked me being here with you like this, for instance."

"Because I'm a woman."

"And because you're not Creek." Jinx paused. "And more than that. Because you're Black. Aunt Angie had a rigid view of the right order of things."

"I can't say that doesn't sting. Racial rejection hurts every damn time, and racial prejudice is a chimera. It repels some people, and attracts others. My mother married a white man she met in business school—my father. Her parents were dead set against it. They wanted her to marry well when it came to money and education, but only to a Black man. So there's that . . . There was always something off about my parents' relationship. I felt it as a child. It was like he loved and hated her at the same time. Her race was part of the attraction, and the revulsion."

"I'm sorry," Jinx said.

Ruth nodded in the darkness, pushing the knot of her fist into the dirt floor.

"It doesn't have to be like that," Jinx added. "The way my aunt was, the way your dad was. Some people respect and trust each other even through their differences."

Ruth unknotted her fist, offering a hand to Jinx in the darkness. Jinx took it in a loose grasp. They sat together breathing, feeling the humid air around them, smelling the dirt of the cabin floor and the raw wood of the walls, hearing the breeze outside rustle the river cane.

Ruth peered at the open doorway where she had seen the girl, where she had tripped when she first entered the cabin all those hours earlier that now felt like days. She sucked in her breath. "The threshold," she said. She leapt to her feet and moved to the doorway. She brushed her hands across the wooden frame, feeling the flow of the grain. "She was standing right here," Ruth said, "the image, the girl. What if she wanted to show me something? What if she had a message?"

She dropped to the floor, inching her hand across the sill. The single plank lay unevenly across the dirt. Why use a wooden door sill on a dirt floor? Ruth shoved her glasses up, squinting in the white light that Jinx was shining on the ground. Near the end of the plank, the floor dipped, forming a subtle indenture.

"I need a tool," Ruth said. "Something to dig with."

Jinx was already gone, shining her flashlight through the dust-coated rooms.

"Here," she said. "I found these in a back room." She handed Ruth a gardening trowel and kept the spade.

They dug at the dip in the ground. Two inches deep. Three to four inches wide. The dirt softened and fell away beneath their tools. They reached a hollow space.

"It's a ground safe, a keeping pit." Ruth's words tumbled over each other. "Enslaved people used to dig them in their quarters, to store food and hide treasured items, sort of like a safe-deposit box."

Jinx laid the flashlight at the edge of the hole and reached a hand inside. She pulled out a conch shell, six silver buttons, a small glass vial, and a pair of green spectacles. Below those was a wooden box. She paused, looking at Ruth.

"Go ahead," Ruth whispered.

Jinx pulled the box out of the ground and gently wiped the dirt from its surface. It was fashioned of light chestnut wood with intricate floral carvings.

Ruth reached over to Jinx's lap and unhooked the small metal clasp, lifting the tight lid open. A square of scarlet silk was spread inside. Jinx unfurled the folds of the cloth. A sheath of manuscript pages, brittle and thin, nestled within the fabric.

"Holy . . . Is this happening?" Jinx whispered.

"I think it is," Ruth answered, breathless. "Take out a page." Ruth grabbed the flashlight from the ground and directed the beam toward Jinx.

Jinx's hand shook as she reached for the sheet of curled paper. The amber edge flaked at her touch. She stilled her hand and read aloud.

The Diary of a Mission to the Cherokees, by Anna Rosina Gamble, Sister in Christ

February 14, 1815

The rain fell and would not stop. It continued, unabated, throughout the last portion of our long journey southward. We passed through the mountains beneath the clear blue of sky, but entered Virginia with the drops constantly upon our backs. It was a bone chilling rain. My husband directed the trembling horses from the front of the wagon, his dark hat a covering over his thoughts. My skirts gathered about my knees, weighted down by the torrent. My sogged hair escaped its pins and hung about my shivering shoulders. From time to time, my husband chanced to glance at me, observing my discomfort. But he did not choose to speak or slow our pace. A higher calling urged us onward. We are expected within two weeks in the territory of the Cherokee Indians, where we will endeavor to spread God's word.

Only when the wagon's wheels stuck fast in the mud did he see fit to stop. He sloshed down to the ground in his boots, and with the help of a stranger, freed us. With our horses fatigued, and us besides, we consented to rest at an inn near Knoxville, the great center city of the Southwest Territory. We retired to our room before supper. My shoes had filled so with water that I thought they were buckets. My hair hung about my face like melted beeswax. I helped my husband to undress first and prepared his coat for drying while he studied his Bible by the fireside. Peeling off my skirt and petticoat, I lay them beside the fire to dry. I cast my gaze about the chamber, from dripping skirts to silent spouse, wishing for the simple comforts of home. I stared into the nascent flames, bright in the dimness, and reflected on all that I had left behind. I sacrificed my post as head teacher to the girls of Bethlehem village in order to answer this sacred calling. When John Gamble was named Head Missionary to the Cherokee Indians, a selection approved by the Lot, our earthly interpreter of Divine will, the elders of the Church agreed that Mr. Gamble should marry in order to ensure the success of the endeavor. Two women from his town of Salem were tried, but failed to gain the Lot's approval. And then, recalling that I had accompanied Brother Loskiel as his secretary on a journey to the Ohio Indians, the elders approached me, my father and mother having both passed on many years before. Upon hearing what my marriage should be—a partnership for the work and glory of Christ— I agreed to wed at the late age of forty years. The Lot approved. There was neither necessity nor time for courtship. I relocated from Pennsylvania to the merchant village of Salem, North Carolina. There, in our foremost Southern Moravian town, I found a neatness and simplicity that could not fail but to excite the feelings. The buildings were remarkably trim, the gardens pretty, and the streets neatly paved. A noxious weed or tangled grass could not be found, for everything was kept in perfect order. We dwelled in Salem for the better part of a year as we prepared to depart, and many dear friendships were sewn there.

This journey from Salem to the Cherokee nation is the first that I have taken with my husband. How I miss my country-women of Salem. How I fondly recall my students of Bethlehem and the specimen garden beyond the schoolyard where we assayed a menagerie of plants. I have packed with me seeds and seedlings, tucked within a burlap wrap which I have not had to moisten due to the constant rain. I have also brought, in linen pockets sewn by my skillful students, a small collection of my favorite tomes: The Book of Common Prayer, An Introduction to Botany, A Botanical Arrangement of British Plants, and Paradise Lost. Besides my good husband, these books will be my only faithful company in the heathen land. And more books yet will be sent, together with sundry supplies, once we have safely arrived in Cherokee country. My sacrifice of the comforts of home is a requirement of this mission, and one that I make willingly. I have long desired to venture again into the unknown wild, taking the Light of our Savior to the aborigines of America.

I stood and turned the clothing beside the fire in the bed-chamber of the inn, lit the candles, and prepared the beds for sleeping. The room smelled of damp and the musk of its former inhabitants. How I wished I could have brought with me a servant to ease the labor of our travels. But none could be spared by the Church, and my husband has been directed to rent one from Mr. Hold, who, we are told, is a very wealthy planter of his tribe with many Negroes to spare. Besides being an aid with the housework, such a servant might also be pre-disposed to understanding the Indians' tongue, of which we have no knowledge.

I folded the woolen blankets back, making a sleeve of warmth for my husband. He settled himself and consented to close his piercing grey-green eyes. When his breathing aligned into a regular pattern of sound and silence, I peeled away the cool, wet underthings that modesty had precluded me from freeing myself of. I lay my soaked shift and stockings beside the fire, pulled on a dry cotton gown, and braided my tangled hair. I turned to the second bed, grasped the blanket, and had only begun to rest myself when my husband called my name. His voice was low within the silent room, and yet cloaked by that firmness that underwrote his character. I turned toward him. His eyes were stern upon me. I rose and answered his call.

Jinx looked up from the wreck of a page and into Ruth's eyes. "I know this woman," she said. "The missionary, Anna Rosina Gamble. I found a reprint of an old Moravian Church history at a secondhand bookstore in Tennessee. It included a summary of Anna Rosina's work in Cherokee territory, as recounted by her student. That student was Mary Ann Battis. Anna Rosina kept a diary of her time on the plantation, a full-length manuscript that was lost."

"Not lost, saved," Ruth said. "And I think we know by who."

"Mary Ann," Jinx said. "The girl you saw. She must have hidden it when she lived here. But she never told the church about it. She kept it secret from them. I wonder why."

"Keep going," Ruth said.

She leaned over Jinx's lap, squinting at the barely legible manuscript pages. The curling script faded into the paper like so many watermarks. How could Jinx make it out, the faded, looping words, the *s*'s that looked like *f*'s, the disappeared punctuation marks? Ruth tried to read along, tried to follow with her eyes as Jinx picked up the story with the next diary entry.

Jinx stumbled while reading at first and then caught a rhythm, the particular cadence of Anna Rosina Gamble's lines. Ruth gave up trying to read along and closed her eyes, letting Jinx's soothing voice carry the story. She felt the hard dirt floor beneath her legs, the humid evening air around her, the paintbrush end of Jinx's braid brushing her arm. She breathed in the smell of the manuscript pages, a scent like crushed leaves, a scent like sifting baskets. Plant matter. Jinx read on, her voice the breeze, her voice the river cane. *Shh, shh.*

March 3, 1815

The journey to Cherokee territory was tedious and slow, with many difficulties to be endured. The greater therefore was our relief when on the first day of March we safely reached the Cherokee settlement called Hold Hill. At evenfall, we were directed to Mr. Hold's plantation by a wandering, paperless Negro, who, when Mr. Gamble inquired, indicated through signs, for he spoke only the Indians' tongue, that he was a free man. Mr. Hold's plantation is a broad swath of land, consisting of a rough set of buildings chiseled out of the wilderness between the woods and a field of river cane so tall that one cannot see beyond it. His own house, a fine and fancy brick affair recently built, is impressive indeed for this country. We have been told that his is the most profitable and civilized of all the Cherokee establishments, for Mr. Hold has put his plantation profits into the development of various mercantile establishments. He owns two trading posts and ferries besides, and seeks to establish a gristmill.

Upon our arrival, Mr. Gamble climbed down from the wagon, removing his hat for less than an instant while he wiped perspiration from his brow. The nearness of the river's flow makes the air here wet, with or without a rainfall. Mr. Gamble has the thin, drawn face of a man always thinking: of what should be done, what must be done, and how it should best be accomplished. Every aspect of his existence is drawn and quartered through the chastening prism of duty. He is held in much esteem by our Church for these qualities of single mindedness and dogged self discipline. He directed me to remain in the wagon and approached a cabin with glass paned windows situated along the road to the main house. There he met Mr. Geiger, Mr. Hold's business manager. I breathed a relieving sigh at the sight of Mr. Geiger, standing at the cabin door in woolen breeches. He is a white man, and German by descent as we Moravians are.

I let my worrying fingers come to rest upon my lap. The details of our stay here have been prearranged by elders of our Church and the Cherokee Agent for the U. States, Return Jonathan Meigs. Agent Meigs pledged to help support our labors from the national Dept. of War funds. The remainder of our support comes from our brethren and sisters in Christ and the profit of whatever goods we might barter with the Indians. The chiefs in council of the Cherokee nation have consented to have a Christian mission, provided that a school should teach their children the English language. Our Church elders insist that such a school, if it be established, must instruct in religion as well as English, and must room and board the children in order to extricate them from the daily influence of their heathen households. None other than the prominent Mr. Hold himself has offered to host the mission on the grounds of his estate.

When Mr. Gamble inquired about water and food for our horses, Mr. Geiger called for servants from the barn. The two men, bulky as barrels and darker skinned than soot, set down our trunks on the dusty, red road and then led our horses away. Mr. Geiger conversed with my husband in English, the language of preference here next to the Indians' tongue, explaining that Mr. Hold was away on business in Charleston, Carolina, and that we should stay in the main house until a cabin of our own can be prepared.

We were accompanied to Mr. Hold's home, where upon we met his wives, as Mr. Hold and the Indians here practice the sin of adultery as if it is indeed a virtue, customarily keeping for themselves more than one wife, and sometimes as many as five.

Mr. Hold has two wives—a younger one, who is quite lovely and speaks the English language much, the daughter of a Cherokee woman and an English trader; and an elder wife, who speaks only her native tongue and is said to be the younger one's half sister. The younger Mrs. Hold lives with her husband in the brick house. The elder Mrs. Hold, having her own peculiar dwelling in a cleared spot within the river cane, was merely visiting the home of her husband on the day we arrived. It appeared, however, that the elder wife took precedence over the younger even in the house that was not her own, for she was the one who bid us to come inside. She gave us gifts of woven cloth and a basket of dried, dark berries, which I judged to fall within the Rubus genus. The younger wife directed a Negro girl of perhaps twelve, who then heated water in a kettle suspended above the fire and made us a refreshment of tea. There was no sugar, for Mr. Hold had not returned from his latest trading venture. Nor was there honey or anything nearly so sweet. To accompany our tea, we were served plain cornbread and a sour hominy meal that reeked of lye.

The contrast embedded in this place is striking. The house, which had stood the better part of a year, according to Mr. Geiger, boasts glass windows, triple stories, and verandas to channel the breeze. On the inside, however, it feels much like the rough hewn dwellings of the Carolina country folk, having none of the refinement of our own Moravian village structures. The rooms are full of dirt and confusion. The walls smell of hominy and wood smoke, and the air is thick with the residue of too many bodies in motion. My husband and I sleep on mats beside the fire in the rear most parlor of the house, for there are neither bedrooms nor beds to spare in this large abode. The younger Mrs. Hold retires in a room on the second floor in the evenings, and the elder Mrs. Hold continues her visit mainly to survey us, sleeping in a spare room in the upper chamber. Various men and women whose names we were never told sleep and visit within the house as if it is an outdoor camp, bringing in food from the separated kitchen, taking their meals in any room they please, and clogging the already fetid air with the swill of pipe smoke.

A host of children also scamper through the house, feeding themselves from a large pot of stew nursed on top of the fireplace coals and otherwise running around the plantation grounds unchecked. When they frolic out of doors, which for them is a constant pastime, the children graze directly from the edible trees and plant life. I am told that the pink blossoms of the Eastern Redbud shrub (Cercis canadensis), are as delightful a treat to these children as pastry cakes to the youths of Bethlehem. There is no school for the Indian children here to attend, and no discipline is exacted from them, so that they dash to and fro like wayward field mice with the Negro children as their sole companions. Some of these Indian youngsters, I have learned, belong to Mr. Hold by paternity. The others are his nieces and nephews, the children of his sisters. The younger Mrs. Hold retains the rosy cheeked blush of unblemished youth. She appears to be less than eighteen years and has no children of her own. The majority of Mr. Hold's children, we are told, live in their mothers' respective towns, for Hold had other wives before, or in addition to, the two whom we have met.

The familial life of these Indians is a complete confusion. No one of organized mind could unwind these tangled genealogical registers. Besides the unnamed persons, upward of twenty of whom seem to regularly dwell here, sundry Indians visit the place from day to day, some, but not all, being distant relatives of the Holds. Many a night we must share our sleeping spot beside the fire, rendering what should have been a fine parlor cramped and malodorous.

March 8, 1815

This tedious phase of our stay has lasted for nearly a week, while we await Mr. Hold's return from southern Carolina. During the days, Mr. Gamble studies the lay of the place, walking about the plantation with Mr. Geiger as his guide. If we were back at home in Salem or my beloved Bethlehem, I too should walk freely about. But here, at my husband's direction, I stay behind, shut up like an invalid in the hazy home of the Holds, with only Christ Jesus, and you, Dear Diary, as my interlocutors.

The younger Mrs. Hold does not often speak, but smiles politely and keeps about her work of spinning thread and weaving cotton in what would be called the drawing room in a proper house of this size. The skills she displays have been lately learned by some of the mixed blood women in this country. The older Mrs. Hold, by contrast, speaks quite freely in my presence. I must confess that the cutting syllables of the Indians' language grate on my ears, like a wind sharpened twig repeatedly scraping against the bubbled glass of a windowpane. The constant flow of voluble, unintelligible sound is reminiscent of the mythical Sibyls. I wonder, as Mrs. Hold mutters her incantations, if they are not directed in protest of our presence here. Most of these people, we have been warned by Agent Meigs, believe in ancient superstitions, in beings above and below this world, in witches taking human form, in magic, medicine men, and ancestor ghosts. Many would be loath to learn the Gospel of the Lord, the one true Savior. Showing them the Light will require dedication and steadfast resolve, qualities which my husband possesses in abundance. But even as the older wife shakes her finger and mutters in a repelling, guttural hum, the younger Mrs. Hold has already begun to touch my heart. Her actions toward me are reserved, it is true. She does not consent to pray with me upon invitation. Nevertheless, she possesses a politeness of manners inculcated, it must be surmised, by her English father. This, together with a light behind her amber eyes that burns intensely when she sets about a given task, instills in me the hope that she might someday be won for the Lord.

A high screech sounded from the rear of the cabin, breaking the rhythm of Jinx's voice. Ruth started where she sat.

"A barn cat," Jinx said, looking up from the page. A streak of matted black fur flashed along the back wall, then faded into the shadows. "This diary . . . incredible. I wonder if anyone's ever seen anything like it."

"We should show Cheyenne," Ruth said after a pause, resistant to finding herself standing up for the woman again, but certain that this discovery should be her means of making peace. Cheyenne was proud, judgmental, and often blind to the needs of other people, but she was also consistent. She usually thought she was doing good. "She'll want to hear this too."

"You're absolutely right. Let's go roll her out of bed." Jinx gave Ruth a smile that warmed her like a hot drink on a cold day.

SIXTEEN

->->->-·-<-<-<-

JINX CLASPED THE chestnut box to her chest as they hurried from the cabin and rounded the house to reach the front door. She rang the bell. Through the windows, she saw Cheyenne traipsing down the staircase in an ivory robe and faux rhinestone-studded slippers. The peach sheen of her pajamas peeked from behind the folds of her robe. Her hair hung straight and loose around her shoulders, as if just released from the protective covering of her bedtime scarf.

Cheyenne flung open the door. "What is all this racket? I'm trying to get my beauty sleep."

"Your beauty will survive, Cheyenne. We have something to show you," Ruth said.

"I thought you left."

"I almost did, but I thought better of it when I realized you need me."

"*I* need *you*?" Cheyenne said, incredulous.

Ruth paused. "What's that awful smell?" She pushed past Cheyenne to get a look at the hallway.

Jinx followed her. The chemical stench of bug spray assaulted their senses.

Cheyenne's confident expression faltered. "It's nothing. I had a few bugs in the drawing room. I sprayed them, and the exterminator is coming tomorrow."

"Trouble in paradise?" Ruth commented with brows raised.

"Nothing I can't handle." Cheyenne fixed her eyes on the box Jinx was cradling. "What's that?"

"A diary," Jinx said. "Written by a missionary. It chronicles daily life here during the plantation's early years. We found it buried in the mission cabin."

"Let me see."

Jinx released the chestnut box into Cheyenne's hands.

Cheyenne's robe slid up her arms as she opened the lid. She peered at the top page tucked inside. "It's completely illegible. The writing's faded."

"It's old cursive script, but Jinx can make out most of it," Ruth said.

"Follow me. We'll sit in the dining room." Cheyenne slammed the front door, turned the lock, and pushed a heavy cardboard box against the lower panel as Ruth and Jinx watched her, then glanced at each other.

The table was set just as it had been that morning—blue and white bone china on a white cloth, silver utensils, goblets. Jinx glanced up at the golden phoenix above one of the silk-draped windows, thinking of what this room had been like, what this house had been like, when Anna Rosina first visited. She imagined the press of people upstairs and down, the squeals of children and smell of pipe smoke. She imagined the warmth of the fires and light of the candles. A bustling home.

"Well?" Cheyenne said, settling in at the head of the table, where James Hold would have sat. "I'm dying to know what's in this thing." She opened the box and handed Jinx several diary pages, careful to keep the rest of them close to her.

Jinx looked at Cheyenne beside her and Ruth across the table. "Let's go back to the 1800s," she said.

March 15, 1815

The Passion Week prior to Good Friday commenced with Mr. Hold's return to his coarse estate. He brought with him a

chain of wagons pulled by thick oxen and filled with an ava-
lanche of useful and frivolous things: kettles, knives, and pot-
tery dishes, bundles of pungent cinnamon sticks, sacks of
sugar, dresses, barrels of rum, bricks of tea, leather shoes with
silver buckles, fine writing papers, coats and coatees, eating
utensils, reading matter, scented soaps, aprons of lace, silk
scarves, hats, gloves, and a coffle of African slaves. All of these
jostled one on top of the other in and behind the open topped
wagons, whose creaking joints testified to their frequent use.

Agent Meigs had informed us that the opening of the federal road adjacent to Mr. Hold's estate has played a large part
in the growth of his fortune. Mr. Hold travels the road fre-
quently to trade his field and orchard crops for manufactured
wares in the finest cities of the South. Piloting each wagon
home is a Negro driver with the wooden face of a painted toy
soldier. Beside the first driver, the master himself sat with a
grim and forceful air. Mr. Hold's skin is as fair as that of any
white man one might encounter along the streets of Salem. He
wore his wavy, pitch black hair shorn at the ears, a tailored shirt
of Irish linen, and a silk cravat. His dark eyes are brooding, his
jaw squarely cut, his lips the color of a bruised summer plum.
When Mr. Hold swung his legs down from the seat, his body
moved all of a piece, as if he were a large cat caught and corralled from the mountains behind his sprawling estate. On Mr.
Hold's left hip, a dirk protruded from its sheath. Inside his
right hand, he grasped a pistol. He strode about in his fine cut
breeches, thick white stockings, and Hessian boots, casting his
eyes over the gathered assemblage of Cherokee women and
slaves. The older Mrs. Hold wore her customary simple shift
with men's deerskin leggings beneath. The younger Mrs.
Hold, having some sense of proper etiquette, dressed herself
for reception in a garnet toned velour frock, soft wool shawl,
and bonnet to secure her from the ever threatening springtime
rains. Mr. Hold seemed not to notice the effort which she had

made to braid and loop her long dark hair. Failing to greet her beyond a nod, he spoke a few brief words to his Negro driver, who wore a turban in the Indian style and a knife at his side like his master. Repeating the Cherokee words that his master had spoken, the driver called to the other black men who had gathered by the side of the dusty road. They then began to unload mounds of supplies, carrying items within their arms or across their backs, to the main house, the barn, and a log storehouse several paces away.

From a wheat or cotton field far off in the distance, a bulky man whom I had not met began a slow approach. His pantaloons were worn at the ankles, his straw hat stiffened with sweat, and his work boots caked with soil and loose sprouts of grass. Unlike Mr. Hold's tightly woven dress shirt, this man's shirt was homespun from coarse linsey wool, a fabric rougher even than the sunburnt skin of his taut, irregular features. I took him to be of Scotch-Irish stock, the descendant of unruly Highlanders, quite like his half breed Indian employer. Upon reaching the motley crowd assembled by the wagons—made up of Mr. Hold's family and slaves, Mr. Gamble and myself, the clerk Mr. Geiger, and a few unaccounted for white men and Cherokees—he shook Mr. Hold's hand, barked an order to the nearest Negro, and came to stand before the line of tethered slaves that stretched behind the wagons like a trail of dried blood.

They were a pitiful sight to behold, those men, two women, and a single small child, whose lives were now entwined by the thick rope that bound them. Their twelve bowed bodies were draped in rags. Their feet were bare. One man limped, his toes chewed away by the morning frosts of a long forced journey. A middle-aged woman with cracked, dry skin crawled on her hands and knees, apparently affected by the same cruel malady. The child, who seemed to belong with her, clung to her neck and sobbed. A young woman beside the pair flicked her gaze about, keenly taking in the surroundings. The smooth skin of her face glowed a buckeye brown. Her eyes flashed the color and shape of almonds. Her hair wound around itself in a series of spiral knots. Her limbs were long and lithe. She stepped slightly forward, as if to shield the weaker two with her half-clothed frame. The man I took for the overseer halted before her, stretched out his arm, and pounded her chin with the force of a gale, pushing her back into line with the others. She reached out an arm behind her, fingers fanned, not to break her own fall, but to cushion the woman and child, who shrunk in the shadow of the man. But it was she who crashed back, rather than they, under the crush of the overseer's fist. "My name is Samuel Talley," he grunted to the woman and line of eleven others in a voice low and thick. "And y'all nigras are mine now."

The crowd loosened as men and women alike stumbled back from the scene unfolding, waves of anxiety fanning out like ripples in a human pond. The younger Mrs. Hold gasped but did not speak. The older Mrs. Hold mumbled something at once furious and unintelligible, beckoned to an aged black man and woman, and began a slow retreat with them across the yard and toward the dense canebrake. Mr. Geiger scribbled on his fluttering leaves, keeping a written inventory for Mr. Hold. I had never in my life seen such a display. The possession of Negroes by our church to assist with the necessary labors of life was quiet and humane. Black servants could join the church if they professed the faith, worship in Home Church sanctuary, and, until recent years when the Strangers' Cemetery became the preferred practice, be buried in God's Acre along with their white brothers and sisters. My husband watched the scene unfold, expressionless.

The stricken woman rolled on her heels, a bloom of blood trickling from the corner of her nose to merge with another sprouting from her lip. Her breasts were now exposed by the sagging neck of her ragged shift. She lifted her eyes from the ground. Talley knotted his fist. Mr. Hold raised his hand, causing Talley to pause. Mr. Hold approached the woman on the ground, rolled his gaze over her flesh—the quaking shoulders, the brilliant blood. When he bent to cup the roundness of her upper arm, the tassels on his Hessian boots swung.

"What is your name?" he murmured, near enough to her ear to bestow a kiss.

"Patience." She was softly crying now, her brown eyes directed toward the ground.

"Give this one to my little wife," he said to his overseer, rising. "Send the men to the field cabins. And these damaged ones," he continued, gesturing toward the shuddering woman and child, "they should do for the missionaries." Mr. Hold looked directly, then, at my husband, rudely acknowledging his presence.

This exchange constituted the first English words that the master of Hold Hill had spoken in our midst, and there was in them no trace of the heathen tongue. Educated from the time of his youth by a private tutor, Mr. Hold was now a perfect chameleon, his colors shifting fluidly from white man to red Indian, leaving no trace from one form to the next. Talley flushed beneath his leathered skin, feeling, perhaps, the acid sting of open rebuke.

Mr. Hold then commenced a long-legged stride toward the big brick house. The wagons had been emptied, the women and child cut from the rope line, the male slaves led away to the fields of wheat and cotton. The slave called Patience was directed to the house by an elderly, coal black woman named Grace, whose calm countenance could not obscure the sadness in her eyes. I followed my husband, who followed Mr. Hold. Behind us, the crippled woman crawled, her young son grasping the hem of her filthy dress. The smell of cinnamon, sweat, and fear clung to the air. I felt within me a stain of shame for having been present at this spectacle, the silent witness to an evil spreading its blackened wings.

March 26, 1815

Easter Sunday. The weather was stormy again. We attempted a morning service in the brick house of the Holds. The crippled woman assigned to us, who answers to the name of Faith, her little son, and the household slaves were our sole co-celebrants. The downcast Patience seemed glad of the chance to escape the bedchamber of Mr. and Mrs. Hold, where she is often retained to administer some service or other, even in the absence of her mistress. Our hope of bringing the Gospel here has yet to find fertile ground. It looks very dark in this land.

March 28, 1815

We have been one month in the home of the Holds. Faith does little more than manage my sewing and stir the coals beneath the stewing pots. Her little son, Michael, a yellow boy about the age of ten, fetches firewood from the nearby forest and tends to my husband's personal effects. Patience cooks for the Holds and their motley stream of ruffian guests, replacing the bumbling machinations of the twelve year old girl whose sour hominy greeted us upon our arrival. Unlike the girl, who was born and raised in Cherokee country and knows only the Indians' dishes and tongue, Patience came to the Holds with suitable experience as a cook for white people. Her yeast rolls we have found quite agreeable, as well as her chicken pie, which she spices with pennyroyal from herbs I have planted in hollowed gourds. The girl, we have learned, has since been sent to Mr. Hold's older sister, where she might find an audience more eager for her savage fare. Her mother was also disposed of at that time, being sent to the wife of the Assistant Cherokee Agent William Lovely, who had put in an order for a Negress.

March 30, 1815

We now have milk. The elder Mrs. Hold brought us a cow from the cattle range at the far edge of Mr. Hold's establishment. There, I have learned from Faith, an elderly couple from Africa who speak only their native tongue, keep the cattle. As we had nowhere to pen this cow, we asked Mrs. Hold to take it back for the time being. Through the younger Mrs. Hold's translations, she entreated us to keep it, lest Mr. Hold become angry with her. Gone was the threatening Sibyl whose presence had commanded this house upon our arrival. Now that her husband had returned, the older Mrs. Hold appeared shrunken in the doorway, her indecipherable words like a dust cloud around her, the faded calico dress hanging loose as a shroud. It was then that I began to suspect a darker side to Mr. Hold, who seems to hold his two wives in invisible chains. She turned and retreated to her peculiar dwelling in the trees, where an aged black couple that she has owned since her childhood live with her as equals. We have tied the cow behind the brick house for the moment, for there are no fences here.

April 1, 1815

All sins and scandals are going full swing and one can see clearly that Satan, the prince of this realm, still keeps the Indians bound with chains of darkness. Mr. Hold's Negroes cart rum by the barrel into the dwelling house, where Mr. Hold, his

Indian guests, his overseer and craftsmen, all partake together. On Tuesday last, Mr. Hold shot at the elder Mrs. Hold because she refused him some meat belonging to her aged slave couple. Her life was spared by a courageous black servant named Demas, who stood between her and the threatening specter of her husband. Demas's life was saved in turn by Mr. Hold's wavering aim, hindered, as he was, by his rum induced state. After the altercation, Mr. Hold had Demas dragged from his bed, disrobed, whipped, and chained to the hitching post for all to see.

April 3, 1815

The elder Mrs. Hold has determined to relocate to Etowah town together with her Negroes to live in the household of her brother. She says that she cannot reside near this husband any longer. Mr. Hold's house has indeed become a Sodom during his stays between trading ventures. He lays about the place in his ruffle fronted shirts, swigging rum and dancing with his slaves to the tune of the Negro Isaac's fiddle. His constant companions are his pistol and dirk, which he hesitates not to unveil at the slightest provocation. His younger wife, appareled in long skirts of somber hues, wilts in the corners on these occasions, trying to disappear herself into the plaster walls. But having no respect for the delicacy of the female sex, Mr. Hold hikes her up, swinging her to his right side in a rough embrace whilst hoisting the slave woman, Patience, on his left. I see from the distant look in her eyes that the younger Mrs. Hold longs for an elsewhere. I speak to her at every opportunity about the salvation of the Lord and the everlasting peace of His Heavens, so that she may one day be brought to the knowledge of her one true friend, Jesus Christ our Lord.

Beyond Mr. Hold's home and fields, his mill at the creek,

and his ferry at the river, lies a wild mountain vastness. We are sequestered at a far remove from Christian civilization. And Mr. Hold behaves like a heathen lord of his manor.

April 5, 1815

In need of a proper place to begin our work in the virgin field of the Lord, my husband requested assistance in building a house of our own. Mr. Hold determined instead to remake his separate log frame kitchen into a mission station whilst building a new kitchen in the cellar of the brick house. He lent ten of his slaves, who proved to be able workmen, to accomplish the task. They added two rear rooms to the one room kitchen, complete with cut glass windows.

They whitewashed the inner rooms until our cabin glowed like a single star of civilization in the firmament of this heathen land.

I have set myself to the task of making our cabin into a house of God. Oh, how I long to bring the light into this little domicile. For surely from our hearth Good News will flow, and a light will be set upon this darkened country. Our public meeting space has been established in the front of the structure, within the former kitchen. The bedchamber that Mr. Gamble and I are to share is situated toward the back of the cabin. The second rear room will be used to house our scholars until such time as it becomes overfull, whereupon the students will be moved to board in the garret of the main house under the care of Mrs. Hold. Our wide brick oven, fashioned to my specifications by Isaac, one of Mr. Hold's most highly skilled slaves, occupies the front room sidewall, where a sleeping enclosure was also fitted for Faith, the crippled woman, and her son, our mission's servants. We procured our furnishings from Mr. Hold's storehouse, where he kept several pieces carved by his former master craftsman, a Negro lately sold for a hefty price to the Nathaniel Russell family of Charleston. The Negro Isaac was the artisan's protégé.

I have sewn curtains of blue cotton produced by the slave women in the weaving house, arranged the woolens we brought with us inside the carved blanket chest, lined our beloved books along the poplar shelving, and hung sage and rosemary from the front room window. The young Mrs. Hold has supplied us with gourds for carrying water and serving. To these, we have added proper dishes sent to us by our dear brothers and sisters back in Salem. The mail is slow to arrive in this part of the country. Mr. Hold has the only contract in the region with the U. States government to deliver it, which he fulfills with the labor of his slave boys, whose minds become distracted, or whose legs cannot go the distance from settlement to distant settlement. But oh, the joy of receiving packages from our old friends, with their accounts of the mission stations around the world, shoes for Mr. Gamble and our servants, fabric for my sewing, and robust coffee beans. We should want for medicines too, for my latent cough and Mr. Gamble's joints, but our crippled slave woman Faith has turned out to have a very fine working knowledge of herbal remedies. Mr. Hold may find in time that he has undervalued that one.

April 9, 1815

On this the second Sunday of the month, the sun rose high and clear above the eastern mountains. I instructed the slave woman Faith on how to bake the potato buns of our traditional Home Church Lovefeasts. She kneaded the dough on her knees and worked at a bench foreshortened by Isaac to accommodate her malady. The cabin smelled of hot bread baking and the fresh butter that I have taught Michael how to churn. I was sorely reminded of home and longed to look upon the faces of my dear countrywomen. Mr. Gamble need not have reminded me that we are here in this darkened land to do the work of the Lord, that our sacrifices are nothing when compared to those of our suffering Savior, who gave all for our sins.

After the praying of the Church Litany, we held our first public service in the mission cabin. Mr. Gamble presided, delivering an enlightening message on the Holy Trinity and leading the singing in German. I stood behind and held a Bible aloft to symbolize to those gathered the sacredness of the book. Sunlight glinted through our single pane windows, casting the light of a thousand angels over the modest room. Our audience consisted mainly of slaves who are not required to labor on Sundays, that being a day that Mr. Hold does not trade or manage the affairs of his plantation, so that he can drink and carouse. Old and blind, young and ignorant, women and men in the full strength of youth, all came of their own accord to hear my husband preach the Gospel. They managed, despite the limitations of their daily working attire, to piece together colorful dresses, deerskin leggings, and hair decorations fashioned, I suspect, from the grosgrain ribbon ordered for Mrs. Hold's bonnets. The eagerness in their shadow-rimmed eyes quelled my disappointment at the absence of many Indians among the congregants. It has long been a mission of our fellowship to minister to the blacks as well. That work was begun seventy years before in the West Indies missions, about which I often read in the Church dispatches that arrive by post.

One of the black congregants at our mission, Samuel Cotterell, a self-described free Ethiopian preacher, at times during the service translated my husband's words into an African language, which he appears to know as well as English. Mr. Cotterell can read the Bible and carries one of his own in a leather pouch at his side. He is white haired and distinctive despite his color. Patience attended along with her mistress, the young Mrs. Hold, who, I observed, listened feelingly to Mr. Gamble's words. Mrs. Hold has taken to Patience and seems to love her like a sister. For Patience is a woman just out of girlhood, close to her mistress's own young age, and possesses, like her mistress, a light behind her almond eyes that shines brightest in the absence of Mr. Hold.

After the service, I served to all of those in attendance the sweet rolls Faith had baked, together with our Moravian coffee, thick with milk and sugar. At the forbearance of her generous mistress, Patience, who possesses a deeply kind heart, stayed behind to help our crippled Faith scour the iron pots. I put the chairs in order, cleaned the floor of grit, folded and stored my husband's white shirt and kerchief. I permitted Faith to feed little Michael the last of the buns, which he ate with early season wild strawberries, having always an eager stomach. I retired to the rear bedchamber with a little book of nature poems lately sent by my former students in Bethlehem. A warm evening breeze drifted through the open window, flickering the flame of my beeswax candle and carrying into my awareness the sharp scents and muffled sounds of the nearest slave quarters. I should have wanted someone with whom to share my observations—of the steady awakening of Mrs. Hold, the rumbling voice of the itinerant preacher, the slave girls dressed in their vibrant hues, the rounded Lovefeast buns. But my husband, with a mind set toward the next day's labors and the importance of making our mission integral to this place, had gone to survey the plantation grounds alongside Mr. Hold.

"Stop," Cheyenne said, raising a hand with spread fingers and breaking their concentration. Her eyes shone in the artificial light with a dazed sheen. "I can't listen to any more of this."

Jinx looked up from the half-read page to find the portrait of James Hold hanging like a threat before her. His penetrating eyes bore down on the three of them from the cobalt-colored wall. His velvet riding jacket, a deep maroon, brought to mind Anna Gamble's description of slaves lined up like a trail of dried-up blood.

"You mean you don't want to hear it," Ruth said. "Wanting to and being able to are different things."

"I didn't buy this house to dig up dirt on all the shit that happened here. Do you hear who James Hold was? Abusive. A tyrant."

Ruth's head jerked up at Cheyenne's words, an involuntary action that drew Jinx's eye.

"If they could live through all that, don't you think the least we can do is learn about it? We honor their memory by being witnesses for their lives. Leave if you have to, but I'm going to keep on reading. Mary Ann Battis is bound to show up sometime soon."

"Battis," Cheyenne repeated, her eyes sharpening, her voice slowing. "As in Adam Battis."

"Exactly," Jinx said.

SEVENTEEN

-+->->-·-<-<-<-

April 22, 1815

The last frost has melted away, and I can finally dig in the ground, setting in place the lines of my garden between our mission cabin and the big house. Each plot shall have a path leading to its center, so that I might tend the plants separately, according to kind. I have brought with me seeds and cuttings from Bethlehem and Salem. I have likewise collected seeds from the Indians who come calling at our mission in the hopes of receiving food or supplies at no expense. My garden shall soon have varieties of peas, large-leafed lettuce, beans, squash (prickly cucumbers), ornamental flowers of various kinds, and a few rows of cotton. It shall also have a supply of medicinal plants. For Faith has proven most knowledgeable in this arena and has already used her skills to treat visiting Indians with salves and teas. Beyond my garden is the mission's large cornfield, which we will soon sow. Mr. Hold, being generous according to the custom of his people in the use of land, apportioned to us a fifth of his cleared fields and peach orchards.

When he is not preaching, leading liturgical service, or secluded in Bible study, Mr. Gamble spends hours traveling with Mr. Hold. He has become in some ways an advisor, keeping a record of Mr. Hold's legal affairs and accompanying him to the nearest Cherokee villages. He hopes that through such careful ministrations and the establishment of trust between them, he might lead Mr. Hold, along with his dependents, to an abiding belief in the Lord. As we yet have no scholars, and I am often on my own save for Faith and her son, I have taken to walking about in search of plant life, as I once used to do along the Lehigh River. Here, the Conasauga's loamy banks afford a home for a vast array of plants. Eager to set my eye upon each one, to sketch them in pencil, describe them in words, and harvest their seeds for planting, I tramp freely about the place with my white cap tied at the neck, hanging loose on my shoulders.

I have begun to assemble a list of plants in the Cherokee area and have commenced sending samples to my northerly brethren in Christ, Rev. Henry Muhlenberg, Rev. Henry Steinhauer, and Rev. Elias Cornelius, who likewise subscribe to the study of Linnaeus's principles of botanical schema and are eager to hear my thoughts. If they knew of my husband's disapproval of my scientific pursuits due to my sex, they might withdraw their interest. I therefore desire to send my specimens and accompanying notes as soon as I collect them so as not to draw his suspicions. I have found Mr. Hold's mail system so sluggish, however, that I grow impatient. I have therefore enlisted his most trusted slave, Isaac the craftsman, to carry these samples as far as Kentucky on my behalf, where he will post them to Pennsylvania forthwith. In the Cherokee nation, no passes are required for Negro slaves in transit, but for his smooth passage through Tennessee I have fashioned him a letter of allowance.

April 30, 1815

Having become accustomed to this place and its natural shape, I pulled on my husband's boots and set out for the woods earlier this day. Great was my anticipation. A fresh spring rain had fallen, and newborn seedlings are already sprouting. I wore a burlap seed pack on my waist looped about the ties of my skirt and petticoat and carried a wax-bound sheath of papers in my hand. The spring air was warm on the bare skin of my neck. The sun shone above like a beacon. Coming over a rise in the Holds' freshly sowed cornfield one mile west of the main house, I scanned the dense wood below. Pine, hickory, oak, chestnut, walnut, mulberry, poplar, and sourwood trees thrive there, thick and inviting.

The Negress Patience was ambling along the forest's interior edge, seeming to take pleasure in the natural scene about her. She did not observe me on the hillside above as she went about her quiet task, gracefully circumventing the sassafras and sumach underbrush while pausing to touch one glossy leaf that beckoned to her. Barefoot, buckeye skin glistening in the afternoon light, Patience hiked her muddy skirt up about her hips, bending low to collect the wild potatoes and onions that are a staple of the Indians' diet. It was then with a lightning speed that Mr. Hold appeared beside her, together with a thundering herd of five other men. They were each of them members of the Lighthorse brigade lately authorized by the Cherokee Council to track and punish horse thieves. Mr. Hold is known as a passionate judge of his fellows, whipping his tribesmen with a fury that even the heathens see fit to question. I lowered myself within the field, sensing that I should not draw notice.

The contingent below became a blur of motion and sound as they dismounted and stomped their thick heeled boots. One man wore a traditional scalplock of knotted hair; another bore a strand of red turkey feathers dangling from his hat. Mr. Hold, in his cleanly knotted blue silk cravat, was the most civilized in appearance among them, and the most brutal. As if to display his power before the others, he knocked Patience to the ground without a word of warning, as if felling a sapling on a field he intended to clear. Her basket of gathered onions tumbled to the forest floor. She grasped for it. But the basket rolled away, and then she had nothing to reach for. When Mr. Hold defiled her, he forced her eyes open, pressing her lashes apart with his thumbs as he crushed her with the weight of his body. Daring the men who esteemed his leadership in the political arena to interfere, he searched her gaze, hunting incessantly for the light which must dim still more each time he looks at her. As her master and possessor, he had and took free reign. Once sated, he threw his servant to her knees, sending her skirts to the treetops. Following this wicked act, he abandoned her in a pool of filth that seeped into the blameless ground. I gathered my skirts about me, fleeing the young woman's shame, which had somehow become my own, scattering my notes and sketches, in which I had taken such delight, to the far corners of the cornfield.

May 1, 1815

Today, as I dug in my kitchen garden, tending the wild transplanted strawberries and looking up from time to time at the penetrating sunlight, Patience emerged from the rear door of the brick house. I watched her approach from the slaves' work yard, it being the only boundary between the Hold family home and our mission cabin. On legs that bowed weakly like violin strings, she passed by the slave women making soap and scalding bed linens. She wobbled into the little gate that marked the entrance to my garden, cut for me from fallen timber by the itinerant preacher Mr. Sam Cotterell. With her slender arms wrapped around a broad bottomed basket woven of river cane dyed a deep crimson with the roots of the Sanguinaria canadensis (bloodroot), she approached me. Her countenance was withholding, her skin everywhere marred by pulpy wounds. She reached inside the basket and drew out handfuls of wild onions and potatoes. "My mistress wishes you to have these, Mrs. Gamble, for next Sabbath service," she said. How, oh how, had she managed to gather each curled onion again? How had she stood? How had she moved? How had she commenced a new day? I accepted the offering. The wild potatoes were small and clean, free of the loose dirt and leaves that should have clung to their skins, given the circumstances of their collection. But the basket Patience carried was well constructed, made to shed grime through its fine grained sifting seams.

Patience reached inside the basket a second time and withdrew my lost papers and seed bag, placing them beside me on the garden ground, speaking not a word about where she had found them. I ducked my head in sorrow for her suffering and guilt for my failure to come to her aid. We were, both of us, helpless members of the weaker sex. The papers had come loose from the thin wax mooring; nothing held them together now. Only the dissected drawings of plant parts showed how the pages had connected before—the stem of a Tradescantia virginica (spiderwort) on one page, its striped, oval leaf on another, the likeness of its seedpod buried at the bottom of the loose leaf stack. I stared at the words and shapes I had formed and began to blindly rearrange them in my mind.

A Beginning List of Plants found in the Neighbourhood of the Conasauga River, (Cherokee Country) where Hold Hill is situated; made by Mrs. Gamble.

Aesculus pavia—The nuts pounded, are used in poultices.

Asarum virginicum—The leaves; fresh, they are applied to wounds.

Cornus florida—The bark of the root is used to heal wounds, and in poultices.

Saururus cernuus—The roots roasted and mashed, used for poultices.

Liriodendrum tulipifera—Of the bark of the root, a tea is made
  and given in fevers. It is also used in poultices.

"Patience," I whispered, withdrawing my focus from the
solace of plant life, "I am sorry."

"Yes, ma'am," was her only reply. Her eyes remained fixed
on her basket until she noticed Faith, who with great effort had
appeared at the cabin doorway.

Faith's frost-gnawed feet still made it necessary for her to
crawl to each destination, but she never complained of this dif-
ficulty. Neither did her features reveal surprise at Patience's
lamentable condition. Faith hears and learns things through a
network of Negroes and poor Cherokees who seem to place
their trust in her maternal wisdom. From her knees, Faith extended a hand toward Patience and pressed a vial of acorn balsam into the young woman's palm. "This will ease your pain,
daughter," she said. Patience nodded, bowed to hug Faith's
waist, then left again with her river cane basket, into which she
placed the vial. I watched her pass through the gate and move
across the slaves' work yard, her lovely neck long and dark
above her overburdened shoulders.

That night, with my husband sleeping beside me, I dreamt
of poison hemlock.

"I want to murder the asshole myself." Cheyenne shot up from her
Chippendale chair and rubbed her upper arms abrasively through
the fabric of her robe. Her face was a crumpled flower, all illusions
shattered. "It's so damn cold in here," she said, squeezing her arms
with a punishing force.

"What he did to Patience . . ." Tears were wet on Ruth's cheeks.

Jinx laid the diary page upside down on top of the one before it.
Her eyes fell on Ruth. "Cheyenne, tissues?"

"Oh, of course." Cheyenne had started pacing in front of James
Hold's portrait, the rhinestones on her slippers flashing in the chan-

delier's muted light. She stopped abruptly and walked through the swinging doors into the kitchenette and butler's pantry. Then came the echo of cupboard doors opening and closing as Cheyenne looked for supplies.

The next sound they heard was a scream. "Cheyenne!" Ruth said, jumping up.

Jinx and Ruth found Cheyenne standing on a step stool beside the open pantry, hand clasped over her mouth. The door was thrown back beside her. Cheyenne stood frozen, gazing at an upper shelf just out of reach. Ruth peered into the storage space. It looked like a stuffed animal at first, soft and orange, glassy eyes the color of grass blades. But the cat was real. Real and dead, its neck twisted unnaturally to one side. There was no smell. Death had been recent—while Cheyenne was resting in bed, or when they had found the ground safe.

"It's Sorbet," Cheyenne said, shoulders trembling beneath the ivory robe. "He did this to her."

"What!" Ruth said, alarmed. She hadn't even known Cheyenne had a pet. "Who?"

"You should come down from there," Jinx said, holding a hand up to Cheyenne who stepped unsteadily to the floor, her face drained of emotion. "When I bought this house, I beat out another major contender. His name is Mason Allen."

"We've heard of him," Jinx said. "And I've seen him in action. He ran into me, literally, at the Marathon station. Scary guy."

"He wanted this place as much as I did. I could see it in his eyes. After the auction, he suggested I go back to Atlanta. Obviously, I didn't. And then strange things started happening around here."

"What kinds of things?" Ruth had dried her face with the backs of her hands and was focusing on Cheyenne.

"Little things that seemed like they could be accidents or bad luck at first. Someone cut the blossoms off my azaleas. I found a bunch of filthy cockroaches in the fireplace. And now the cat is dead. She was a stray, a smart, pretty thing, but I took to her." Cheyenne caught and held Ruth's gaze.

Ruth dipped her head, breaking the contact.

"And you think Mason Allen is doing this?" Jinx asked.

"Maybe the blossoms blew off. Maybe the roaches were in the walls. Maybe Sorbet was already sick and climbed up there to die. But I don't think so. That man was . . . He was . . . determined. I should have paid closer attention."

"You had no idea he would act on his twisted belief that he owns this whole town," Jinx said. "Adam said he's been digging up the African American cemetery."

Ruth gasped.

"He's trying to intimidate me. I know it now. But to kill a helpless animal?" Cheyenne stared into the cupboard at the carcass.

Jinx reached around her to shut the door. "We'll have Sorbet removed tomorrow."

"You should sit down," Ruth said. She rummaged in the kitchenette drawers, then made tea in the microwave. She returned to the dining room with a tray of full Styrofoam cups.

"Next time, use the good china." Cheyenne reached for a cup, breathed into the steam, and then added in a quieter voice, "Thank you, Ruth."

Ruth wrapped the cashmere throw from a side chair around Cheyenne's shoulders before taking a seat at the table. "You're welcome."

Cheyenne grasped the fringe edges of the covering, pulling them tightly across her breasts. "I owe you an apology, for what I said about your mother. It was wrong and insensitive of me."

Taken aback by this turn, Ruth squinted at Cheyenne, all the while feeling Jinx's eyes on her. The room fell silent as Ruth hesitated beneath the glare of James Hold's portrait.

"Apology accepted. And Cheyenne, about the bulimia, I should never have—"

Cheyenne looked away from Ruth this time, toward the china cabinet. "Honestly, we're all works in progress. I have some things to improve on too."

Ruth waited a moment for Cheyenne's gaze to return before giving her a sad smile. "Should we call the police? About the cat?"

"What would I report without looking like a hysterical urbanite?"

"Vandalism? Harassment? Breaking and entering? There must be some legal term for this crap," Ruth said.

"Not until I can prove it was him." Cheyenne straightened her back in the chair. "People around here respect him for some imperceptible reason."

"It's his family's money, and maybe political influence too." Jinx warmed her hands around a Styrofoam cup as she watched the other two women. "Sally Perdue and Adam both say the Allens have dominated this area for generations."

Cheyenne turned up her nose at the sound of Sally Perdue's name. "I can't put my reputation at risk in this town by accusing their golden boy of infantile pranks. I'd be the one to suffer for it, not him. I have a business to launch, and it *will* be successful."

"We're all tired," Jinx said. "It's the end of a very long day. We can make sure the house is locked tight and revisit the police question tomorrow when our minds are clear. But we're not leaving you alone here tonight. Right, Ruth?"

"Fine with me," Cheyenne said, relief in her voice beneath the bluster. "You two can sleep in the guest room."

"And you're sleeping in there with us," Ruth said, "whether you want to or not. We should stay together."

"Do you have any bags?"

"In our cars."

"I'm not walking you ladies out to the driveway, of course. But I will stand by the door with the porch light on while you go."

Ruth stood and directed a stare at the formal oil painting hanging over the sideboard. "Watch your back, James Hold," she said aloud to his brooding visage. "We're moving in."

*

In the small first-floor bathroom, Jinx unwound her braid, brushed her teeth, and changed into a heather tank top and boxer shorts. Ruth emerged from the bathroom next, smelling like cherries from a fresh application of body lotion, and wearing a nightshirt that read HOLD ON WHILE I OVERTHINK THIS. The nightshirt clung to Ruth's curves and revealed the strong muscles of her full thighs. The headband was gone. Tight curls tumbled over her forehead, threatening to overtake her eyes. Jinx glanced away, until she sensed Ruth looking back, and then she smiled.

Cheyenne left all the lights on downstairs and mounted the grand staircase. The two guests followed her. The old home settled in sighs while each of them found a spot in the guest room. Cheyenne took the queen-sized bed, propping the embroidered pillows behind her. Ruth sat on the end of the mahogany sleigh bed—carved, by the look of it, from a single piece of wood. Jinx joined Ruth, at the other end, draping a lace coverlet over both of their knees that tented in the middle like two mountain ranges meeting at a narrow pass.

"It looks like this old house is still full of surprises," Cheyenne remarked obliquely as she glanced their way.

The deep darkness of midnight had gathered outside the windows. Jinx adjusted a pillow behind her back and smoothed the loose strands of hair that shadowed her now-straining eyes. She sipped the tepid tea from her cup and tugged the chain of the tulip-shaped lamp. She could hear the breathing of the other two women as they waited for her to begin. She reached for the chestnut box.

EIGHTEEN

❖❖❖·❖❖❖

May 7, 1815

All is calm about the place since Mr. Hold has been away at the government trading post in Tellico, Tennessee. In his absence, the house Negroes do what they please, and Mrs. Hold declines to exert authority over them. The field slaves too take their liberties, refusing to work at night, and the overseer, a vile, lazy man, slips in his vigilance. Mr. Gamble complains that our mission slave Faith has been infected by this wanton attitude of the Hold slaves, and as a result has slowed down the housework that she can accomplish even on crippled feet.

But to my understanding, she has been occupied with far more worthy endeavors. Our thriving garden now includes 32 medicinal plants, of which Faith is the chief alchemist. Faith receives many visits from the Negroes as well as the Indians, who seek her healing salves. She confirms that among the Negroes, Isaac is suspected of taking his leave, and among the common Cherokees, whose language Isaac speaks, having been born in this country and raised among the Indians, he is much missed. Tongues wag about where Isaac has gone, how long he will stay there, and by what means he made his escape. I dare not speak a word to another soul on this subject. I pray fervently on my knees each day that the Lord may forgive my poor judgment in sending Isaac on so foolish a journey. I pray too that my husband does not discover my indiscretion. For even in our Church, where women's talents are valued, men stand at the helm. As Head Missionary to the Cherokees, my husband could send me away from this place and these people, around whose hearts I have begun to twine my own.

May 14, 1815

Mr. Hold is still away on his trading venture. And so the loveliest month of the year has brought with it a welcome warmth and seven new scholars for our fledgling boarding school. Three of the children, Joseph, Mary, and Jesse, are Mr. Hold's own, sent to us by their various mothers. Three come from prominent Cherokee families of Coosawattee and Coosa towns, whose parents entrust to us their instruction in reading, writing, arithmetic, and moral reasoning. One is an older girl called Mary Ann Battis, sent to us from a Methodist mission school in Creek country. Mulatto in color with pensive dark eyes and bean-like limbs, she is said to be the unfortunate child of a poor Creek woman and a Negro. Her father having run away, and her mother unable to feed all her children begotten by him, Mary Ann was sent to the Creek mission by the Indian Agent from the U. States, to be housed and educated there. By native right, she was born free and eligible for full support at the school, where she distinguished herself among the Indian pupils. Quick of mind, she is also quick of hand, for Agent Meigs related that the girl is suspected of having set fire to the place and was therefore expelled. Even now, she has been sent to us while her old mission schoolhouse lies in ashes on the ground of the Alabama-Georgia border. The Creek Agent has begun an investigation, and the head Missionary, accused of improper management and other improprieties beside, has been sent back to his home in South Carolina.

I wonder at the wisdom of this troubled girl of questionable parentage having been sent here to us, and can only surmise that my husband's reputation for sound judgment and a firm hand has traveled as far as the Creek territory to the west. The girl reads and writes well, and keeps to herself in the main, often burying her face in the pages of her spelling book. She refuses to let Mr. Gamble meet her eyes. When he gestures to her in simple greeting, she jerks her hand away as if his touch might sear her flesh. She seems not to have faith in the majority of humanity, suspecting every action of secret motivations. Even my own gentle direction she tolerates with suspicious looks. She seems to have taken only to the Negro preacher, Sam Cotterell, who remains in the vicinity. Perhaps Mr. Cotterell reminds the girl of her own lost father.

Isaac has not yet returned. He has been absent nearly three weeks, and even the lazy overseer has begun to ask questions.

May 18, 1815

I am in receipt of a letter from Rev. Muhlenberg in Philadelphia. He has received the plant samples and predicts this Cherokee collection that I am amassing to be the only one of its kind. Meanwhile, the Negro Isaac who delivered the samples has not come back. I grow anxious by the day that Mr. Hold will miss him upon his return.

May 22, 1815

One day this month, I awoke and departed my bedroom to find a strange thing had occurred. The Negroes who are often about pleading for food or Faith's medicine had come this day bearing plants of all description. They crowded into our mission hearth room, having with them cuttings and seedpods gathered from the far corners of Mr. Hold's acreage. I hesitated at this curious outpouring and reached for my white cap, which, having just awakened, I had not yet placed on my head. Across the cabin, Faith sat on her low wood bench, wearing an indigo head wrap and kneading dough. She watched me while appearing not to. Our new and promising student of the Creek nation, Mary Ann, also watched from the side of the room, where she sat with a book in Faith's sleeping enclosure. Her pensive eyes fixed on my face, awaiting my response with greater anxiety, perhaps, than the crowd of suffering humanity before me. Little Michael had pulled the Sunday meeting chairs into a haphazard row for the older members of the visiting party. I paused by Faith's side and bent to her ear, smelling the St. John's wort and sage that she had been crushing the evening last. "Faith, what is this? Do you know?" I whispered.

"No, ma'am, I surely don't," she answered, then paused. "Unless it has to do with Isaac."

"Isaac?" I repeated, my heart hurtling.

The itinerant Negro preacher, Mr. Sam Cotterell, then made himself visible at the end of the line, his white hair a thundercloud atop his head and his Bible in its leather pouch at his side.

"I understand that you are a student of plants," he said, his voice a rumble, his eyes steadily searching mine, "that you collect 'em and send 'em beyond the Cherokee lands to your associates in the North. Gander, Caty, Bob, Peter, Sam, Big Jenny, and Hannah, here, have gone to great lengths to bring these cuttings to you. May be that you see fit to send one among 'em on an errand someday."

I was beyond shock at his boldness. My knees buckled beneath my petticoat. I had not time to ascertain how he surmised my role in Isaac's journey. I looked at the assemblage gathered before me, at the plant stems tucked into baskets, wrapped in squares of woven cloth, gathered with twine, dried between bark, and grasped in worn, callused hands. "Mr. Cotterell," I said firmly, my eyes fixed on his Bible pouch, "I fear to what misunderstandings I owe these gifts."

"You might see that you find a use for 'em, sometime or other." He nodded to the gathered Negroes, who heaped their supply of dazzling plant life upon the center table as if it were a beloved's grave. Mr. Cotterell departed from the cabin. The line of slaves trickled out behind him.

Faith has indeed made good use of these cuttings, isolating some of the seeds to enhance our medicinal garden and learning of their applications from an old Cherokee man named Earbob, who comes from time to time to talk with her. These include the use of Acer rubrum—the inner bark boiled to a syrup, made into pills, and these dissolved in water for cases of unseeing eyes, the eyes washed therewith, and of Podophyllum peltatum—a drop of the juice of the fresh root in the ear, is a cure for deafness. Earbob is held up by the Cherokees as a healer, though his methods are far from verifiable. Besides his use of herbs, which is at least within reason, he places red and white corals afloat in vessels of water for divination purposes. If the corals rise in the water, this is taken as a sign that the patient will recover from his, or her, malady.

May 27, 1815

Mr. Cotterell has seen fit to continue his sojourn here to urge the bondsmen of Mr. Hold to the light of salvation. Mr. Gamble is not present enough to worry over the competition this might cause to our home church. I am quite open to any method of saving souls for Christ, and I see in Mr. Cotterell a gift of experience. It is said that Mr. Cotterell was once a slave of the Indians himself before purchasing his freedom, converting to Methodism, and taking to the road. He has collected on his journeys a working knowledge of many languages, not only the Cherokee and English spoken here, and an unnamed African tongue, but also the Creek tongue. He visits our mission often to soothe the children who cry in the night, longing for their mothers' cooking fires. Mary Ann especially takes his words to heart, as he can converse with her in her native language. In the heat of the afternoon beneath the peach trees that line the boundary of our mission, he takes off his hat, abandons his walking stick, and lowers himself to the ground, regaling the children with stories of wily rabbits and dancing billy goats. He has asked me to teach him the German word for this or that and at times punctuates his stories with the gems of his new vocabulary. On these occasions, we are quite alone—the children, Mr. Cotterell, and I, except for a visit from Mr. Hold's slaves, who drift over from their work yard to hear about the goings on of Brer Rabbit the story character, and the younger Mrs. Hold, who seems drawn to the sound of children's laughter floating freely across the garden.

June 1, 1815

The meadows are alive with green grass and clover. Summer has come. I have taken chief charge of our little school, guiding the pupils in reading and script. All whom we accept are the children of heathen Indians. We make no distinction here between Indians and half castes, as the Cherokees themselves do not. For several hours in the morning and afternoon, the students are in classes. Otherwise, they are kept busy in the field, garden, or yard.

Mary Ann is so talented as to serve as my teaching assistant. She works in the main with the youngest scholars. Her eagerness to absorb new knowledge has gotten the better of her resentment at having been sent here among us, when she had hoped that by setting a fire she would be rid of the teachers and returned to her mother. On Saturdays while the Indian pupils run about the woods in the company of the Negro children, a habit which they cannot be broken of, I devote my time to instructing Mary Ann in my own beloved subjects of botany and the poetic arts. Even the work of Linnaeus and Bartram is not beyond her grasp. Mary Ann in turn has taken to tutoring Mrs. Hold, who is determined to learn how to read and write the English language, so that she might decipher the Holy Book for herself.

Mr. Gamble leaves the schooling to me and spends his days all about the place, making rounds on behalf of Mr. Hold in his absence and planning for the Sunday message, which he now preaches to a room crowded with Indians and slaves, so that Faith and I can hardly keep abreast of the baking.

June 15, 1815

Our house overflows with scholars. Three more have joined our sundry flock, nieces and cousins of Mrs. Hold, whose parents have become convinced of the good purpose of our enterprise. They squeeze in, head to toe, on cots in the rear sleeping room, while my own little Mary Ann has forfeited her cot to share my chamber, where ample room is to be found, due to my husband's frequent absences. Faith complains of the washing for our nearly dozen scholars, so much so that I must aid her over the boiling pots. Little Michael assists by hanging the clothing out to dry in the sunlight.

My work in the garden suffers for want of time. It has been weeks since I last gathered wildflowers, which show off their spectrum of color now in the fullness of their beauty. I am kept busy here, so that I have not the time to collect the plants that tempted me to the woods last spring.

July 1, 1815

Patience is with child. The younger Mrs. Hold is in a state of near despair, fearing not that the child is her husband's, which everyone has suspected, given the occurrences that transpire here, but that her husband might sell Patience away, along with the unborn babe. I have taken the opportunity to have a heart to heart talk with Mrs. Hold, our dear burdened Peggy, for her to know the Savior and find comfort in His Word. She shows great change. She seeks the Savior and is not without the feeling of His love in her heart. She continues to study writing with Mary Ann on Saturdays and to come to service on Sundays, accompanied by Patience, so that we almost have a little church family here in the Indian wilderness.

On Sunday evenings, after Mr. Gamble has gone to walk about the grounds or consult with the visiting chiefs who often stop by the plantation, I find myself settled before the hearth with a small circle of unexpected but beloved companions: Mrs. Hold and Patience, whose belly grows by the day, Faith and little Michael, my protégée Mary Ann, and Mr. Sam Cotterell, who has become like a father to the latter. I read to them aloud from the dispatched diaries of our brethren and sisters in the West Indies mission field. It seems that Patience, Faith, and likewise Mary Ann are most feelingly moved by the stories of people of their own race seeking the truth of the crucified Savior in faraway lands. Mr. Cotterell, who possesses a deep, melodic voice, shares in the reading when I become tired, stokes my tea with freshly crushed leaves, and opens the door to let in the breezes in the warm summer nights. Except for a stubborn one or two who strain to stay awake, our little red scholars sleep through these evenings, rolled onto their mats and cots in the rear bedroom, bare limbs stretched wide in the heat.

July 3, 1815

Mr. Hold has lately returned from an extended sojourn northward, where he traded slaves for cattle with his business partner, a fellow Scot to whom Hold is linked through his late father's connections. He called for Isaac to play the fiddle, and hence has discovered Isaac's absence. Mr. Hold presumes him to have run away. Enraged, he acts as if he has lost his mind. The suffocating summer heat only drives him on. Last night, he was in his house shooting, burning, and ravaging, such that no one's life was safe. I dare not speak a word about my part in this to anyone but the Lord.

July 4, 1815

We heard horrible things about what Mr. Hold had done overnight, especially that he mistreated his wife so badly that it cannot be repeated. When the opportunity presented itself, Mrs. Hold escaped to our cabin. Her tender face was a sea of blue where her husband had struck her. The Cherokee scholars were fast asleep on their mats in the rear of the building, but Mary Ann was alert and stiff in the hemp gown I had sewn for her, attuned like a fawn to the scent of men with muskets. I inquired after Patience. Mrs. Hold shook her head, closing her eyes against a blinding thought. I persisted with my questioning until she reported that Mr. Hold has shut Patience up in the garret, binding her with the steadfast rope of the Annona bark.

   I pulled Mary Ann to my chest and covered her ears with my hands. I did not wish her to know the cruelty and tyranny which is practiced in that house. Her small body trembled against mine, damp with sweat. Her long braids fell like open wings around me.

July 6, 1815

We missed Patience for three days and two nights. When we saw her again, she could not stand and support the weight of her protruding belly. It is rumored that Mr. Hold is not beyond torture. He has been known to hang his slaves by fingers or toes from log beams in his garret. Patience's offense, we learned through Faith, was alleged relations with the absent Isaac. Faith tended the wounds. Mrs. Hold stayed with us until Patience regained strength. And then she returned, God help her, to the prison house of her husband.

It is further revealed with each passing day that Mr. Hold brought us here solely for the betterment of his own position—to educate his children in the English language, strengthen his trading outlets by gaining our brethren as purchasers, and increase his status with the government Agent who oversees the tribe. Mr. Hold does not care anything about our religion, or about our warnings of hellfire and the vengeance of the Lord. Oh, if the Savior would only have mercy on him and free him from the hands of the evil enemy who has him completely under his power!

July 9, 1815

Mr. Hold was drunk again last night. He lit a torch and rampaged through the slave quarters, burning down three cabins of his Negro men, whom he accused of aiding in Isaac's escape. He would have burned more if his clerk Mr. Geiger had not stopped him with his pistol. We had to listen to the noise of shooting and shouting all through the night. I prayed in the dark on my knees, asking the Lord to forgive me for my part in this travesty and to show Mr. Hold that the Savior died for him as well. My dear Mary Ann prayed beside me, gripping the bed quilt in her hands. Might God free our evil host from Satan's chains which bind him. Might God free us all.

July 10, 1815

On the breaking of dawn, I sought out my husband to impress upon him the need of our mission for a second Negro woman.

A servant is indispensable for milking, laundering, cooking, baking, and the like, and one cannot deny that this work, which is no small matter in our establishment, has hitherto been done incompletely by Faith. An additional servant would aid in getting the necessary work done, which has been much increased by boarding and washing for our eleven Indian scholars. Mr. Gamble sought to persuade me that the Church could not consent to such luxury, but on this notion I would not be moved. We might forgo our monthly supply of coffee, I told him, for I could roast our own from the seeds of the wild Cassia occidentalis (coffee senna) weed. "It is for the benefit of the students. Our crippled Negro woman cannot keep pace with the labor of the mission. We must have Patience," I said.

Assessing my request with the calm calculation that is his chief strength, my husband narrowed his eyes. "Yes, I see," he said, observing my ardent state. "You desire a second Negro woman from among Mr. Hold's stock. But Patience will not do, for her master will never part with her."

I looked into my husband's eyes, wondering what dark knowledge he held secret there. Had he witnessed scenes such as that which I endured in the cornfield, during his frequent visits to the Hold house? I saw in his eyes that he had shed the mantle of God and now shared one mind with those thieves of spirits and bodies that polite society refers to as "planters."

"Patience must do," I boldly persisted. "She must." I knew that my eyes were as fierce now as those of the wild cats that live in the corners of the barns here, jumping and biting people at the least provocation. I could feel the sweat damped strands of my hair sticking to my cheeks and tongue. I grasped for my Bible, which is never far from my side. "Our crucified Christ loves all," I said. "He watches over all, and gave all for all. The Holy Spirit is no respecter of persons."

My husband glanced at the Holy Book and, I thought, relented. "Yes, I see. I will speak with Mr. Hold," he said, striding from the room. He turned at the doorway to look at me. "Provided that Isaac can be convinced to return," he added, and was gone.

His words stopped my heart. I lost my bearings in the swirling space of the hearth room and grabbed at the table for support. The edge was firm in my hands, solid as the pine tree that a slave had carved to shape it. I have never felt the natural love of a wife for her husband. In pursuit of the higher aim of spreading the light of the Gospel, I have endured my husband's disdain for my feelings and grasping hands in the night. And all the while, he had corrupted his calling, becoming nothing more than a purveyor of flesh, worse, as he is a man of God, than a common Georgia slave trader.

Jinx placed the manuscript pages back in the box, enraged and incredulous. She glanced at her companions. Cheyenne had drifted off to sleep. Ruth had removed her glasses, watching the pictures in her mind as Jinx read the words. Jinx sat up, wondering if the sleigh bed that held them had been crafted by the missing Isaac, wondering what would happen—what had happened—to Patience, Isaac, and Mary Ann.

"What's that?" Ruth whispered, her voice husky from the nearness of sleep. Her face took on a waxen cast as she stared out the window. She leaned into the glass, elbow pressed against the frame, feeling for her glasses on the end table.

Jinx circled to Ruth's side of the bed, handed the glasses to her, and peered over her shoulder. She saw nothing but shape and shadow in the light of the full moon. "What do you see?"

"The girl who called me. I think she's come back." Ruth flung off the coverlet and slid from the bed. "Cheyenne, wake up."

Cheyenne lifted her eye mask and snapped open her lids, registering Jinx's bare feet, Ruth's crooked glasses, the unkempt hair flying around each of their heads. "What time is it?"

"Four," Ruth said. "We need to go out to the gardens."

"What? Why?!"

"Yesterday in the mission cabin, I thought I saw a girl in the doorway, but then she disappeared. I didn't know what she was at the time, but later, when I could come up with no other explanation, I realized she had to have been a . . . ghost. Now I'm convinced she was the spirit of Mary Ann, showing me where to find the diary. I think I see her again right now, but I'm too far away to be sure. I'm going down there."

"You think there's a ghost in the garden, so you're running toward it, instead of away? This is exactly how Black people die in the horror movies, Ruth. Investigating when common sense says duck and cover."

"I feel like she's calling me, and I have to listen." Ruth slapped on her clogs.

"This is *not* real," Cheyenne said. "Lanie Brevard was full of shit when she hinted the house was a stigmatized property."

"Reality is a gray zone," Jinx said, grabbing and flinging on an oversized hoodie and gathering up the diary pages to tuck them under her arm. "And if you want to be a true caretaker of this place, you should probably face up to its haunted past."

NINETEEN

❯-❯-❯· ·❮-❮-❮

RUTH'S GLASSES STEAMED in the humid morning air. She wiped them, leaving behind blurry streaks. Followed by Jinx, who carried the diary, and Cheyenne, who swore beneath her breath, she crept through the back door, breathing in the fragrance of rose petals. Ruth had heard the shakiness in Cheyenne's voice, felt anxiety rising from Jinx, and she could smell the pungent perspiration clinging to her own flushed skin. They plunged into the garden. Rambling wildflowers gave way to river cane stalks tipped with open tufts. Ruth wrapped her arms across her chest, wishing she were wearing something more substantial than a flimsy nightshirt. She felt exposed to the elements, and afraid of what might come next.

Out in the canebrake, someone stood beckoning to Ruth from the shadowed opening of the round earth house: a girl on the cusp of womanhood, ribbons dangling from her hair, a floral print skirt banding her legs. The girl seemed to stand within a spidery light. Her ribbons of black, red, and white danced in that light, as though filtered through a kaleidoscope held in the hands of a child. Ruth could not deny her a second time. Mary Ann Battis was really there, leaning against the doorframe, staring at her.

"You see her, don't you?" Jinx said.

"She's standing in the doorway of the round house."

Cheyenne squinted at the shadows. "Bullshit. There's nothing there."

Ruth moved forward. Her stomach was a knot. She rushed across the garden, reached the phosphorescent light, could almost stretch out a hand to touch the apparition. And then the girl was gone. Ruth plunged into the gap where the figure had been, feeling a cool mist like the dissipation of mountain clouds.

She heard the uneven rush of Jinx's breathing behind her.

"Did you feel that?" Ruth said. Inside the dark enclosure, she breathed in the rich smell of silt. "What did she want us to find here?" Ruth paced the tight, dark space—once, again, three times, a fourth, pressing her fingers to the mud walls, squatting beside the fire pit and examining the ground. "I don't feel anything."

"What about the diary?" Jinx said. "Maybe that's how she's talking to you, and she'll just keep returning until whatever she came back for is accomplished. And it *is* you she's communicating with, or communicating through."

The mud enclosure echoed with silence until Ruth spoke again. "It's our mothers," Ruth said, her eyes filling with tears again. "We both lost our mothers as girls."

Jinx's gaze softened as she watched Ruth speak in the darkness of early morning. "She set a fire to reunite with her mother. Instead, the missionaries sent her here."

Ruth would not say aloud what she was feeling—that she had been a coward compared to Mary Ann. Her father had kept the truth of her mother's death buttoned down like the broadcloth dress shirts he wore. A drowning accident—that was all Ruth knew, all she had managed to extract from him. Her mother was taken by a wave on her parents' second honeymoon, the Caribbean escape they had planned to save their rocky marriage. Her father had shielded her from the garish local news coverage. He couldn't protect her, though, from the lurid whispers that trailed her at school like clouds of gnats—the rumors that her father had her mother's blood on his hands, that he had snapped from envy of her mother's professional success. In the twenty-two years since, Ruth had never dared search for answers to the questions of why, how, or who was responsible. Her father's cloak of silence had been complete—and somehow a comfort. She had willed herself into forgetfulness, until she came to the Hold House, walked through the rose garden, and saw Mary Ann. If Mary Ann had any message especially for her, perhaps it was to dig.

Ruth looked up at her companions. "Maybe she has a message for you too," she said to Cheyenne. "The Black preacher—Samuel Cotterell—you have to be wondering why you share his last name."

The vein at Cheyenne's temple pulsed, but she said nothing. Ruth knew the story wasn't what Cheyenne had expected. Her ancestor, by the sound of things, was a homeless man who had lived a simple life of faith. Cheyenne slowly lowered herself to the floor, sacrificing her ivory robe to the dirt. She took the flashlight Jinx held out and shone it on the page. Jinx began to read.

July 11, 1815

There was only one man I could turn to with my confidence, a man who had already intuited too much. I sought out Samuel Cotterell and told him all. If he knew where Isaac was, a message must be sent to him. Mr. Hold would continue to torture Patience and terrorize the slave quarters until the day of Isaac's return. Though Mr. Cotterell consented to help me, his eyes held the sorrow of a million men. I pressed my hand to the jagged white hairs that rose from his face. He leaned his bearded jaw into my palm before quickly, self consciously, withdrawing. He turned on the heel of his travel boots. I touched the offending hand to my forehead. It was hot, as if with fever.

August 27, 1815

Isaac has returned of his own accord. The first few nights after his arrival, he has slept, under cover of secrecy, on the floor of the mission barn. He applied his last free hours to his craft. And before submitting himself to the authority of his master, Isaac presented us with gifts: a chair fashioned of river cane reeds affixed to wheelbarrow casters for Faith to move about in, and an image of the Holy Cross formed in the likeness of sweetgum leaves carved upon the mantel of our hearth.

The Head Missionary to the Cherokees was true to his sordid word. Upon Isaac's appearance at Hold's rear doorstep, Patience was released for purchase by the mission. I have this evening penned a letter of explanation of this expenditure to our elders in the Church, of which follows a true copy.

To Our Brethren of the General Helpers Conference, Salem:

This letter confirms that a week ago today Mr. James Hold, master of Hold Hill, transferred to us a Negress who is to be under my direction to help with the housekeeping for the Cherokee mission and school. Head Missionary Gamble has lately received power of attorney over her. Mr. Hold sold this Negress, called by the name of Patience, for only 130 dollars cash, though she is with child and therefore hampered in her work for a time. Once the child is born, however, the mission will acquire another little Negro or Mulatto servant to be added to the credit side of our ledger. Patience, a strong, black one of nearly twenty years, can now be counted among the assets of the Church. With gratitude for your unceasing support of this mission, we continue our efforts in the salvation of the heathen.

Yours in the Wounds of Christ, Anna Rosina Kliest Gamble

My head grew dizzy as I placed my pen beside the pot of ink and cast my eyes about the rooms of our cabin. In the crevice by the stove, Mary Ann dozed in Faith's loft enclosure, her spelling book and a pair of my spectacles grasped loosely in her hand. The younger Cherokee pupils, together with Michael, slept on cots in the rear bedroom. Before the hearth, a bean soup simmered in readiness for the next day's afternoon meal. Patience, who was now, praise be to God, out of the reach of her former master, tended the soup with a steady hand on the ladle. And good Faith, my steady companion, rested on her knees at her kitchen workbench, mixing a salve for a Cherokee pupil stung by a honeybee that day. Beside her was a vessel of water left behind by the healer Earbob for a patient undisclosed. Crystalline corals floated across the surface, having risen to the top.

I found that I could not breathe as I took in this peaceable scene. These women could be bought, sold, traded, and used for a spiteful man's spittoon; even Mary Ann might be snatched away by illegal traders due to her Negro patriliny. I felt my chest constrict. I needed God's air. I plunged through the fog of stewing soup, baking bread, and sweat-soaked children that filled the mission cabin with the scents of life. I escaped into my garden that night to find my equilibrium, but utterly failed even there.

August 28, 1815

Mr. Sam Cotterell appeared at the garden gate past evenfall bearing a seed specimen. Speaking in a muted voice so as not to awake Faith and the children, I bid him remain outside. I joined him beneath the white peach tree, under whose canopy we had sat many times as he conversed with Mary Ann in her language and regaled our students with stories. We spoke in low tones of Isaac's bravery, of Patience's improved fate, of Mary Ann's progress. The night air felt balmy on my cheeks, intoxicating with the scent of evening primrose which shone, ever so softly, in the darkness. I held my hand out to Sam Cotterell and accepted his gift. He took my hand in his, wrapping his warmth around me. In more than forty years of life, I had never experienced a touch so sincere. I vowed that I would plant in my garden the seeds that he so tenderly gave me and tend whatsoever should grow there.

When I awoke later in a blanket of dew and wildflowers, I felt first the sensation of a new day's sun on my uncovered head. My hair had come loose from its braid in the night, and it fell to the ground around me, tangling with the switchgrass and plant stems. I realized then where I was and what nature of thing I had done. I cast my eyes about with a start, searching first for Sam Cotterell, and then for any other soul who might have witnessed my transgression. Sam Cotterell had left his linsey shirt drawn about me and disappeared into the early morning light, latching behind him the garden gate that he had carved as a gift for me. I pressed my eyes closed, ashamed at my instinct toward self protection. It mattered not what man had seen. I could not hide from the face of the Lord. I rose from a supine position to my hands and knees, digging my palms in the dirt, praying to He who forgives all to have mercy on his straying daughter.

I felt a touch on my shoulder and started, thinking that Sam Cotterell might have returned, wishing that God might make possible a new life for us on this earth. But Peggy Hold knelt beside me, dampening her dress in the dew, worrying her silver buttons. She brushed her fingers to my hair and gently gathered it back, but did not at first attempt to meet my eyes. She smelled of the lavender oil and sage that she daily smoothed through her long, black tresses. "I had only one husband," she whispered, "whom I no longer love. You had only one husband, whom you never loved. Surely the spirit above understands these things better than you and I. The dance of the

Green Corn comes very soon. We will go there and be cleansed. All will be forgiven. A new fire will be lit."

I looked at her through tears, this young Indian woman whom I had sought to bring to God, and before whom I was now lowered in a base state of sinful humanity. I had no doubt that her ardent faith sprang from a lingering heathen superstition. And yet, in a single aspect, her people were correct. The one God, the true God, does forgive all—in exchange for the dearest sacrifice.

I rose then, straightened the length of my skirts, and returned to the mission cabin. I refused to let little Michael collect the water for my bath, and instead purged myself in the muddy waters of the Conasauga.

August 29, 1815

Mr. Hold has made an example of Isaac and hanged him from the oak tree beside the stone wall. I am beyond sorrow.

August 31, 1815

On the night of the day that Mr. Hold took Isaac's life, he sent to the mission for Patience. Mr. Gamble came to deliver the message to me, giving consent for Mr. Hold's Negro driver to rip her from my grasping arms. Then, his face a shadow beneath the brim of his hat, Mr. Gamble left our cabin for the comfort of Mr. Geiger's house, where all manner of evil is witnessed.

I cannot say how horribly Mr. Hold treated his good wife and her servant in his drunkenness. Peggy stumbled into the mission after the ordeal, unable to speak a word to us, silenced by the cruelty she had endured as both victim and audience of her husband's aggressions. Patience accompanied her former mistress to the shelter of our cabin, her flax gown torn, her black face a stone, her belly suspended before her like a melon on the vine. The blood on her thighs made me fear that she might lose her child.

I could not hold back my tears at the sight of them. Mary Ann clung to the wall, her eyes wide and fearful. In a flurry of words and signals, Faith sent our Cherokee scholars along with her son Michael out to the mission barn. She instructed us to lay the two women on rolls of soft bedding. Faith was the doctor, Mary Ann and I her assistants. The voiceless Peggy Hold was ensconced on one of our scholars' cots before an open window, through which a relieving breeze flowed. Faith sent Mary Ann to glean from my red apothecary rose, then concocted a most unusual conserve, which she said was a curative for hoarseness. Throughout the long night, Peggy took a teaspoonful of the brew at regular intervals from Mary Ann, while I assisted Faith with the birth of Patience's child back in my sleeping chamber. For Patience's baby was indeed born that night, too early and deathly weak, its face punctuated with the plum colored lips and brooding eyes of Mr. James Hold.

Patience would not look at the babe, and gave Faith leave to name him. "Adam," Faith said. She dropped her eyes, and for an instant I glimpsed the pain in them. How many infants had she seen die from ill health of the mother? How many children had she seen sold away in her forty some years? She treated Patience with mother wort to calm convulsions of the womb and gently kneaded the younger woman's slack skinned belly.

September 2, 1815

Today, under the untiring ministrations of Faith, Peggy recovered her speaking voice. She spoke her first words to Patience in the Cherokee language, which Patience, having become her former mistress's most intimate companion, readily understood. The eyes of the two women communicated much more.

No translation was given me, but Mary Ann seemed to comprehend some part of what was spoken. She rose and began to make preparations, setting aside changes of clothing, dried meat and apples, and a walking stick that Sam Cotterell has taken to leaving in the corner of the hearth room. Then she sat at the center table to write in the elegant, sweeping cursive that I was so proud to see her master. I watched her while a dawning awareness and trepidation came over me. Her purpose was a counterfeit letter of manumission.

September 3, 1815

This country affords several species of Rosa. The climbing, moon-flowered Cherokee rose seems to be used purely as ornament, admired as it is for its tenacious beauty. The Indians boil the roots of the wild ground rose as a treatment for dysentery. Only the slaves seem to know the foreign red rose as a cure for lost voice. I have given a detailed description of Cherokee country roses—their cups, flowers, chives, pestles, seedboxes, stalks, leaves, and uses, together with drawings, in my botanic papers. The recipe for making a conserve of red roses in the manner of the slaves follows herein: Take rose buds, and pick them; cut off the white part from the red, and sift the red part of the flower through a sieve to take out the seeds; then weigh them, and to every pound of flowers take two pounds and a half of loaf sugar; beat the flowers pretty fine in a stone mortar, then by degrees put sugar to them, and beat it 'til it is well incorporated; then put it into gallipots, tie it over with paper, over that a leather, and it will keep seven years.

September 5, 1815

Peggy and Patience walked into the outside air for the first time since the ordeal. Arms interlinked like ivy, they made their way to the bubbling waters of a spring on the property, called sacred by the Indians. There, with Peggy holding each of Patience's hands to guide her into the deep sand creek, together they bathed.

September 6, 1815

We could not risk the observation of the Cherokee scholars, for three of them are the offspring of Mr. Hold himself, and most of the children are the progeny of other slaveholders. Neither could we risk the witness of Faith's Michael, who has already seen and heard more than his young soul should have to bear. The mission is also often full of the many Indian visitors who crowd in to seek Faith's medicines, beg for food, or ask for aid in translating some exchange with the white people. Most of these common Cherokees appear sympathetic with the plight of the Negroes, but nevertheless caution must be taken with the future of one so dear to us.

It was at Peggy's urging, therefore, that we moved our talks to the old mud hut at the edge of the settlement. The clay and mica house, half hidden in a field of cane reeds, was built with an ancient design. The older Mrs. Hold, Peggy's sister, had made this hut her home during her time as Mr. Hold's wife. It was a round dwelling with a small aperture at the apex for the escape of smoke from the old time cooking fires. Late in the night, a week before the Green Corn festival, the four of us met in this place. Faith stayed behind to manage the mission kitchen, mind the scholars, and deflect any queries regarding our whereabouts.

Inside the mud hut, Peggy held the infant Adam to her bosom while I outfitted Patience with sturdy clothing and the pass that she will surely need once she makes it to the U. States. Adam was born too small to suckle from his mother's breast, which I bound with layered gauze to blot the flowing milk. Faith has been feeding him the boiled down juices of collards and cabbage by way of a hollow river cane rod, and he is growing by the day on this concoction. His eyes shine like onyx from beneath the swaddle of Peggy's scarlet scarf.

The fact of his son's birth would be impossible to hide from the master of Hold Hill, who, given his impetuous nature, might seize the babe or sell him down the river for a good price. But Mr. Hold took leave on the day following the ordeal, and Mr. Gamble departed with him, covered, in my humble view, with shame. Peggy has resided at the mission cabin since that time, helping to care for Patience and nurse the child whom Patience has not the heart left to notice. The babe's eyes follow Peggy now as if she is his natural mother. But to protect him from the ravings of his capricious father, he will be raised under the cover of anonymity as a sickly black child, born in the slave quarters and taken in by the mission for medicinal care. By the time Mr. Hold returns with the Head Missionary to the Cherokees, Patience will be gone from this place and the child she birthed vanished into the slave population. Mr. Hold will be told that Patience's issue did not survive.

Mary Ann changed into young men's pantaloons, stockings, and boots that I procured from the clothing sent by our brothers and sisters in Christ for the use of the Cherokee scholars. I unbraided and combed her thick, dark hair and watched in silence while Peggy cut it in the Indian style. Like a torn swath of midnight, her hair fell to the floor. Without it, Mary Ann looks small, fragile, and more like a girl of fourteen years than she ever has before.

Mary Ann and Patience will travel together to the boundary of Cherokee territory, posing as a young Indian master and his slave. I have instructed Mary Ann to go no farther than the border of Kentucky and Tennessee. I think of wolves, poisonous snakes, and land hungry squatters' camps. My heart shuddered as I watched them step into the iron darkness.

September 13, 1815

My Mary Ann has returned, lovely to behold. She reports that along their journey, she and our fugitive sister followed in the footsteps of a dearly departed friend, for along the route north, a growth of wild strawberries stretched through the woods in the likeness of a trail. Mary Ann, having studied with me in the garden behind the mission, recognized the star-like flowers of the plant which Isaac had carried along with 150 other specimens. Knowingly or unknowingly, he had dispersed the strawberry seeds all along his way. In the heavy rains of April, they had taken root.

September 20, 1815

Patience has been gone two weeks, and Mr. Hold, now returned, knows not where to direct his rage. Peggy spends her days in the mission cabin, and because she has lately accepted Jesus as her Lord and Savior, the Head Missionary to the Cherokees dares not insist upon her removal. Mr. Gamble now chooses to reside all of the time in the home of our un-Christian host.

September 25, 1815

Mr. Hold attended our last Sunday's church meeting. The Head Missionary to the Cherokees continues to preach on the Sabbath and gave Mr. Hold the choicest seat at the forefront of the hearth room. I could not bear the sight of his cruel lips and smoldering eyes. I busied myself with cooking, serving, and whispering encouragements to our newest Cherokee scholars. Peggy kept company with Faith in the kitchen, the joy of our faith communion having been pierced by her husband's presence. When I turned away briefly from the boy over whose head I bent, pointing out the English words in his hymnal, I saw it like the gust of air that blows the candle out: Mr. Hold's wolfish eyes falling on Mary Ann as she stood in her pure white blouse and cap. With Patience as good as gone, he had now fixed his desire on Mary Ann, and whether for a slave or a wife, it matters not to her future. My thoughts raced. What means have I to protect her? My breath flew from my body and out the window of the stifling room. My heart and strength went with it. I was left a bag of bones. Not Mary Ann. Not my daughter. No.

September 26, 1815

These are words that should never be written. With the aid of the Head Missionary to the Cherokees and a hired slave tracker from the Georgia settlements, Mr. Hold retook Patience beyond the border of Kentucky. Upon her return, he had her dumped in ropes at the doorstep of his overseer, who used and beat her beyond this life within the space of an hour.

We were in the mission garden when we heard the news, brought to us by Sam Cotterell, whose hat was in his hands. Mary Ann's eyes widened in terror at her future, for Mr. Hold's admiration has grown nakedly apparent in the passing weeks. Peggy could not be consoled. Her grief at the loss of this sister was consuming. With baby Adam strapped to her back amidst a tangle of loosened hair, she fell to her knees and wailed to the Heavens, as is the custom in this country.

Faith and I knew without speaking what must be done.

September 27, 1815

Peggy has not yet returned to the home of her husband. She says she will never do so again. Mr. Hold has sent a message, by way of the Head Missionary to the Cherokees, that he wishes our Mary Ann to move into the brick house and assist in the care of the Cherokee scholars who will soon board there.

Faith has begun the preparations in her kitchen. I have begun to write my letters with the aid of Mary Ann, who duplicates my work with the grace and skill of a trained scribe. We put the letters into the hands of little Michael and bid him rush to the closest mail station beyond the range of Mr. Hold's estate. Michael took off like buckshot through the trees, having some inchoate knowledge of the import of his mission.

I pray to the Lord for forgiveness and guidance, bowing my head. Mary Ann joins me on her knees, fervently adding the sweet tones of her innocent voice to my own.

September 28, 1815

Patience was buried yesterday at evenfall on the edge of our mission garden. The ceremony was beautifully conducted by our dear Sam Cotterell. The Negro people sang a hymn soothing to the gathered mourners, who represented every shade of humanity. Our Cherokee pupils read a series of poems that they had themselves written about the mercy of God and the peace of His Heavens. There was not one among the Negro population upon whom Patience had not smiled with her shining almond eyes. We, the women of this mission, have planted a variety of roses around and about her grave in remembrance. The Cherokee rose (Rosa laegivata) predominates, as it is native here, and will grow in time to crown this spot in pure white blooms. Besides these wild creeping ones, which Peggy adores, there are roses here that have never been grown together in one spot of earth.

A lifetime ago, before I set out for the Cherokees' wilderness, before I saw all manner of evil that goes on here, a wagonload arrived in Salem from Cape Fear, N.C. with numerous special goods, among them white and red rosebushes (Rosa alba, R. Gallica officinalis). I brought samples of them with me hither, harvested the seeds, and planted them in my botanic garden beside the mission. These are the same roses that revived Peggy's will to speak after the ordeal. Among an assortment of wild plants, they have fared well in this foreign soil—better, perhaps, than they would have done in the orderly gardens of Salem.

The night of Patience's burial, a lunar eclipse cloaked the sky in a darkness deep as winter. We were prepared for this, having heard tell of its coming by the Cherokee healer Earbob. Under this cover, Peggy, Mary Ann, and I led those Negroes who wished to come to the old hut built of mud and mica. Inside, we lit a candle to cast a circle of light. We girdled the gathered men, women, and children, altogether a party of twenty-eight, with clothing, provisions, letters of purpose, maps, and knives. We have divided them into groups for greater efficiency of movement. They will follow routes north, seeking out the trail of the strawberry plant, the leaves of which they carry in their sacks for point of reference. I have enlisted them for the express purpose of carrying seeds to a select few of my botanical colleagues in Philadelphia, who await their packages, and are of like mind. It is in Patience's honor, for her stolen life, that I violate the legal principles of property. Christ's love, not man's law, reigns supreme.

September 29, 1815

The eclipse of last night was followed by a swell of storms that felled three oak trees and studded the mission buildings with hailstones. Mr. Hold was away doing business in the city of Augusta with the Head Missionary to the Cherokees as his companion. We women kept about our work. Faith ran the operations of the mission while secretly making her preparations.

I monitored arrivals to and departures from the Hold house. At the urging of an elderly woman who speaks her native African tongue, Mary Ann has memorialized the ones who have left, casting the shape of their names in shells on the inside walls of the hut. It is tradition in the old woman's country that those now departed who once brought wealth to the master's house must never be forgotten. Together, they represent nearly a quarter of Mr. Hold's human property. Haste is required by the pilgrims before the Godless Talley makes a full accounting of the Negroes lost during the unusual hailstorms. One thought alone brings me comfort. Should Mr. Hold learn of their absence from Mr. Geiger and seek to recapture them from afar, due solely to his rampant greed, he could not, would not, kill them all.

TWENTY

September 30, 1815

Our plan continues its forward motion. Within one week's time the major festival of the Cherokees will commence. This is the ritual of the new green corn, through which transgressions are atoned and crossed relations mended. Peggy is adamant that all must be completed before this ritual begins. The long absent Mr. Hold paid an overnight visit home with plans to set out again next day for this annual ceremony. I have learned he attends yearly in the various host towns for the ceremony, more for the purpose of intermingling with other powerful chiefs than for observing the sacred aspects of this communal ritual. A chance has been presented to us. I pray that he will not have time to walk through the slave quarters and look upon the faces of his now depleted property. Against my best judgment, but with the wise counsel of Faith, I determined to send my beloved daughter to Mr. Hold. My heart was in my mouth as I watched them follow the stone path that the now deceased Isaac had laid across my garden floor. Peggy, with Mary Ann at her side, approached the house, bearing gifts for Mr. Hold in river cane baskets: honey laced corn cakes prepared by Faith, and freshly picked cherries gathered by the Cherokee scholars. Desiring reconciliation with his estranged wife and currying the favor of young Mary Ann, Mr. Hold readily admitted them. Peggy held her husband at length with fervent promises that all should soon be reconciled. After the sacred festival of renewal, she told him, she would return to his home accompanied by Mary Ann.

By design, Faith's preparation will be slow acting. She has baked the seeds of Calycanthus floridus (sweetshrub) into the golden corn cakes. These are used by the Cherokees for poisoning wolves, among which Mr. Hold can be counted as kin.

October 1, 1815

Mr. Hold set out at dawn for the appointed town where the Green Corn ritual will be held. A turbaned Negro driver saddled the finest horses and mounted a steed beside his master. The Head Missionary to the Cherokees, having long disavowed such ceremonies as nothing more than heathen superstition, remained behind in the brick house. I remained in the mission cabin with the baby Adam in my care, aided, at times, by Mary Ann. I did not know that Peggy would follow behind her husband's party on her own stout bay horse, cloaked in a woven hood that covered her hair, and carrying one of her husband's fire-arms. I should never have known, had Michael not glimpsed her from the loft of the mission barn, where he often plays with the Cherokee pupils.

Hours before Peggy returned covered in road dust, her hair a storm cloud, Faith and I learned of the shocking occurrence from Indian passersby who often visit the mission. Mr. Hold is dead, shot by a pistol, it is presumed, and his body then badly burned. The shooting occurred in the vicinity of the tavern of Mr. Buffington, where Mr. Hold had stopped for whiskey while en route to the festival. The perpetrator is as yet undiscovered.

Mr. Hold was buried in an unmarked grave near where he

fell. All was done quickly and without fanfare by those who had been his companions in drink and vice. Patience, the object of his torture, had garnered more mourners than this famed captain of enterprise, a prominent chief of the Cherokee tribe, nevertheless known for his deception and avariciousness. Due to Mr. Hold's great number of enemies, it is said his assailant will not be searched for and may never be found.

At Peggy's insistence, we put out our fires and rode all evening to watch the Green Corn dances, the Indians' festival of thanksgiving. The night sky was a whorl of ethereal light above us. Faith and I were seated in the front of a wagon driven by Sam Cotterell. I felt every dip and rise of the rough road and thought that I might be sickened, as I have been often of late. Faith unwrapped a square of cloth and handed me a slice of flat bread. Mary Ann sat behind us in the bed of the wagon humming in a low voice to baby Adam, who slept fitfully in her lap. Michael and our Cherokee scholars were tucked in snugly beside her. Peggy led the way on the back of her bay horse, hair loose and flying wild into the air behind her.

Once we arrived at the encampment, Earbob the healer, with the assistance of Peggy, Sam, and the older boys, built temporary structures for our party beyond the square ground. We feasted on the first day, during which Earbob came to speak with Faith and made her a comfortable place to sit. As we camped there, a new fire was made by a conjurer and his assistants. The green corn was sanctified, after which the women and men danced, tortoise shell rattles shaking like seed packs about the women's legs. All who were gathered feasted again on new corn, dried meat, fish, beans, pumpkins, and fruits.

After the ceremony, each family came forward to collect a spark from the fire to carry back to their homes. Peggy's face glowed in the reflection of the virgin flames. Mary Ann seemed to likewise glimpse a renewed path before her. I touched my hand to my belly on the bed of straw that Sam Cotterell had prepared for me, certain of the new life growing within. No dance, no fire, can ever restore me to my former self.

October 3, 1815

The seeds of the new fire have been planted in the hearths of every dwelling on the plantation—Cherokee, Negro, and white alike. The houses of Hold Hill have been cleansed.

October 5, 1815

The weather is russet in its warmth; the leaves have begun their turning. With Mr. Hold now gone and his enterprises shut down, the white traders rarely come to our isolated mountain location. Even the Agent for the U. States has turned his attention elsewhere, devoting his time to meetings with the other big men in the tribe: Chief Doublehead, Mr. Ross, Mr. Ridge, and Mr. Watie, the father of our former students Buck and Stand. Peggy thrives in the midst of this neglect, trying an experiment that has perhaps never been ventured before in slavery's territory. Peggy has set the slaves at liberty to work for themselves, and they have run off the Godless Talley, threatening him with knives and sickles. The Head Missionary to the Cherokees, in fear or in shame, has departed for our Home Church and left me as sole proprietress of this mission until such time as the Church appoints his replacement, which I suspect they will be reluctant to pursue now that Mr. Hold, our sponsor, is dead.

October 10, 1815

Peggy has sent to Charleston, repurchased Mr. Hold's master craftsman Butler, and reunited him with his family. Like the other slaves on this estate, he now has the liberty to come and go as a free man. She has, besides, enlisted Butler to renew the character of her home to dispel the memory of her dead husband's presence. She has selected a palette of earthly hues and has envisioned a beautiful floral design. The likeness of the Cherokee rose, being her favorite flower and its seeds having been planted at the grave of Patience, shall be made in repetition and set in place throughout the house.

Peggy has renamed her home the Cherokee Rose in sympathy with her affections for the sister she has lost, who lies on the hillside even now, covered by a blanket of roses. Hold Hill remains the name written upon the maps and records drawn by the Cherokee Agent of the U. States. But to Peggy, it is Cherokee Rose, and to the slaves as well, who respect her now as a friend.

November 1, 1815

Fall is waning with the sun, and winter waits with bated breath. The Cherokee and Negro women rush to dry their peaches. I have word that my seed packets have been delivered to the North. And trails of strawberry plants stretch in four directions spreading out from the Conasauga River valley.

December 10, 1815

All things must begin and end, and so it is with Mr. Hold's grand plantation enterprise. Mr. Hold entrusted his legal affairs to the Head Missionary to the Cherokees with whom he had developed an unholy bond. This ensured the protection of Mr. Hold's property in the Georgia courts. The appointed administrators of the estate have seen to it that while Peggy can retain the house, mission complex, outbuildings, and furnishings at the insistence of the Cherokee Council, she has no jurisdiction over the slaves, save for the ones that she brought with her from her father's house at the time of her marriage. The others must be sold at auction to satisfy Mr. Hold's contracts and debts. Peggy has seen to it that baby Adam be known hereafter as the child of Mary Ann Battis, so that he might never be counted among Mr. Hold's enslaved population.

December 25, 1815

We gathered this holy day with Peggy, our Cherokee pupils, and a large number of the neighboring Negroes, for the celebration of Christmas. For this purpose, the floor of the hearth room was scattered with green spruce branches, and a window was decorated with a wreath of the same. At the top of the window, beautifully lit by burning candles, were the words "Christ Is Born!" written in gold letters by my dear Mary Ann. After singing a few stanzas, Sam Cotterell spoke on the meaning of this celebration. Then he read the story about the birth of our dear Lord, and, along with all those present, fell to his knees. We finished with a splendid repast prepared by Faith and a number of the Negro women, who had been laboring over their festive dishes for the better part of a week.

There was sadness, together with joy, in the demeanor of those in attendance. Accompanied by the evident presence of God Incarnate, the service was closed, and all bid their farewells.

January 1, 1816

A new year has commenced. The administrators of the estate have finally arrived from Charleston to find the plantation empty of slaves, save for those belonging on paper to Peggy Hold or the Cherokee mission. The others have gone the way of seeds in the wind, and Peggy could not give a clear account of them to the administrators. Women, they presumed, have no heads for the careful management of property, and thus the widow will not be held liable. They will now begin the sale of Mr. Hold's trading post, ferry, cattle, horses, and gristmill to raise the proceeds needed to settle his debts. And so this once thriving plantation has become a spirit town, and we few who remain are left to ourselves.

February 2, 1816

My pregnancy is far advanced, and the pains in my chest are such that it is evident the child and I cannot both survive. I have requested that all my earthly possessions here, in Salem, and in Bethlehem be sold. As much as I detest the act itself, I have used the collected sum to purchase Faith as well as Michael from the church and set them at their liberty. Faith holds their free papers, and Mary Ann possesses a copy.

February 17, 1816

Cold shakes the windows of our cabin. I keep to my bed day and night, waiting for the change. I continue to read with my dear Mary Ann in the subjects of botany and poetry. In the main, she reads to me now, her eyes clouding when she looks upon me. Sam Cotterell is often about the place, doing whatsoever chores Faith has for him and sitting long hours by my bedside, telling stories about magic grapevines and reading from his Bible. He has given up the road and is no longer an itinerant preacher. He will make his home here, he promises me.

March 12, 1816

My body can no longer bear the strain of the child who curls beneath my heart. I feel time growing short. I have instructed my dear Mary Ann, who tends to me with tearful eyes, not to speak a word of my eventful life. She and Sam Cotterell will adopt my unborn child as if it is their own. Peggy has bestowed on them the mission cabin, where they will make their home as adopted father and daughter, and continue the teachings of the Lord in this land. Patience's son Baby Adam is quite a handsome child with a serious disposition and precocious mind. Now that the administrators have left, Peggy prepares to bring him into the brick house, where she intends to raise him with Mary Ann's steady help. After convincing the parents of our pupils to entrust their children to her care even in the wake of Mr. Hold's violent demise, she has likewise made her home a lodging for those students. I have no doubt that the work of the mission school will go on in my absence.

April 5, 1816

Easter draws near. My Mary Ann has traversed the fields and riverbank as I once loved to do. She has collected a bouquet of wildflowers in wanton bloom and placed them atop my writing desk. Sun glints through the windows, touching the verdant leaves.

April 18, 1816

Though I am weak with the effort, I must write of joyous news. On this day I gave birth to my own precious babe, Isaac Samuel Cotterell, on the Cherokee Rose Plantation. He bears the name of Isaac, a noble soul, and of his father, a true man of God. I pushed Isaac out into Faith's hands amidst the piercing pains of my heart. My body could hardly bear up to it. My breaths came as mere flutters and will soon not come at all. The good Faith bid me drink a cup of tansy tea, which will soon soothe me into forever sleep.

I trust my dear Mary Ann to destroy this diary as I have requested. The work of the mission that brought me here is not yet complete, and would forever be tainted by the truth of my story. Little Mary Ann, do not cry as the baby does, flailing in our dear Faith's able arms. For surely our reunion will occur in Heaven a mere lifetime from now. Merciful God, Your forgiveness is perfect, and Your vengeance is true. May this place live on to prove the truly miraculous works which only a just God can authorize. I remain in death as in life a servant of our loving Christ, whose sufferings were not in vain.

TWENTY-ONE

✦➤➤➤·◄◄◄

THE SILVER GLOW of early morning light filtered through the doorway as Jinx turned over the final page of Anna Rosina Gamble's diary. The three of them sprawled on the dirt floor of the mud shelter shoulder to shoulder, spines bent and necks arched toward the stack of yellowed papers. When the sound of Jinx's voice sank into silence, she felt the others jerk beside her in a somatic jolt of confusion. Their bodies did not immediately know where their minds had gone. They had been transfixed by the words just like her over the last two hours, and now they had to reacclimate as if awaking from a dream. Jinx flexed her fingers and rolled her shoulders. She adjusted her eyes to the dawning light and turned first to look at Ruth, whose chocolate eyes were still full of tears. Ruth swiftly wiped them away with the back of her hand, then flopped the hand, palm curled, into her lap.

"He killed her," she whispered, staring at the empty doorway and disturbing the strange quiet that seemed to cast the round house in an otherworldly stillness.

"We know," Jinx said, reaching out to touch her fingers to Ruth's back as if that small gesture of support could be a buttress. She was unsure if Ruth was referring to Hold or Talley, but it didn't matter. The accusation fit them both. They were guilty of unspeakable crimes, and so was the missionary who abetted Hold's abuses, and all the men in the United States and Cherokee Nation whose actions ensured the rampant abuse of vulnerable people. "But Patience was loved during her lifetime, and her memory was cherished after the tragedy."

"She's talking about her mother," Cheyenne said, her mascara-smudged eyes bleary and set in dark circles of fatigue. "Aren't you?"

"My mother's death was not an accident," Ruth said, her voice rising above a whisper. "I was the only one who believed that story, but I always felt deep down that he killed her. He pushed her off the side of that cruise ship and watched her drown. How could I live with him for eight years after that? How can I stay in touch with him now?"

"Maybe because you were only a kid when your mother died?" Cheyenne leaned toward her so that Ruth couldn't avoid her eyes. "You needed him to take care of you. And old habits die hard. I know."

"You did what you had to do to survive, just like Mary Ann," Jinx said. "You can't blame yourself." Ruth had a terrible childhood, that much was evident to Jinx, but now Ruth knew through example that love and friendship could temper the pain.

Ruth looked up in surprise as Cheyenne reached out a hand to take hers, squeezed, then let go.

Jinx noticed the gesture, feeling in that moment that she had found what she came here for, and discovered what Deb Tom had suspected was true all along. Mary Ann Battis had not given up on their tribe or her own mother; she had extended her kinship circle and fought to defend it.

And Mary Ann Battis was not Adam Battis's lineal ancestor—Patience was.

How would Cheyenne take it? Which old habits had Cheyenne meant when she was reassuring Ruth? Her eating disorder, or her fantasy that she was Cherokee? What would she do when she next saw Adam Battis, the rightful heir to this property on moral, if not legal, grounds? Jinx knew Cheyenne could not deny the fact known to them all now—that she descended from two missionaries, Anna Rosina Gamble and Samuel Cotterell, not Chief James Hold. These weren't the Cherokee roots Cheyenne had longed for. But were they the ancestors she would come to accept and honor?

Ruth's voice broke through Jinx's thoughts. "What matters is they got him," she said. "The women won."

*

A low rustling sound penetrated the silence of their enclosure, yoked to the smell of acrid smoke. A burst of molten light curled against the canebrake, and Ruth's heart pounded. She straightened on the floor where she sat, pulling away from Jinx's fingers at her spine. All the nerves in her body had switched into alert mode, focusing her attention on the sign of a threat.

As Cheyenne leapt to her feet and whispered, then shouted, "Fire!" Ruth's pulse surged. She levered up, pulling Jinx with her, watching the greenery burn through the slim poplar door of the round house. Waves of grass and tall weeds glowed hot before her eyes. The foot of a cane stalk caught just yards in front of them. The fire was spreading.

Ruth knew in an instant that although Peggy, Mary Ann, and Faith had ultimately survived this plantation, the three of them might not.

The scene in the yard seemed to unfurl in slow motion—the fire, the smoke, the stench. Cheyenne pushed through the doorway, cursing as flames approached the mud walls, scorching the cane stalks she had planned to upend herself.

Ruth knew she should follow Cheyenne, that they should run to safety. But she couldn't help holding back to see if Mary Ann would appear again.

Ruth turned at the mouth of the mud house, peering back inside. "Oh," she exhaled when she saw it.

The earth house was set aglow by the light of the fire outside, revealing a sheen to the mica-strewn mud. Tiny alabaster bits of precious stone, crushed into the plaster mix, glittered in the darkness. White seashells were interspersed among the stone flecks, pressed into familiar linguistic patterns.

Jinx and Cheyenne turned when they heard her exclaim. A constellation of floating symbols shaped in shells spiraled around them on the walls.

"Is that writing?" Cheyenne said.

"Yes," Ruth whispered, squinting at the lines and loops. "Who would have done this?" She seized a breath, knowing the answer at once.

"These are the names," Jinx said, tracing her fingers across the shells. "The ones Mary Ann fixed to the wall for those who ran during the hailstorm."

"A list of names," Cheyenne repeated, her voice going flat. "*The* list of names. It was only a list of runaway slaves?"

Ruth watched emotions shift across Cheyenne's face, her cheeks streaked with trails of sweat. Cheyenne had repeated the story of the secret list her grandmother spoke of enough times that Ruth knew what was at stake. Cheyenne thought that list would be proof that her ancestor was Black and Indigenous, evidence that she herself belonged in the tribe. Ruth reached out to touch Cheyenne's arm. Cheyenne's eyes locked on hers.

Through the doorway, Ruth saw cane stalks tipping over like dominoes. The closer the fire inched, the brighter the shells and mica shone, flashing like precious gemstones.

"These names matter, Cheyenne. All the names matter. Whether the people were beautiful or plain, grand or humble, Native American or Black—like me and you. We have to remember them. You have to read the wall. Jinx, can you record this?"

Ruth began a frantic tapping on her cell phone to capture images of the names as Cheyenne read, raising her shaking voice above the hiss of the fire.

"Isaac the First, Patience, Gander, Bob, Peter, Sam, Caty, Renee, Old Ned, Big Jenny, Little Isaac, Hannah, Will, Candace, Peter, Magdalena, Matthew, Butler, Mila, Infant Rose, Grace with her Jacob, Aged Betty, Aged July, April, May, Hagar."

The sound of the names filled the old clay dwelling, making the smoky air hum.

"Got it!" Jinx shouted.

They grasped for each other's hands, crawling low as the smoke pushed in, then rising and running toward the mission cabin and gardens. Ruth barely registered the changing scent of the smoke or the sound of rushing water. They made it as far as the work yard before they heard the barking. A hound dog with three legs had run through the haze and was circling them while emitting high warning yips.

A man with sandy hair, slate eyes, and a stiff gait commanded the dog to sit as he approached. He was wearing taupe pants and a camouflage shirt. He was carrying a repeating rifle. If his eyes showed a flicker of surprise when he saw that Cheyenne was not by herself, he did not comment.

Ruth froze where she stood, paralyzed with fear at the sight of the man, and the dog, and the weapon.

"Stay away from us!" Cheyenne shouted, her hair a loose skein of dark strands around her face.

"No need to get yourself in a tizzy, Miss Cotterell," the man said with a measure of calm that communicated menace. "You don't know this property. There's cogon grass here. Highly flammable, and with this hot summer weather continuing into the fall . . . Well, things happen. Perfectly natural for grass to burn every so often. Fortunately for you, it was an isolated blaze, far enough from the house to leave it intact. It'll burn out within a few hours."

"Well, isn't that convenient," Cheyenne said, sounding a tone of defiance that surprised Ruth, as her white silk robe dragged on the ash-darkened grass. "The house was never at risk from the fire because it's the one thing you want. It was you."

"You're damn right. It was me who saved your hide."

"You set that fire."

"I tamed that fire. There's a hose by the barn on the east side of the mud hut, but you wouldn't know that."

"What were you doing out there?"

"Hunting in the woods that border this property, like I have all my life." He rubbed the butt of his rifle, which was dark brown and well oiled.

"This conversation is a very bad idea," Jinx inserted. "The fire is dying down. We should go inside."

"I don't believe you." Cheyenne stepped toward the man that Ruth assumed was Mason Allen, holding the flashlight toward his face as if it, too, could fire deadly shots. "You cut my azaleas. You planted roaches. You killed my cat, and now you've committed arson."

"Deer eat flowers. Insects like houses. And whatever you used to treat your roaches might well be what killed your cat." He spoke through a smug, close-lipped expression that was almost a smile.

"You want me to think I'm crazy."

"Are you? I can't say it seems entirely right-headed for a young woman like you to move up here all alone."

"She's not alone," Jinx said, stepping closer to Cheyenne.

"Is that another threat?" Cheyenne said, pushing farther out in front of Jinx and Ruth. "Like the thing you said about my windows and doors? Get off my land, or I'm calling the police."

"You tell them I said hello while you're at it. They're old friends of mine."

"You will not intimidate me, Mason Allen. You have no idea what I'm made of."

"Maybe one of these nights I'll find out." He did not adjust his stance. His voice retained its casual air, but Ruth heard the threat behind his words. She heard her father's voice in her head, addressing her mother. *My gold coast.*

"We have to get back to the house. Now," Jinx said in a low voice. And then, when Cheyenne did not move, "Cheyenne!"

Cheyenne started to back away toward the house, aiming the beam of her flashlight at his face. Only when she came even with the stone path that led to the porch and saw that Allen had not moved, did she turn her back to him.

All three women ran as the hound dog barked after them.

Cheyenne yanked open the door at the back of the house. The three of them stumbled inside, breathing hard while Cheyenne slammed the lock into place. Jinx pushed a stool against the door and wedged it beneath the metal knob. Cheyenne rushed toward the hall-way, where the coal-black telephone sat on the secretary. But Ruth did not stop running.

She saw Cheyenne dial the old rotary through a haze, vaguely heard her speak to someone. But she didn't wait while Cheyenne de-scribed the scene to the dispatcher. She snuck off like she always had, needing to get far away from the sight and sounds of violent struggle, needing to hide. She climbed the stairs to the second floor and lunged for the arabesque of the bridge.

"Ruth?" Jinx called after her. "Ruth!"

Ruth turned to look over her shoulder, and the heel of her clog caught on the bridge. She fell to the floor and shut her eyes against the memory of blood on her mother's face and clothing. "No, no, no," she stammered. The pictures descended upon her, surrounded her, and took her under. She saw her father slam her mother against a wall, saw herself crouched in a closet, silently begging him to stop. Ruth was drowning in a wave of images crashing through open flood-gates. Vomit was welling up as her throat constricted. *She. Hated. Him.*

"Ruth!" Jinx wrapped an arm around her, sitting with her on the floor of the bridge. "Breathe. You need to breathe. It's okay. We're here with you." Jinx held Ruth against her, trying to take some of the weight. Ruth ripped her glasses off, wiping at her tear-blurred eyes.

"She needs air," Cheyenne said tightly, moving toward the tall window on the staircase landing. She lifted the latch and opened the glass. A firm, wet, driven breeze swept up the scrim of smoke outside and carried it into the house as raindrops fell. The sweet scent of soaking grass mixed with the curling smoke.

Jinx urged Ruth up, walked her off the bridge and down several steps to the open window.

"The fire truck is on its way," Cheyenne said quietly.

Ruth squinted into a pearlescent early-morning sky. And there she was. Mary Ann. Floating in the old rose garden with a fan of incandescent pages dangling from her backlit fingers. Ruth watched as Mary Ann raised her arms, wrapping the smoke around her like a spirit gown, then lifted her arms a second time and gave wing to the spectral pages. They seemed to fly from her hand into the churning, rain-washed air. She was releasing it all to them, all of the pages, all of the pain. She was letting it go.

"Where's the diary?" Ruth suddenly said.

"I . . . it's . . . oh God." Jinx slapped a hand to her mouth and spoke through her fingers. "I had it in the round house. The fire . . ."

"You mean it's gone?" Cheyenne said.

And so was Mary Ann. Ruth was certain.

Without the diary Cheyenne had no proof of her link to this place. She was back at square one. Ruth turned to look at her.

"I don't know which is worse," Cheyenne shook her head, gazing out onto the hazy grounds, "having or losing the evidence that this place belongs to Adam Battis."

Flashing lights penetrated the darkness as a fire truck sped up the avenue of oaks.

"You'll stay with her?" Cheyenne asked. Jinx nodded. And Cheyenne pounded down the steps in a sullied silk robe to meet the firefighters.

Part III

Our Mothers' Gardens

-→->- · -<-←-

I began to look about me and saw . . . the
most beautiful roses I ever beheld, another of
these exquisite southern flowers—the Cherokee rose. The blossom is very large, composed
of four or five pure white petals, as white and
as large as those of the finest Camellia, with a
bright golden eye for a focus.

—Frances Anne Kemble,
Journal of a Residence on a Georgian Plantation
1838–1839

-→->- · -<-←-

TWENTY-TWO

"HELLO? WHERE ARE y'all?" A bright voice lilted through the lower corners of the house. "Are y'all all right? Hello?"

Jinx felt the stair-rail balustrades pressing against her spine like bone spurs. She breathed in through her nose. The smoke had begun to clear, leaving behind a scent like tanned deer hide. The smell reminded her of home, of smoked meat, fry bread, and dried fruit packed together inside Aunt Angie's stomp-dance tent. She turned toward Ruth sitting beside her, whose full legs tapered beneath the nightshirt. Jinx indulged in a look at the smooth skin of Ruth's face, the rounded dark caramel shoulder bared by her skewed neckline. Cheyenne had rejoined them on the stair landing after the fire crew had left. The three of them sat, shell-shocked.

"It's me. Sally Perdue from the gas station?"

"Cheyenne?" A deep drawl echoed Sally's from the first floor. "Jennifer? Ruth?"

Cheyenne reached up to smooth her hair at the sound of the second voice. Jinx wouldn't be the one to tell her it was hopeless. Footsteps sounded on the stairs, and the solid figures of Sally Perdue, a wriggling baby, and Adam Battis materialized.

"There y'all are." Sally's cornflower-blue eyes, framed by a tumble of short red curls, peeked above the steps. She was as charged as the day Jinx had met her, those same faint lines of exhaustion beneath her inquisitive eyes. The infant on her hip sucked intently on a pacifier and stared at them with his mother's bright baby blues. He wore a white onesie with SATURDAY emblazoned on the chest. Jinx guessed Ruth would be charmed by this wordy outfit, especially since it was actually Thursday. The baby kicked his chubby bare feet as Sally held him close.

"I was worried sick when I saw the smoke from the station lot this morning. I called Adam, and we got here as fast as we could. But it looks like y'all are all right and the Hold House is still standing." She switched the baby to her other hip.

Jinx pushed back a swath of hair that had worked itself free from her braid. "Thanks for coming to check on us. Sally Perdue, these are my friends Ruth Mayes and Cheyenne Cotterell. Cheyenne owns the house."

"Oh, I know that." Sally swatted the air with her hand. "Word travels fast around here. I hope you liked the muffins and jam Adam left for you. I didn't have time to make the muffins from scratch, but the Jiffy folks do a pretty good job in a pinch. The jam, now, that I always make myself."

Cheyenne's eyes widened at the onslaught of enthusiasm. "Thank you," she said. Cheyenne glanced at Sally's worn Lee jeans and MUR-RAY COUNTY COOK-OFF T-shirt, but Jinx could see her thoughts were focused on Adam, who held a door key in his hand.

"So what the heck happened here?" Sally asked with a familiarity that made it seem as if she had known them all their lives. She settled in next to them on the landing, baby on her lap. "You three look like you've seen a ghost."

Ruth gave Jinx a private look before she said, "And that's exactly how we feel."

Adam mounted the stairs and halted near the landing, one knee jackknifed up to a higher step. He wore loose jeans and a wash-softened T-shirt the color of summer plums. He turned his pensive gaze to where they sat, a tangle of wild dark hair, wrinkled pajamas, and sweat-dewed faces.

"Sorry to barge in like this, Cheyenne," he said. "We wanted to stop by to make sure everything was all right. Sally told me she saw smoke. She was worried. I was worried."

Jinx looked at Cheyenne, who stared without speaking at Adam's brass key.

"There was a grass fire in the yard. By the time the firefighters arrived, the rain had almost put it out." Jinx paused. "Cheyenne thinks Mason Allen may have set it."

"Shit," Sally said. "I never could stand that Mason. He's nothing but a burner set on low, waiting to explode. Are y'all okay? Is anybody hurt?"

"We were scared," Ruth said. "It was like a *Psycho* sequel out there for a hot minute. But we'll be okay."

"You should press charges against that jackass. And if you don't, I will. A fire like that could have spread for miles, and our fire department's all-volunteer," Sally said.

Adam listened, a quiet storm gathering on his face. "It would be hard proving he started a grass fire, but that doesn't bar me from having a talk with him."

Cheyenne stared through Adam as though her eyes were fixed on a distant scene. Jinx imagined the silent film scrolling in her mind: a premature, sickly infant born in the missionaries' cabin to Patience and James Hold. That child was the first Adam Battis, whose name would never appear on any Cherokee census roll, even though he was the son of a chief. The man standing before them was that boy's descendant and the holder of his name. Jinx wondered if Adam knew of his family members in Oklahoma, if his family knew about him. She hoped the descendants of James Hold's wives and siblings would listen to Adam's side of the family story, that they would see the past as a stage of possibility and unexpected occurrences.

Cheyenne wrapped the ivory robe, dingy with dust and ash, around her delicate waist. She descended the stairs, meeting Adam where he stood, aligning her eyes with his. "You have a key to this house. An original key. Where did you get it?"

Adam sighed, glancing away, but only for a millisecond. "It's been in my family for generations. My grandfolks said it was given to Mary Ann Battis by Peggy Hold herself. I shouldn't have used it, though, now that you own the house. No one answered when we knocked. We wanted—I wanted—to be sure you were okay."

"Do you know who you are?" Cheyenne demanded. Adam froze, startled by her directness.

"Do you know who you really are? Your tie to this plantation?"

Adam shifted his gaze from Cheyenne's searching eyes to the faces of the women beside her. "Yeah," he nodded after a pause. "I know where I come from. I know my family's history, if that's what you mean. It's in our family stories, the things that happened, and the things that had to be kept hidden for safety. What about you? Do you know who you are, Cheyenne?"

"I thought I did when I bought this place," Cheyenne said quietly. "But now I have to figure that out all over again. I must look like a fool to you. Buying this plantation, treating it like a dollhouse, acting like it was my own personal inheritance while I waited for DNA results to pop into my inbox." Her staccato words signaled confidence, but her chin trembled.

Adam lifted his hand and touched a palm to her temple, where perspiration was spiraling her straightened hair. "You had a right to bid on the Hold House. You did nothing wrong."

But Cheyenne's crushed expression said she knew differently. Her hunger for this land had been as selfish and blind as Mason Allen's. Cheyenne's eyes were wet, her mouth set in a colorless line. Jinx had seen that crestfallen look on someone's face before, back when she was doing dissertation research deep in the basement of the Oklahoma Historical Society. A starry-eyed genealogist questing for Indian roots had emerged from the microfilm machines disillusioned, coming up empty-handed—and worse, in his mind, finding an ancestor on the Dawes Rolls recorded as *Freedman* instead of *Indian by Blood*. Cheyenne's forebears had been teachers, preachers, and freedom fighters, but they had not been American Indian. Could she turn the page?

"This property, this land, should never have been put up at auction," Cheyenne said. "This is not my house. And as long as I can fight it, it will never be Mason Allen's either. Peggy, her family, the Cherokee people—it still belongs to them." Her voice dragged as she pushed against the catch in her throat. "It still belongs to you."

Adam hesitated before speaking, his eyes going dark with unspoken feeling. "Maybe this isn't your house in the way you mean. But that doesn't mean it couldn't become your home."

Cheyenne's shoulders quaked as she stood on the stairs of her manor house, dirty, sweaty, with all her makeup washed away. Ruth stood to wrap her in a hug. Turning into the sooty cotton of Ruth's nightshirt, Cheyenne leaned on the strength of her childhood friend.

"No offense, but y'all are a mess," Sally said, breaking the silence. "Let's get you dressed and out of here and find some breakfast. And you," she added, looking pointedly at Cheyenne, "are in need of a slice of this county's best strawberry pie."

Jinx smiled, thinking of Deb's pie back home, and of Mary Ann's second family on the Cherokee Rose Plantation. Ruth, Cheyenne, Adam, Sally, and the little baby with a word on his chest: these were also her people.

*

When dusk fell, Ruth lay on the thinning rug in the rear parlor of the plantation house. The hand-woven Persian textile swirled with color, its rich shades forming the intricate pattern of a hunt. Turbaned men rode astride long-necked steeds, chasing their antlered prey in an endless, searching circle. Ruth had showered, changed into a clean T-shirt and knee-length white denim skirt, and pulled her hair back with an orange bandanna. She lay on her back beside the fire Adam had built from kindling and logs that he had cut and stacked back when he was employed at the place. The fire did its humanizing work, flickering before the four of them like a miniature dance of the sun, making them feel safe, alive, connected.

Ruth looked from the fire to Jinx, who sat with her back against the legs of an upholstered chair, her braided hair, wet from a shower, dampening her shirt. Jinx had fashioned a makeshift library carrel on the carpet before the hearth, using a throw pillow for a lap desk. She sat within a nest of books and loose legal-pad pages, intent on putting the fragments together, connecting the dots of the story. Over fried eggs and grits at Adam's cabin that morning, she had told Ruth and Cheyenne about the digital photos she had taken of the diary pages as they were all preparing for bed the previous night, before the fire. Then she had put Adam through a battery of questions about the oral history of the Battises and the Holds. Now that Sally had gone home with Junior, leaving behind a fresh strawberry pie, she wanted to get all of their thoughts about the history of the plantation down on paper. The scratching of her pen and popping of the fire echoed in the room.

Cheyenne lounged on a silk settee, legs neatly folded beneath the pressed lime skirt of her poplin dress. Adam sat nearby, grinning at her as she took experimental bites of gooey strawberry pie.

"Are you still going to write that column, Jinx, about Mary Ann?" Cheyenne asked, after swallowing a mouthful as delicately as possible and taking a sip from her crystal water glass.

Jinx pulled her eyes from her notepad, folded her legs beneath her, and straightened her back. "I am. Some people in my community, owing in part to me, think Mary Ann abandoned her family when she converted to Christianity, that she chose to stay behind in the South and turned her back on her Muscogee kin because she was a traitor. But it turns out she was a child taken from her family, like so many others since colonization began. She wanted to stay here where her adopted mothers were buried to carry out their work and tend their graves. Mary Ann was a witness for all of them: Anna Rosina, Patience, Peggy, Faith, even those whose names she inscribed on the mud house walls. And now I'm a witness for her, so I have to pass the story on."

"How?" Ruth said.

"In more than a single column. I'd like to write a history of this plantation, if Adam agrees."

"I do think people should know what happened here," Adam said. "But is that what Anna Gamble would have wanted? You-all said she told Mary Ann to burn that diary." He gestured toward the cell phone and the empty chestnut box beside Jinx on the rug.

Jinx tucked damp strands of hair behind an ear, gathering her answer. "Mary Ann buried it for someone to find instead of destroying it. She led Ruth to the pit and the names. She wanted us to know what happened here; she made sure we knew. All stories have their time, and I think this one's time has come."

"And what about Mary Ann?" Ruth said. "Shouldn't we find a way to say goodbye?"

*

The moon was high overhead when they waded into the garden. They left the rear doors of the house open behind them, allowing the September breeze to flow in. They each held a beeswax candle Adam had produced from the bottom of a Chippendale credenza. The lights of their candles burned over the singed garden flowers as the wide sea of river cane swayed at a distance before them. Some of the reedy stalks—the ones nearest the mud house—had lost their fullness in the fire, but most retained their feathery heads, forming a loose, fibrous net between earth and sky.

A heap of clay was all that remained of the earth house. *Ashes to ashes, dust to dust,* Ruth thought. She slowed as they neared the center of the flower garden, letting Adam lead. He knew this place better than any of them. He could find where the bodies were buried.

Adam stopped beside the place where the hill dipped, where Ruth had first noticed the roses. The cluster of mounds he pointed out appeared at first as natural features of the landscape. But the rise in the center was covered with roses of every description, some in bloom, some at rest after a full summer's show. Three slight mounds surrounded that middle plot, complemented by rosebushes less thickly planted.

Jinx grasped the braid of sweetgrass Aunt Angie had made for her, which she had once sworn never to burn. She held the tip of the braid out to Adam. He lit it with his candle, releasing smoke and a rich aroma to float around them. Jinx fanned the smoke toward her face and torso. She turned to the others, inviting them to mirror her.

Adam was the first to speak: "Lord, help us remember this woman and all those who dwelled here."

"Mary Ann," Ruth said, "it's time for you to go back."

"Rest in peace," Cheyenne whispered.

Sweetgrass smoke rose above the burial mounds and hillside. Jinx took Ruth's hand and reached out for Cheyenne, who extended her left hand to Adam. The four of them stood before the graves, thinking of the ones below and also the ones above, the ones who had come before and the ones who would come after, hoping that Mary Ann Battis, a spirit no longer alone, would find her rightful place among them.

TWENTY-THREE

-+>-+>·-<-+-<

CHEYENNE WATCHED THE incredulous faces of the state attorneys as she sat next to Adam in a paneled anteroom of the courthouse. She had dressed in an Eileen Fisher pantsuit, loose and flowing like the spun silk of a cottonwood tree, to communicate her sense of assuredness. Instead of straightening her hair with her blow-dryer and flat iron, she had decided to let it find its natural wave.

The rectangular conference room table was overpopulated with representatives from almost every conceivable constituency. Her father's lawyer had driven up from Atlanta for the last-minute meeting in a rush that had left him on edge. After trying to dissuade her from her decision, Dan Shapiro had given in to Cheyenne's will. His pinstriped suit contrasted with Adam's dark blue jeans and plaid buttondown shirt. The broker, Lanie Brevard, was there, too, wearing a black pencil skirt and a frown. She sat next to the title-company representative, who was struggling to facilitate the unwieldy deal.

Adam handed over the cashier's check for twenty-five thousand dollars, prepared for him in a rush by the local bank that morning. It was only at his insistence that Cheyenne had agreed to accept any down payment at all. She had been prepared to carry the mortgage for as long as it took. She still had her job at Swag. She still had her family's money. She could even sell her condo in Candler Park, if it came to that.

Cheyenne fingered the glossy pearls around her neck. With a

deep breath that was as much release as resignation, she started to sign the mountain of documents before her. Adam signed his corresponding stack, followed by their witness, Sally Perdue.

*

"I know what I'm doing, Dan," Cheyenne whispered to the balding man who had represented her father for as long as she could remember. His hazel eyes showed concern behind the wire-rimmed glasses. She touched a hand to his arm as he shook his head with combined affection and disbelief. "Or at least I have a decent idea. Can you make one more stop with me before you head back to the city? I'll fill you in on the drive."

"I can," he said, beckoning Cheyenne into the passenger seat of his BMW.

"Follow him," Cheyenne said to the lawyer, smiling through the open window at Adam, who had climbed into the driver's seat of his Bronco. Sally sat beside him, her red curls catching the September sunlight, her baby strapped into a car seat in the rear.

They followed Adam through the town center, past Hold Hill. They turned away from the road leading to the mountain and snaked down behind the Hold property line to cross a one-lane bridge. As the poplars and chestnuts parted beyond the riverbank, Cheyenne saw a construction site that appeared like an open wound. Burly men were shouting in English and Spanish, lifting and hauling materials. The land had been cleared for two hundred feet, and a cement foundation had been poured inside the square indenture. Bright machines with sharp teeth and elongated necks stood at the ready. A black Grand Cherokee squatted on the edge of a road that was dirt now but would soon be paved to accommodate more traffic if Mason Allen had his way.

Adam parked next to the SUV. Dan Shapiro followed. The four of them stepped out of their vehicles to see Mason Allen, wearing a yellow hard hat and ironed denim, break away from a huddle and stride forcefully toward them. "Sally, Adam," he said, nodding his head in a clipped greeting. "Miss Cotterell. Mason Allen," he said to the law-yer, holding out a hand. "And you are?"

"Daniel Shapiro, Mr. Allen. I represent Cheyenne Cotterell in the matter of the Hold House property sale."

Mason Allen's eyebrows arched over his slate-gray eyes, his jowls turning pinkish as he looked from the attorney to Cheyenne to Adam. "So it's true"—he addressed his words to Adam—"what I've been hearing around town this morning. You went and bought the Hold place from her behind my back. We've lived in this town a long time together, Adam. Our families have ties. And you're going to throw it all away. For what? A chance to fail at something too big for you to handle?"

Cheyenne doubted his meaning was lost on anyone in that tense circle. He was telling Adam to know his place.

"I won't fail, Mason, because I'm not alone in this. And I want you to know right here and now, in front of these good people, that if you come near the Hold House or anybody living there with ill intentions ever again, we'll take it to the law and slap you with a restraining order."

"Is that so?" Mason Allen widened his stance and lowered his voice, his narrow nostrils flaring. "Feeling big in your britches today, Adam? Remember, these people aren't from here. We are, and that goes for you too, Sally. Long after they're gone, we'll have to maintain a certain . . . comfort level with each other."

"I didn't want to have to raise this," Cheyenne said. "But I'm not so sure how comfortable you'll be around here, and certainly with your Atlanta business partners, if this gets out." She slid her phone out of her handbag and pressed PLAY.

On the morning of the fire, after recording Cheyenne's recitation of the names on the walls, Jinx had forgotten to tap her recording app off and accidentally captured the exchange in the work yard. Mason Allen's rude insinuations were clear in the audio.

"The two friends you saw me with that morning are both journalists writing about the Hold House," Cheyenne continued. "Won't it be interesting when their stories describe the local builder who violates professional and personal boundaries?"

"And I am also prepared to represent the Hold House Historical Association with regard to this burial ground," Dan Shapiro stated, as he coolly held the other man's gaze, barely masking his disregard.

"There is no such thing," Mason Allen countered.

"There is now," Adam said. "And you're looking at the first president." He gestured to Sally.

"Adam, if you own the place, well, that's that," Mason Allen said, avoiding a reply to the lawyer and refusing to look at Cheyenne. "I'm sure you and I can get along. A property like that is expensive to maintain unless you make it work for you. I can help you do that. We'll talk over a couple of beers. The two of us, at my club next week."

"That would be the three of us," Cheyenne said. "Adam is my business partner. We own the property jointly. If you plan to deal with him, you're going to have to deal with me, and I can tell you right now I'm not available next week." Cheyenne watched Mason Allen's head spin from her face to Adam's before Dan Shapiro cut in again.

"I have to inform you that we have reason to believe you're building on a burial ground of historical significance. The National Historic Preservation Act and the Native American Graves Protection and Repatriation Act say you can't do that without going through federal channels. We'll be requesting a cease-and-desist order from your county court by the end of the business day."

"And another thing, Mason," Sally said with Junior bouncing on her hip. "I quit."

*

Jinx skidded to an abrupt halt, leaned forward, and pressed her hands to her knees. She had struggled to keep pace with Ruth during their run on the mountain trail, and now she inhaled draws of the sweet-smelling mountain air like an addict.

"How—far—was—that?" she managed to say to Ruth, who had

slowed to a walk and was gesturing to Jinx to follow suit. Jinx managed to walk a haggard circle before she stopped again.

Ruth, who was wearing navy running shorts with white trim and an orange scoop-neck top, shifted to stretching her legs. She propped one bent leg on the wooden step of the building of her former camp and pressed forward.

Jinx plopped down beside her on the step, not even pretending to continue this farce. She was a regular walker, but this was excessive.

"Two miles. You did a good job! It's tougher on a trail. The inclines are challenging, and the pinecones, sticks, and rocks mean you have to watch your feet."

"And you choose to torture yourself like this regularly?"

"Just once a week." Ruth pulled the blue and white paisley-patterned bandanna from around her forehead. She wore her hair in a Scunci that barely held the springy curls in a short ponytail.

Jinx wiped a bead of sweat from her own forehead, then pressed her cool water bottle to her hairline. She leaned back against the step and stared into the spaces between the trees in the forest. "Do you ever wonder where she got the money?" she said.

"Cheyenne? Never. She gets every cent from her parents." Ruth opened her reusable water bottle and took a swig.

"Peggy Hold. She redid the house after James Hold died. She repainted the walls and added carved woodwork to all the fireplace mantels. She had copper knobs etched with roses made for the doors."

Ruth nodded. "And she may have added the front veranda. Cheyenne's brochures point out it wasn't original to the house."

"Okay, that too. So how did she afford it?"

"She was a plantation mistress. She had her husband's money, or family money."

"In the early 1800s, when estates still typically passed to firstborn male heirs, that would have been unusual. And the South was even more traditional than the North when it came to women's roles and rights. Anna Rosina Gamble said her husband arranged James Hold's affairs through a U.S. court. As a widow under most American state laws, Peggy would have gotten a portion of the house to live in, or she would have been assigned to a small exterior dwelling. This kind of division of living space became known as the 'widow's third.' She wouldn't have retained the whole estate and total control of the house . . . unless specific provisions—creative, ingenious provisions that found legal loopholes—had been made."

"Maybe she had a legal advocate. One of Anna Rosina Gamble's Pennsylvania contacts?"

"Or James Hold's eldest son, when he came of age. The diary said he lived and studied at the mission," Jinx said.

"Right! He was one of their first pupils."

"And he went to live with Peggy like the other students after the death of James Hold. Maybe they became close."

"Even if she did have assistance in acquiring the estate, that still doesn't answer your question about how she afforded it." Ruth looked perplexed, then thoughtful, and then excited as Jinx watched her face. "With all those renovations Peggy undertook, why didn't she change that odd bridge on the second floor? The thing is impractical. It chops up the house in an awkward way, and as I found out two days ago, it's a tripping hazard."

"You think she left it alone to avoid drawing attention to it." Jinx inhaled sharply, placing her water bottle on the step. She was staring hard at Ruth as the ideas turned in her mind.

Ruth nodded vigorously. "Because she was the only one who really knew its purpose. That bridge was her husband's safe, hidden in plain sight."

"Holy shit! Let's go."

The two women jogged to Ruth's Beetle, jumped in, and maneuvered back to the Hold House, with Jinx damning the inconveniently slow curves of mountain roads while Ruth laughed.

They found the house empty. Cheyenne was still at the courthouse with Adam. Ruth used her borrowed key, and they pressed inside, dropping their water bottles on the secretary to take the stairs two at a time. The satin light of late afternoon shone through the landing window as they knelt on the wood at the step that adjoined the base of the bridge.

Jinx leaned to the side, craning her neck so that her eyes were level with the floorboard. "What are we looking for? A notch or a lever?"

"Probably something very small, almost invisible. Maybe wood grain that's slightly discolored. Maybe a loose joint."

"Nothing here." Jinx crawled across the bridge, examining the floor.

"Watch your knees in those shorts," Ruth said, awkwardly squat-walking beside her like a crab. "Splinters!"

On the far side of the bridge, where the structure leveled off toward the hallway leading to the master bedroom, Jinx paused. "Wait."

"What!"

"A corner of this slat seems . . ." Jinx scrambled to the hallway floor and turned back to face it, still on her knees, ". . . off." She pressed her hands against the panel, putting pressure on all areas of the board, which was slightly lighter in color than those around it.

Ruth wedged in beside Jinx on her knees, the threat of splinters forgotten as she felt around the panel. When both their hands, aligned like the wings of a butterfly, pushed against the same swirl of wood grain at the same time, the single board swung open.

"Holy . . ." Jinx said.

"Shit," Ruth finished.

The narrow compartment was lined with a double layer of wood and filled with variously sized rocks that reflected the light of the window.

"Gold," they said at the same time.

As Jinx stared, her thoughts spinning, she saw Ruth reach her hand into the enclosure.

"Watch it! Who knows what else is in there?"

"I see something!"

Ruth flattened out to lie on her stomach, extending her legs across the hall, with her orange and blue trainers pointed toward the door of the main bedroom.

"Careful," Jinx cautioned again.

Ruth took her glasses off and handed them to Jinx so that she could press her cheek against the wood, close her eyes, and wiggle her hand around the gold to touch the back of the safe.

When Ruth withdrew, her ponytail was pressed to one side, and her arm was coated with dust. In her hand she held a pistol with a bronzed body, matching trigger, gold tip, and tarnished silver joints engraved with the name of the gunsmith.

"Be careful with that!" Jinx breathed.

Ruth pushed back to sit on her butt, turning the finely crafted gun over in her hands. It was thin, long, and surprisingly delicate. "It has to be Peggy's," Ruth said.

"One of the murder weapons."

"One of the *purported* murder weapons," Ruth said. "I did some quick online research into the plants from the diary while we were at Adam's. Anna Gamble mentioned the sweetshrub seeds that Faith baked into cornbread, but even if Faith had a stash of those seeds on hand—and why would she, as a healer who tried to make people well—there wouldn't have been enough in those pastries to actually kill a man."

"So when Anna included this detail in her diary—"

"Maybe she was obscuring the facts, clouding the story to make it harder for anyone who might read it to know who had killed James Hold if suspicion had fallen on the women of the mission."

"But she told Mary Ann to destroy the diary after she died," Jinx said.

"Maybe she knew Mary Ann wouldn't be able to let go of her writings. I still have every card and note that I could find in my mother's room the day I learned she had died. That diary, which no one would have questioned since it exposed Anna Gamble herself to criticism, would have protected Mary Ann, Peggy, and Faith if an investigation were to be launched."

Jinx sat quietly for a moment. "Who did kill him, do you think?"

"Mary Ann," Ruth said in a voice ringing with clarity. "We know she started at least one fire in the past. She didn't shy away from dangerous means of self-defense. And we know she traveled to the ceremony. She might have gotten James Hold alone, and—"

"And his body was burned after the alleged shooting."

"Mary Ann extinguishing a threat through the best method she knew—fire."

"Wait," Jinx said, inhaling sharply, watching Ruth's face. "You don't think Mary Ann, her spirit, still has the ability to—? That Mason Allen was telling the truth about the fire?"

"I think it's possible." Ruth absent-mindedly stroked the burnished barrel of the gun.

Jinx's eyes flicked toward the motion, and worry surfaced in the wrinkling of her brow.

"I saw her again afterward—when we were all on the steps that morning. I saw her through the window. It was like she was floating above the fire, wearing the smoke. And then the rain started."

Jinx stared at Ruth, open-mouthed.

"I think it's possible she knew Mason Allen was there before we did. Maybe she saw him hunting or, more likely, planning to gaslight Cheyenne with another trick. Maybe she tried to stop him."

Jinx was quiet. She considered Ruth's words as she looked from the hallway toward the door of the bedroom where James Hold had slept two centuries ago, toward the guest bedroom where she, Ruth, and Cheyenne had slept just days ago, toward the stifling closet that led to the attic, and across the bridge to the staircase and the double front doors.

"When we first talked during Cheyenne's impromptu tour, we realized we'd read the same article—remember?" Jinx asked, her voice softening on that last word.

"Of course. I had a strange feeling that we had been drawn together." Ruth ducked her head as if to disguise her shyness and twined a finger of her free hand around a curl.

"I had that feeling too. And I'll never tell anyone but you this—I think Mary Ann was behind it. I think she wanted us here, drew us here, to protect the plantation because she knew Mason Allen was a threat to the graves of Anna, Peggy, and Patience."

"And when he became a threat to us, she risked the place she loved to defend us."

"Stranger things have happened," Jinx said.

"Have they?" Ruth laughed.

"The world is a mysterious place." Jinx swayed to bump her shoulder into Ruth's. "So what are we going to do about all this gold?"

"Make Cheyenne Cotterell's life even better than it already is?" Ruth said with sarcasm undercut by the mirth in her eyes.

"And the gun?" Jinx gave a pointed look to the antique weapon in Ruth's hands.

"In that case, what Cheyenne doesn't know won't hurt her."

*

On Sunday morning, Ruth and Jinx had packed Ruth's car and Jinx's truck with luggage, laptops, notebooks, papers, and cases of Sally's fruit preserves. Now Ruth turned to wave at Cheyenne, who posed beside Adam on the front veranda, wearing a belted trench dress, matching Ferragamo flats, and perfectly applied makeup. Cheyenne waved back like a princess on a parade float, her hair drifting down in loose waves around her face. Her DNA results had come in with no evidence of Native American ancestry, and after she had involved her father's attorney, she had to admit to her parents that she had failed to fully vet this property purchase. But far to the positive side of the ledger, Cheyenne now had an even grander story to tell about her historic home, which had turned out to be a treasure trove. She and Adam were having the gold Ruth and Jinx had found appraised, but the expert they spoke with through Cheyenne's attorney speculated the nearly 540 ounces would be worth as much as Cheyenne had paid for the house at auction. Cheyenne had managed once again to maintain her glass-slipper footing in a world that had rapidly turned under her feet—but not, Ruth knew, without first wrestling her own secret losses and insecurities to the ground.

Jinx was in her idling truck, finishing up a call with her cousin while Ruth said her goodbyes. Ruth then climbed into the driver's seat of her own car, trying to gather her courage to follow Jinx down the drive of the Hold House estate and into the next chapter of their lives.

She pushed her tortoiseshell glasses up on her nose and readjusted the bandanna she wore as a headband. She still had more weeks than she wanted to count left of her vacation, and she had agreed to caravan with Jinx out to Oklahoma. She would stay in the small cottage Jinx had described, with 1920s Craftsman-style details and flower beds that hadn't been planted in years. Jinx had a column to write, a library to staff, and a dissertation to rediscover. Maybe Ruth would spend part of that time writing in the cottage beside her, with sunlight streaming through a kitchen window. Ruth had pages full of notes for her article on the plantation, and haunting photographs of the grounds. She was feeling inspired, too, to craft a field guide to Southern flowers based on the varieties her mother had selected for Canebrake Botanicals. And in the right light, in the right mood, when she let her thoughts wander to the dark places, she had a mind to write a ghost story.

Or maybe she would never see Jinx's sunlit kitchen. Maybe she would make an excuse, peel off when they hit the interstate, and take the road she knew north.

Ruth didn't know how long she had been sitting there with her hands squeezing the steering wheel and her engine off. She looked up to find Jinx standing by the open car window. Jinx leaned in toward Ruth, her long braid brushing Ruth's arm. Ruth breathed in the scents of Twizzlers, cola, and Jinx's shampoo.

"Are you ready?" Jinx said, her eyes questioning. "Or are you just going to sit there being cute?"

Ruth laughed, then wavered. "What if I said I'm just going to sit here?" She bit her bottom lip.

"Then I'd say scoot over and let me drive. We'll find another way to get my truck to Ocmulgee. Maybe one of those two will drive it out." She turned her head to point her chin toward the veranda. "They owe you a favor now that you've made them precious metal moguls. Besides, how long do you think it's going to take before Adam feels like Cheyenne's hostage and starts itching for a road trip?"

Ruth laughed. "You know I can tell when you're pandering to me, right? And actually, I think he really likes her."

"And I think I really like you. So what will it be, F.D., caravan or shotgun?"

"F.D.?" Ruth countered, curious but also stalling.

"Freaking Delightful," Jinx supplied with a playful smile. "That shirt was my first clue that I had to find out more about you."

"We'll see if you still think so in two weeks." Ruth spoke through sputters of laughter, but her eyes betrayed her uncertainty, about her capacity to be with someone, about the road ahead. "Caravan. You lead—at first. Then we switch."

Jinx nodded, reaching into the car to lightly place a hand over one of Ruth's on the wheel.

When Jinx started her engine this time, Ruth did too. She looked toward Jinx who was settled into her pickup truck with her sweetgrass braid repositioned on the dashboard and an open can of Coke in the cup holder. She watched as Jinx fiddled around with her stereo and smiled when she heard the music. The fusion of sax, flute, and drum filled the air as they flew down the winding road in sync. Driving behind Jinx near enough to keep her close and far enough for safety, Ruth caught a view of the Hold House in the rearview mirror, a study in handmade brick and homespun brutality, haloed by gardens of memory.

EPILOGUE

The Song of the House

✦→✦→✦・✦←✦←✦

In search of my mother's garden, I found my own.

—ALICE WALKER,
In Search of Our Mothers' Gardens

JUNIOR WAS THE first to greet them, toddling down the winding gravel path. At twelve months, he was brave and boundless, happy enough to stay on his feet or tumble to the ground. He was dressed in designer baby blue jeans and a top featuring the Hungry Caterpillar in hand-stitched appliqué. *Cheyenne's doing,* Ruth thought, shaking her head.

Beside Junior, the elegant bank of azalea bushes had just begun its spring showing. The bushes blazed hot pink in the cool April air, bringing out the color in the bricks of the home behind them. Cheyenne and Adam had put their gold fortune to immediate use, paying off the loan on the property, and making the main floors of the old house shine again. An ornate wooden sign beneath the azaleas announced THE CHEROKEE ROSE BED-AND-BREAKFAST.

In the side yard, the weaving house, corncrib, and smokehouse had been refurbished with clean white paint and glistening windows. The old, battered wooden sign picturing a flushed summer peach had been rescued from the Ball Fruit Stand and hung now as an artifact on the outside wall of the weaving house. A matching sign introduced SALLY'S WHOLE FRUIT JAMS & PIES.

"Hey, y'all," Sally said, bounding three steps behind Junior, her short hair pinned back in butterfly-shaped barrettes. She raced for-

ward to throw her arms around Jinx, then Ruth. "We weren't expecting to see you 'til suppertime, and you 'til midnight."

"Jinx flew in from Oklahoma City and waited at the airport in Atlanta while she speed-read a book. Then I flew in from Minneapolis,
and we rented a car," Ruth said.

"Coordination has its benefits," Jinx said.

"I'll say. Adam's out in the orchards now, pruning the trees. Cheyenne's in the cabin, probably trying to do some last-minute planning.
The inn opens the first of May, and she's been in more than a tizzy
this month."

"The cabin?" Ruth said, glancing at Jinx.

"There's been quite a few changes around here," Sally said. "You
two are in for a treat."

They stepped onto the wide veranda filled with white wicker
rockers, potted pink geraniums, and pale, delicate ferns. A bronze
National Register of Historic Places plaque had been affixed to the
brick beside the antique doorbell.

Jinx took in the scene as Sally led them inside, Junior hitching a
ride on her hip. The preternatural chill she had felt when first crossing this threshold was gone. She reached for Ruth's hand and
squeezed, amazed as always at the reassurance of feeling her touch
returned.

A reception table had been placed in the foyer. Printed brochures
described the history of the plantation and all its former residents,
listed times for historic tours, and outlined hiking trails on Fort
Mountain. Gleaming oak barrister bookcases housed Adam's nonfiction collection. A gourmet kitchen with granite counters and
industrial-quality appliances had been built into the east side of the
house, swallowing the pantry and a fair amount of hallway space.

"The drawing room will be a common area for B&B guests," Sally
explained. "The bedrooms upstairs are named for the women who
lived here back when. Junior and I have the room in the back on this
floor—the rear parlor with the fireplace. It's the Anna Gamble Room."

Jinx smiled to herself, remembering the thoughts Anna Rosina

Gamble had expressed about that parlor in her diary. The Hold House, the missionary had thought upon her arrival, was too bustling, too foreign, and too crowded for her delicate senses. By the looks of things, it would soon be full again.

"Cheyenne giving up her master suite and mountain view?" Ruth said as Sally led them to their room. "Has that girl lost her mind?"

"You might think so," Sally said. "But I know a thing or two about losing your mind, after living seven years with Eddie Senior. So I'd say she's just changed a bit, like all the rest of us." Sally smiled as she took in the way Ruth and Jinx walked together so that their arms and hips occasionally touched. "After you get settled, come on down. I know Cheyenne will want to show you the gardens."

Jinx and Ruth took a turn around the largest suite, named for Patience, which looked nearly the same as it had when they were in the house last fall. The linens had been replaced with high-thread-count cotton that smelled faintly of rose petals, and Cheyenne had added the promised luxury bath.

They headed down the staircase and through a narrow hallway that closed off Sally's room from the back exterior doors.

The garden, which was making a comeback after the fire, still held its wild character. Cheyenne had not torn down the cane that dipped to the river below or built her glass breezeway to frame a water view. She had left the yard as she found it, as Anna Rosina would have remembered it. Newly planted vegetable and herb gardens fanned out from the old mission cabin, punctuated by raised soil lines and markers in the ground. The building was designated the MARY ANN BATTIS HOUSE on a sign beside the front step.

"The prodigal sisters return," Cheyenne said, sashaying out of the mission cabin with a ponytail rolling down her back and an orange kitten twining around her legs. "Long time since September," she said. "And believe it or not, I missed you ladies." She hugged them and ushered them inside.

Ruth took a moment to absorb it all. The raw space where she and Jinx had dug out the diary was now a shabby-chic country cabin fit for an *Abode* magazine spread. The walls were a soothing eggshell white, from milk paint common to the structure's original era. The front room was filled with overstuffed white linen furnishings, English-country-house floral throw pillows, and a thick sisal rug. A painted iron chandelier hung from the cabin's rafters. A half wall had been built around the original brick oven, which had been coaxed back to life and was emitting the heavenly smell of cornbread.

"Cheyenne," Ruth said, her mouth dipping open in shock. "You live here? And you . . . cook?"

"Of course I live here, Ruth." Cheyenne flashed a wicked smile and winked. "But Adam cooks."

The round antique table Cheyenne had placed in the center of the room overflowed with blossoms. A Simon Pearce glass vase was filled to cascading with every species of plant life then in bloom on the Hold estate.

Ruth looked at Jinx in her cargo pants and Cheyenne in her ocean pearls. Three vastly different women enlisted to carry on the same story. As she breathed in the fragrance of fresh spring flowers and watched the clear sunlight glinting on their leaves, Ruth thought Mary Ann would have approved.

*

Ruth tried to rise from the canopied bed she had shared with Jinx in the Patience Suite, their bodies curved together like question marks on the plush mattress and fine sheets. They had slept late, awakening to a high morning sun and a house that was quiet around them.

"Where do you think you're going?" Jinx reached out, pressing her face into the coils of Ruth's hair.

Ruth adjusted to put space between their bodies. Even after months of visits between Minneapolis and Ocmulgee, Ruth had to quell her impulse to withdraw and give herself permission to accept the comfort of Jinx's arms.

Jinx waited as Ruth breathed, inched back toward her, and spoke.

"There's something I never got to do here last fall. Sometimes when I wake up in the night, I think about it."

"The attic," Jinx said.

"How did you know?"

"I remember the look on your face when you saw that river cane basket in the stairwell . . . It reminded you of your mom."

Ruth wrapped herself around Jinx in a shy hug, breathing in the scent of licorice, before sliding out of bed.

"Come with me if you want."

"Try and stop me, F.D."

Jinx gave her a quiet smile while Ruth ducked her head at the ridiculous nickname, pulling on her clothes from the day before, a cutoff denim skirt with fringe at the bottom and a T-shirt that read ALL PEOPLED OUT. Jinx dressed quickly in cargo pants, a library book-sale T-shirt, and unlaced high-tops.

Ruth stepped into the stillness of the hall. She cracked the closet door that led to the attic, breathing in the stale smell. She pushed aside the discolored mops, nearly tripping over a fallen broom handle.

Jinx grabbed Ruth's hand, stepped over the handle with her, then settled the broom upright against the wall.

"I've got you," Jinx said. "Do you want me to go first?" she added as Ruth paused.

"I'll go." Ruth stepped gingerly forward into the darkness, feeling the warmth of Jinx close behind her. She lightly touched the sifting basket that still hung on its hook and stared into the closet's depths before climbing the narrow staircase.

At the top of the steps, she scanned the only part of the house that Cheyenne and Adam had left untouched. The attic was a long coffin-like room, capped on opposite ends by semicircular eyebrow-shaped windows. Except for an antique wheelchair woven from river cane, a torn hoop skirt, and an infant's crib, the floor was bare. The emotional residue of human suffering still clung to the air. But other than that cloying stench that Ruth could smell inside her mind, James Hold's torture chamber appeared almost mundane—just another attic in an old plantation house down a winding Southern road.

Ruth arched her neck to look up. The ceiling was formed of hand-hewn beams held together by thick wooden pegs. Her eye caught high in the tented rafters, where a bird had left a nest and the gossamer webs of spiders past draped like nets.

"Look," Ruth whispered placing a palm on the small of Jinx's back and pointing toward the apex.

The rough-plank trusses were embellished with delicate floral carvings. Alabaster Cherokee roses, too many to count, clustered around the joints of the beams. The petals were formed of mica stone, pearly and brilliant. And at the center of each decorative flower, shining in the late-morning light, was a dot of pure gold.

"It's a golden rose garden," Ruth said on the intake of a breath. "Peggy was memorializing Patience, even here."

"Especially here," Jinx said, staring in awe at the detailed craftsmanship that might have been accomplished by Isaac's mentor, Butler, the artisan. "It reminds me of the floral motif made of gold on the dome of the Library of Congress."

"You don't have to show off for me, Dr. Micco." Ruth reached out to take Jinx's hand, squeezed, and let go. "I already know you're the bomb."

Ruth cast her eyes around the room, finding the oddly shaped window facing east and letting her gaze settle there. She imagined a female figure brooding at that window, fingertips softly disturbing gray dust on the sill. She imagined she could still see fingerprints. The house seemed to inhale and exhale in the silent moment that followed.

Ruth walked across the room to stand at the window. This was what Mary Ann had wanted Ruth to see and safeguard—the memories of the Cherokee Rose built into the bones of the house, planted in the soil of the garden, holding warnings and hope.

Ruth fixed her eyes on the view of the garden, picturing her mother tending those plants, coaxing them to grow and bloom even after the damage of fire. She knew now that shame had kept her mother away from Georgia. Shame at the bruises and shattered bones she had tried to hide from Ruth, and shame at having married a man—stayed with him, made a child with him—who turned out to be a monster. But even though her mother had chosen isolation, Ruth could choose to form a new family like the women of the Cherokee Rose.

Ruth smiled to herself as she felt Jinx close behind her, wrapping an arm around her waist. She turned in surprise when she felt something cool at the crook of her arm. Jinx had slid the two-toned river cane basket onto her elbow.

"You think there might be some heirloom seeds to collect down there?" Jinx asked. "Our cottage garden could use some flowers."

"*Our* cottage?" Ruth said, turning around in Jinx's arms to look her fully in the face—because Jinx lived alone.

"Maybe it's time the Cherokee Rose B&B held its first wedding," Jinx said. Her touch was warm on Ruth's arms, but her eyes were uncertain as she watched for Ruth's reaction, waiting to see if she would bolt.

"And make Cheyenne Cotterell's misguided dreams of plantation romance come true?" Ruth protested. "Give her a showstopper event to plan? A marketing gold mine for her website?"

As Jinx's steady gaze faltered, Ruth kept talking. "And the chance to boast that her matchmaking skills brought her first houseguests together forever?"

"Shit." Jinx pressed her lips together, shook her head, and drew back an inch. "I didn't think . . . I didn't mean . . . A plantation wedding, like those people who cluelessly pose on the lawn and honeymoon in slave quarters . . ."

"I know you didn't." Ruth's lips turned up at the left corner. "But did you notice, Dr. Micco, that when we stepped into the closet just now, we jumped over a broom?"

Jinx's eyebrows lifted, but her body was rigid with worry as she waited for the rest.

"So according to the marriage ritual that would have been observed by the original enslaved residents here, the deed might already be done. Sometimes I think this house has a mind of its own. It's not James Hold's place, or James Hold's story anymore. It's theirs . . . and ours."

"So does that mean—"

Ruth raised her arms, basket and all, to clasp them around Jinx's neck, and, on tiptoe, close enough to Jinx's ear to flutter the tendrils of hair that had escaped her braid there, whispered, "Yes!"

Jinx exhaled, pulling back to see Ruth's face. She grinned as if Ruth had just bought her a Cherry Coke at an old-fashioned soda fountain. Jinx leaned down to press her lips to Ruth's, then broke the kiss to take Ruth's hand.

Ruth gave the garden a long, last look from the attic window. She had learned intriguing things while writing and illustrating her field guide to Southern plants. The Cherokee roses she saw below flashed in resplendent bloom, and come autumn, if the weather conditions were exactly right, they would bloom a second time. She knew these flowers were hardy, with thick roots and sharp thorns, preferring to twine through barren, obscure, and difficult places. And she trusted that in the fullness of time, the wild roses would creep and spread, gracing the ground of the round house and the Strangers' Graveyard.

Author's Note

(from the original 2015 edition, with updates)

THE CIRCUMSTANCES AND characters described in this novel are drawn from my research on African American and Native American relationships, conducted over more than fifteen years. The predominant historical context for the story is Cherokee slaveholding—the practice of owning people of African descent adopted by some Cherokees (mostly, but not solely, individuals of dual Cherokee and European heritage) with the formal support and, indeed, participation of the Cherokee national government. A minority of Native Americans in the Southeast (of the Cherokee, Creek, Choctaw, Chickasaw, and Seminole nations, the so-called Five Civilized Tribes) owned Black slaves in the eighteenth and nineteenth centuries for the purpose of increasing their agricultural productivity and demonstrating their level of "civilization" to American officials. A handful of Native American families became wealthy through their use of slave labor and developed plantations that rivaled those of the white South. The Cherokee Nation of the Georgia and Carolina region, and later of the Indian Territory, was the largest of these slaveholding tribes; its citizens held just over 2,500 Black slaves on the eve of the Civil War. The Cherokee government allied with the Confederacy during the war in large part to protect the right to own slaves. After the Civil War, the Treaty of 1866 enacted between the United States and Cherokee governments required the Cherokees to adopt former slaves as members of the nation.

Just over twenty years later, in 1887, Congress passed the Dawes

Act, or General Allotment Act, which called for the dissolution of tribal governments and the division of communal tribal landholdings. Each Native American family would be assigned 160 acres within Cherokee territory, and each individual over the age of eighteen 80 acres. The General Allotment Act was a policy meant to detribalize and assimilate American Indians by weakening community ties through the notion of amassing private property, which a minority of tribal members had already embraced in the first half of the century in the form of slave ownership.

In order to carry out the allotment process, the United States government organized a massive census of Native Americans who qualified for tribal membership, and hence allotments of land. In the Cherokee Nation (and other nations in the Indian Territory, where the Dawes Act was implemented through the Curtis Act of 1898), this census (called the Dawes Rolls) was segmented into racial categories: "Indians by Blood," "Freedmen," and "Intermarried Whites." "Indians by Blood" were considered biologically or genetically determined Cherokees for the purposes of the census, and blood-quantum ratios were recorded for people on this list; "Intermarried Whites" were Euro-Americans who had married into the tribe; and "Freedmen" were former slaves of both sexes, and their descendants. No blood quanta were recorded for "Freedmen," which meant that no historical record was kept of the Cherokee Indian ancestry of former slaves, some of whom were in fact descended from Cherokees and would have qualified as Cherokees by blood. The structure of the Dawes Rolls codified tribal membership in racial terms that disregarded evidence of mixed Afro-Cherokee heritage.

When the original edition of this novel was published in 2015, the Cherokee Nation of Oklahoma still traced membership through documented lineal descent from an individual on the established Dawes Rolls. Through the late nineteenth century and most of the twentieth, formerly enslaved people and their descendants with an ancestor on the Dawes "Freedmen" roll were considered tribal members. At various points in the twentieth and twenty-first centuries, the Cherokee

Nation of Oklahoma's elected officials and citizens have argued that citizenship should belong only to those who can trace their ancestry to the "Indians by Blood" category of the Dawes Rolls. They have further argued that, as a consequence, descendants of "Freedmen" are not rightful citizens eligible for tribal government services and voting rights. The Cherokee district and supreme courts have sometimes disagreed and sometimes agreed with this argument, while the United States Department of the Interior holds that the Treaty of 1866 guarantees citizenship. Thus, the place of "Freedmen" descendants in the Cherokee Nation has been and continues to be a longstanding source of internal and public controversy. The conflict (now ameliorated, as the new introduction to the novel attests), is a painful, ongoing legacy of Cherokee slaveholding.

*

This novel, *The Cherokee Rose,* is set on a fictionalized plantation similar to that of a historical figure, the wealthy Cherokee entrepreneur and planter James Vann. In the early 1800s, Vann was one of the richest members of the Cherokee tribe. He was also an influential political leader who held the title of chief on the Cherokee Tribal Council. Vann owned a plantation called Diamond Hill near the Conasauga River and the western edge of the Blue Ridge Mountains of what is now Georgia, where he held 115 slaves at the time of his death in 1809. He had at least two Cherokee wives on the premises, a handful of former wives and consorts in the vicinity, and several children. Vann, of Cherokee and Scottish parentage, and his young wife, Peggy (or Margaret Ann) Scott Vann, of Cherokee and English parentage, were firmly ensconced in Cherokee cultural practices and community circles, and spoke Cherokee as their primary language.

In 1801, with Vann's assistance, the Moravian Church of North Carolina established a Protestant mission in the Cherokee Nation. In 1805, head missionary John Gambold and his wife, Anna Rosina Gambold, took charge of the Moravian mission and school on land adjacent to Vann's plantation. (In the novel, I have changed their last name to Gamble, in an effort to respect the feelings of some religious

readers, who would not wish to see the historical Anna Rosina Gambold engaging in fictional acts that take place in the book. I also
hoped the altered name would signal something of the psychological
and physical risk that Anna Rosina the character undertook when
moving to Cherokee territory.) Anna Rosina Gambold was a German
American botanist (the first published woman botanist in Georgia)
who meticulously recorded her observations about native plants in
Cherokee country. Her vegetable and medicinal garden at the mission
was widely respected, and she sent plant specimens to colleagues in
North Carolina and Pennsylvania for further study. (In 2006, both the
Southern Branch and the Northern Branch of the Moravian Church
apologized for the church's involvement in enslaving people of African descent.)

For more on Anna Rosina Gambold, see: Daniel McKinley, "Anna
Rosina (Kliest) Gambold, 1762–1821, Moravian Missionary to the
Cherokees," *Transactions of the Moravian Historical Society*, vol. 28
(1994); *Records of the Moravians in North Carolina*, vol. 6, ed. Ade-
laide L. Fries (North Carolina Historical Commission, 1943). My rendering of Anna Rosina's interests, skills, and turns of phrase were
inspired by and derived from her actual diaries and letters. My description of Anna Rosina's writing and labors in Jinx's history book
comes from Anna Rosina's fellow missionary, Heinrich Gottlieb
Clauder, 1836, in the John Howard Payne Papers, Newberry Library,
Chicago. My description of Anna Rosina's garden in Jinx's Moravian
history book and in the diary comes from McKinley, as well as from
Anna Smith, "Unlikely Sisters: Cherokee and Moravian Women in
the Early Nineteenth Century, *"Pious Pursuits": German Moravians
in the Atlantic World*, eds. Michelle Gillespie and Robert Beachy
(Berghahn Books, 2007); and from Henry Steinhauer, "Extract of a
Letter from Anna Rosina Gambold," *Periodical Accounts Related to
the Missions of the Church of the United Brethren*, vol. 7 (1818).

Within the documented historical story of the Vann plantation,
several remarkable figures have emerged. A woman named Pleasant
and her son, Michael, were the missionaries' slaves, owned by the

Moravian Church. (In the novel, I have changed Pleasant's name to Faith to avoid confusion with the character Patience.) Among James and Peggy Vann's slaves were individuals named Patience and Isaac. Patience was beaten by Vann's overseer, Samuel Tally, after which she falls out of the historical record. It is possible and even likely that Patience died from that beating. Isaac was burned alive by James Vann as punishment for participating in a conspiracy to steal from Vann and then running away. Samuel Kerr was a free Black itinerant preacher who spent time at the Moravian mission with the pupils enrolled there. (I have changed his last name to Cotterell in the novel.) Earbob was a Cherokee spiritual leader who visited the plantation for long spells and administered a cure to Pleasant on at least one occasion. Like Anna Rosina, Pleasant was greatly admired for her garden.

Peggy Vann inherited the original Diamond Hill plantation house after James's unsolved murder in 1809, but she chose instead to live in a small cabin on the grounds. James Vann's favored son, Joseph Vann, known as "Rich Joe," inherited the plantation as a whole and commissioned builders to construct the formal brick manor house that has become an icon in Cherokee history.

After newly elected president Andrew Jackson championed Indian removal in his 1829 State of the Union address, Congress passed the Indian Removal Act. This legislation led to the relocation of numerous tribes east of the Mississippi and the forced expulsion of Cherokees from the South to Indian Territory (what is now eastern Oklahoma) during the historical event known as the Trail of Tears. Concurrently, the Georgia legislature passed laws to repress Cherokee autonomy after gold mines were discovered on Cherokee lands. One of these laws expelled Cherokee owners from their property and redistributed it to Georgia residents through a lottery system. Joseph Vann lost the plantation to white residents during the repressive period of the Georgia gold rush and federal Indian removal, and the Vanns moved west to Indian Territory with their slaves to begin new lives.

Mary Ann Battis, another historical figure on whom parts of the novel are based, was a young woman of Creek, Black, and white ancestry. In the 1820s, Mary Ann attended the Asbury Manual Labor School and Mission for Creek children, run by Methodist missionaries near Fort Mitchell, Alabama. A star pupil whose special accomplishments were noted by visitors, Mary Ann lived at the school between the ages of twelve and eighteen and was in residence at the time of Creek removal. Mary Ann's mother and uncle begged for her to accompany them west to Indian Territory, but the missionaries protested. An unusual conflict developed over Mary Ann's future, as her Creek family, missionary teachers, the United States Indian agent to the Creeks, and the secretary of war argued about whether she should stay in the Southeast or move with her family and tribe. In the end, Mary Ann remained in Alabama with her missionary teacher, Jane Hill. By 1832, she married (becoming Mary Ann Rogers) and was living in Georgia. Historians know little more than this outline of Mary Ann's life, and her presence on the Cherokee plantation at the center of the novel is imagined.

While I have altered or imagined details of their lives, the historical characters in the novel are based on people who lived on James Vann's plantation, at the Moravian Springplace Mission in northwestern Georgia, and at the Methodist Asbury Mission School. The first names of many of those characters have been retained as an act of remembrance.

In contrast, all the present-day characters are fictional, though they, too, draw on the experience of real life. My description of the role, methods, and means of inspiration of a tribal historian was inspired by a presentation given by the late Cheyenne tribal historian John Sipes to the Native American Studies Program at the University of Michigan. Sipes described a method that combined oral and written sources and was responsive to community needs, and said he knew he needed to pursue a topic when he kept feeling prodded toward it in inexplicable ways.

Most of the events in the historical section of the narrative did, in fact, take place on or around Diamond Hill in the early 1800s, including the arrival of a missionary couple and the establishment of a mission school, the bravery and punishment of Demas, the departure of James's elder wife, the slave order by Agent Lovely, the presence of Earbob the healer, the arrival of Sam the Black preacher, the dispatch of plants to Pennsylvania by Anna Rosina, the Christian conversion of Peggy, the treatment of Patience and Isaac, the lunar eclipse and hailstorms, and the murder and burial of James. However, I have added fictional elements including the relationship between Anna Rosina and Sam, Peggy's adoption of an enslaved child, and Mary Ann's negative experience at the Methodist mission school. Peggy's friendship with Patience is an elaboration of a reportedly close relationship that the actual Peggy Vann had with a slave named Caty. In two important instances—the murder of James Hold and the fire that damages the Methodist mission—events are historically accurate, but their attribution to the actions of certain characters is purely imagined. Although all the actual events took place in the early nineteenth century, I have modified precise dates throughout the narrative in order to accommodate the alignment of Cherokee and Creek story lines and an expanded scope of action for the characters.

For a nonfiction account of the historic site and the Vann family, I invite you to see my previous work of history, *The House on Diamond Hill: A Cherokee Plantation Story* (University of North Carolina Press, 2010). For a modern translation of Anna Rosina Gambold's original mission diary, which deeply influenced the novel, see: *The Moravian Spring Place Mission to the Cherokees,* ed. Rowena McClinton (University of Nebraska Press, 2007). For published translations of Cherokee Mission letters that also informed the novel, see: *Records of the Moravians Among the Cherokees,* vols. 1 & 2, eds. Daniel Crews and Richard W. Starbuck (Cherokee Heritage Press, 2010). For my scholarly take on the young adulthood of Mary Ann Battis, I invite you to see my article "Notes from the Field. The Lost Letter of Mary Ann Battis: A Troubling Case of Gender and Race in

Creek Country," published in the *Journal of the Native American and Indigenous Studies Association* (Spring 2014).

The garden theme of the novel was inspired by the historical realities of Anna Rosina's passionate study of plants, Pleasant's coveted garden, and the rose carvings preserved throughout the Vann family's brick plantation house. In addition to its cultural meaning for Cherokees as a symbol of hope during the hardships of the Trail of Tears, the Cherokee rose is the state flower of Georgia. The memory-garden concept described in the narrative is derived from an African American cultural tradition of growing a plant cherished by a loved one who has left, often attached to a story about that person. Memory gardens were especially meaningful in the Northern cities to which many African Americans moved during the Great Migration of the late nineteenth and early twentieth centuries.

I drew information about Cherokee and native Georgia plants and their uses from the following sources: Anna Rosina Gambold, "A List of Plants found in the neighbourhood of the Connasarga [*sic*] River," in *Plants of the Cherokee Country* (*American Journal of Science*, 1818–1819), which is noted in Anna Rosina Gamble's fictional diary; William H. Banks Jr., *Plants of the Cherokee* (Great Smoky Mountains Association, 2004); Paul B. Hamel and Mary U. Chiltoskey, *Cherokee Plants, Their Uses—a 400 Year History* (Herald, 1975); Flora Ann L. Bynum, *Cultivated Plants of the Wachovia Tract in North Carolina, 1759–1764* (Old Salem, Inc., 1979); Kay Moss, *A Backcountry Herbal, 18th Century Backcountry Lifeways Program* (Schiele Museum, 1993), which contains the rose remedy for hoarseness; Daniel E. Moerman, *Native American Medicinal Plants: An Ethnobotanical Dictionary* (Timber Press, 2009); the Georgia Native Plant Society's website (http://www.gnps.org/indexes/Plant_Gallery_Index.php); the *Rivercane* website, Department of Plant and Soil Sciences, Mississippi State University (https://www.rivercane.msstate.edu/node/4); and Amy Stewart, *Wicked Plants* (Algonquin, 2009). For an enlightening study of the life and work of a formerly enslaved gardener, see Myra B. Young Armstead, *Freedom's Gardener: James F. Brown, Horticulture, and the Hudson Valley in Antebellum America* (New York University Press, 2012).

The Chief Hold House museum, central to the contemporary portion of the novel, is based on the Chief Vann House State Historic Site, located in Chatsworth, Georgia. The site is owned by the state and operated by the Georgia Department of Natural Resources. Unlike the house museum in the novel, the real Vann House has not been closed or sold. However, staffing has been drastically cut and hours reduced. In recent years, the Georgia State Archives narrowly avoided being closed due to budget cuts. It was saved for public use thanks to mass organized protest and the intervention of the governor. I cannot help noting the irony that this novel portrays a present time—our time—in which stories of the past are meaningful and necessary, at a moment when access to historical sites and sources seems to be under threat in Georgia.

I will leave you, though, with a symbol of hope and a treasure hunt. If you ever pay a visit to the Chief Vann House (and I hope you will), look for the many carved flowers on the walls and porches of the building. It seems that each time I tour that grand, old, storied home, I notice a small white rose where I had not seen one before.

*

I'd like to express a depth of gratitude to the many people who, knowingly or unknowingly, helped this book along its way over the course of many years. I am grateful, as always, to my loving parents, Patricia King, Benny Miles, Montroue Miles, and Jim King; my wise husband, Joe Gone; my incredibly patient children, Nali, Noa, and Sylvan Gone (who are here with me reading their bedtime books as I write this); my sister and brother, Erin and Erik Miles; my in-laws, Stephanie Iron Shooter, Sharon Juelfs, Roxanne Gone, Bertha Snow, Rena Gone, and Alicia Werk; and my uncles and aunts, Steve McCullom, Deborah Banks, and the Walker family. I have fond memories of, and owe a warm thanks to, my past creative-writing companions,

Sunita Dhurandhar and Josie Fowler. I am blessed to have had brilliant writing-group members, writing confidantes, and dear friends in Ann Arbor: Martha Jones, Kristin Hass, Liz Cole, Angela Dillard, Kelly Cunningham, Meg Sweeney, and Magda Zaborowska.

I am thankful to many colleagues and friends for being sources of information, inspiration, and aid: Julia Autry, Rowena McClinton, Sian Hunter, Celia Naylor, Stephanie Morgan, Rebecca Walkowitz, Barbara Spindel, Barbara Krauthamer, Sharon Holland, Barbara Savage, Darlene Clark Hine, Beth James, Mary Kelley, Phil Deloria, Greg Dowd, Emily Macgillivray, Angela Walton-Raji, Angie Parker, Richard Starbuck, Chase Parker, Dave Roediger, David Chang, Craig Womack, Jennifer Brody, Claudio Saunt, Michael Witgen, Penny Von Eschen, Eisa Ulen, Alexandria Cadotte, Soraya Binetti, Andy Smith, Meg Noodin, Audra Simpson, Dale Turner, Robert Warrior, Dennis Tibbetts, Scott Lyons, Derek Collins, and Wayne High.

I am grateful to the organizers of the Bear River Writers' Conference, to my wonderful teachers there (Elizabeth Kostova, James Hynes, Michael Byers, and Valerie Laken), and to my fellow workshop participants; to the organizers of the Scribblers' Retreat Writers' Conference on St. Simons Island, where I always felt revived by the sea; and to the Loft Literary Center's Mentor Program and its speakers and teachers, particularly Jewelle Gomez, Ellen Hart, and Lee Young Lee, whose personal words inscribed in my book of his poems ("Sister maker, keeper of the treasure") have always stayed with me. I am likewise grateful to Debby Keller-Cohen and the Institute for Research on Women and Gender at the University of Michigan, which funded me to begin a serious draft of this work (the funding included childcare, a godsend to mother-writers), and to Kevin Gaines and the Department of Afroamerican and African Studies at Michigan, for funding that allowed me to attend writing conferences. I have drawn more satisfaction and inspiration than I can measure from students in my women of color courses at Michigan, Chicago, and Berkeley; I thank those students, as well as my fellow young women writers of *The Rag* feminist collective at Radcliffe when I was a student there.

Finally, I am deeply grateful to my agent, Deirdre Mullane; the president of John F. Blair, Publisher, Carolyn Sakowski; and my dedicated editor there, Steve Kirk, for taking a chance on a first novel by an academic writer of hidden histories. If I have forgotten to name you, I am nevertheless thankful to you; please forgive the omission.

—Bozeman, MT,
Autumn 2014 and Summer 2022

Gardens of Memory

GHOSTS, GROUNDS, AND THE ARCHIVES

Reprinted from Historical Fiction Now (Oxford University Press)

THE CHEROKEE ROSE turned out to be many things: a ghost story, a love story, a mystery, a teaching tool, and what I like to think of as a temporal bridge novel—a work of both historical and contemporary fiction that illuminates the meaning of the past for the present and future. It was the first and only one of my books that my women family members read all the way through, and that, for me, was among its highest achievements. I was, in fact, writing for them, for my sister, sisters-in-law, mother, stepmother, and aunts, and writing for the many women like them (including myself) who might be more inclined on some days to pick up a thoughtful romance about the history and legacy of racial and gender issues rather than a dense historical tome. In other words, I aspired to write in the Black feminist literary tradition of Pauline Elizabeth Hopkins and Frances Ellen Watkins Harper. These were African American public intellectuals whose late-nineteenth/early-twentieth-century pedagogical genre fiction about Black women's difficult pasts, American racial and sexual politics, and Black community strategies for uplift I had analyzed in my undergraduate thesis in Afro-American Studies, and in my master's thesis in Women's Studies.[1] To Hopkins's and Harper's exemplary models, I added the spectral fiction of science fiction writer Octavia Butler, whose 1970s time-traveling novel *Kindred* is set on an antebellum Maryland plantation and features Black women and white men embroiled in a tangle of complex and exploitative romantic and sexual relationships.[2]

In addition to being drawn to an audience with whom I wished to communicate and a literary tradition that I hoped to speak back to and update, I felt compelled to contend with emotional and political story lines that felt present and yet unfinished just below the surface of my second academic book, a multiracial history of the largest extant plantation in the Cherokee Nation of present-day Georgia.[3] I was propelled by divergent desires: to write Black feminist genre fiction for women readers, and to retell a historical account of slavery and race in the Native American South, in a form that would allow me to craft a more emotionally satisfying and hopeful ending than the textbook histories of racial slavery and forced removal allow.[4]

In the story that became *The Cherokee Rose,* the three main characters are Jennifer "Jinx" Micco, a Creek-Cherokee tribal historian and graduate student from Muskogee, Oklahoma; Cheyenne Cotterell, a wealthy African American interior designer and BAP ("Black American Princess") from Atlanta, Georgia; and Ruth Mayes, the daughter of a Black mother and white father who writes for a "shelter" magazine in Minneapolis, Minnesota. Each is pulled out of her restless everyday life by spiritual forces unknown to her and compelled to travel to the same place: a nineteenth-century plantation home in the foothills of the Blue Ridge Mountains on land that once belonged to Cherokee slaveholders. The person who has called them there, the ghost of a young Afro-Creek woman who has access to both West African Indigenous and southern American Indigenous spiritual knowledges, needs their historical engagement as well as their personal growth in order to stop a sacrilege upon the land. On the hallowed ground of that plantation where so many had lived, loved, and died, the women travelers find that an old garden holds secrets of the past that, once uncovered, show them not only what they share with one another across their many differences, but also what they have in common with the African American, Native American, and Euro-American women who once fought for freedom on those same grounds. After facing one another and the travails of history by way of emotional time-travel, set in motion through a diary discovered in the

slave quarters, the women of the contemporary story emerge strength-
ened and connected, ready to face their futures and protect the place
and people that they have come to love.

These characters, and the journey into the past that they would
embark on together, took many years to coalesce in my thinking. The
germ of an idea sprouted before I had any notion of what expressive
form it would take. In the late 1990s I was a graduate student researching my dissertation on slavery in the nineteenth-century Cherokee Nation, when the first image for the novel that would eventually
become *The Cherokee Rose* appeared, unbidden and free-floating. I
had, for this research, visited historic plantation sites, which is surely
what had begun the shaping of this picture in my unconscious mind.
One day, perhaps while daydreaming when I should have been reading my secondary sources, I saw a young woman in my mind's eye.
She was walking through a field of flowers toward a spacious, deterio-
rating plantation house, oblivious to the pageantry of nature around
her because of an unseen weight of past pain that narrowed her sen-
sory and emotional range. The image came and went in a flash. It was
merely a snapshot of a woman alone, slowly moving uphill through a
field of beauty that she could not recognize due to historical trauma.

The specific personal and communal history that I would eventually wrap around that woman—who turned out to be Ruth, the
daughter of an abused and murdered mother—and her peers, was
inspired by primary research and the vivid image of an enslaved
woman that I first read about in the archives and then imagined on
plantation grounds over a decade later while researching my second
history on slavery in the Cherokee Nation. Some of the richest first-
hand accounts on this topic were the letters and diaries penned by
Christian missionaries from the Moravian Church who had traveled
to Cherokee country, in what is now Georgia, to start a school and
mission on the land of a wealthy Cherokee slaveholder named James
Vann. In the small basement reading room of the Moravian Archives
(Southern Province) in Old Salem, North Carolina, I had immersed
myself in translations of the old German missionary script, reading

about Vann, his family members, his missionary associates, and the enslaved people owned by both Cherokees and the Moravian Church. A woman named Pleasant stood out to me in these records. Pleasant was an enslaved mother of a young mixed-race boy, Michael, brought by the missionaries from North Carolina to the Cherokee Nation. The missionaries criticized Pleasant for cursing at them when they gave her orders, and carrying out her assigned tasks slowly and belligerently. Although the missionaries who sought to extract her labor saw Pleasant as a lazy, ungodly nuisance, I saw her as a person of remarkable inner fortitude. She exhibited intelligence, bravery, and creativity throughout her time in the Cherokee Nation by pushing back against her missionary-masters' wishes, seeking to protect her son from sale, forming bonds with other enslaved Blacks as well as Cherokees, and growing a garden that others in her community envied.

Pleasant had been enslaved on the Vann plantation, an estate that was known as Diamond Hill in the 1800s, and, by the 1950s, was preserved, marked, and open to the public. I walked those grounds (the Chief Vann House State Historic Site, operated by the Georgia Department of Natural Resources) several times while working on my book about the family that had owned the estate and the people they had enslaved. It was during one of these visits in the sticky heat of July that the second seed of *The Cherokee Rose* sprouted.

I was walking among the trees by a live spring once considered sacred by Cherokees, and which had also inspired the name of the former Moravian Cherokee mission station on the grounds: Springplace. A generous senior colleague, Dr. Rowena McClinton, accompanied me. She was an expert on Moravian documents and a translator of the Springplace Mission diaries, who often sent me loose sheaths of translated pages in the mail when she came across Pleasant's name.[5] I was discussing research with Rowena and feeling the soft, welcome breeze beside the waterway, when I let my mind wander. I looked up at the trees, through the canopy of leaves filtering the day's languid light, and I imagined that I saw Pleasant there, sitting astride a sturdy branch and demanding my notice beyond distant academic interest. Glimpsing Pleasant by the spring that day, I felt moved by a sense of the untold stories of the more than a hundred enslaved people who had lived on that land alongside her, and pushed to try to capture revelations about their lives that were perhaps unprovable, but nevertheless true to the human experience.

I do not say that I saw a ghost that late summer afternoon. I do say that I saw a figment—a figment of the historical record augmented by my imagination once it had been set free. Seeing Pleasant on that branch in her calico dress and headscarf unveiled for me a living sense of the past, and a means of connecting to that past beyond the realm of my accustomed mode: academic history writing. Pleasant, the historical person held captive by missionaries, became the character Faith in *The Cherokee Rose.* The spectral woman in the tree transformed into Mary Ann, the spirit guide to Jinx, Ruth, and Cheyenne, who was modeled on a Creek historical figure whom I had uncovered in a Native American history research seminar taught by the Ojibwe historian Jean O'Brien.[6] I hoped that by writing the stories of women who lived in the past in a way that allowed for a deeper emotional connection than is often possible in historical writing, I could prepare the ground for a richer understanding of their struggles and strengths with women readers who enjoy climbing inside of stories and who feel that the histories we inherit make us who we are today.

I knew for years that I should heed Pleasant's call, but knowing and doing are entirely different enterprises. I was an academic with three young children, classes to teach, articles to publish, and no time to spare for creative writing. Soon after my youngest child was born, I attended an annual conference of the Native American and Indigenous Studies Association in Minneapolis. One evening, I wandered into a fairy-tale-like bookstore in the Uptown neighborhood where the bookseller happened to be dressed like Mother Goose. With my four-month-old son in the stroller beside me, I browsed the shelves and came across a book by Walter Mosley, my stepfather's favorite crime novelist. *This Year You Write Your Novel* was the book's title. I bought it and tucked it inside my diaper bag. By the time that academic year of 2008–2009 ended, I was ready to follow Mosley's prescription.

My family moved to Montana for the summer while my husband was engaged in wellness intervention research in a community partnership on the Blackfeet Reservation. During the days, I snatched time around caring for our five-year-old twin daughters and eight-month-old son to start the creative endeavor that Pleasant's visage had sparked years earlier. The project before me was daunting, but a single question guided my thinking, enabling me to cross the (arguably fluid) boundary between historical and fictional narrative construction. I had by then conducted extensive primary research on the Diamond Hill plantation. My book on the history of that place and its residents was in production at the University of North Carolina Press. I knew that the owner of that plantation, the legendary Chief James Vann, had been murdered under mysterious circumstances. His unknown assailant had never been apprehended, but historians believed that the perpetrator was his compatriot-turned-enemy. Knowing what I did of the lives of enslaved women, as well as Cherokee women, on Diamond Hill, I thought that in a world of my own creation, a fictional world, an alternate scenario was entirely plausible. Who killed James Vann? This became the mystery, the question around which I might weave a story. And my answer would be that the women of the Vann plantation, acting in an alliance built of love and necessity, had taken this abusive man's life in collective self-defense. I needed, then, to craft a story that realized that version of events, made it believable, and showed its relevance to the lives of women in our contemporary society, women that I knew and loved, like my family, friends, and the readers in a mystery book club that I had briefly joined during a parental leave after our twins were born.

I felt a devotion to this story that pushed me through the difficult moments when time was scarce, children were noisy, and faith in my ability to complete the thing wavered. But writing fiction after fifteen years of writing academic history proved the most challenging part of this enterprise. I had been trained to accurately render the past as best as I could reconstruct it, to offer my analyses backed by evidence fairly and rationally interpreted. Over the course of my professional career, I had labored to build narratives that I could reasonably and responsibly support through primary and secondary sourcing. Now that I was trying to write fiction set in both the past and present, in a real place where historical lives had unfolded in ways I had already documented, I had a tough time letting go of the "known" past. In my initial efforts I adhered so closely to historical dates and events that I gave myself no room to develop a new plot. I had to resist a gravitational pull to write in footnotes (and settled for an Author's Note that explains the background for the story). Finally, I found my way out of a data-bound tunnel when I reread the evocative, detail-rich diary of missionary Anna Rosina Gambold. Although I had read pages of her diary many times before when mining them for historical information, now I read decades of her daily journal straight through while sitting outside in the sunshine. Her observations were so sharp, her turns of phrase so captivating, that I became absorbed by her world. Anna Rosina Gambold, herself a writer of diaries, letters, and botanical papers with a literary quality, opened the door to fiction writing for me. I began anew by free-writing new entries of her diary in my best estimation of her voice. At first these diary pages adhered to the originals, duplicating the missionary's recorded dates, locations, and words. But before I realized a shift had occurred, the entries that I was writing, in the voice of a character modeled on Anna Rosina, took on a life of their own.

The historical Pleasant had inspired me to write this story about the Vann plantation and its inhabitants. The historical Anna Rosina had guided me into the heart of that story's pages. Shaping the lives of the wholly manufactured contemporary characters—Jinx, Ruth, Cheyenne, Adam, and Sally—was an extremely challenging second

phase of the creative process. I struggled with making these characters real as people, with giving them things to do and words to say
that were not mere reenactments and recitations of the historical information that I sought to share with readers. In the end, with the
feedback of editors and fiction-writing workshop leaders who helped
the manuscript along, I was able to enliven these characters, although
I realize that my skills in dialogue and plotting are far from mature. By
the time I finished the final draft of *The Cherokee Rose*, more than five
years after stumbling across *This Year You Write Your Novel*, I wanted
to travel back in time to 2009 and visit my characters at their restored
and repurposed historic site. The fiction had worked on me. I nearly
believed that they lived on the former Vann estate, making new relationships and histories.

While I was completing an early draft of the novel and, coinciden-
tally, spending time in Detroit for research on a different project, I
learned about the practice of tending memory gardens. I picked up
on this idea while hearing gardeners in the city talk about planting
gardens in memory of loved ones who had moved away, as the city's
population began its steep decline. A friend might care for the old
garden of someone who had moved and left a vacant yard behind. A
relative might transplant flowers from a departed loved one's garden
into her own, or a daughter might replicate the shape and colors of
her mother's previous plantings. Even if a loved one was long gone—
having relocated to a new city, or even a place farther away, like heaven
or the deep, star-dusted universe—a plant would bloom in that person's cherished memory. A plant would be the reminder of that loved
one's life and stories. This beautiful notion of the memory garden
became an essential element in the novel as I revised.[7] I finally completed and published the book in 2015, my willingness to let the story
go and to take the ensuing professional risk having been encouraged
by the life-changing gift of a MacArthur Fellowship.

Now, I like to think of myself as the keeper of a memory garden,
too, in the form of new seeds in the soil and new pages on the past. As
a first novel, and as a suspension bridge between my dutiful work as a

historian and my fever dreams as a fiction writer, *The Cherokee Rose* contains many flaws.[8] Still, I hope that by sharing in the experiences of these characters and finding inspiration there, readers can bend their own lives toward care, remembrance, and justice, and, like the flowers in the rose garden: grow.

Notes

INTRODUCTION

1. Tiya Miles, *The House on Diamond Hill: A Cherokee Plantation Story* (Chapel Hill: University of North Carolina Press, 2010). This book, my second, was awarded prizes by the National Council on Public History, the Georgia Historical Society, and the American Society for Ethnohistory.

2. I have written more extensively, in various essays and a book, about how I think plantations where enslavement was practiced might be constructively interpreted for the public. See Tiya Miles, *Tales from the Haunted South: Dark Tourism and Memories of Slavery from the Civil War Era* (Chapel Hill: University of North Carolina Press, 2015). Tiya Miles, "What Should We Do with Plantations," *The Boston Globe,* August 8, 2020. Hannah Scruggs and Tiya Miles, "A Way Forward for Plantation Sites: Reimagining Space and Relations in the Wake of Black Lives Matter," in *Revisiting the Past in Museums and at Historic Sites,* eds. Anca I. Lasc, Andrew McClellan, Änne Söll (New York: Routledge University Press, 2021). Tiya Miles and Rachel Miller, "Critical Place-Based Storytelling: A Mode of Creative Interaction at Historic Sites," in *Bending the Future: 50 Ideas for the Next 50 Years of Historic Preservation in the United States,* eds. Max Page and Marla R. Miller (Amherst: University of Massachusetts Press, 2016).

3. The history scholars in this cohort that I became part of included Claudio Saunt, Celia Naylor, Barbara Krauthamer, and David A.Y.O. Chang. I learned a great deal about historical methods from them, as we often collaborated and crossed paths at conferences. For reasons that are still unclear to me, most scholars working on the topic of Black presence in Native nations in the late 1990s and early 2000s were other

Black women, including Naylor and Krauthamer, as well as Fay Yarbrough.

4. Tiya Miles, "Uncle Tom Was an Indian: Tracing the Red in Black Slavery," in *Confounding the Color Line: Indian-Black Relations in Multidisciplinary Perspective,* ed. James F. Brooks (Lincoln: University of Nebraska Press, 2002).

5. Audre Lorde, "Eye to Eye: Black Women, Hatred, and Anger," in *Sister Outsider: Essays and Speeches* (Berkeley: Crossing Press, 1984).

6. Lindsey Bark, "Cherokee Nation Removes 2 Confederate Monuments from Capitol Square," *Cherokee Phoenix,* June 16, 2020, https://www .cherokeephoenix.org/news/cherokee-nation-removes-2-confederate -monuments-from-capitol-square/article_dec30c2c-52c2-5ff1-a837-c561 58ff2f96.html.

7. "Osiyo: Voices of the Cherokee People," Wherever We Are, 2022 Freedmen Edition, https://youtu.be/JXfqobnoelM.

GARDENS OF MEMORY:
GHOSTS, GROUNDS, AND THE ARCHIVES

1. Pauline E. Hopkins, *Contending Forces: A Romance Illustrative of Negro Life, North and South* (1900; reprint: Schomburg Library of Nineteenth-Century Black Women Writers, New York: Oxford University Press, 1988). Pauline E. Hopkins, *The Magazine Novels of Pauline Hopkins* (reprint: Schomburg Library of Nineteenth-Century Black Women Writers, New York: Oxford University Press, 1988). Frances E. W. Harper, *Iola Leroy, or Shadows Uplifted* (1892; reprint: Schomburg Library of Nineteenth-Century Black Women Writers, New York: Oxford University Press, 1990). Frances Smith Foster, ed., *Minnie's Sacrifice, Sowing and Reaping, Trial and Triumph: Three Rediscovered Novels by Frances E. W. Harper* (Beacon, 1994).

2. Octavia E. Butler, *Kindred* (1979; reprint: Beacon, 2004).

3. Tiya Miles, *The House on Diamond Hill: A Cherokee Plantation Story* (University of North Carolina Press, 2010). Also see Tiya Miles, "Showplace of the Cherokee Nation: Race and the Making of a Southern House Museum," *The Public Historian* vol. 33, no. 4 (November 2011): 11–34.

4. For a detailed description of my experience of writing fiction as a way of doing public history, as well as the anxieties, risks, and fallout involved, see Tiya Miles, "Edges, Ledges, and the Limits of Craft: Imag-

ining Historical Work beyond the Boundaries," National Council on Public History Keynote Address 2015, *The Public Historian* vol. 38, no. 1 (February 2016): 8–17.

5. Rowena McClinton, ed., *The Moravian Springplace Mission to the Cherokees, Vols. I and II, 1814–1821* (University of Nebraska Press, 2007). Also see Rowena McClinton, ed. *The Moravian Springplace Mission to the Cherokees, Abridged* (University of Nebraska Press, 2010).

6. For more on my research on the historical figure of Mary Ann Battis, see Tiya Miles, "The Lost Letter of Mary Ann Battis: A Troubling Case of Gender and Race in Creek Country," Notes from the Field, *Native American and Indigenous Studies* vol. 1, no. 1 (Spring 2014): 88–98.

7. In draft form, I had titled the novel "Our Mothers' Gardens," inspired, of course, by Alice Walker's classic work of womanist theory. My literary agent, Deirdre Mullane, suggested the new title of *The Cherokee Rose,* also fitting and more immediately explanatory for readers regarding the subject matter. Alice Walker, *In Search of Our Mothers' Gardens* (Harcourt, Brace, Jovanovich Publishers, 1983).

8. *The Cherokee Rose,* though imperfect, was named "A Book All Georgians Should Read" by the Georgia Center for the Book. It was a finalist for a Lambda Literary Award in the category of Lesbian Fiction, and a winner of a Bronze Medal in Multicultural Fiction, Independent Publisher Book Awards.

The Cherokee Rose

-⊁->->-·-⊰-⊰-⊰-

TIYA MILES

A BOOK CLUB GUIDE

A Q&A WITH TIYA MILES

What inspired you to write fiction after a decade of writing histories?

While doing research on my second work of history, I immersed myself in letters and diaries penned by Moravian missionaries who had traveled to Cherokee country in the early 1800s to evangelize. These missionaries brought an enslaved woman named Pleasant along with them as they settled on the grounds of the wealthy Cherokee slaveholder James Vann. The missionaries saw Pleasant as a belligerent, incompetent laborer who drove them mad with her back talk. But I saw Pleasant as a woman who persistently showed courage, intelligence, and creativity. Despite the vulnerability of her circumstances, she consistently spoke up for herself and her son, and was sometimes able to further her own ends.

Pleasant never left my mind as I read those records and visited the Chief Vann House State Historic Site in Georgia. On one such visit, I was walking among the trees by a clear flowing spring when I let my mind wander. I looked up at the trees, through the thick leafy canopy filtering the day's languid light, and I imagined that I saw Pleasant seated on a high branch, demanding that I notice her. That fleeting vision led me to feel that I had to tell the stories of Pleasant and her community members—even if that meant looking beyond the facts available in the historical record.

Seeing Pleasant sitting there in her headscarf unveiled for me a living sense of the past and a means of connecting to that past outside the realm of my accustomed mode of academic research and writing. Pleasant, the historical person, the figure in the tree, became the character Faith in *The Cherokee Rose*. My experience of sighting her became Ruth's experience of encountering the ghost of Mary Ann. By writing fiction about women who experienced slavery, I hoped to capture emotional struggles and strengths that can be difficult to access in historical writing, and to share those elements with readers who feel the histories we inherit make us who we are today.

How did you go about turning history into fiction?

As a scholar, I had not been happy with how the real story ended for enslaved women and Cherokee women on the Vann plantation, many of whom faced lifelong exploitation, familial separation, and domestic violence. But as a novelist, I had the opportunity to write my own ending. In *The Cherokee Rose,* the weak are strong, and the ne'er-do-wells get their comeuppance. As Jinx suggests indirectly at the end of the novel when she plays music by the Indigenous jazz group Poetic Justice, making the leap from history to fiction gave me the chance to achieve poetic justice for women who saw little or no social justice in their lifetimes. In the historical record, the legendary Chief James Vann of the Cherokee Nation had been murdered under mysterious circumstances. I started this novel by posing the question "Who killed James Vann?" and allowing myself to invent an answer. That invention was the creation of a plantation world in which diverse women constructed an alliance built at first of necessity, and then of love.

How did you develop the characters in The Cherokee Rose?

The characters in the nineteenth-century story line are all based on historical figures that lived in the Cherokee Nation or the Creek Nation during the heyday of the Diamond Hill plantation, owned by James Vann, on which the Cherokee Rose Plantation is based. These were individuals whose hard lives and creative means of survival captured my imagination while I was conducting historical research on the intersections of African American and Native American histories. The characters in the modern-day story line of the novel are composite characters inspired by my observations, and in some cases my experience, of the complexities of Black, Native, mixed-race, and "Black Indian" identity, particularly where these complexities have included dynamics of gender and women's issues. Jinx's character was influenced by a tribal historian whose story I had the privilege of hearing about, and also by the many talented graduate students who struggle with questions of professional calling. Ruth was inspired by family and friends who have suffered domestic violence, as well as by a brief time I spent working at a domestic violence shelter on an Indian reservation after college. And as one reader of the novel joked on Twitter, every Black woman knows a Cheyenne.

Is the plantation house itself a character?

The house has a life of its own in the novel; it has eyes (windows), an austere personality, and a sense of place on its hilltop. The house is animated by both the materials that make it up, derived from nature (such as the bricks fashioned by enslaved people), and by the spirits of residents who have gone before. I was inspired to describe a living house by a number of sources, including the creative work of the Creek poet and musician Joy Harjo (her book *A Map to the Next World,* and her work with the jazz ensemble Poetic Justice), whose words open Part II of the novel; and by my own sense of the closeness of history when I enter very old structures. Places that humans construct, as much as natural places on the land, shape our lives and take on lives of their own.

Why are gardens so important in this book? Have they always been important to you?

Many of us have grown up with gardens. When I was a girl, I spent time working with my grandmother in her vegetable garden alongside the house that she had worked thirty years to purchase. Working in the garden soothed my grandmother's soul, brought us closer together, and also produced essential nourishment for the family. Later in life, I read Alice Walker's classic book *In Search of Our Mothers' Gardens* and was captivated by her depiction of Black women's gardens as sites of creativity. In fact, my original working title for this novel was "Our Mothers' Gardens." In the history that I researched, gardens also played a prominent role. The Cherokee plantation mistress kept a garden, as did the Moravian missionary diarist and the enslaved woman possessed by the missionaries. Gardens were important to these historical women who occupied vastly distinct social positions; plants were a potential form of interpersonal connection for them. I wanted gardens to be important, as well, to the women in the contemporary story line. This comes out most strongly in Ruth's personal history and arc of change. It is also apparent in the life of Ruth's mother and Jinx's great-aunt. The love of the garden and recognition of its healing power was something that I thought could bring the women together in both the historical and contemporary timelines.

What role does the ghost play in The Cherokee Rose? *What purposes do ghosts serve in real life?*

Although this novel was inspired by the flash across my imagination of an enslaved figure on the grounds of the Vann House historic site, the first draft did not include a ghost. Ghosts are tricky to pull off in fiction; plus, the symbol of a ghost of the Middle Passage had already been perfected in Toni Morrison's classic novel *Beloved*. My ghost, the figure of an Afro-Native adolescent girl, became a character only after I began a study of ghost tours at historic sites in the South. I was finding that many of these ghost tours included stories of Black slave ghosts, which was intriguing because ghosts often represent the past in popular culture and encourage engagement with history for popular audiences. However, my research (detailed in the book *Tales from the Haunted South*) indicated that these enslaved ghosts were often resigned to the system of slavery rather than resistant to it. My find-

ings led me to want to create a fictionalized ghost at a historic plantation site that undercut the romanticization of slavery and represented
the need for justice. My plantation house ghost represents history in
the story, serves as a vehicle for the contemporary characters' connection to the past, and stands as an indictment to the abuse of Black
women in slavery.

QUESTIONS FOR FURTHER DISCUSSION

Have you ever researched your family tree? What is your most precious family document or heirloom? Why do you cherish it? What have you learned about yourself from your family's oral stories?

If you could go back to a past time and place to learn about the history of your family or social group, where would you go? What would you hope to find there?

Have you ever visited a house museum or historic home on the state or national register? What was that experience like for you? Do you feel citizens or governments have a duty to protect historical sites like the Cherokee Rose?

What aspects of the history presented in the novel surprised you most? Do you think fiction is a good tool for teaching about lesser-known people and events of the past? What can fiction achieve that a work of history, perhaps, cannot?

The main characters in the contemporary story line of this novel have something in common: they are all women of color. And yet, there are key differences in their experiences that have shaped their identities and act as barriers to their connection. What differences keep the characters apart? How do they begin to recognize and break down those differences?

Members of marginalized groups—such as African Americans, Native Americans, women of all racial backgrounds, people of non-heteronormative sexual orientation or gender expression, and people with a disability—experience collective and individual pain connected to devaluation and discrimination in mainstream society. In what ways, big and small, do you see the characters experience or confront prejudice based on their race, class, gender, sexuality, or physical ability? How do they recover from these painful experiences?

Part of the psychological weight that each woman carries in this novel is linked to trauma that took place in a past time in her own life or the lives of her forebears. How would you define historical trauma? How can individuals and groups heal from historical trauma?

Who should own the Cherokee Rose Plantation? Adam? Cheyenne? The state of Georgia? The Cherokee Nation of Oklahoma? What does the battle over ownership in the novel suggest about Indigenous places and the return of land in contemporary American society?

The Cherokee Rose includes traces of a Southern past that is fading away in the face of suburban development and corporate expansion: a family fruit stand, a summer camp for African American youth, a preserved plantation home, and natural forested landscapes. What does the loss of these places mean for memory and identity, as well as for the environment that makes the American South special?

About the Author

TIYA MILES is the Michael Garvey Professor of History and Radcliffe Alumnae Professor at Harvard University, and the author of *All That She Carried,* a *New York Times* bestseller that won the National Book Award for Nonfiction, the PEN/John Kenneth Galbraith Award for Nonfiction, and several other historical and literary prizes. She is a recipient of the MacArthur Foundation Fellowship Award, the Hiett Prize in the Humanities from the Dallas Institute of Humanities and Culture, and fellowships from the Mellon Foundation and the National Endowment for the Humanities. Her recent book *The Dawn of Detroit* received the Hurston/Wright Legacy Award in Nonfiction, an American Book Award, and a Frederick Douglass Book Prize, among other historical prizes. Additionally, Miles is the author of *Ties That Bind, The House on Diamond Hill,* and *Tales from the Haunted South.*